THE LAND OF STORIES

A GRIMM WARNING

THE LAND OF STORIES
A GRIMM WARNING

CHRIS COLFER

ILLUSTRATED BY BRANDON DORMAN

LITTLE, BROWN AND COMPANY

NEW YORK   BOSTON

Copyright © 2014 by Christopher Colfer
Excerpt from *The Land of Stories: Beyond the Kingdoms* copyright © 2015 by Christopher Colfer

Little, Brown and Company

Hachette Book Group
1290 Avenue of the Americas, New York, NY 10104
Visit us at lb-kids.com

Little, Brown and Company is a division of Hachette Book Group, Inc.
The Little, Brown name and logo are trademarks of Hachette Book Group, Inc.

The publisher is not responsible for websites (or their content) that are not owned by the publisher.

First Paperback Edition: June 2015
First published in hardcover in July 2014 by Little, Brown and Company

Library of Congress Cataloging-in-Publication Data

Colfer, Chris, 1990–
The Land of Stories : a Grimm warning / by Chris Colfer ; illustrated
by Brandon Dorman. — First edition.
pages cm
Sequel to: The Land of Stories: the Enchantress returns.
Summary: After thirteen-year-old Conner returns to the Land of Stories and reunites with his twin sister, Alex, who is training to become the next Fairy Godmother, war breaks out in the fairy-tale world.
ISBN 978-0-316-40681-9 (hardback)—ISBN 978-0-316-40682-6 (pb)—ISBN 978-0-316-40683-3 (ebook edition)—ISBN 978-0-316-40684-0 (ebook library edition)
[1. Fairy tales—Fiction. 2. Characters in literature—Fiction. 3. Magic—Fiction. 4. Brothers and sisters—Fiction. 5. Twins—Fiction. 6. War—Fiction. 7. Youths' writings.] I. Dorman, Brandon, illustrator. II. Title. III. Grimm warning.
PZ7.C677474Lal 2014
[Fic]—dc23

2014012462

11

LSC-C

Printed in the United States of America

To J. K. Rowling,
C. S. Lewis, Roald Dahl, Eva Ibbotson,
L. Frank Baum, James M. Barrie, Lewis Carroll,
and all the other extraordinary authors who taught
the world to believe in magic. When I think of all
the time I spent inspecting wardrobes, spotting
second stars to the right, and waiting for my
Hogwarts acceptance letter—it's no wonder
I didn't get good grades.

Also, to all the teachers and librarians
who have expressed their support for this series
and incorporated it into their classrooms.
It means more to me than words can describe.

"YOU HAVE ENEMIES? GOOD. THAT MEANS
YOU'VE STOOD UP FOR SOMETHING,
SOMETIME IN YOUR LIFE."

—WINSTON CHURCHILL

GUESTS OF THE GRANDE ARMEE

1811, Black Forest, Confederation of the Rhine

I t was no mystery why this part of the countryside had been christened the Black Forest. The abnormally dark leaves and tree bark were nearly impossible to see in the night. Even though a bright moon peeked out from the clouds like a shy child, no one could be certain what was lurking in the thick woods.

A chill lingered in the air like a veil spread across the trees. It was a remote and mature forest; roots sank as deep into the ground as branches reached high into the sky. Had it not been for a modest path winding through the terrain the forest would have seemed completely untouched and unseen by human eyes.

A dark carriage pulled by four strong horses shot through the forest like a cannonball. A pair of swinging lanterns illuminated the path ahead and made the carriage resemble an enormous creature with glowing eyes. Two French soldiers of Napoleon's Grande Armée rode beside the carriage. Black cloaks covered the soldiers' colorful uniforms so they could travel in secrecy—the world was never to know what their agenda was tonight.

Soon the carriage arrived at the edge of the Rhine River, dangerously close to the border of the ever-growing French Empire. A large camp was being set up, with dozens of pointed beige tents pitched every moment by hundreds of French soldiers.

The two soldiers following the carriage dismounted their horses and opened the carriage doors. They yanked two men out from inside. The men's hands were tied behind their backs and they had black sacks over their heads. They grunted and yelled muffled messages—both men had been gagged as well.

The soldiers pushed the men to the center of camp and into the largest tent. Even with their faces covered, the bound men could tell it was very bright inside the tent and they felt a soft rug beneath their feet. The soldiers forced the men into two wooden chairs farther inside.

"J'ai amené les frères," they heard one of the soldiers say behind them.

"Merci, Capitaine," another voice said in front of them. *"Le général sera bientôt là."*

The sacks were pulled off the men's faces and the cloths around their mouths were removed. Once their eyes adjusted to the light they could see a tall and muscular man standing behind a large wooden desk. His posture was authoritative and his scowl was anything but friendly.

"Hello, Brothers Grimm," the tall man said with a thick accent. "I am Colonel Philippe Baton. Thank you for joining us this evening."

Wilhelm and Jacob Grimm stared up at the colonel. They were cut up and bruised, and their clothing was disheveled—clearly it had been a struggle getting them here.

"Did we have a choice?" Jacob asked, spitting a mouthful of blood on the rug.

"I trust you're already acquainted with Capitaine De Lange and Lieutenant Rembert," Colonel Baton said, referring to the soldiers who had brought them.

"*Acquainted* is not the word I would use," Wilhelm said.

"We tried to be polite, Colonel, but they would not cooperate," Capitaine De Lange informed his colonel.

"We had to be *aggressive* with our invitation," Lieutenant Rembert explained.

The brothers looked around the tent—it was impeccably decorated for having been so recently assembled. A grandfather clock ticked the night away in the far corner, shiny twin candelabras burned on either side of the tent's back entrance, and a large map of Europe was spread across the wooden desk with miniature French flags pinning the conquered territories.

"What do you want with us?" Jacob demanded, struggling against the ropes tying his hands.

"Surely if you wanted us dead you would have killed us by now," Wilhelm said, struggling against his own restraints.

Their discourteousness made the colonel scowl even harder. "General Marquis has requested your presence tonight not to *harm you*, but to ask for your *assistance*," Colonel Baton said. "But if I were you, I would change my tone so he does not change his mind."

The Brothers Grimm looked at each other nervously. General Jacques du Marquis was one of the most feared generals in the French Empire's Grande Armée. Just hearing his name sent shivers down their spines—but what on earth did he want with them?

An undeniable musk suddenly filled the tent. The Brothers Grimm could tell the soldiers smelled it, too, and grew tense from it, although no one mentioned it.

"*Tsk, tsk, tsk*, Colonel," said a wispy voice from outside the tent. "That is no way to treat our guests." Whoever it was had obviously been listening the entire time.

General Marquis stepped into the tent from between the candelabras, causing the flames to flicker from the sudden burst of air. The tent immediately filled with the strong musky smell of his cologne.

"General Jacques du Marquis?" Jacob asked.

For a man with such an intimidating reputation, his physicality was a bit disappointing. He was a short man with large gray eyes and big hands. He wore a large rounded hat that was broader than his shoulders and several badges of honor were displayed on his tiny uniform. He removed his hat and placed it on top of the desk, revealing a perfectly bald head. He took a casual seat in the large cushioned chair behind the desk, neatly folding his hands over his stomach.

"Capitaine De Lange, Lieutenant Rembert, please untie our visitors," General Marquis instructed. "Just because we are living in hostile times does not mean we have to be inhospitable."

The captain and lieutenant did as they were instructed. A pleasant smile appeared on the general's face but it didn't fool the Brothers Grimm—his eyes were empty of compassion.

"Why have you forced us to come here tonight?" Wilhelm said. "We pose no threat to you or the French Empire."

"We're academics and authors! There's nothing to gain from us," Jacob said.

The general gave a little laugh and then placed an apologetic hand over his mouth.

"That is a nice story, but I know better than that," Marquis said. "You see, I've been watching you, Brothers Grimm, and I know that, like all your stories, there is more to *you* than meets the eye. *Donnez-moi le livre!*"

The general snapped his fingers and Colonel Baton retrieved a large book from inside the desk. He dropped it with a *thud* in front of the general, who began flipping through its pages. The Brothers Grimm instantly recognized the book—it was theirs.

"Does this look familiar?" General Marquis asked.

"That's a copy of our book of children's stories," Wilhelm said.

"*Oui.*" The general didn't look up from its pages. "I am a major admirer of yours, Brothers Grimm. Your stories are so imaginative, so *merveilleuses*—where did you come up with all these stories?"

The Brothers Grimm looked at each other cautiously, still unsure what he was getting at.

"They're just fairy tales," Jacob said. "Some are original but most are just folktales that have been passed down from generation to generation."

General Marquis slowly nodded as he listened. "But passed down by *whom*?" he asked, and slammed shut the book of stories. His pleasant smile faded, and his gray eyes darted back and forth between the brothers.

Neither Wilhelm nor Jacob knew what answer the general was looking for. "By families, by cultures, by children, by their parents, by—"

"Fairies?" the general said in total seriousness, not moving a single muscle in his face.

The room went dead silent. Once the silence reached an uncomfortably long amount of time Wilhelm looked at Jacob and they both forced a laugh, making light of the assertion.

"Fairies?" Wilhelm asked. "You think fairies gave us these stories?"

"Fairies aren't real, General," Jacob said.

General Marquis's left eye began to twitch violently, which took the brothers by surprise. The general closed his eyes and slowly massaged his face until the spasms stopped.

"Forgive me, Brothers Grimm," the general apologized with another fake smile. "My eye always begins to twitch when I am being *lied to*."

"We aren't lying to you, General," Jacob said. "But if our stories have convinced you otherwise then you have given us the greatest of compliments—"

"SILENCE!" General Marquis ordered, and his eye began pulsing again. "You insult my intelligence, Brothers Grimm! We have been following you for quite some time. We know about the sparkling woman who brings you the stories!"

The Brothers Grimm went completely still. Their hearts were racing, and beads of sweat appeared on their foreheads. They had both been faithful to a vow of secrecy for years, but still the greatest secret of their lives had been uncovered.

"A *sparkling woman*?" Wilhelm asked. "General, do you hear what you are saying? This is ludicrous."

"My men saw it with their own eyes," General Marquis said. "She wears robes that sparkle like the night sky, has white flowers in her hair, and carries a long crystal wand—bringing you a new story for your books every time she returns. But from *where* does she appear? That's what I've been asking myself. After countless days of looking over every map I own, I must assume she's from a place that can't be seen on any map of mine."

Wilhelm and Jacob shook their heads, desperately trying to deny all that he said. But how could they deny the truth?

"You military men are all alike," Jacob said. "You've already conquered half of the known world and yet you still want *more*— so you make up things to believe in! You're King Arthur obsessing over the Holy Grail—"

"Apportez-moi l'oeuf!" General Marquis ordered.

Capitaine De Lange and Lieutenant Rembert stepped out of the tent and returned a moment later carrying a heavy box wrapped in chains. They placed the box on the desk directly in front of General Marquis.

The general reached into his uniform and removed a key he wore safely around his neck. He unlocked the chains and opened the box. First he pulled out a pair of white silk gloves and placed them on his hands. He reached farther into the box and retrieved a giant egg made of the purest gold the brothers had ever seen. The golden egg clearly wasn't of this world.

"Is this not the most beautiful thing you have ever laid eyes on?" General Marquis said. He was almost in a trance as he stared at the golden egg. "And I believe this is only the beginning—I believe this is just a small sample of the wonders waiting in the world your stories come from, Brothers Grimm. *And you're going to take us there.*"

"We can't take you there!" Jacob said. He tried to stand but Lieutenant Rembert pushed him back into his seat.

"The Fairy Godmother—the sparkly woman you speak of—brings us the stories from her world to share with ours," Wilhelm said.

"She's the only one who can travel between worlds. We've never been there nor can we take you there," Jacob said.

"How did you even get the egg in the first place?" Wilhelm demanded.

General Marquis carefully placed the golden egg back in the box. "From another one of your acquaintances, the *other* woman who gives you stories to share. *Apportez-moi le corps de la femme oiseau!*"

Colonel Baton left the tent and returned a moment later pulling a wagon with bars built around it. He yanked off a sheet covering it and the Brothers Grimm gasped. Lying inside the wagon was the lifeless body of *Mother Goose.*

"*What did you do to her?*" Wilhelm yelled, trying to stand, but he was forced back into his seat.

"I'm afraid she was poisoned at a local tavern," General

Marquis said without remorse. "So sad to see such a spirited woman leave us, but accidents do happen. We found the egg in her possession. Which makes me wonder—if *this old lush* has managed to find a way to travel between worlds, I'm very confident you two can as well."

The brothers' faces were bright red, and their nostrils flared. "And what are you going to do once you get there? Claim the fairy-tale world for the French Empire?" Wilhelm asked.

"Why, yes," General Marquis stated, as if he had made it obvious already.

"You'll never stand a chance!" Jacob declared. "That world has people and creatures you could never imagine! People and creatures more powerful than you will ever be! Your army will be destroyed as soon as you set foot there."

General Marquis let out another laugh.

"That is highly unlikely, Brothers Grimm." The general giggled. "You see, the Grande Armée is planning something very big—there are many territories we're planning to conquer by the end of next year. The fairy-tale world is only a crumb of the cake we're after. As we speak, thousands and thousands of French soldiers are being trained, and they will form the greatest army the world has ever seen. I very much doubt anything will stand in our way—not the Egyptians, not the Russians, not the Austrians, and certainly not a bunch of fairies and goblins."

"So what do you expect from us?" Wilhelm asked. "What if we can't supply you with a portal into this other world?"

The general smiled, but it was sincere this time. His eyes filled with greed as he finally told them what he wanted.

"You have two months to find a way into this world of stories, Brothers Grimm," Marquis said.

"But what if we can't?" Jacob said. "Like I said, the Fairy Godmother is very mysterious. We may never see her again."

The general's face fell into a cold and malicious stare. "*Tsk, tsk, tsk*, Brothers Grimm," he said. "You won't fail, because the future of your friends and family depends on you. I know you won't let them down."

A quiet snort filled the tense room—but it didn't come from either of the Brothers Grimm. Jacob looked toward the caged wagon and saw Mother Goose smack her lips. To the amazement of everyone in the tent, Mother Goose stirred back to life as if she was waking up from a long night's rest.

"Where am I?" Mother Goose said. She sat up and rubbed her head. She cracked her neck and let out a long yawn. "Oh no, did Spain start another Inquisition? How long have I been knocked out?"

The general slowly got to his feet and his eyes grew in bewilderment. "But how is this possible? She was poisoned!" he said to himself.

"Well, I wouldn't say *poisoned*... but maybe a little *overserved*," Mother Goose said as she looked around the tent. "Let's see. The last thing I remember is being at my favorite alehouse in Bavaria. The barkeep there has a very generous pour—his name is Lester, he's a sweet man and an old friend of mine. Always said I would name my first child after him if I ever had one—*wait a second! Jacob? Willy? What in the name of Merlin are you two doing here?*"

"We've been kidnapped!" Jacob told her. "These men are planning to invade the fairy-tale world in two months. They're going to harm our family if we don't provide them with a portal!"

Mother Goose's jaw dropped and she looked back and forth between the brothers and the soldiers. She was having enough trouble regaining consciousness in general, but this information made her head spin.

"But... but... but how do they know—?"

"They've been following us," Jacob said. "All of us—they have your golden egg! They have an army of thousands and want to claim the fairy-tale world in the name of France—"

"Silence!" Colonel Baton demanded of the brothers.

General Marquis raised a hand to silence the colonel. "No, Colonel, it's fine. Because this woman is going to *help* our friends fulfill our request. After all, she wouldn't want anything to happen to the Grimm family, either."

He peered through the bars at her as if she were an animal. Mother Goose was no stranger to waking up in peculiar places and situations but *this* took the cake. She had always feared the secret of her world would be revealed but never thought it would be under such extreme circumstances.

Her cheeks turned bright red and she began to panic. *"I gotta go!"* she said. She reached out an open hand and the golden egg floated straight out of the box and into the wagon where she sat. And with a blinding flash, Mother Goose and the golden egg disappeared into thin air.

The soldiers around the tent began to yell, but the general remained very still. The determination in his eyes grew as he stared at the wagon Mother Goose vanished from—it was the most amazing thing he had ever witnessed and had proven everything he was after was *real*.

"Général, quelles sont vos instructions?" Colonel Baton asked, anxious to know what his next instructions were.

The general looked to the ground as he decided. *"Emmenez-les!"* he said, and gestured to the Brothers Grimm. Before they knew it, the brothers were gagged again, their hands retied behind their backs, and the black sacks placed over their heads.

"Two months, Brothers Grimm," the general said, unable to tear his eyes away from the wagon. "Find a portal in two months or I'll make you watch as I personally kill everyone you love!"

The Brothers Grimm moaned under their masks. Capitaine De Lange and Lieutenant Rembert forced them onto their feet and out of the tent. The whole camp could hear their muffled moans as they were pushed into the carriage and sent away into the dark forest.

General Marquis sat back in his seat. He let out a pleased sigh as his heartbeat and his racing mind caught up with each other. His eyes fell upon the Brothers Grimm storybook on his desk and a soft chuckle surfaced from within him. For the first time the fairy-tale world didn't seem like an overly ambitious Arthurian quest—it was a victory within reach.

The general took one of the miniature French flags from the map of Europe and stabbed it into the cover of the storybook. Perhaps the Brothers Grimm were right—maybe the fairy-tale world had wonders he couldn't imagine—but he was imagining them now. . . .

CHAPTER ONE

AN EDUCATIONAL OPPORTUNITY

It was half past midnight and only one light was on in all the homes on Sycamore Drive. In the second-story window of Dr. Robert Gordon's house was a shadow that moved back and forth: It was his stepson, Conner Bailey, pacing around his bedroom. He had known for months he was going to Europe but had waited until the night before his departure to pack.

Reruns of a dramatic television show set in outer space did nothing to stop his procrastination. There was just something about a female captain piloting her crew away from an evil alien race that he couldn't take his eyes off. But looking up at his clock and realizing he only had seven hours before he needed to be at the airport forced him to turn the television off and focus on packing.

"Let me think," Conner said to himself. "I'll be in Germany for three days... so I should probably bring *twelve* pairs of socks." He confidently nodded, and tossed a dozen pairs of socks into his suitcase. "You never know, there could be a lot of puddles in Europe."

Conner retrieved ten or so pairs of underwear from his dresser and laid them out on his bed. It was more than he needed but a traumatizing sleepover in kindergarten that ended in a wet bed had taught Conner to always be generous when packing underwear.

"Okay, I think I have everything," Conner said, and he counted the items in his suitcase. "I've got seven T-shirts, four sweaters, my lucky rock, two scarves, my other lucky rock, underwear, socks, pajamas, my lucky poker chip, and my toothbrush."

He looked around his room, wondering what else a kid could need in Europe.

"Oh, *pants*!" he said, thankful that he'd remembered. "I need pants!"

Once he had added the missing (and vital) articles to his suitcase, Conner sat on the edge of his bed and took a deep breath. A big boyish smile came to his face. He couldn't help it—he was *excited*!

At the end of the previous school year, Conner's principal, Mrs. Peters, had called him into her office to present him with a very exciting opportunity.

"Am I in trouble?" Conner said when he sat down in front of her desk.

"Mr. Bailey, why do you ask me that every time I call you into my office?" she said, eyeing him over the top of her glasses.

"Sorry. Old habits die hard, I guess." He shrugged.

"I've called you in here for two reasons," Mrs. Peters said. "First, I was wondering how Alex is acclimating to her new school in—where is it again? Vermont?"

Conner gulped and his eyes grew very big. "Oh!" he said. Sometimes he forgot about the lie his family had told the school about his sister. "She's doing *great*! Never been happier!"

Mrs. Peters bit her lip and nodded, almost disappointed to hear this. "That's wonderful, good for her," she said. "Although sometimes I selfishly wish she would move back and be one of our students again. Your mother was telling me all about the educational programs they offer up there, though, so I'm sure she is enjoying them."

"She sure is!" Conner said, and looked to his left to avoid eye contact. "And Alex has always *loved* trees... and maple syrup... so Vermont suits her."

"I see," Mrs. Peters said, squinting. "And she's staying with your grandmother? Is that correct?"

"Yes, she's still with my grandma... who also loves trees and maple syrup. It's a family trait, I guess," Conner said, and then looked to the right. He panicked for a second when he couldn't remember which direction people tended to look in when they were lying—he had seen a special about it on TV.

"Then give her my warmest regards and please tell her to visit the next time she's in town," Mrs. Peters said.

"I will!" Conner said, relieved to be changing the subject.

"Now, on to the second reason I called you in today." Mrs. Peters sat up extra straight in her seat and slid a pamphlet across her desk. "I have just heard exciting news from an old colleague of mine who teaches English in Frankfurt, Germany. Apparently the University of Berlin has uncovered a time capsule that belonged to the Brothers Grimm. I'm assuming you remember who they are from my lessons in the sixth grade."

"Are you kidding? My grandma knew them!" Conner said.

"Excuse me?"

Conner just stared at her for a moment, mortified by his carelessness. "I mean...yeah, of course I remember," Conner tried to cover. "They're the fairy-tale guys, right? My grandma used to read their stories to us."

"Indeed," Mrs. Peters said with a smile—she had grown so used to Conner's strange outbursts that she didn't even question this one for a second. "And according to the University of Berlin, three brand-new fairy tales were discovered in the capsule!"

"That's amazing!" Conner was genuinely excited to hear this and knew his sister would be thrilled, too.

"I agree," Mrs. Peters said. "And even better, the University of Berlin is planning a big event to reveal the stories. They're going to read them to the public for the first time this coming September, three weeks into next school year, at St. Matthäus-Kirchhof cemetery, where the Brothers Grimm are buried."

"All great things!" Conner said. "So what does this have to do with me?"

"Well, since you've become a bit of a *Grimm* yourself—"

Conner awkwardly laughed and looked back to his left. She had no idea how close to home this compliment was.

"I thought you'd be interested in the trip I'm planning." Mrs. Peters slid the pamphlet even closer to Conner. "I've decided to invite a few select students such as yourself—students who have proven to be passionate about writing and storytelling—to venture with me to Berlin and be among the crowd that hears the stories for the first time."

Conner picked up the pamphlet and stared down at it with an open mouth. "That sounds *awesome*!" He flipped it open and looked at all the attractions the city of Berlin had to offer. "Could we check out these nightclubs, too?"

"Unfortunately, missing more than a week of school for any trip is frowned upon by the school district. So no *nightclubs*, I'm afraid. We'll only be there for three days, but I thought this might be an opportunity you wouldn't want to miss," Mrs. Peters said with a confident smile. "I feel like a little piece of history is waiting for us."

Conner's smile faded when his eyes fell to the bottom of the pamphlet. He saw how much this trip would cost.

"Eek, this is a *pricey* educational opportunity," Conner said.

"Travel is never cheap, I'm afraid," Mrs. Peters said. "But there are many school fund-raisers I can get you information about—"

"Oh wait! I keep forgetting my mom just married a doctor! We're not poor anymore!" Conner said, and his smile returned. "But wait, does that mean *I'm* still poor? I'll have to ask them. There's so much to this stepson thing I haven't figured out yet."

Mrs. Peters raised her eyebrows and blinked twice, not sure what to tell him. "That's a conversation you'll have to have with them, but my office phone number is on the bottom of that pamphlet if you need help convincing them," she said with a quick wink.

"Thanks, Mrs. Peters!" Conner said. "Who else have you asked?"

"Only a handful of students," Mrs. Peters said. "I've learned the hard way that bringing more than six students to one chaperone on a trip can lead to a scene out of *Lord of the Flies.*"

"I understand," Conner said. He couldn't get the image out of his head of tribal sixth graders tying Mrs. Peters to a spit and roasting her over an open fire.

"But Bree Campbell has signed up," Mrs. Peters said. "I believe she's in Ms. York's English class with you?"

Conner could feel his heart rate rising. His cheeks went red and he pursed his lips to hide a smile. "Oh, good," he said softly while his inside voice was screaming, *Oh my gosh, Bree Campbell is going to Germany! That's amazing! That's the best news ever!*"

"She's quite the talented writer herself. I can imagine the two of you getting along nicely," Mrs. Peters said, oblivious to Conner's increasing pulse. "I hope you'll be able to join us. You should head back to class now."

Conner nodded as he got to his feet, and continued nodding all the way back to his Biology class. He didn't understand why the room always seemed to get warmer every time he saw or heard someone mention Bree Campbell. He wasn't even sure how he felt about her—but for whatever reason, Conner always looked forward to seeing her around and really wanted her to *like him.*

He couldn't explain it no matter how much thought he gave it. But one thing was certain: *Conner had to go to Germany!*

Telling his mom and stepdad after school went as well as Conner could have imagined.

"It's a really great educational opportunity," Conner stressed. "Germany is a really super-smart place with a lot of history, I think some kind of war happened there at some point—*can I go? Can I go?*"

Charlotte and Bob sat on the couch in front of him looking over the pamphlet. They both had just gotten home from working at the children's hospital and hadn't even had time to change out of their scrubs before they were attacked by a very enthusiastic Conner.

"This seems like a great trip," Charlotte said. "Your dad would have been so excited to hear about the Brothers Grimm time capsule!"

"I know, I know! Which is why I need to go—so I can experience it for all of us! Please, can I go?" he asked, bouncing in little hops. Whenever Conner asked them for something he acted like a hyper Chihuahua.

They only hesitated for a second but Conner felt like it was an hour. "Oh, come on! Alex gets to live in another dimension but I can't go on a school trip to Germany?"

"You can absolutely go," Charlotte said.

"YES!" Conner threw both hands into the air.

"But you'll have to pay for it," Charlotte quickly added.

Conner's hands instantly fell and his excitement deflated like a crashed hot air balloon. "I'm thirteen—I can't afford a trip to Europe!"

"True, but ever since we moved into Bob's house you've been getting an allowance for helping out around the house and your fourteenth birthday will be here before you know it," Charlotte said as she did the math in her head. "If you add those together with a little fund-raising at school, you'll be able to afford—"

"Half of it," Conner said. He had already done every possible math equation in relation to any parental scenario he thought they might throw his way. "So I'll be able to get there but I won't be able to come back."

Bob looked down at the pamphlet and shrugged. "Charlotte, what if we met him halfway? This is a really great opportunity. Besides, he's always been such a great kid, it couldn't hurt to treat him a little."

"Thanks, Bob! *Mom, listen to your husband!*" Conner said, and gestured toward him like he was directing a plane into a terminal.

Charlotte humored the idea for a moment. "That's fine by me," she said. "If you earn half and show us that this trip is something you really want, we'll give you the other half. Do we have a deal?"

Conner wiggled from all the excitement building up inside of him. *"Thank you, thank you, thank you!"* he said, and shook both their hands. *"Pleasure doing business with you!"*

And so, after four months of saving his allowance, birthday money, and taking part in school fund-raisers selling candy, baked goods, and hideous pottery (which Charlotte and Bob bought most of), Conner had earned his half of the trip and was ready for Germany.

At the beginning of the week leading up to his departure, when Conner should have started packing, Bob walked into his bedroom with another surprise. He plopped a very old and dusty suitcase onto his stepson's bed. It was brown and covered in stickers of famous locations, and made Conner's room smell like feet.

Bob placed his hands on his hips and proudly looked down at the suitcase. "There it is!" Bob said.

"There *what* is?" Conner said. "Is that a coffin?"

"No, it's the suitcase I used during my own Euro trip after college." Bob gently petted the side of it like it was an old dog. "We've had some pretty good times together—covered a lot of ground! I thought you could use it for Germany."

Conner couldn't imagine taking it overseas—he was shocked the suitcase wasn't instantly decaying like a mummy exposed to the elements after thousands of years. "I don't know what to say, Bob," he said, hiding his reservations under a fake smile. He couldn't refuse it after Bob had helped make the trip happen.

"No need to thank me," Bob said, although a thank-you was the furthest thing from Conner's mind. "Just do me a favor and get a sticker from Berlin for her."

"It's a *she*?"

"Oh, yes, her name is Betsy," Bob said as he headed out of his stepson's room. "Enjoy her! Oh, almost forgot, her left buckle needs a good push to lock. Just put your back into it and you'll be fine."

At the end of the week, Conner discovered exactly what Bob was talking about as he struggled to shut it with the new addition of pants. After three good pushes that almost threw out his back, he surrendered to Betsy.

"All right, maybe just six pairs of socks, four T-shirts, five pairs of underwear, two sweaters, pajamas, my lucky poker chip, a toothbrush, and *one* lucky rock will be enough," Conner said. He removed the excess items from the suitcase and finished packing.

He was overdue for bed but Conner wanted to stay awake for a little while longer. He wanted to feel the excitement as long as he could. Thinking about the trip to Germany had been a great way for Conner to ignore the other thoughts he had been having lately. As he looked around his bedroom and listened to the absolute silence of the house, Conner couldn't fight off the loneliness he had been suppressing. Something was missing from his life . . . *His sister.*

Conner opened his bedroom window to break the silence around him. Sycamore Drive was just as quiet as the house and did little to comfort him. He gazed up at the stars in the night sky. He wondered if Alex could see the same stars from wherever she was. Perhaps the Land of Stories was one of the stars he was looking at but it hadn't been discovered yet. Wouldn't that be an uplifting discovery? That he and his sister were only separated by light-years and not dimensions?

When Conner couldn't stand the solitude anymore, he asked himself, "I wonder if she's awake?"

Conner snuck down the stairs and into the family room. A large golden mirror hung there, on a wall it had all to itself. It was the mirror their grandmother had given them the last time they were together—it was the single object that allowed the twins to communicate between worlds.

He touched the golden frame and it started to shimmer and glow. It would glow for a few moments until Alex appeared in the mirror or return to its normal shade if she didn't—and tonight she didn't.

"She must be busy," Conner said quietly to himself. "She's always so busy."

When he first arrived home from his last adventure in the fairy-tale world, Conner talked to his sister in the mirror every day for a couple of hours. She told him all about the lessons their grandmother was teaching her and the magic she was learning to use. He told her about his days at school and everything he had been taught, but her stories were always much more interesting.

Unfortunately, as Alex became more and more involved with the fairy-tale world, the twins' daily conversations happened less and less often. Sometimes more than a week passed before they spoke. Sometimes Conner wondered if Alex even needed him anymore. He had always known that one day they would grow up and lead separate lives—he just never imagined it would happen so soon.

Conner touched the mirror again and waited, hoping his sister would arrive. He didn't want to leave for Germany before having a chance to talk to her.

"I guess I'll have to tell her about it when I get back," Conner said, and headed to bed.

Just as he reached the stairs, he heard a small voice behind him say, "Conner? Are you there?"

Conner ran back to the mirror and his heart jumped. His sister was standing in the mirror before him. She wore a headband made of white carnations and a sparkling dress the same color as the sky. She seemed cheerful but Conner could tell she was very tired.

"Hi, Alex! How are you?" he asked.

"I'm great," Alex said with a big smile. He could tell she was just as excited to see him as he was to see her. "You're up late."

"I couldn't sleep," Conner said. "Too excited, I guess."

Alex scrunched her forehead. "Excited about what?" Before Conner could say anything, Alex had answered her own question. "Oh, you're leaving for Germany tomorrow, aren't you?!"

"Yes," Conner said. "More like later today. It's super late here."

"I completely forgot! I'm so sorry!" Alex said, disappointed in herself for letting it slip her mind.

"No worries," Conner said. He couldn't care in the slightest, he was just happy to see her.

"I've been so busy with magic lessons and preparing for this silly Fairy Inaugural Ball," Alex said. She rubbed her eyes. "I even forgot about our birthday! Isn't that crazy? Grandma and Mother Goose made a cake and I had to ask them what it was for!"

It was Conner's turn to scrunch his forehead. "Fairy Inaugural Ball? What is that?"

"It's this big party the Fairy Council is throwing to celebrate me joining the Fairy Council," Alex said, as if it were just any old fact.

"That's amazing, Alex!" Conner said. "You're joining the Fairy Council already? You must be the youngest fairy that's ever joined!"

A proud and eager smile grew on her face. "Yes," she said. "Grandma thinks I'm ready. I'm not sure I agree with her, though; I still have so much to learn—"

"You know how protective Grandma is. She would protect the ocean from a raindrop," Conner said. "If she thinks you're ready then you must be!"

"I suppose," Alex said, still very unsure of herself. "It's just a lot of responsibility. Being part of the council means I'm automatically part of the Happily Ever After Assembly—which means having to give my input on so many decisions—which means so many people and creatures will look up to me for guidance—"

"There wouldn't still be a Happily Ever After Assembly if it wasn't for you," Conner reminded her. "That whole world is in your debt forever after defeating the Enchantress. I wouldn't worry."

Alex looked into his eyes and smiled. "Thanks, Conner." His reassurance always meant more to her than anyone else's.

"How is Grandma, by the way?" Conner asked.

"She's good," Alex said. "She misses you and Mom terribly—almost as much as I do. She's taught me so much over the past couple months. Really, Conner, you would be so impressed with some of the things I can do now."

Conner laughed. "Alex, I've been impressed by you since the womb. I'm sure your part of the uterus was much neater and more organized than mine."

Alex laughed out loud against her will—she missed her brother's sense of humor but she still didn't want to encourage it. "Really, Conner? A uterus joke? Come on. You're lucky Mom isn't awake to hear you," she said. "Is Mom doing all right? She's always very happy when she talks to me but we both know what a great front she can put up."

Conner nodded. "She's doing good, actually. She misses you but I've only caught her crying over an old photo of us together once or twice since we got back. Bob makes her really happy. I had almost forgotten what it was like to see her so happy all the time—it's like Dad is around again."

"That's great to hear," Alex said. "Dad would have been so excited about your Germany trip. He'd probably be going with you if he was still alive—I wish I could go."

Conner looked at the clock. "Speaking of which, I better get to bed soon. I leave for the airport in, like, three hours."

Alex's face fell. "Aw, that's too bad. I've missed you so much—it's been great to catch up," she said. "I've just been so busy. Sometimes a whole week will pass and I'll feel like it was only a day or two."

"You're still happy, though, right?" He looked at her with a raised eyebrow. He would know if she was lying to him.

"Um..." Alex thought about all her lessons, all her tasks, and despite how overwhelmed and tired she was, she told him the truth. "Honestly... *I've never been happier!* I get up every morning with a smile on my face because living here is like waking up to a dream that never ends!"

The twins shared a smile, each knowing this was the truth. As hard as it was to be without her, Conner knew Alex was where she belonged and was having the time of her life.

"I wish there was a way I could take you to Germany with me," Conner said.

"Me too!" Alex said. "But I doubt there's a story the Brothers Grimm wrote that we haven't heard from Grandma or Dad or— *wait a second...*" Her eyes fell to the bottom of the mirror. "Is the right side of your mirror's frame loose?"

Conner inspected the corner of his mirror. "Nope—but wait, I think the left side is."

"Can you gently pull it back and uncover the corner of the glass?" Alex asked as she did the same on her side.

"Check!" Conner said.

"Oh, good!" Alex said. "Now, can you gently chip off a piece without cracking—"

Clink! Conner held up a piece of glass bigger than the palm of his hand. "Like this?"

Clink! Alex broke off a piece of her own mirror—it was a smaller and neater piece than her brother's but neither commented on that.

"Perfect! Now look into it!" Alex looked down into hers.

Conner looked into the small piece of mirror in his hand and saw his sister's face staring up at him. "Amazing!" he said with a laugh. "Now I can keep you in my pocket the whole time! It's like video chat!"

"Terrific!" Alex said. "I've always wanted to see Europe! Now go get some rest; you don't want to be exhausted before you get to Germany."

"Okay. Good night, Alex," Conner said. "I'll call you—or, um, *reflect you* rather—as soon as I get off the plane!"

"I'll look forward to it," Alex said, so pleased she would be a part of his trip. "I love you, Conner!"

"I love you, too, Alex," Conner said. And with that, the twins faded from each other's mirrors and returned to their separate lives.

Conner climbed the stairs and placed his piece of mirror gently into his sticker-covered suitcase. He lay in bed and closed his eyes tightly but couldn't fall asleep—seeing his sister had rejuvenated him completely, causing all the excitement about the following day to come rushing back.

He laughed at himself as he lay there. "I've ridden a magical goose, climbed a giant beanstalk, swum to an enchanted underwater cave on a sea turtle's back, and sailed on a flying ship across the skies of another dimension....," Conner listed to himself. "But I'm excited about *getting on a plane tomorrow*! Oh, brother..."

CHAPTER TWO

THE HALL OF DREAMS

Alex woke up the next day wearing a big smile. She had woken up with a smile every day since she began living in the Land of Stories, but her smile was especially big today because she had talked to her brother the night before. And although her new home had brought her huge amounts of happiness, spending time with her family made her feel better.

The Fairy Palace was the most beautiful place Alex had ever lived. She marveled at its beautiful golden pillars, archways, staircases, towers, and vast tropical gardens. However, one downside was that there were very few walls and ceilings in the

Fairy Palace—it was always so pleasant outside the fairies had no need for them. So every morning when the sun rose over the Fairy Kingdom, Alex had no choice but to rise with it.

Luckily she had been able to enchant a magnolia tree to grow its branches and blossoms around her room like drapes. This gave her an extra few minutes of rest each morning before she forced herself out of bed and started her day. Other than the enchanted drapes, Alex kept her chambers quite simple. She had a large comfy bed with white rose-petal sheets, a few shelves filled to over-capacity with her favorite books, and a small wardrobe in the corner, which was practically unused thanks to a few magical tricks her grandmother had taught her.

Alex stepped out of bed, picked up her crystal wand from her nightstand, and waved it around her body. Her plain nightgown was instantly turned into a long, sparkling dress the color of the sky and a headband of white carnations appeared on her head—it was her standard fairy uniform and resembled her grandmother's.

"Good morning, Mom, Conner, and Bob," Alex said to a framed photo on her nightstand. "Good morning, Dad," she said to another framed photo, this one of her late father.

Alex took a deep breath and closed her eyes. "All right, three wishes by noon, three wishes by noon," she said to herself. "You can do this, you can do this."

Every day at noon Alex met her grandma in her grandma's chambers for a new lesson. Sometimes the lessons were magical, sometimes historical, sometimes philosophical, but whatever it was, the lesson was always highly enjoyable.

And although it wasn't expected, Alex had recently taken it upon herself to grant at least three wishes every day to the villagers nearby using the little magic she knew. It was very ambitious of the fourteen-year-old fairy-in-training, but Alex didn't feel like herself unless she was overachieving. Alex also found that the busier she kept, the less homesick she felt—and the less she thought about her home in the Otherworld, the better her training went.

She briskly walked out of her chambers, through the palace, and down its front steps. The shimmering golden walls and floor had taken some getting used to but they didn't make her nearly as dizzy as they had the first week she lived in the palace.

Alex passed Rosette, who was trimming a luscious rose garden just outside the palace. The roses and thorns were as big as her head.

"Good morning, Rosette!" Alex said.

"Good morning, dear!" Rosette waved at her as she walked by. "Another early morning, I see?"

"Yes, ma'am!" Alex said. "Three wishes by noon, that's my daily goal! I haven't missed a day in two months!"

"Good for you, dear! Keep up the good work!"

Alex continued through the gardens until loud snoring to her left startled her. She looked at the ground and saw Mother Goose sleeping against a large boulder, clutching a silver flask. Lester was passed out beside her—obviously the two had had a late night in the gardens.

"Good morning, Mother Goose!" Alex said loudly enough to wake them both.

Mother Goose snorted as she came to life. "Is it?" she said with one eye open. Lester yawned and stretched his long neck.

"Did you sleep outside all night?" Alex asked.

"Well, the last thing I remember was taking a walk with Lester after dinner and we stopped to sit for a moment," Mother Goose said. "It looks like we've been here ever since. *Lester, you mattress filler! You were supposed to wake me up! I'm getting a bad reputation.*"

Lester rolled his eyes as if to say, "That ship has sailed."

"Why do we have to live in a *morning* kingdom?" Mother Goose said to the goose. "I swear I'm going to move to the Eastern Kingdom. At least people know how to sleep there!" Mother Goose climbed on top of Lester and took his reins, and together they flew toward the Fairy Palace.

Alex chuckled as she watched them fly away. Then she reminded herself of her schedule and proceeded with her walk. She reached the edge of the gardens and found herself in a large meadow.

"Cornelius!" Alex called out. She smacked the side of her leg loudly. "Here, boy! Where are you? Cornelius?"

Across the meadow, sipping from a stream, was a unicorn—but he was unlike any other unicorn in the kingdom. Cornelius was frumpy with a big tummy that swung underneath him when he walked. A silver horn grew out of his head but had broken in half during an accident when he was a baby.

"There you are, Cornelius!" Alex said.

Cornelius was glad to see her and trotted over so she could pet his large nose.

"Good morning, boy." Alex sensed something off about her horned friend today. He didn't have as much of a bounce in his step. "What's wrong, Cornelius? You seem sad."

Cornelius lowered his massive head and looked gloomily across the stream. Alex looked, too, and saw a herd of magnificent unicorns in the distance. Each was more beautiful than the next, with their long, lean bodies and perfect horns that glistened in the sunlight.

"Oh, Cornelius," Alex said, and stroked his mane. "You've got to stop comparing yourself to the other unicorns."

Cornelius nodded but Alex could see the self-consciousness in his eyes. He was never good at keeping any emotion to himself—he wore his heart on his hoof.

"Do you know why I chose you to be *my* unicorn, Cornelius?" she asked him.

The troubled unicorn opened his lips and showed off his large pearly white teeth.

"Yes, I know you have a good smile, but that's not the only reason," Alex said.

Cornelius stood on his back legs and moved his front legs in tiny circles.

"Yes, you're a good dancer, too, but those aren't what I'm talking about," Alex said. "I chose you because you are different from all the other unicorns in the Fairy Kingdom. Your horn may be broken and small, but your heart is big and strong."

Cornelius exhaled a gust of air and turned the other way. Alex had made him blush, the pink showing through his white hide.

"Are you ready to help me grant some wishes today?" Alex asked him. He neighed excitedly. "Good, then let's get going!" Cornelius bent down and Alex hopped aboard his back. She waved her wand over his head and whispered into his ear, *"Take us to someone who needs us, Cornelius."*

Cornelius's broken horn began to glow, his head jerked northwest, and he started galloping at full speed to wherever it was the magic was leading him. Unicorns ran much faster than normal horses and Alex had to hold on to her headband as they went.

They zoomed through the trees, over a river and two streams, and eventually found a path that led them into the Charming Kingdom. A small and simple village came into view in the distance and Cornelius slowed down. He took Alex into the heart of the village—his horn was guiding him like a hound's nose. Many of the villagers stopped in their tracks as Alex and the unicorn strode by them.

"Hello, good people of the Charming Kingdom!" Alex said. She awkwardly waved at them. "Don't mind us, we're just granting wishes!"

The villagers weren't as excited as she was hoping they'd be, and went back to their daily errands. Cornelius came to a halt right in front of a tiny cottage with stick walls and a hay roof.

"Are you sure this is the right place?" Alex asked. Cornelius nodded confidently and his horn stopped glowing.

Alex hopped down from her unicorn and walked to the door. She knocked lightly but the sticks broke under her knuckles, leaving a small hole in the door.

"Oh dear," Alex said. She wasn't off to a good start.

"Who's there?" a faint voice asked from behind the door. Alex looked through the hole she had just made and saw a pair of eyes staring out at her.

"Hello," Alex said. "My name is Alex and I'm a fairy! Well—technically I'm a fairy-in-training—but I've come here today to grant wishes. My unicorn has led me to this location. Does someone inside this cottage have a wish they'd like granted?"

The wrinkled eyes looked her up and down. Alex knew her introduction was as much of a work in progress as her magic, but to her surprise, the door opened and an elderly woman appeared before her.

"Come in," the woman said, although she didn't seem thrilled to have company.

"Thank you," Alex said. She took a step inside and looked around the small home. It was dirty and dim, as frail on the inside as it was on the outside. "You have a lovely home," Alex said politely. "What can I help you with?"

"These are my granddaughters. I'm assuming you've come to help them," the woman said. Had she not addressed them, Alex wouldn't even have seen the identical triplet girls standing against the wall. They were so dirty they blended into the rest of the house.

"Nice to meet you," Alex said but they wouldn't shake her hand.

"They need nice clothes for school," the woman said. She sat down at a table covered in thread and fabric. "We can't afford to buy new dresses so I tried making them myself, but my hands aren't what they used to be." She raised two hands that shook with arthritis.

"Say no more!" Alex said. "I'll turn their tattered clothes into beautiful dresses they'll be proud to wear at school!"

The triplets looked at one another with wide eyes—*could she actually do it?* Alex was asking herself the same question. She raised her wand and flicked it at each of the girls like she was conducting a symphony. One by one, a bright sparkly light circled each girl, transforming her dirty clothes into a vibrant pink dress with a white collar.

The girls looked down at their new dresses in total silence. Alex figured they were shocked from witnessing magic—but she was very wrong.

"Gross, they're pink!" one of the girls said.

"I hate pink!" another said.

"Can you make them another color?" the third asked.

Alex was taken aback by their ungrateful remarks. She looked at their grandmother, expecting them to be reprimanded.

"Don't look at me. You never asked them what color they wanted," the woman said.

"Oh, sorry! My mistake," Alex said. She raised her wand and flicked it three more times at the girls, transforming the dresses into yellow, purple, and blue.

"Better?" Alex asked.

"I don't like my collar," one of the girls said.

"I want green," another said.

"I liked the pink one better," the third said.

Alex's nostrils flared and she bit her tongue. "Fine," she said with a tight jaw. She flicked her wand to grant their requests. "Are we all happy?"

"Sure," one of the girls said unenthusiastically.

"It's *fine*," another said.

"Can I have my old clothes back?" the third said.

Alex was floored. She wanted to tell them that beggars can't be choosers, but as a fairy she couldn't bring herself to say it. After all, she wasn't helping them because they were poor; she was helping them because that's what she was supposed to do.

"Girls, I want you to thank the nice fairy lady for the new dresses even though she doesn't know what she's doing," the old woman said.

The triplets frowned. "Thank you," they said in unison, not meaning a word of it.

"You're welcome," Alex said, not meaning it, either. "Enjoy school."

She left the house in a huff and found Cornelius nibbling on a piece of the roof. She convinced herself that even though her first deed of the day had been unappreciated, it had still been a good one. Alex jumped on Cornelius's back and waved her wand over him again.

"One wish down, two more to go," she said. "Take us to our next stop, Cornelius!"

The unicorn's horn glowed again and he began to run in another direction. Soon they arrived just outside an even smaller village in the northern part of the Charming Kingdom. Cornelius took Alex straight up a hill and dropped her off beside a well where two village children stood staring down into it.

Alex smiled and struck a pose for them with her wand raised. "Hello, children!" she said, but they continued staring down the well. Alex cleared her throat. "How can I help you? Did you drop something down there?"

The children finally looked up at her, but their subdued expressions didn't change.

"No," the boy said. "It's been dried up for a while."

"Our mom sends us here every day with a pail, hoping there'll be water," the girl said. "But every day we return with nothing."

Alex was happy to hear of their misfortune. "I can help you with that!" she said, feeling useful.

"How?" the boy asked.

"Are you going to build us another well?" the girl asked.

"No, I'm a fairy!" Alex said, a bit disheartened that she had to tell them. She was certain her grandmother never had to tell people who *she* was. "I can cast a magic spell to make the water come back."

The village children both raised an eyebrow at her, not buying it.

"If you're a fairy, then where are your wings?" the boy asked.

"Not all of us have wings," Alex said. "We come in all shapes, sizes, and variations."

The children cocked their heads and stared at Cornelius behind her. "Is that a unicorn?" the boy asked.

"It sure is! He's the reason I'm here—he brought me to this spot knowing I could be of service," Alex explained. Cornelius lifted his head proudly, showing off for the children, but they were a tough crowd.

"Why is he so fat?" the boy asked.

"Is his horn broken?" the girl asked.

Cornelius lowered his head and looked at the ground sadly.

"He broke his horn when he was a baby and he eats his feelings, okay?" Alex quickly told them. "Now do you want me to fix your well or not?"

The village children shrugged. "I suppose," the boy said. "It can't get any worse."

Alex was so glad to finally get to the point. She instructed the children to stand a few feet behind her. She peeked inside the well and saw nothing but dirt at the end of a very long drop. She raised her crystal wand and swung it toward the well. The sound of water echoed up the well as the bottom of it was magically filled. The village children jumped and clapped for joy.

"You fixed our well!" the boy said happily.

"You *are* a fairy after all!" the girl said.

"Let's take you back to the village so they can reward you!" the boy said.

Alex shrugged and her cheeks went a little rosy. She was very pleased to be appreciated. "No need to reward me," she said. "Everything I do is for the greater good and I never expect—"

Alex stopped talking and the village children became very still. The ground underneath their feet shook and a loud whistling sound came from the well as it filled with more and more water rushing to the top.

"Oh no," Alex peeped. She and the children and Cornelius slowly backed away. A massive geyser shot out of the well and into the sky like an erupting volcano.

"I was wrong!" the boy shouted. *"This is worse! This is worse!"*

"Run for your life!" the girl yelled.

The children ran down the hill and back to their village as fast as they could, screaming their heads off. Villagers dashed outside their homes and shops to see what all the fuss was about—they couldn't believe their eyes. Water from the geyser rained down on the village, drenching everyone and everything.

Alex and Cornelius were getting drenched, too. "Cornelius! Sit on the well! Plug it up until I can think of something to do!" she said. The unicorn looked at her like she was out of her mind. *"Please?"* Alex pleaded.

Cornelius carefully went to the well. His hooves were messy from all the fresh mud the geyser was creating. He lifted his tail and sat right on the well, plugging it up and stopping the geyser. It was a degrading experience for him but it proved to be useful. The village cheered from below, but it only lasted a moment. The water built up inside the well and shot the unicorn straight into the air. He landed on the muddy hill and slid toward the village like an avalanche. All the villagers ran back into their homes and shops to avoid him.

Cornelius crashed into the side of a barn. He was covered in so much mud he looked like Black Beauty.

"Dry!" Alex yelled, and pointed her wand at the well. "Dry up, I said! *Dry! Dry! Dry!*"

Suddenly a huge ball of fire erupted from the tip of Alex's wand and hit the well, blasting half of it into pieces. Thankfully, the water pressure diminished and the geyser died down. The well was broken but full of water—and the village was covered in it, too.

"I fixed it!" Alex happily called down to the village below. The villagers peeked out from their homes and stared up at her, each soaked, dripping, and furious. "The good news is you have water again." Alex tried to laugh it off, but no one joined her.

The muddy unicorn joined the young fairy at the top of the hill. "Okay, Cornelius, let's get out of here."

She climbed on his back and they took off—not in the direction of their next stop but just as far away from the soaked village as they could get for the moment. They found a tiny stream in the woods and cleaned themselves up. Cornelius had a hard time looking at his reflection in the water; he was fat, broken, *and* dirty.

"Would you like me to use my wand to make you clean again?" Alex asked Cornelius. The unicorn shook his head—he didn't want what had happened to the well to happen to him. "Okay, then," said Alex, "let's move on to our final stop."

It was a couple hours till noon and Cornelius's magic horn steered them to the southwest corner of the Eastern Kingdom. A farm appeared in the distance that Alex thought she recognized.

"Haven't we been here before?" Alex asked Cornelius, but he was certain his horn was leading them to the right place. Up ahead Alex saw a farmer building a fence around his vegetable garden and figured he was the man they were looking for.

"Excuse me? Do you need any help?" she asked the farmer.

The farmer wiped the sweat off his brow and looked over his shoulder at her. He instantly got to his feet and waved her away like she was a wild animal he didn't want to deal with.

"Whoa, whoa, whoa," the farmer said. "I don't want any trouble, lady!"

Alex was insulted. What about her could possibly make him believe she was bringing trouble?

"Sir, I'm not trying to cause any harm," Alex assured him. "I'm a fairy. I'm here to help."

The farmer placed his hands on his hips and squinted at her. "That's what you said the last time," he said.

"The *last time*?" Alex asked. "So I've been here before?"

The farmer regretfully nodded. "Yes, you *helped* me put a fence around my yard to keep out the rabbits and deer," he informed her.

Alex pressed her index finger to her mouth as she recalled. "Oh, I remember you! You're Farmer Robins!" she said. "But what happened to the fence I gave you?"

Alex heard a door shut. She looked up and saw Farmer Robins's son coming out from their house—Alex didn't have any trouble remembering him. He was tall and strong, no more than a year older than her, had wispy hair that covered his face, and in Alex's opinion, was very handsome.

"The animals ate your fence," the farmer's son said with a brash smile. "It was made of vines and leaves—it was fun to watch you make it magically grow out of the ground but it wasn't ideal for keeping out herbivores."

"Don't you have a table to build?" Farmer Robins asked his son.

"I'm on a break," the son said. Clearly he wanted to stick around now that Alex was there. She tried her best not to look him directly in the eyes—she could feel herself blushing when she did.

"Well, why didn't you tell me the fence wouldn't work the last time I was here?" she asked the farmer.

"You didn't give us much of a chance," the farmer's son answered for him. "You just sort of waved your wand and then left, insisting there was no need to thank you."

Alex shook her head and rolled her eyes. "Gosh, no good deed goes unpunished," she said to herself. "Well, then I insist you let me make it up to you!" Alex raised her wand; she was just about to make a new fence appear when the farmer blocked her.

"Young lady," Farmer Robins said rudely, "I've got a full day of chores ahead of me and building this fence is just the beginning. The best thing you can do is leave us alone and stop wasting our time."

"That's silly," Alex tried to argue. "All I have to do is wave my wand and the fence will be done—"

"I said *LEAVE!*" Farmer Robins yelled, losing his patience with her. "We don't *want* your help and we don't *need* it. I know you people solve everything with just a flick of your wrist, but people like us know how to take care of ourselves. So please go turn a maid into a princess somewhere before I do or say something I'll regret."

Alex's mouth dropped open. She wasn't going to let someone speak to her like that, especially after the awful morning she had been having. Farmer Robins had picked the wrong day to mess with this fairy.

"No!" Alex yelled back at the farmer.

"What?" the farmer said.

"No, I will not *leave*," Alex said.

The farmer's son perked up—this was going to be interesting.

"I'm really sorry for going out of my way to help you but you aren't the only one with a job, buddy," Alex said. She stepped closer to Farmer Robins. "The fact is, you need my help whether you want it or not, and that's why I'm here! That's why my unicorn brought me! So swallow your pride, step back, and get out of my way because I'm not leaving until this fence is built!"

Farmer Robins looked genuinely terrified of Alex. His son bit his fist and choked on the laughter building up inside of him. Alex set her wand on the ground and rolled up her sleeves. She walked over to the farmer and reached for his hammer.

"What are you doing?" the farmer asked.

"Give me your hammer," Alex demanded. "I don't need magic to build this fence."

She yanked the hammer out of his hand, picked up a couple pieces of wood, and continued to build what the farmer had started. Farmer Robins and his son stood motionless and watched the young fairy work.

"If you two have so much work to do today, I suggest you get to it while I build this," she snapped with a dirty glare. They didn't argue. Farmer Robins went to work a few feet away, pulling carrots out of the ground, and his son went back inside the house to finish the table.

Alex built the fence at a very quick pace. Fueled by frustration, she had the whole thing done in just under two hours. She pounded the final nail into the last piece of wood and returned to her unicorn.

"I'm done!" she called to Farmer Robins. His son stepped back outside to see the completed fence—he was very impressed by the young fairy's craftsmanship. She retrieved her wand from the ground and jumped onto Cornelius's back.

"Have a nice day, gentlemen!" Alex said. "And by the way, *no need to thank me! BECAUSE I'M A FAIRY, IT'S MY JOB!*"

Alex and Cornelius galloped away, leaving the two stunned farmers in the dust behind them. It was a few minutes past noon by the time Alex made it back to the Fairy Kingdom. She left Cornelius in the meadow at the edge of the gardens and hurried toward the Fairy Palace, not wanting to keep her grandmother waiting a minute longer.

"Oh come on now, they aren't going to sting you!" said a perky voice in the garden. Tangerina was feeding acorns to a family of squirrels in a tree when Alex ran past her. The bees flying around Tangerina's beehive were making the squirrels very apprehensive.

"Hi, Tangerina," Alex said.

"Oh my goodness, what happened to you?" Tangerina asked when she saw Alex hurrying past her. Between fixing the well and building the fence, Alex had become filthy. "You look like you fell into a stream!"

"It's a long story," Alex said, trying to avoid getting wrapped up in an explanation.

"Did someone say stream?" an airy voice asked from across the garden. Skylene surfaced in the nearby pond. Her long, silky hair and gown were one with the water as she floated through it.

"Poor Alex has had a rough morning," Tangerina said.

"Just trying to help as many people as I could before my noon lesson with Grandma," Alex told her fairy counterparts.

"Don't work too hard, Alex," Skylene said. "You've got a big day coming up!" She floated through the pond and gently touched the surface with her finger, causing gorgeous white lilies to appear around her. "I'm getting a head start on the decorations. I've always loved a good fairy inauguration celebration. It's an excuse for the kingdom to look its best!"

"I can't wait for the Inaugural Ball! My bees are making me a brand-new honeycomb gown as we speak!" Tangerina said.

"How fancy is this Inaugural Ball?" Alex asked them, feeling a hurricane of anxiety forming inside her. "I thought it was just a simple ceremony. Do I have to dress up?"

Tangerina and Skylene exchanged the same worried look—as if she had asked them what the sun was.

"Sweetheart, the Fairy Inaugural Ball is how you're introduced to society," Skylene said. "You need to look how you want to be remembered."

"Every fairy in the kingdom will be there," Tangerina said. "And they'll all be there to see you!"

Alex closed her eyes. "Oh great...," she said, "as if joining the Fairy Council wasn't enough, now I'll have to worry about looking nice in front of the whole kingdom. Why does it seem like fairies always spare the details until the very last minute?"

"Not to worry, dear, you'll look fine in whatever you choose," Tangerina said.

"Yes, just don't choose that," Skylene said, and pointed to the dirty dress she was currently wearing.

Alex sighed quietly. She waved her wand over her body and her dress sparkled until it was like new again. "Well, good talk, girls! Thanks!" she said, and continued to the Fairy Palace.

Alex rushed up the golden front steps of the palace, down the main hall, and up a flight of stairs to the top floor, where her grandmother's chambers were. They were some of the only parts of the palace that had four walls, so Alex had to knock.

"Come in, dear," Alex heard her grandmother say, and she stepped inside. It didn't matter how many times she had been there, her grandmother's rooms always dazzled her.

To call the Fairy Godmother's chambers anything but spectacular would be an understatement. The furniture was made of rosy-dusk clouds and floated around the room. Her bed was under the branches of a white willow tree with crystal leaves. Instead of a fire burning in the giant fireplace to one side of the room, bubbles emitted from it and filled the air. A chandelier made of a hundred perched doves floated above the center of the room, although there was no ceiling for it to hang from.

Every surface in the room was covered with the Fairy Godmother's collectibles. Jewels given to her by monarchs from both worlds over time covered the mantel. A large table near the fireplace was covered with colorful bottles of potions and elixirs. A glass display case mounted to the wall contained the Fairy Godmother's wand collection. A mini-library of books of spells, fantasy, and history covered the wall across from the fireplace.

But in front of all these valuables were countless family photos of Alex and Conner and their dad, crayon drawings they had done for her as kids, math and spelling tests they had received

A's on, and horrific macaroni creations the twins had made her for Grandparents' Day. She hadn't thrown out anything the twins had ever given her.

In the back of the room, elevated on a platform, was the Fairy Godmother's desk, made entirely of glass—although Alex never saw her sitting behind it. She always found her standing by one of the four tall windows behind it that looked out to a breathtaking view of the Fairy Kingdom.

"Hello, Alex," Grandma said by one of the windows. She was in her trademark blue robes that sparkled like a starry sky.

"Sorry I'm late, Grandma," Alex said. "Things got a little carried away today when I was granting wishes."

"Oh?" Grandma asked. "Why is that?"

Alex sighed. "Sometimes I don't know if I should be a fairy," she confessed. "Don't get me wrong: I love magic and I love helping people. There are days I'll get up and feel so good about what I'm doing for people, and then others when I feel like I'm just screwing everything up. Some days I don't think I'm helping enough people, and then other days I don't think people even want my help. And when I don't feel confident, my magic suffers—it becomes so unpredictable. And when that happens I feel like I have no business being on the Fairy Council."

Alex sat on the steps of the platform and rubbed her tired eyes. Her grandmother walked over to her and gently stroked the top of her head.

"You're overexerting yourself, Alex," the Fairy Godmother told her granddaughter. "You're only one person. No matter how hard you try, you can't help *everyone*. And you're beginning to learn that some people can't be helped, not because they're helpless, but because they don't want to be helped."

Alex looked at the floor—this was a hard lesson to learn.

"I'm glad you brought this up," Grandma said. "There is something I wanted to show you. Follow me."

The Fairy Godmother helped her granddaughter to her feet and escorted her out of the room and down a very long hallway. They stopped at a large pair of doors in an impressive arched entryway. Alex had never seen these doors before.

"Where are we, Grandma?"

"*This*," Grandma began with a smile, "is the *Hall of Dreams*."

The Fairy Godmother pushed open the doors. Alex gasped and her eyes grew to twice their size. The room inside was unlike anything she'd ever seen. It was a dark and endless space that seemed to stretch for miles in every direction. Bright orbs of all sizes floated around them. It was like the whole galaxy had been squeezed into the room in front of them.

They stepped inside and shut the doors behind them. Alex wasn't sure how they were standing since there was technically no floor.

"This room has been here since the beginning of fairies," Grandma said.

"What are they?" Alex asked as the orbs flew around her.

"They're *dreams*, each and every one of them," her grandma told her. "No matter how big or small the dream, a record of every *wish* or *want* can be found in this room."

"There are thousands—no, millions of them!" Alex said.

"Oh, yes, possibly more!" the Fairy Godmother said. "As you can see, even with all the fairies in the world, it would be impossible to make every dream come true. When you look inside them you can see what they are and who they belong to."

A medium-size orb floated directly into Alex's hand. She peered into it closely and could see a small girl wearing a paper crown inside.

"That little girl dreams of becoming a princess," Grandma said. "You'll find a lot of those in here. We tend to pay special attention to the ones more like *this*."

One of the largest orbs floated into her hand and they both looked into it. Inside the orb a sad little boy watched over his younger sister, who sat in a wooden wheelchair.

"This little boy would give anything just to see his sister walk again," Grandma said. "It's one of the larger orbs because it's one of the larger dreams—and it's easier to hold because it's selfless. I'm going to save it and see if there's anything I can do for them later." Grandma promptly placed the orb in a pocket of her robes.

"So *this* is how you find all the people you help?" Alex asked.

"Indeed," the Fairy Godmother said. "Much more efficient than unicorns, don't you agree?"

The two exchanged a smile. Alex tried to reach for another large orb, but it wouldn't stay in her hand.

"Why can't I grab that one?" Alex asked, afraid it was something to do with her.

"Because whoever that dream belongs to doesn't want your help, and from the looks of it, they don't even want you to know what their dream is," Grandma said.

"That's silly," Alex said. "Why wouldn't they want me to see it?"

"To know someone's deepest desires is to risk knowing them more than they want to be known," the Fairy Godmother said. "I've had to learn that lesson the hard way many times."

Alex thought for a moment and stopped trying to grab the orb. "It must be so frustrating to see all these dreams and know you can't make them all come true," she said.

"When I was younger, perhaps," the Fairy Godmother said. "But we should do what we can, and not torture ourselves over the things we can't. It's unfair and unrealistic to expect yourself to solve every problem in the world. Never forget that no matter how many dreams you find in here, there would be many more if it weren't for people like us. Every wish granted by the magic from a fairy's wand inspires a dozen more that will be achieved by the magic within people themselves. Take a look at that one."

The Fairy Godmother gestured at an orb floating in front of them that slowly faded away until it disappeared.

"What happened to it?" Alex asked.

"The dream came true," Grandma said. "And it had nothing to do with us. After years and years of being inspired by other dreamers, that person made their own dream come true and probably inspired countless others to do the same. We wouldn't want to live in a world where no one believed in themselves enough to make their own dreams come true."

A shy smile came to Alex's face. "I think I get what you're trying to teach me, Grandma."

Grandma smiled back at her. "I'm glad to hear it." A small

orb landed in the Fairy Godmother's hand but it instantly faded away.

"Whose was that?" Alex asked.

"Mine," Grandma said. "Every lesson that you learn is a dream come true for me. And I have to say, you're learning much faster than I ever did."

Alex smiled again. Despite how frustrating her day had been, her grandmother made her feel like she was accomplishing her *own* dreams. She knew that somewhere in this room an orb that belonged to her had just disappeared.

"Now, aside from our lessons, I want you to relax for the rest of the week. You can't help anyone if you don't know how to help yourself first," the Fairy Godmother instructed her.

"All right," Alex reluctantly agreed. "Thank you for the lesson, Grandma." She hugged her and left the Hall of Dreams. She didn't know what to do with herself for the rest of the day— it'd been a while since she had allowed herself any free time.

Once her granddaughter left, the Fairy Godmother closed her eyes and tiny tears formed behind her lids. She had never thought it would be possible to be as proud of someone as she was of Alex. She knew that one day Alex would be an even better fairy godmother than she was.

And unfortunately, due to some changes the Fairy Godmother had recently felt inside herself, she knew that day was going to arrive much sooner than either of them wanted. . . .

CHAPTER THREE

THE BOOK HUGGERS

Conner was having a whimsical dream. He was skipping through the German countryside in bright green lederhosen, merrily swinging a basket of freshly picked flowers. He yodeled happily as he skipped toward a picturesque village ahead of him. Everything was so peaceful and happy—he never wanted to leave. But suddenly, a screeching alarm sounded through the area—it was a familiar sound, one that he had heard many times before. Conner looked to the sky and saw the evil alien race from the television show he had watched the night before descend upon the village and begin attacking it!

The dream came to an abrupt stop when Conner realized the sound was coming from his alarm clock. He smacked it a couple times more than necessary to shut it off. He was so tired he didn't even feel alive. He felt like his head was filled with a giant cloud that made it difficult to keep his eyes open.

Even though he was glad he'd gotten to spend time with Alex the night before, he was seriously regretting his decision to stay up so late. He got dressed and dragged Betsy down the stairs one step at a time. Bob and Charlotte were waiting for him by the front door—they had always been *morning people*, a race Conner never understood.

"Ready, champ?" Bob asked, spinning his car keys in his hand.

Conner grunted something that sounded like yes. Charlotte had an early morning at the hospital and was already dressed for work. She put her arms around her son and hugged him tightly.

"Make good choices, Conner," she said. "But most important, have fun!"

"Mom, I can't go to Germany if you're still hugging me," Conner wheezed through her tight grip.

"I just need another minute," Charlotte said. "You're the only kid I've got left to hug."

Once his mother finally let go, Conner threw his suitcase into the back of Bob's car and they left the house. They stopped at a fast-food drive-in for a greasy breakfast, one they wouldn't have gotten away with if Charlotte was with them, and headed to the airport. Bob happily reminisced about his own European adventures as he drove. Conner faded in and out of the conversation—the subtle bumps and vibrations of the car kept putting him to sleep. Eventually they arrived at the airport and Bob pulled up to the curbside.

"Before you get out, there's something I wanted to give you," Bob said in a very serious tone.

"It isn't the birds-and-the-bees talk, is it?" Conner asked, fearing the worst. "Because I've already seen all the videos at school."

"Um, no . . . ," Bob said. He paused for a moment, wondering if that was the talk he should have been giving him instead, but then proceeded as planned. "I got you something your mom doesn't know about."

Bob reached into his front pocket and pulled out a credit card. He handed it to his stepson and Conner was shocked to see "Conner Jonathan Bailey" written across the bottom.

"That's my . . . my . . . *my name*," Conner said. "You got me a *credit card,* Bob?!"

"I did," Bob said. "The pin number is the year you were born. It's only for emergencies and only for this trip, understand? As soon as you come home safe and sound I'm going to take it back. I know your mom is against things like this but I'd rather you were safe than sorry—so it's our little secret, okay?"

Conner excitedly bobbed his head up and down. "Absolutely! Bob, you're slowly becoming my favorite person ever! Thank you so much!"

Bob smiled and chuckled to himself. "Glad to hear it." He patted Conner on the back. "You're my family, Conner. I need to make sure you'll be all right. Now go have an adventure—I mean, you know, one by normal standards. Try to avoid the evil enchantresses and talking animals as much as possible."

Conner spotted Mrs. Peters standing outside the terminal entrance. She was surrounded by a group of four girls from school who had all just arrived as well. As excited as he was about the trip, Conner wasn't looking forward to traveling with *these* girls.

"Don't worry," Conner reassured Bob. "The scariest thing on this trip is waiting for me over there."

Conner gave Bob a hug, grabbed Betsy from out of the back, and waved good-bye as Bob drove off. He joined Mrs. Peters and the group of girls by the entrance. All the girls looked as tired as Conner. Mrs. Peters, however, looked exactly the same as she always did, which furthered Conner's theory that she was a robot.

"Good morning, Mr. Bailey," Mrs. Peters said, perky as ever.

"Good morning, Mrs. Peters," Conner said. "Good morning, Mindy—Cindy—Lindy—Wendy."

None of the girls responded, and Conner hadn't expected them to. They hadn't said a word to Conner since the school year began. Instead, they would just stare daggers at him from afar—as if he had publicly humiliated them in the past and never apologized for it. Conner couldn't think of a reason they did this but he never spent too much thought on it. He knew girls tended to get very strange at their age—and these four were already some of the strangest girls he had ever met.

Mindy, Cindy, Lindy, and Wendy had been inseparable since the first grade when they were grouped together by their teacher for a rhyming project. Together they made up the Reading Club at school and spent every moment they could in the library. They would have reminded Conner of his sister had they not been so eccentric.

Mindy was the shortest, the loudest, and the self-appointed leader of their group. She wore her hair in pigtails every day as if she was contractually obligated to. Cindy was the youngest and to this day proudly told everyone that she had skipped kindergarten. She also had a mouthful of braces with enough metal to build a satellite. Lindy was African American and the tallest girl at school. She even towered over all her teachers. She stood a bit hunched over from all the time she spent looking down at people. Wendy was painfully shy and usually let the other girls do all the talking. She was Japanese and had very dark hair and the largest eyes Conner had ever seen on a human.

He had known for a while that the four girls were going on the trip and it had almost convinced him to stay home. But luckily, Bree was going, which somehow made the whole trip worthwhile.

"We're just waiting for Ms. Campbell to arrive and then we'll get checked in," Mrs. Peters said, looking up and down the curb. "You're the only boy on the trip, Mr. Bailey. Are you sure you can handle it?"

"Oh yeah," Conner said. "I'm used to it. My mom and sister used to talk about all kinds of girl things in front of me... usually over dinner, too, which I never appreciated."

The girls exchanged dramatic eye rolls with one another as soon as Conner mentioned his sister. He couldn't figure out what their problem was.

"Oh, here comes Ms. Campbell," Mrs. Peters said.

Conner jerked his head in the direction she was looking and saw Bree Campbell walking toward them. The exhausting clouds filling his head instantly deflated. Just seeing her made Conner feel like he had drunk five energy drinks.

Bree Campbell was unlike any girl Conner had ever met. She was always very calm and cool, never raised her voice for anything, and never seemed to let anything or anyone affect her in any way. She had blonde hair with a streak of pink and blue in her bangs. She usually wore bracelets and wristbands by the dozen, always wore a purple beanie, and had an earbud plugged into one ear whenever she could.

"Good morning, Ms. Campbell," Mrs. Peters said.

"Good morning, everyone," Bree said with a yawn. She even *yawned* cooler than everyone else, Conner thought.

"Let's go inside and get checked in," Mrs. Peters instructed, and they followed her with their luggage. One by one they showed their passports to the lady behind the counter and checked in to their flight.

Conner was standing in line right behind Bree. He couldn't explain the anxiety she caused him. He was so excited to be near her, yet terrified at the same time.

She's just a girl, not a python, he said to himself over and over in his head. *Be cool. Don't try to be funny. Just act normal. And when you get back home you need to see a doctor about this.*

"Mindy, Cindy, Lindy, and Wendy are in row thirty-one, seats A, B, C, and D," Mrs. Peters said as she passed out their plane tickets. "And Conner and Bree are in row thirty-two, seats A and B."

Conner's heart was doing cartwheels. *I'm sitting next to Bree! I'm sitting next to Bree! Woo-hoo!* he thought. *But why does that seem like the best news of my life?*

He got a glimpse of Bree's passport photo—which was, to no surprise, far better than his—and Bree caught him staring at it. Conner had to think fast so he didn't seem like the creeper that he was.

"Your passport picture is much better than mine," he said. "I got mine over the summer and made the mistake of asking if I was supposed to smile right as they took it."

He flipped his passport open so she could get a glimpse of it.

"It kind of looks like you sneezed and it scared you," Bree said blankly. There was no trace of judgment or mockery in her voice. It was a perfectly honest description.

"Would you like to check your bag, sir?" the lady at the counter asked. It took Conner a second to realize she was talking to him; no one had ever called him *sir* before.

"Oh, please! Take her!" Conner said and handed Betsy over to be tagged. The lady gave him a strange look, hearing that his suitcase had a gender. "I mean take *it*. Take *the suitcase*."

Betsy was loaded onto the conveyor belt and slowly traveled farther and farther away from him. The next time he'd see her would be in Germany. Conner and the girls went through the security line and their group was boarding the plane within the hour.

The plane was massive. Conner couldn't wrap his head around how something so big could get into the air. Even after witnessing all the magical things he had seen in the Land of Stories, it was still fascinating to him. They walked down the aisle and found their seats. Conner gulped when he realized how long he would have to spend in such a small area.

"Where is your seat, Mrs. Peters?" Mindy asked. All the seats around them were filling up fast.

"I'll be in first class," Mrs. Peters said. "But don't worry; if any of you need me, just have a flight attendant notify me. I'll be in row one, seat A. It's going to be a long flight, so get comfortable."

And with that said, Mrs. Peters promptly turned on her heel and pushed her way past the oncoming travelers to the front of the plane. Conner sat down in his seat by the window and Bree sat next to him. He stared at the back of the seat in front of him for a moment; he had no idea how to start a conversation with her.

"Are you okay by the window?" Conner asked her.

Bree looked confused. "But *you're* by the window," she said.

Conner wanted to smack his head against the stupid window—they weren't off to a good start. "Oh, right, what I meant to ask was if you wanted to sit by the window," he said. "I wouldn't mind switching seats."

"I'll be fine," Bree said. "I'm just going to read for most of the flight." She gestured to her bag and Conner saw it was full of thick murder-mystery novels. Bree kept getting cooler by the second.

"Great. Let me know if you change your mind," Conner said, and returned to staring at the seat in front of him until he thought of something else to say. "So, Mrs. Peters was telling me you like to write, too."

"Uh-huh." Bree nodded. "Short stories mostly. I read some

of yours when I TA'd for Ms. York last year—they're cute. They remind me of classic fairy tales."

Conner couldn't believe his ears. "You've read *my* stories?"

"Yup," Bree said. "I liked them a lot—especially the one about the Curvy Tree and the Walking Fish. Those were very clever."

"Thanks," Conner said, and blushed a deep shade of red. Not only had she read them but she also *remembered* them. "Those were originally called the Curvy Giraffe and the Flying Frog, but I changed the titles to sound more...um...realistic. What kind of stories do you write?"

"I just finished one called 'Cemetery of the Undead,'" Bree said. "It's pretty self-explanatory."

Conner nodded a little too much to seem normal. "Sounds lovely."

He felt like an idiot talking about his fairy tales knowing that she wrote about things like cemeteries and zombies. How was he going to convince her he was cool when she was obviously the coolest person that ever lived?

"I've thought about changing up my genre," Conner said. "I think it'd be fun to write darker stories about things like that. Stories with vampires and werewolves, but no love triangles or anything—"

"Oh, Conner—I forgot I had something I was going to ask you," Bree said.

"Ask me anything," he said.

"Do you have a crush on me or something?" Bree asked him point-blank.

Conner was positive everything in his body came to a complete stop, starting with his brain. He could feel his cheeks filling with so much blood he was worried his head would explode.

"What?" he asked, as if she had asked him if he was a leprechaun. "No! Of course not! Why would you think that?"

"Because you turn bright red and ramble whenever I'm around you," Bree said. She was neither accusatory nor suspicious; she was just stating the facts calmly as ever.

Conner forced a laugh that was too loud to be genuine. "Oh, *that*? That's nothing. That's just my *sodium allergy*." He was as surprised to say it as she was to hear it.

"Sodium allergy?" Bree asked. "I've never heard of such a thing."

"It's very rare," Conner said. "Makes me ramble and turn bright red for no apparent reason.... So that explains all that...."

He wasn't sure how far he was planning to go with this. He could tell she wasn't convinced.

"Sorry, I just thought since we're going to be sitting next to each other for half a day on this plane I would ask," Bree said.

"I appreciate you asking," Conner said. "That would have been totally awkward....Just sitting here...for hours and hours...one of us crushing on the other...glad that's not the case..."

Conner wanted to die. He fantasized about crawling out the window and curling up in the plane's propeller. He couldn't decide what was more mortifying: giving the impression that he had a crush on her or that there may have been some truth to her suspicion. Conner had never had a *crush* before; he wouldn't have known if he had. But after being accused of having one, it slowly dawned on him that that must have been his problem—*he had a crush on Bree!*

He looked out the window, too horrified to look at anything else. What was he supposed to do now that he had been diagnosed with a crush? Was there an anti-crush pill he could take? Was there a gland on his heart that could be removed? Was it terminal?

Soon the plane pulled away from the gate and proceeded to the runway. It took off with a jolt and Conner watched in amazement as the airport below them became smaller and smaller.

"Amazing," Conner said under his breath.

"Have you ever flown before?" Bree asked him.

"Not on a plane," Conner said without thinking.

Bree squinted. "Then what did you fly on? A magic carpet?" she asked.

It took Conner a moment to realize she was being sarcastic. "I've been—um—*ballooning* before. It was really neat but nothing like this. Technology is almost like magic these days."

"You know, Arthur C. Clarke said that magic is just science we don't understand yet," Bree quoted.

Conner smiled. "Not always," he said to himself.

"Pardon?" Bree asked.

"Oh, nothing," Conner said. "That's a great quote."

Bree narrowed her eyes and stared at him suspiciously. "Where did you go ballooning?" she asked.

"It's a long story." Conner shrugged it off. "It was with my sister in my grandmother's—um—*state*. But this is my first time being on a plane."

"Looks like you're having all kinds of *first experiences*,"

Bree said with a smile of her own. Luckily for Conner, she then popped an earbud into her other ear and began reading one of her books before he could panic or respond with something else embarrassing.

If this was just the beginning of the trip, he didn't want to think about what the rest of it would entail. Conner wanted to crawl out of his skin but Bree didn't seem at all affected by their conversation. She just kept turning the pages of her murder-mystery novel, completely immersed in every word.

An hour or so into the flight Conner got up to use the rest-room. When he exited the shoebox-size stall he was accosted by Mindy, Cindy, Lindy, and Wendy. They stood right in front of him, blocking his way back to his seat.

"Can I help you?" Conner asked.

"We need to talk to you," Mindy said. They all scowled at him with the same serious eyes. They looked like a pack of hungry cats.

"Here?" Conner asked. "At the bathroom on a moving plane?"

The girls nodded. "We figured it was the best place to talk to you privately," Cindy said. "And so you couldn't get away."

Conner looked for help but the closest flight attendant was serving drinks on the other side of the cabin.

"Have you been planning this ambush?" Conner asked.

Wendy nodded.

"Since the end of the last school year," Lindy said.

"Okay...," Conner said. "What's up?"

All the girls looked to one another, excited to finally interrogate him.

"How's Alex doing, Conner?" Lindy said. She crossed her arms. Her left eyebrow was raised so high it almost touched the ceiling.

"She's fine," Conner said. "She's going to school and living with my grandma in Vermont. Why do you ask?"

Mindy threw her hands into the air. "*Vermont! Vermont,* he says!" she declared as if Conner had said his sister was living on Mars. "Do you have any proof of this? A photo or a postcard with Alex's handwriting, perhaps?"

"You think I'm lying to you?" Conner asked. He was beginning to worry they might be on to something. How much did they already know?

Cindy stepped closer to him and looked directly into his eyes. "We practically live in the library, and last year we saw some *things,* some *questionable things,*" she said.

"Like what?" Conner asked.

"Well, for starters, Alex used to come into the library every day at lunch," Mindy said. "And every day she would go to the back and take *one* book off the shelf."

"She would hug it and whisper sweet nothings into its spine!" Lindy continued.

"Why would she do that, Conner? Your sister was the smartest girl in the school. It was so out of character for her to be talking to inanimate objects, don't you think?" Cindy said.

Wendy squinted and nodded.

"So you're ambushing me on a plane because my sister hugged a book?" Conner asked, trying to make them seem crazy.

"We think she was *talking to someone*!" Mindy said. "She used to say things like 'Please take me away' and 'I want to go back!'"

"And then the next thing we know, Alex is gone," Lindy said.

"Left for *Vermont*, or so you say," Cindy said, and swiveled her head.

Conner tried to make his face as expressionless as possible. He didn't want to give them any hint that their suspicions were remotely valid. "You guys are insane," he said. "What are you implying? Do you think Alex ran away?"

Mindy clenched both her fists in frustration. "I don't know if she ran away, is working for the government, was abducted by aliens, or something else," she said intensely. "All I know is, something isn't right and I know you know the truth! And even if you don't tell us what's going on, we're gonna find out!"

"Because that's what the Book Huggers do," Lindy said. "We read between the *lies* and get to the bottom of things."

Wendy nodded again and punched the palm of her hand in a threatening manner.

"The Book Huggers?" Conner asked.

"That's what we've renamed the Reading Club," Cindy said. "In honor of Alex ... wherever she is."

However close they were to discovering the truth, they were still the most obnoxious people Conner had ever had to deal with and that kept him from spilling any of his family's secrets.

"I think you guys read too much," he said. He pushed his way through them and went back to his seat. He could feel their cold glares on his back as he went.

When Conner sat down he noticed Bree wasn't staring as attentively at her book as before and she had pulled an earbud out of her ear. Had she been listening to the Book Huggers assault him?

"So your sister lives in Vermont now?" Bree asked.

"Yes, with my grandma," Conner said. Bree's questions were much more difficult to dodge. He felt himself wanting to tell her the truth about his sister—and anything else she may have wanted to know.

"Vermont's pretty far," she said.

"It is," Conner said. "But we talk on the phone a lot."

"So that's where you went ballooning, then, I take it?" she questioned him further, starting her own interrogation.

"Um...yeah," Conner asked. "Why?"

"Just curious," Bree said blankly. "So if you've never flown before, how did you get all the way up to Vermont?"

He knew she could see the uncertainty in his face. "Train?" Conner peeped.

A coy smile spread across her face. "Interesting...," Bree said. "I see why they'd be suspicious."

She wasn't looking at him like a boy she thought had a crush on her anymore, but rather the way she looked at her novels: He was the mystery she was invested in now.

Bree placed the earbud back into her ear and returned to her book, occasionally side-eyeing him over the course of the flight. Conner made himself as comfortable as possible in his tiny seat. His first flight would also undoubtedly be the longest flight of his life.

CHAPTER FOUR

A WEDDING IN THE WOODS

Alex spent the following afternoon on the grand balcony of the Fairy Palace. She leaned on the railing and gazed at the beautiful sights around her. Everywhere she looked she could see fairies of all shapes and sizes preparing the palace and the gardens for the Inaugural Ball. Every flower bloomed a little brighter, every pond rippled a bit clearer, and every bird's chirp was a little merrier. The whole kingdom was buzzing with excitement for the ball...except for Alex.

A year ago Alex had wanted nothing more than to live with

her grandmother in the Land of Stories. Just the idea of learning magic and becoming a fairy had seemed like a stretch, but here she was, days away from being introduced to society as a new member of the Fairy Council. It was more than she could ever have wished for, more than she would ever have thought possible, and maybe more than she could handle.

After defeating Ezmia, the evil Enchantress, she had proven herself capable of leading the fairy-tale world—but perhaps she still hadn't proven it to *herself* yet.

A large shadow eclipsed the balcony and Alex looked up to see Mother Goose and Lester descending from the sky above.

"Hey, kiddo! I've got something to tell you!" Mother Goose called down. Lester landed on the balcony and Mother Goose dismounted and joined Alex at the railing.

"What is it?" Alex asked. She eyed a questionable sack of gold coins Mother Goose was clutching to her side.

Mother Goose cautiously looked around the balcony to make sure no one was in earshot. "Now, don't tell anyone you heard this from me, but I just ran into some friends of yours in the Dwarf Forests," she told her.

"What were you doing in the Dwarf Forests?"

"I was playing my weekly card game with a few of my gambling buddies, but that's not the point." Mother Goose held the sack of gold coins a little tighter. "I bumped into Jack and Goldilocks. They had some very exciting news to share with me and wanted to pass it along to you."

"What is it?" Alex asked eagerly. The last time she saw Jack and Goldilocks had been the night Bob proposed to her mom at the Charming Palace. She had always wondered what kind of mischief they had been up to since then.

"Apparently they're getting *married*!" Mother Goose said.

Alex happily clapped her hands. "That's incredible news!"

"I guess Jack popped the question while they were in combat with a gaggle of Corner Kingdom soldiers—he said he knew it would make Goldilocks swoon," Mother Goose said.

"When are they getting married?" Alex asked.

"*This evening!* Just before dusk in the Dwarf Forests! Talk about short notice," Mother Goose told her. "They decided it would be best to do it with as little notice as possible. You know how cautious fugitives get about their whereabouts. They asked me to officiate the ceremony and pass along an invitation to you."

"Well, that *is* short notice but I wouldn't miss it for the world!" Alex was suddenly happy that her grandmother was forcing her to take the week off. "But where in the Dwarf Forests?"

"They told me to meet them in the clearing just south of the dwarf mines," Mother Goose said with a shrug and an eye roll. "I don't know why they want to have their wedding there— maybe all the swamps were booked? Anyway, the guest list is very exclusive; only a few people know it's even happening, so keep it to yourself, especially around here. You know how judgmental these fairy folks get when any of us try to have a little fun now and then."

"How exciting!" Alex said. "I can't wait. I think a wedding is just what I need to distract myself from all this Inaugural Ball business."

"Tell me about it," Mother Goose said. "I hope I'm still good for it. The last time I officiated a wedding, Puss in Boots drank all my bubbly and started playing a fiddle, a cow convinced everyone he could jump over the moon, and an enchanted dish ran off with a spoon. You know it's a good party when even the china gets into a little hanky-panky—but I'll tell you more about that another time."

Mother Goose hopped aboard Lester, took his reins, and they flew back into the sky.

Alex was thankful to have something to think about besides the Inaugural Ball. She left the Fairy Palace a good hour or two before dusk to meet Cornelius so they would have enough time to travel to the dwarf mines. However, when she went to meet him in the field just outside the gardens, an even greater distraction was waiting for her.

"Hello there," said a smooth voice Alex wasn't expecting. She stopped in her tracks. Across the field near the edge of the stream, she saw Cornelius lying on his back and Farmer Robins's son rubbing his belly like a kitten.

"What are *you* doing here?" Alex asked, and placed a hand on her wand. She couldn't be too sure what his intentions were.

"I hope you don't mind the intrusion," the farmer's son said, walking closer to her.

The truth was Alex didn't mind at all, but she wasn't about to let him know that. "How did you find me?"

"I didn't—I found your unicorn," he explained. "He wasn't hard to pick out. I assumed if I found him I would eventually see you again."

Alex had to assess the situation twice. First, as a fairy, she assumed the boy whom she had recently helped was probably seeking her help again. Second, as a fourteen-year-old girl, hearing that a cute boy wanted to see her made her blush.

"Well, here I am. What can I help you with?" Alex said collectedly.

"I don't need help with anything," the farmer's son said. "I just wanted to thank you for what you did at our farm. My father hates fairies, especially when they help us out, but I know deep down inside he's grateful, too."

Alex nodded. "You're very welcome—wait, what's your name?" she asked.

"My name is Rook," he said. "Rook Robins."

"It's very nice to meet you, Rook," Alex said. "And you never have to thank me. Helping people is what we do best. Now if you'll please excuse me, Cornelius and I have somewhere we need to be—"

"Wait." Rook stepped between her and Cornelius. "Before you go, I have something I wanted to ask you."

"What's that?" she asked.

Rook looked at his feet and kicked a rock near his foot. "The truth is, you're *different* from any other fairy I've ever met. You're not all sparkles and bubbles, and you aren't afraid to get your hands dirty. I really like you and I've been thinking about you an awful lot since I saw you at the farm."

Alex could feel her heart start to beat a little faster, but she ignored it, not wanting to get her hopes up. Where was he going with this?

"You can say no and I would understand, but I was wondering, would you like to take a walk or something with me sometime?" Rook said. He was scared to ask the question and terrified to hear her answer.

Alex stopped completely: She stopped breathing, she stopped thinking, and she was pretty sure her heart stopped beating. She forgot about everything on her mind—the Fairy Inaugural Ball, Jack and Goldilocks's wedding, her name, who she was, where she was, and everything else important. All she could think about was the attractive boy in front of her, his floppy hair, his hazel eyes, and how he wanted to take a walk with her.

With every second that Alex stayed quiet, Rook's face fell a little more into a frown.

"That's all right, I understand," Rook said. "You're a fairy and I'm just a farmer's son. I should have known better than even to have asked."

He turned around and headed out of the field, muttering to himself how stupid he was.

"No, wait!" Alex barely regained control of her senses before it was too late. "I would love to go for a walk with you sometime."

Rook jerked his whole body back toward her. "You would?" he said with a goofy grin. "Well, that's . . . that's . . . *splendid*!"

The two stood silently for a moment with giddy smiles frozen on their faces.

"When will you be free?" Rook asked.

"Is tomorrow evening good? Same place, same time?"

"That would be wonderful," Rook said. "I'll meet you in this field tomorrow."

"I'll look forward to it," Alex said.

"Enjoy the rest of your day—wait, what's *your* name?"

"My name is Alex," she said. "Alex Bailey."

Rook was smiling from ear to ear. "Then I'll see you tomorrow, *Alex*." He jogged out of the forest with a confident jump in his step.

Alex finally understood what people meant when they said they had butterflies in their stomach. She felt a jittery tingling sensation sweep through her whole body as if a thousand butterflies were migrating inside of her. A huge smile appeared on her face.

Cornelius got to his feet and walked to Alex's side. He blew a gust of air in her face and bared his teeth in a flirty smile.

"Oh stop it, Cornelius," Alex said. "We're just two people who have decided to go on a walk together, that's all. It's nothing more than that."

Cornelius neighed; Alex wasn't fooling anyone, especially herself. This was a much bigger deal than she wanted to admit.

"Oh my gosh, the wedding! We better get going or I'll be late!" she said. "It's crazy how fast time goes by when you're—"

Cornelius batted his eyelashes and sighed, teasing her to no end.

"No, when you're *running late*," Alex said.

Alex climbed onto Cornelius's back and the two headed west to the Dwarf Forests as the sun began to descend. Galloping across the land at Cornelius's magically enhanced pace made the trip go by fairly quickly, and the thoughts percolating in Alex's head made it seem that much faster.

After all the tribulations she and her brother had gone through in their young lives, until this moment Alex had never had any head space to think about *boys*. She'd always assumed *one day* she might meet someone and fall in love, but as she got older it never dawned on her that *one day* could be getting closer. And now she couldn't help but ask herself if that moment had arrived already.

Was Alex at the beginning of her own classic love story or just entering a stage of adulthood? Was she about to experience romance for the first time in her life or just a mild case of puppy love? Did Alex even want to be invested in someone this early in her life or should she put all her energy into her fairy training?

She couldn't believe how much excitement and mystery one boy had brought into her life so quickly. Was it too early to say she was enjoying this newfound excitement? Would it lead to more exciting experiences? Could Rook Robins be the love of her life or would there be other boys in her future? And if there would be others, did that mean Rook would break her heart?

Alex knew she of all people needed to protect herself. She had been working too hard to let a silly boy come in and ruin everything she had achieved. She couldn't let him hurt her, distract her from her goals, and—most important—if things went askew she couldn't let him turn her into something or someone she wasn't: She couldn't let anything turn her into *Ezmia*.

Since he had caused her head to spin in so many directions just by asking her to go on a walk, she realized how deeply a bad experience might affect her. The purer the heart, the easier it was to scar, and Alex's heart was as pure as they came.

"Alex, get ahold of yourself," she whispered under her breath. *"Just because you're a fourteen-year-old girl doesn't mean you need to* think *like one. He just wants a walk, not marriage."*

Thankfully, before she could overanalyze the situation to death, Alex and Cornelius crossed into the Dwarf Forests. It didn't matter how old or powerful she became, the thick and dangerous woods of the Dwarf Forests always gave Alex the creeps. These woods were home to some of her worst memories and to some of the worst creatures that lived in the Land of Stories.

She guided Cornelius up one of the only paved paths in the territory and followed a sign that pointed in the direction of the dwarf mines. Just before they reached the mines, a spacious clearing came into view. The clearing had been staged like an outdoor chapel. Two dozen logs had been positioned like bench seats facing the front where a large boulder stood like a pulpit. Carved into the pulpit were the initials J & G, surrounded by a heart.

"Go find some grass to eat, Cornelius," Alex said as she hopped off the unicorn. "I'll come get you as soon as the wedding is over. But don't go too far; these woods aren't exactly unicorn friendly."

Cornelius trotted over to the other side of the clearing while Alex looked for a place to sit. She was one of the first guests to arrive.

A man with a thick, curly mustache and a heavy black cloak sat at the front near the pulpit. A witch who was missing her left arm and most of her teeth sat in the very back with a small troll that had gray skin and large horns.

Sitting in the center of the makeshift chapel was a woman Alex could have picked out in any crowd. She was sitting alone, wearing a large, fluffy red coat that covered most of her body. A tiny red hat with a matching feather was perched on top of her very stylish blonde hairdo, and she wore a pair of round glasses with red lenses in an attempt to conceal her identity. She glared at the people and creatures around her, anxious about being in their presence.

"Red, it's so good to see you!" Alex said and took a seat next to the covered queen. "I wasn't expecting to see you here—"

"*Shhh!*" Red said, and pressed a finger against her mouth. "Keep your voice down. I don't want anyone to know who I am."

Alex looked at her like she was joking. "You're trying to hide in *that* outfit?"

"Well, forgive me, but I didn't know what the proper attire was for a fugitive wedding in the woods," Red said and hid her face deeper in her coat. "I wouldn't be here except that Charlie talked me into it. Look at the characters around us! Where did Jack and Goldilocks meet these people—a child's nightmare?"

"Where *is* Froggy?" Alex asked. She couldn't spot her formerly cursed friend anywhere in the clearing.

"He's in the woods somewhere with Jack waiting for the wedding to begin," Red said. "He's Jack's best man."

"Oh, that's adorable!" Alex said. "Who's Goldilocks's maid of honor?"

Red gave an irritated snort she didn't mind the other guests hearing. Clearly this was a sore subject. "The horse is."

Alex had to bite her lip to keep from laughing. "I suppose that makes sense," Alex said. "She and Porridge have been through a lot together. You two, on the other hand, have always had a—how do I say this—teetering relationship."

"Yes, it's always been very give and take—*I give* and *she takes*," Red said. "But we made up once she gave me back the diamond necklace she stole from me. She thought it was just a joke, I thought it was an act punishable by death, blah, blah, blah ... but we reconciled and here I am."

"That's good news," Alex said.

"So how are you doing, my dear? How's your grandmother and everyone in the Fairy Kingdom?" Red asked. "Shimmery as always, I imagine."

Alex let out a long sigh. "Everyone is getting ready for the big Fairy Inaugural Ball coming up. I'll officially be a part of the Fairy Council and the Happily Ever After Assembly when it's over," Alex said. She hesitated to bring up the other major subject on her mind, but figured there weren't too many people in her life she could talk about it with. "And, I sort of met *a boy*."

Red did a double take and yanked off her glasses. Her big blue eyes grew even bigger and a crooked smile stretched across her face. "*A boy!*" Red said loudly, the topic obviously so exciting she couldn't be bothered to worry about disguising herself anymore. "Tell me everything! Where did you meet him? How old is he? How tall? What class? What race? What species?"

Alex had difficulty remembering all the questions. "He's the son of a farmer from the Eastern Kingdom. He's older and taller than me. And as far as I know, he's human."

"For now," Red said. "Trust me, being involved with someone who has been cursed to live on and off as a grotesque creature can put a strain on the relationship. But he sounds very promising! I love a good working-class man. What's his name?"

"Rook Robins," Alex said, and she couldn't help but smile just mentioning his name.

"I can tell you really like this boy," Red said with a raised eyebrow.

Alex sighed again as she felt the butterflies reappear in her core. "I'm not sure I'm even ready for all of this," she confided. "I just have so much on my mind these days I'm not sure it's a good time to add a boy into the mix. I keep worrying that it may turn into something really special or really awful—and to be honest, I'm not sure which would be worse."

"Oh, Alex, you need to relax and just enjoy the moment," Red said. "You only have a first love once. What's the worst that could happen?"

"I could get my heart broken and take my aggression out by enslaving the world like the Enchantress did," Alex said matter-of-factly.

"That's a tad extreme," Red said. "But you're nothing like her so you have nothing to worry about."

"Who's to say I'm not?" Alex said. "This is the first time something like this has ever happened to me. If I'm not prepared enough going into it, I might be scarred for life!"

Red placed a hand on her shoulder and smiled warmly. "The first cut is always the deepest, but not every cut leaves a scar," she said. "If you spend your whole life worrying about getting hurt, then you aren't really living. You don't want to shield yourself so much from the bad stuff that nothing good gets to you, either. Meeting up with a cute boy who likes you isn't going to hurt you."

"Thanks, Red, that was really insightful," Alex said, a little surprised Red had so much knowledge on the topic.

"Well, if there's one thing I know a lot about it's first loves," Red said. "Then again, when I was fourteen I ruined two lives by trying to be with the boy I liked, so I'm not sure how good the advice I'm giving you is. There's a thin line between *in love* and *insane*—and I crossed it many times. But looking back, had I not experienced all those awful things I would never have met Charlie, so in the long run it was all worth it."

They smiled at each other. Red was probably the closest thing to a big sister Alex would ever have. Red had spent years of her life chasing after a boy she could never have, and yet here she was today, happily supporting him at his wedding to another woman. Red had come a very long way, and if Red could overcome heartbreak, Alex figured she could, too.

"So when do you see him next?" Red asked.

"Tomorrow evening," Alex said. "We're going for a walk."

"Oh, how adorable! I've always wondered what poor people do for their first dates," Red said. "I insist you stop by my castle tomorrow before you see him. We can talk about boys and I can help you pick an outfit."

"Are you sure you wouldn't mind?" Alex said. "Aren't you busy being the queen of your own kingdom and all?"

"Oh no, I'd be delighted," Red said. "I just have this silly little meeting at the House of Progress but you can come with me and we can chat during all the boring parts."

"What's the House of Progress?" Alex asked. Surely she must have heard her incorrectly.

"Didn't I tell you?" Red said. "It's just like that place you were telling me about from your world, the one with all the representatives?"

"Congress?" Alex asked.

"Yes, that's the one!" Red said happily. "I decided to copy it! I have a representative from each neighborhood in the Red Riding Hood Kingdom help me make all the decisions. That way every decision is a well-rounded one and I can't be solely blamed for anything that goes wrong. But *Congress* sounded so dreary and bleak; I wanted my house of representatives to sound promising and uplifting. I thought *Queen Red Riding Hood's House of Progress* had such a better ring to it."

There was movement in the trees around them. They could hear several people approaching the clearing from different parts of the forest.

"Speaking of *ring*, I think the wedding is about to start," Alex said.

Like clockwork, as the sun began to set in the horizon the remaining wedding guests emerged from the trees around them. Each guest was shadier than the next. There was an ogre covered in yellow warts who took a seat in the front. He was followed by a woman with bright red eyes who knew the witch in the back and sat beside her. A rugged dwarf led a blind dwarf with two eye patches to a seat near Alex and Red. A goblin couple with green-scaled skin sat in front of them.

A woman covered in maroon robes sat close to Alex and Red. The only part of her body that was exposed was her beautiful green eyes. She seemed friendly enough, but like Red, Alex didn't want to make herself too known in this environment.

Red looked to the sky and took deep breaths, trying to fight off the anxiety that the newcomers caused her. A loud *swoosh* made Alex jump as Mother Goose swooped down from the sky on Lester's back. They landed at the front of the clearing and Mother Goose took her place behind the stone pulpit. She took a large swig from a flask she had hidden in her hat and cleared her throat before starting the ceremony.

"Hello, ladies, gentlemen, and whatever the rest of you are," Mother Goose said. "We understand a lot of you are on a tight schedule due to being on the run from the law, or have tried to eat or kill each other in the past, so we'll make this celebration as short and sweet as possible to avoid any discomfort. Let the wedding begin!"

The crowd cheered, which was an interesting combination of hoots, hollers, and growls. Jack and Charlie, the man forever known as Froggy to the twins, appeared from the trees behind the pulpit. They both wore sharp dress shirts and looked as handsome and charming as ever. Jack looked as anxious as Red about being there, but in a good way.

A soft series of *thump*s came from the back of the clearing and Alex turned to see a white-and-brown-spotted foal walking down the aisle. He held a basket of rose petals in his mouth and was breathing very heavily, blowing the petals out of the basket and scattering them across the ground with every exhale.

"That's adorable! Who is he?" Alex whispered to Red.

"That's Porridge's new son," Red whispered back. "They call him Oats."

Not too long after Oats reached the front of the clearing, his cream-colored mother trotted down the aisle behind him with a bouquet of daisies in her mouth. Once she joined her son and the others by the pulpit she quickly chewed up the flowers in her mouth and swallowed them.

"Everyone, if you still have your legs, please stand for the bride," Mother Goose asked.

The guests stood and turned to the back of the clearing. Red stayed seated until Alex pulled her up to her feet.

A flock of sparrows perched high in the trees began to sing a beautiful ballad as Goldilocks appeared. She was stunning. She wore a simple but elegant white lacy dress with a long train. She was barefoot and her golden locks of hair flowed all the way down to her waist. Wildflowers had been wrapped around the handle of her sword and she carried it down the aisle like a bouquet. It was beautiful but lethal, just like Goldilocks.

Despite all the gruesome guests, no one could deny that the ceremony had turned out to be beautiful. Goldilocks arrived at the pulpit and she and Jack faced Mother Goose with tears of joy in their eyes.

"Well, sit down already," Mother Goose ordered the crowd. Once they'd obeyed she continued officiating. "Four score and seven years ago—*whoops, wrong speech! sorry*—Dearly beloved, we are gathered *God knows where* today to celebrate the joining of these two wanted fugitives."

Mother Goose turned to face Jack. "Jack, do you take Goldilocks, a woman charged with countless burglaries, breaking and entering, and running from the law—"

"Don't forget attempted murder!" Red called toward the pulpit.

"I wasn't going to," Mother Goose said. *"And* attempted murder, to be your outlawfully wedded wife, in sickness and in health, in arrest and in imprisonment, until death do you part?"

There was no question in Jack's mind. "I do," he said with the biggest smile he had ever been seen with.

Mother Goose turned to Goldilocks. "Goldilocks, do you take this man, a national hero whose reputation you single-handedly ruined, to be your outlawfully wedded husband, in sickness and in health, in arrest and in imprisonment, until death do you part?"

Goldilocks had never looked so happy in her life. "I do," she said.

"Well, in that case let's get this thing over with!" Mother Goose called out. "With the power semi-entrusted in me by the Happily Ever After Assembly, I now pronounce you husband and wife! You may kiss the—"

Before she could permit it, Jack and Goldilocks locked lips and their crowd of guests cheered wildly. Once they were done kissing, they climbed astride Porridge and galloped back down the aisle and off into the sunset with Oats following closely behind.

Mother Goose snapped her fingers and a sign magically appeared over Porridge's back. It read:

Just Married

Watching the wedding had somehow made all of Alex's fears and doubts about taking a walk with Rook go away. She wanted to be just as happy as Jack and Goldilocks one day and she didn't care how many emotional obstacles she'd have to go through to get there.

"All right, now everyone get out of here before I'm seen with you," Mother Goose said. "And to that ogre in the back—you still owe me seventeen gold coins from our card game last week! I haven't forgotten!"

All the guests disappeared into the forest as quickly as they had appeared. Froggy joined Alex and Red in the center of the clearing and gave Alex an enormous hug.

"Hello, Alex! It's always wonderful to see you!" he said. "Lovely wedding, don't you think?"

"It was beautiful," Alex said. "Don't you think it was beautiful, Red?"

Red didn't respond. Her arms were crossed and she was frowning in the direction Jack and Goldilocks had ridden off in.

"Darling, what's wrong?" Froggy asked. "Didn't you enjoy the ceremony?"

"I did," Red said unconvincingly. "Especially the dress—because it was *mine*! She stole it from me!"

CHAPTER FIVE

INSIGHT AT THE GRAVE SITE

After being on the plane for what felt like a week, Conner and the others finally reached London's Heathrow Airport, where they boarded their connecting flight to Berlin. Seeing so many people of different cultures and nationalities traveling around them made Conner feel very worldly. He was sure he'd return home much more dignified than when he left—dignified but exhausted, that is. By the time their second flight touched German ground, Conner had only slept three hours of their fifteen-hour journey, and wondered if his neck would ever recover from sitting in a cramped position for so long.

"I recommend we try to sleep as soon as we get to the hotel," Mrs. Peters instructed her group as she led the way to the baggage claim area. "We don't want to be too jet-lagged for the readings tomorrow."

Mrs. Peters, Bree, and the Book Huggers collected their luggage at the baggage claim with no problem, but Betsy was nowhere to be found. Conner wasn't worried about his luggage being lost, though. On the contrary, he thought wearing the same clothes for the next few days might be worth not having to lug the decaying trunk around Germany. Just as he had happily come to terms with the idea, Betsy slid down into the luggage carousel, making more noise than any other suitcase had. Betsy had arrived in Germany and she wanted everyone to know about it.

The group followed Mrs. Peters through the crowded Berlin airport as they made their way toward the *Ausgang*, or "exit." They shuffled their way outside where Mrs. Peters had arranged for a small van to pick them up. The driver was a stern older man with a plump face and a thin mustache. He held up a sign that said PETERS.

"Guten Tag," Mrs. Peters said to the driver. "I'm Evelyn Peters, so nice to meet you."

"HELLO," Cindy said very loudly to the driver, and forced him to shake her hand. "WE'RE FROM THE UNITED STATES. IT'S AN HONOR TO BE IN YOUR COUNTRY."

Everyone rolled their eyes at her except the driver. Clearly this wasn't his first experience with a tourist like Cindy, the type who gave tourists a bad name.

"I'm German, not hard of hearing," the driver said in perfect English. "Let me load your bags into the van and we'll be on our way to your hotel."

As the driver drove them away from the airport, all eyes in the group widened as they took in the first sights of a new country. Seeing his first glimpses of Germany reminded Conner of seeing the Land of Stories for the first time; they were so far away from home, yet a very familiar world of its own existed here. The Book Huggers took out their cameras and started taking pictures of everything they saw.

"Look, it's a telephone pole!" Lindy said, and showed the others the photo she'd taken of it.

"It looks just like the telephone poles back home," Bree said.

"But it's a *German* telephone pole," Lindy said, as if Bree was missing something.

Every street the van drove down gave them something new to gawk at that they would never see at home. A massive cathedral with gargoyles stood next to an office building made entirely out of glass. An abstract art installation of a balloon dog was planted near a statue honoring a famous German opera singer. Tiny shops that looked like gingerbread houses were across the street from strip malls similar to ones in the United States.

Berlin was unlike any city Conner and the girls had ever been to. It was a combination of new and old, with monuments celebrating people and events of the past, alongside tributes encouraging thoughts and ideas for the future.

"Of all the cities in the world, Berlin is very much among those that shaped the world into what it is today," Mrs. Peters said. "There is history everywhere you look, some noble, some terrible, but highly important nonetheless."

Conner took what she said to heart. He looked out the window and wondered just how many people had traveled down these streets before him, and what their lives had been like.

"It seems more *dirty* than *historical* to me," Mindy said, not showing any enthusiasm. "Look at that wall over there—it's covered in graffiti!"

"That's the Berlin Wall, Mindy," Bree said. "It's one of the most important and historic sites on earth."

The driver let out an amused snort under his breath and Mindy turned bright red. The other girls instantly started taking as many pictures of it as they could.

"Oh," Mindy said. "Well, you'd think there would be a sign or something."

Occasionally they would see a brown poster taped to a bus stop or pinned to a message board advertising the Brothers Grimm event.

At a couple stops, they found the poster had even been translated into English:

The University of Berlin Presents
A Grimm-Fest
Be among the first to hear three never-before-told stories
by the Brothers Grimm as the University of Berlin opens
a time capsule left by the famous storytelling duo.
Wednesday, 12:00 noon
St. Matthäus-Kirchhof cemetery
Contact the University of Berlin for ticket information

Seeing the posters around town made the group even more excited about the readings. Mrs. Peters pulled a thick itinerary out of her purse and went over it with her fellow travelers.

"Let's all take a quick nap when we arrive and then perhaps we can go for a walk around the city before dinner," she said. "The stories will be read at the cemetery at noon tomorrow, so we'll meet in the lobby at ten o'clock for the complimentary breakfast, or if you want to sleep in, we'll be leaving the hotel at eleven o'clock sharp. Then after the readings we can have lunch in a café of our choice and I've scheduled a bike tour of Tiergarten Park. Then on Thursday we'll visit the Brandenburg Gate, the Chancellery, and a couple museums. On our last day I thought we could visit some of the local shops before our flight home."

They all nodded excitedly although Conner wasn't as thrilled at the idea of spending a whole day shopping as the girls were.

Soon the group arrived at Hotel Gewaltiger Palast, which Mrs. Peters told them meant the "Enormous Palace Hotel" in German. However, the translation didn't live up to their expectations. There was nothing very big or grand about the hotel at all. It was fairly small, very plain, and had only a few staff members. According to what the group could make out from the photos framed on the wall, the hotel had been owned by the same family since before World War II.

The older woman behind the front desk also looked like she had been there since before the war. She was tall with curly gray hair, and her beaded eyeglasses chain was the most colorful thing in the lobby. Her English wasn't as good as the driver's had been but she was able to check them in without a hitch.

There was obvious annoyance in her eyes as she helped them get settled. Conner couldn't tell if she didn't like Americans specifically or just people in general. Mrs. Peters helped her pass out the hotel room keys.

"Although I doubt I have to worry about anything with this particular group, I must remind everyone that even though we're in a different country, all school rules and policies will strictly be enforced while we're on this trip," Mrs. Peters warned them. "Now, everyone, try to get some sleep."

They boarded the elevator. Wendy and Lindy were sharing a room on the second floor. Bree was sharing a room with Mindy and Cindy on the third floor. Conner had his own room on the fourth floor, but Mrs. Peters stayed in the elevator after he got off.

"Where is your room, Mrs. Peters?" Conner asked, holding the elevator door open.

"I've booked myself the Chancellor's Suite," she told him. "When you get to be my age, Mr. Bailey, you'll learn that nothing is worth traveling for unless you can do it in absolute comfort. Sleep well."

The elevator doors closed and Conner found his room. He wasn't surprised to see how bleak the room was. The bed was small and looked stiff, the carpet was brown and smelled as old as it looked, and the beige wallpaper was peeling in the corners. Conner didn't mind too much, though; he knew his accommodations reflected the budget he was traveling on.

He tossed Betsy on the chair in the corner and dived into the bed. It was even stiffer than he'd thought and the sheets felt like they were made of paper. As uncomfortable as it was, Conner still expected to fall asleep instantly upon becoming horizontal, but even after lying there for ten minutes with his eyes closed, Conner was wide awake. He was either jet-lagged or just too tired to sleep.

"I wonder if Alex is around," Conner said to himself. "She'll get a kick out of seeing this room."

He opened Betsy and retrieved the small piece of mirror he had chipped off at home. He tapped the glass with his index finger and it started shimmering as it tried connecting him to his sister in the fairy-tale world. He stared at his reflection, hoping it would change into his sister's at any moment. Unfortunately, the reflection didn't change.

"I wish magic mirrors had answering machines," Conner said, and tossed it back into his suitcase.

He went to the window and looked out at the small piece of Berlin he could see. A little part of him felt at home knowing he was in the part of the world where the Brothers Grimm had lived. Perhaps the Brothers Grimm had met his grandmother and the other fairies on the very street his hotel was on. Perhaps before it was a hotel the building had been an old tavern where Mother Goose had met them for a drink one afternoon.

Mrs. Peters was right: There was so much history in this city—more than Conner could have imagined. He could have sworn he felt Berlin's old and experienced heart beating in the ground far beneath him.

Conner's gaze eventually returned to the hotel and he saw Bree leaning out a window below him. Both earbuds were plugged into her ears and she was looking out at the city just as he had. He wondered if she was thinking the same things he was. He imagined how excited Bree would be if he told her about the history of Germany that only he knew. Surely she would then think he was as cool as she was.

Bree looked up and caught Conner staring at her. Conner froze and his face went white. He couldn't believe he had been so careless. Bree just laughed and waved up at him. Conner waved back, acting like he had just noticed her. He quickly shut the window and the drapes before he could seem any creepier and lay down for the recommended nap.

When he woke up from the nap, Conner was so jet-lagged he felt like he was underwater. He went on a walk with Mrs. Peters and the girls, and they got a quick bite to eat at a small restaurant down the street from their hotel. Conner tried to avoid looking at Bree altogether—he was positive his cheeks would explode if she caught him looking at her for another second.

When he returned to his hotel room, Conner tried contacting his sister again, but there was still no reply. He figured she was deep in preparations for the ball.

The next morning Conner awoke just as tired as he'd been when he went to bed—he was worried jet lag may have been a terminal illness. He glanced at the clock on the nightstand and panicked when he realized he had overslept and only had five minutes before they were supposed to leave. He jumped out of bed like he was in the middle of a fire drill and quickly threw on his clothes and brushed his teeth.

Conner didn't even wait for the elevator—he ran down the

stairs to the lobby. He quickly grabbed a piece of toast at the complimentary-breakfast table, and met Mrs. Peters and the girls by the hotel entrance at five *past* eleven. They were standing by a pamphlet rack looking at all the things there were to do in the area.

"Sorry I'm late," Conner said. "I overslept."

The Book Huggers glared at him as if he had committed a federal offense.

"Not to worry, Mr. Bailey," Mrs. Peters said. "Five minutes late is not a tragedy."

"Good thing you're not a paramedic or a train operator," Mindy said, and crossed her arms. She and the Book Huggers were going to take any opportunity to scold him that they could.

"Let's get on our way to the cemetery so we can enjoy some of the festivities before the readings begin," Mrs. Peters instructed.

They left the hotel and found the driver from the day before waiting for them outside. They climbed aboard the van and all sat on the edge of their seats, excited about their first German adventure. The van hurried through the Berlin streets and the girls once again took pictures of everything they saw. They drove through Tiergarten Park, which stretched through the center of the city like a German version of Central Park, and past the iconic Brandenburg Gate. Conner instantly recognized the gate's pillars and its statue of a chariot at the top. A few minutes later, once they'd driven through a winding maze of buildings, they finally arrived at St. Matthäus-Kirchhof cemetery.

Although Conner hadn't been sure what to expect, the cemetery was different from what he had imagined. It was at the end of a long cul-de-sac and almost looked like a courtyard to the tall apartment and office buildings that surrounded it. A domed playground sat a few feet away from the hundred-and-fifty-year-old cemetery's entrance; even it was no exception to Berlin's integration of old and new.

A massive stone gate guarded the entrance to the cemetery. It was covered with traces of dead ivy and had a crucifix at its peak. Although it was the oldest structure in this part of the city, it had maintained its authoritative and imperial prestige over the years. There was something about the gate that demanded respect.

Brown welcoming posters advertising the Grimm-Fest were placed all over the gate. Their van was one of many vans and buses dropping people off for the readings. There were even a couple news crews covering the event.

"Here we are!" Mrs. Peters said. She led her group out of the van and through the stone gate.

"This place is creepy," Lindy said, and Wendy nodded along with her. They were hesitant to go very far inside.

"This place is awesome," Bree said, and took a picture of the gate with her phone; it was her first picture of the trip.

Beyond the gate, the cemetery was very festive. Everywhere they looked they saw students from the University of Berlin in brown shirts that matched the posters answering attendees' questions. Teachers and students of all ages, from all corners of the globe, were clumped throughout the cemetery, speaking in different languages.

Most of the attendees were gathered around the miniature chapel in the center of the cemetery. A red velvet rope blocked the front steps, making the porch into a stage of sorts. In the center of the porch was a white pillar with a glass display case on top of it. Inside the case was a very old wooden chest. Without a doubt, Conner knew he was looking at the Brothers Grimm time capsule. He smiled from ear to ear. Alex and his grandmother would have been as happy as he was to see so many people so enthusiastic about the work of the Brothers Grimm.

"Mrs. Weiss! Mrs. Weiss!" Mrs. Peters called out to the crowd ahead of her. A woman who could only be described as the German version of Mrs. Peters turned to face them. She wore almost the exact same pair of glasses and dress that Mrs. Peters had on.

"Mrs. Peters! It's so wonderful to see you!" Mrs. Weiss said, embracing her old friend.

"Students, allow me to introduce an old colleague of mine, Mrs. Weiss," Mrs. Peters said to Conner and the girls. "She's the reason we're here. She teaches English in Frankfurt and contacted me immediately once she heard about today's event."

"I'm so happy you could make it," Mrs. Weiss said, and looked down at her watch. "The readings should begin in twenty minutes or so, but until then, please have a look around the cemetery. There is face painting and a short story contest on the south lawn."

"Yes, please enjoy yourselves while Mrs. Weiss and I catch up," Mrs. Peters instructed them. "Just don't go too far."

The group split up, going in separate directions like moths drawn to different lights. Mindy and Cindy went to check out the face painting while Lindy and Wendy hurried to see if it was too late to enter the short story contest. Conner wandered deeper into the cemetery to discover it by himself.

The perimeter of the cemetery was lined with enormous mausoleums while smaller graves and tombstones were scattered across the center of the lawns. The dates of birth and death spanned to more than two hundred years ago. Conner almost couldn't believe how long most of the dead had been buried there. He did, however, have an inkling of what it would be like, after flying internationally and being stuck in his own cramped space for a long period of time.

He walked along the mausoleums admiring the pillars, statues, and stained-glass windows. He figured these must be the grave sites of the very important and wealthy—he was sure he would find the graves of Wilhelm and Jacob Grimm among them. But after walking the perimeter of the graveyard twice, he still hadn't found their place of rest.

A cluster of people were gathered around a row of smaller graves in the center of the cemetery. Conner's curiosity got the best of him and he went to see what all the fuss was about.

Finally, he pushed his way through the crowd and saw who all the excitement was for. Everyone was huddled around four identical graves lined up in a row. Each tombstone was tall, dark gray, and square. Conner had to read the names on the last two in the row twice before he believed his eyes. He was staring at the very humble graves of Wilhelm and Jacob Grimm, buried alongside Wilhelm's sons Rudolf and Herman.

"I don't believe it," Conner said to himself.

"What don't you believe?" said a familiar voice. Conner looked to his right and saw Bree standing beside him. She had also just pushed her way to the front of the observers.

"I can't believe this is it," Conner said. "You'd think the most important storytellers who ever lived would have flashier graves. I expected a big crypt with statues of fairy-tale characters and stained-glass windows of castles and gingerbread houses. But this is pretty dull."

"I kind of like it," Bree said, and snapped a picture of the graves with her phone. "Very simple and refined, that's how I'd like to be remembered, I think. Besides, I have a suspicion they don't care very much anymore."

"I guess," Conner said. He was disheartened by the whole thing. He felt the Brothers Grimm deserved much more.

Bree seemed to find his disappointment charming. "I don't think anyone gets remembered exactly the way they want to," she said. "You just have to do the best you can with what you have and hope you're recognized for it. But I doubt there's anyone else in this cemetery that can draw a crowd this size."

A horn sounded through the graveyard. Everyone turned to the chapel and saw a man dressed in ceremonial lederhosen blowing a trumpet on the porch. Noon had arrived and the readings were about to begin. The crowds of people scattered across the cemetery grounds migrated toward the front steps of the chapel, eager to hear the untold stories of the Brothers Grimm. Conner and Bree walked over together and regrouped with Mrs. Peters and the Book Huggers.

"I'm so excited," Cindy said, and clapped her hands.

"I hope one of the stories is about an awful curse like in 'Sleeping Beauty,'" Mindy said. "I've always loved a good curse!"

"I hope one of them is a sequel or a prequel to one of their other stories," Lindy said. "It would be amazing to hear what happened to our favorite characters before or after the stories that we know."

Conner chuckled—he knew, but he wasn't going to share it with them.

"Is something funny, Conner?" Mindy asked.

"Oh no, I'm just excited, too," he said with a shrug.

A woman emerged from the chapel and the crowd greeted her with warm applause. Conner figured she must be a local celebrity. She was tall and plump with a round, rosy face. She wore a bright orange dress with large buttons that matched her short, curly orange hair perfectly. She stood at a microphone that had been placed next to the time capsule, and waved to the crowd.

She greeted the onlookers first in German, then in French, and then in English.

"Good afternoon, everyone, and welcome to St. Matthäus-Kirchhof cemetery," she cheerfully greeted in a German accent. "My name is Sofia Amsel and the University of Berlin has given me the pleasure of reading to you three brand-new fairy tales written by the Brothers Grimm. They have never been heard before today."

The English speakers in the crowd cheered. Sofia removed the wooden chest from the glass case and held it delicately in her hands.

"This chest was recently found in the archives of the University of Berlin from 1811. It was the will of the Brothers Grimm themselves that the stories inside be opened and read to the public two hundred years later," Sofia announced. "I will read each story in German first, then in French, and finally in English. The stories will be translated into other languages and made available on the University of Berlin's website. Now, it is my honor to read the first story."

The crowd happily cheered. She gently opened the wooden chest and removed an aged scroll of parchment wrapped in a white ribbon. The man in the lederhosen carefully took the chest from Sofia and held it while she read the first story into the microphone.

As she had promised, Sofia read it first in German and second in French. Conner and the girls heard the German- and French-speaking people in the crowd squeal and laugh in delight as the story was read, clapping at the parts that tickled them the most.

Conner's anxiety bubbled up more and more the closer she got to telling the story in English. He couldn't wait to hear who or what the Brothers Grimm had written about, and wondered if it would be anyone he or his sister knew.

Sofia cleared her throat before beginning to read in English. "The first story is called 'The Curvy Tree,'" she announced.

Conner's face instantly went red. He gasped so quickly and so hard that he started coughing. He could feel Bree's suspicious glare on the side of his face.

"How funny," Conner said to her when he caught his breath. "That's the name of *my* story. What a coincidence."

"Yeah, a *coincidence* . . . ," Bree said. Her suspicion was short-lived, though, and soon faded away. After all, what else could it have been but a coincidence? She looked back at Sofia as she began reading from the scroll.

Once upon a time, in a faraway forest, there lived a tree that was different from all the other trees in the woods.

While the other trees grew perfectly straight toward the sky, this particular tree grew in loops, twists, and turns. It was known as the Curvy Tree by all who saw it, and many humans and animals came from far and wide to see its splendor.

When the humans and animals were away, in a language that only could be heard by the plants of the forest, the other trees would taunt the poor Curvy Tree. 'We hate your bark and your branches and your leaves that twist and turn! One day they will chop you into firewood and you will forever burn!' It made the Curvy Tree very sad, and if you spoke Plant you would hear it cry itself to sleep every night.

Years later, on the last day of winter before spring began, loggers traveled to the forest looking for wood, not to burn, but to build with. They cut down every tree in the woods to build houses, tables, chairs, and beds. When they finally left the forest, only one tree remained, and I bet it will come as no surprise when I tell you it was the Curvy Tree.

The loggers had seen how its trunk and branches twisted and turned and they knew they could never use its wood to build with. And so the Curvy Tree was left alone to grow in peace now that all the other trees were gone. The end.

The English speakers met the conclusion of the tale with thunderous applause.

Conner kept his hands at his sides. "How amazing," he said to Bree with a guilty chuckle. "I came up with almost the exact same story as the Brothers Grimm. I must be a better writer than I thought." He was all fake laughs and smiles but he could tell this was no laughing matter to her.

Bree side-eyed him like she had on the plane. "Yeah... amazing," she said through the corner of her mouth, but *amazing* was far from the word she was looking for.

Sofia retrieved the second scroll from the chest, also tied with a white ribbon, and began reading it in German. She eventually finished reading it in French, and began her English translation.

"The second story is titled 'The Walking Fish,'" Sofia declared to the eager crowd.

Conner's eyes grew twice in size—he was in serious trouble now. Bree shook her head; surely she had heard it wrong.

"Wait a second, did she just say the second story was called 'The Walking Fish'—" Bree began, but before she could finish Sofia had already started the second story.

Once upon a time there was a fish who lived in a deep lake all by himself. Every day the fish would watch with envy as a boy from the nearby village played with the animals on the land. The boy would run with the horses, wrestle with the dogs, and climb the trees with the squirrels. The fish wanted so badly to play with the boy, too, but he knew that as a fish it was impossible.

One day a fairy flying high above the lake dropped her wand in the water. The fish, being the gentleman he was, retrieved the wand for the fairy.

'As a reward for this kind gesture, I will grant you one wish,' the fairy told the fish. He thought long but he didn't think hard, for the fish knew which wish he wanted the fairy to grant him.

'I want legs, just like all the animals on the land, so I, too, can play with the little boy from the village,' the fish said. With one simple flick of her wand, the fairy magically turned the fish's fins into legs and feet and he walked on land for the first time.

The next day when the boy appeared, the fish happily showed him his new legs. The two became very good friends and every day they ran with the horses, wrestled with the dogs, and climbed trees with the squirrels. However, one day the little boy was playing too close to the edge of the lake and fell into the water. The fish ran to the edge of the lake and tried to save him, but he couldn't go in the water without his fins. The little boy couldn't swim, either, and drowned in the lake.

The fish wished he had never wished for legs, because had he just stayed the normal fish God had intended him to be, the little boy would still be alive to this day.

The English speakers, including Mrs. Peters and the Book Huggers, all made an *aww* sound at the sad ending. Conner and Bree were the only ones who didn't make a sound. Both their mouths had dropped open while the story was read.

"Wow, *another* coincidence" was all Conner could say to Bree, but she didn't respond.

"It's a very sad story, but I think we can all agree that great lessons come from tragic tales," Sofia said to the crowd. "'Be careful what you wish for' is what the Brothers Grimm are trying to tell us with this story, I presume."

Mrs. Peters was inquisitively furrowing her brow. "I swear I've read these stories before somewhere," she said to herself, and Conner's pulse rose. "Didn't *you* write similar stories, Conner?"

"I did!" Conner said, deciding it was in his best interest to seem excited about it. "My stories are creepily similar—it's crazy."

The Book Huggers unanimously rolled their eyes at him. Mrs. Peters smiled and patted Conner on the back, thankfully not spending any more thought on it.

Bree was as quiet as ever but her expression was so intense Conner could practically *hear* her trying to logically assess the situation. She was a girl who loved a good mystery, but *this* was baffling. How could Conner have known these stories before the rest of the world did? Bree must have known this was more than a coincidence.

Conner couldn't believe his bad luck. What were the chances that two of the three stories the Brothers Grimm had locked away in their time capsule were stories Conner had tried passing off as his own? At least the odds were in his favor: The situation was so unlikely that the worst thing he could be accused of was *psychic plagiarism*. But from the way Bree was looking at him, he knew *plagiarism* was the last thing on her mind.

"Now it's time for our third and final story," Sofia regretfully told the crowd. "Since our English-speaking friends have been so patient, I will read this one in English first."

Conner let out a long, heavy sigh, bracing himself for whatever trouble the third story might cause him. Sofia removed the last scroll from the chest. Unlike the others, this scroll was tied with a red ribbon.

"This must be a very important story if it was tied with a different ribbon from the rest," Sofia said. She opened the scroll. "The last story is called 'The Secret Castle.'"

Conner slumped a few inches with relief. He definitely had never heard or written a story about a secret castle. With any luck, the third story would be so good Bree would forget about the first two. He looked at his feet, wanting this whole event to end as soon as possible.

Sofia cleared her throat again and began reading.

Once upon a time, in a faraway kingdom, there lived two brothers who liked to tell stories. Everyone in their village loved to hear their stories and thought the brothers were very creative, but the brothers had a secret. The stories they shared with their village didn't come from them, but from someone else.

Conner's eyes shot straight up toward Sofia. There was something very familiar about this story—something *too* familiar.

Every day the brothers traveled into the forest where they would meet a beautiful fairy. Each time they met, the fairy gave the brothers a new story to share with the people in their village. The fairy lived in a Secret Castle far away from anywhere man had ever been, and her stories were usually about one of the many magical creatures that lived with her in the castle. The brothers were very grateful to the fairy and never told a soul that she and her castle were real.

Conner could feel his heart beating in the back of his throat. He was listening so intently he forgot about everyone in the crowd around him. Many troubling thoughts filled his head as the story became more familiar. Had the Brothers Grimm staged this whole event to come clean about the origin of their stories? Were they about to admit to the world that the Fairy Godmother was real and had supplied them with their greatest work?

One day the king got word of the brothers' stories. The king was very smart and had a hunch that there was truth to their tales. He had his soldiers follow the brothers into the forest the next time they met the fairy, and their secret was unveiled. The king ordered the brothers to come to see him at his palace and demanded that they take him and his army to the Secret Castle where the fairy lived so they could conquer it.

The brothers pleaded with the king, and told him they didn't know where the Secret Castle was. The king showed them no mercy and said that if they didn't supply him with directions to the Secret Castle he would have everyone in their village killed.

Not wanting to trouble the fairy who had been so kind to them, the brothers asked a great magical bird that also lived at the Secret Castle for help. The magical bird gave the brothers a map to give the king, showing a way to the Secret Castle. But what the king didn't know was that this map was of an enchanted path; it would take him and his army of thousands two hundred years to reach the Secret Castle.

The magical bird assured the brothers that by the time the king and his army arrived at the Secret Castle, it would be prepared to face them. The brothers gave the map to the king and he and his army immediately began their quest to find the Secret Castle.

With the king and his army gone, the brothers' village was saved from the greedy king's wrath. However, the brothers never saw the magical bird or the fairy again. As time went by, the brothers worried that the magical bird, being old and careless, would forget to warn the other magical creatures in the Secret Castle that the army was coming. So the brothers decided to write their last known story themselves and they knew it would be the most important one they would ever tell.

The brothers wrote a story similar to their own lives, about a Secret Castle and magical creatures and a greedy king who wanted to conquer it all. They spread the story across the land, from one generation to the next, hoping the tale would eventually reach someone who would recognize it for what it really was—not a fairy tale, but a warning in disguise.

There was a long pause before the crowd realized the story was over. Their applause was as confused as their expressions—it seemed like such an odd, unfinished story.

"That is all there is, I'm afraid," Sofia said. "I certainly hope the Secret Castle was warned of the approaching army. Perhaps the Brothers Grimm purposely left their last story unfinished, so that we would all finish it ourselves in our own imaginations. Now I will read the story in French. . . ."

Conner felt light-headed and sick to his stomach. His mind was racing with so many questions he couldn't focus. He didn't even hear Sofia read the story in French or German; everything was white noise around him. He replayed the story again and again in his head—everything the Brothers Grimm had written in the third story was so obvious and so carefully planned. They were the brothers in their own story, the fairy was Conner's grandmother, the magical bird must be Mother Goose or one of the other fairies, and the Secret Castle was the Land of Stories. And just like in the story, the story wasn't actually a story—it was a warning.

The Brothers Grimm were trying to warn *someone* that *something* was on its way to the Land of Stories. And since they had so carefully planned for the story to be heard two hundred years later, whatever was approaching the Land of Stories must be arriving soon.

It was all so blatant; Conner looked around the crowd hoping to see someone else who had interpreted the story for what it was, but there was no one who had interpreted it like he had. The fairy-tale world was in great danger and he was the only one in the Otherworld who realized it.

"Conner, are you okay?" Bree asked him. "You just went from bright red to pale white in a couple seconds."

"I'm fine," Conner lied. "It's just that story...it was just so strange..."

"Was it coincidentally close to something you were planning on writing?" Bree asked him playfully, but she knew from the look on his face that something was terribly wrong.

Conner was looking right at her, but none of his thoughts had anything to do with her. He didn't care if she knew he had a crush on her, and he didn't care if she or the Book Huggers were close to finding the truth about his sister; all he cared about was warning his grandmother and his sister that they were in danger.

Before he knew it, Sofia had finished reading the story in the other languages and the Grimm-Fest had come to an end.

"On behalf of the University of Berlin, I'd like to thank you for joining us today," Sofia said. "I hope you've enjoyed the festivities today as much as I have."

She placed the third scroll back into the chest the man in lederhosen held for her and together they disappeared into the chapel. The crowd began heading out of the cemetery and Mrs. Peters rallied her group to do the same.

"Wasn't that a remarkable reading?" Mrs. Peters asked. "I'm certain to remember it for the rest of my life."

"Mrs. Peters, I'm starving! Can we get something to eat?" Mindy asked.

"Of course," Mrs. Peters said. "Mrs. Weiss was just recommending we meet up with her and her students at a little café near our hotel if no one objects—"

"Mrs. Peters!" Conner interrupted. "Can I just go back to the hotel? I'm not feeling very well and I think I need to lie down for a bit."

Mrs. Peters was disappointed but not surprised to hear this given the look on his face. "I'm so sorry, Conner," she said. "Of course you may. I'll have the driver drop you off before he takes us to lunch."

The van couldn't drive back to the hotel fast enough. Conner even thought about faking a few dry heaves to speed things up. As soon as they pulled up to the hotel Conner jumped out and ran inside before anyone could say good-bye. He zoomed through the lobby, almost knocking into three guests on his way, and ran up the four flights of stairs to his room—he didn't want to waste any time waiting for the elevator.

He burst into his room and locked the door behind him. He immediately searched through Betsy until he found his piece of mirror. He impatiently tapped the glass and anxiously waited for it to connect him to his sister. Conner prayed Alex would be available. Unfortunately the only reflection he saw in the mirror was his own.

"Come on, Alex!" Conner said. "You've got to answer! Trust me, nothing is more important than this right now!"

He tapped the mirror again and again, trying to reach his sister, with no luck. He spent the rest of the day trying—and still, no result. They were the most frustrating hours of his life. In the evening Conner heard a knock on his door. Mrs. Peters had come to check on him. She and the girls had returned from their bike tour of Tiergarten Park.

"How are you feeling, Mr. Bailey? Any better?" she asked at the door.

"I'm all right, just really nauseated," Conner told her. "I think I caught a bug at the cemetery."

"Do I need to call for a doctor?" she asked.

"No, I think I'll feel better in the morning," Conner said. "I should be fine as long as I get some sleep."

"I certainly hope so," Mrs. Peters said. "I would hate for you to waste your whole trip locked in your hotel room."

She left him alone to rest, but rest was the last thing Conner got that night. After trying to reach his sister for a couple more hours, he couldn't stand being in the hotel room any longer. He couldn't sit around while he knew something very wrong was going on somewhere.

Conner decided to go back to the cemetery, for clarity if not for answers. He grabbed his coat and quietly left his room. He took the stairs again, trying to avoid as many people as possible. He snagged a map from the pamphlet rack in the hotel lobby and followed it all the way back to the cemetery. It took him an hour to walk there in the dark, and to make matters worse it also started to rain.

When he reached St. Matthäus-Kirchhof cemetery all the posters had been taken off the gate and all the guests were gone. It was so much more peaceful now that it was empty. He retraced his steps to the modest graves of the Brothers Grimm. The ground around the graves was littered with flowers and gifts from the attendees of the readings earlier that day.

Conner squinted at the graves as if he were looking not at two big blocks of stone but rather two very silent people.

"So that was some story," he said to the graves. "Was there anything else you failed to mention? Were there any clues you forgot to include?"

The rain increased with Conner's frustration. He was actually upset that the graves weren't responding.

"What army is approaching the fairy-tale world? Where did it come from? Are my grandmother and my sister in danger? Please, I need to know," Conner said, this time asking the rainy sky above him.

Unfortunately, there was no sign for Conner to witness. He had to rely solely on what his gut was telling him. Conner knew he had been meant to be in the cemetery earlier that day, he had been meant to hear and correctly interpret the story, and now he was meant to warn the fairy-tale world of the approaching danger.

He just didn't know how.

CHAPTER SIX

QUEEN RED'S HOUSE
OF PROGRESS

The Fairy Inaugural Ball was just a day away but it was only one of the major things occupying Alex's mind. As soon as she'd agreed to go on a walk with Rook, she found herself juggling two fixations at the same time. One minute she was obsessing about what to wear and how to behave at the ball, and the next she was daydreaming about how wonderful or tragic her walk might be. It was an exhausting and constant balancing act between the two worries.

On the one hand she was thankful to have two subjects on

her mind, as each distracted her from the other; on the other hand Alex would have given anything just to clear her mind for a moment or two. Alex thought the best way to deal with the stress of the two pending events would be to get away from reminders of both, so she happily took Red's offer to meet the morning after Jack and Goldilocks's wedding.

It was a bright sunny morning when Alex and Cornelius journeyed into the Red Riding Hood Kingdom. They traveled northwest, around the Troll and Goblin Territory—or Troblin Territory as it was now called—and soon the tiny kingdom came into view.

A high wall was being constructed around the kingdom. Dozens and dozens of stonemasons worked tirelessly on it, building it up brick by brick. From the looks of it, the new wall would be exactly like the old one, which the Enchantress had eliminated.

Alex and Cornelius had no trouble at all crossing into the kingdom. Many of the guards at the south gate even bowed to Alex, recognizing her as an acquaintance of the queen. Cornelius regally trotted through the rural hills of Bo Peep Family Farms, showing off for all the livestock they passed, and went to the town in the center of the kingdom, where Queen Red's castle stood.

The town was as delightful as when Alex saw it for the first time with her brother. It was a friendly and picturesque village with many shops, barns, houses, and landmarks. A baker stood outside his shop sharing trays of free samples with the townspeople moving past. A locksmith had a table set up outside his store and demonstrated how he made keys to a crowd of onlookers. Farmers pulled their stubborn animals and children through the streets as they went about their day.

The Red Riding Hood Kingdom had recovered handsomely from the turmoil the Enchantress had caused.

"Excuse me? Do you know where the House of Progress is?" Alex asked a shepherd passing by.

"It's across from the castle at the other end of the park," the shepherd told her.

"Thank you," Alex said, and followed his directions. She had been to the castle many times and it was easy for her to steer Cornelius there.

The House of Progress looked just like a miniature version of the US Capitol, except it had been painted red and the dome had been replaced with the world's largest square basket.

"That is *so* Red Riding Hood," Alex said, and shook her head. Even Cornelius moved his head back and forth at the ridiculous sight.

They traveled through the park and Alex left Cornelius at the foot of the building's wide front steps. Statues of Queen Red posing heroically in her favorite outfits lined the steps all the way up to the doorway. Alex couldn't believe this was the woman she had come all this way to get advice from, but at least the journey had gotten her out of the Fairy Kingdom.

The House of Progress's entrance hall was decorated with dozens of paintings of the young queen. Alex was used to Red's narcissistic decorating by now and it didn't faze her, but there were two incredibly large paintings on the walls that made her laugh. One was of Red regally speaking to her people just before setting sail on the enormous flying ship the *Granny*. The other was a painting depicting the moment when Red refused to surrender her kingdom to the Enchantress.

Alex had been around for both of those moments and didn't remember either one as dramatic as the paintings suggested, but she thought they were amusing nonetheless. In the very center of the entrance hall was another statue of Red, but of epic proportions: Queen Red sitting on her throne, looking exactly like the Lincoln Memorial.

"I've got to stop showing Red pictures of the Otherworld," Alex said under her breath.

A line of waiting townspeople started in the entrance hall, curved around the giant statue, and ended just before the open doorway to the next room. Alex followed the line and found herself stepping into a large circular room directly under the building's gigantic basket.

"ALEX, LOOK OUT!" Red shouted from the back of the room.

The next thing Alex knew, she was being tackled to the ground by an enormous black wolf. Her wand was knocked out of her hand and it rolled away from her. The wolf pressed his massive paws against her chest near her throat. He opened his large snout and Alex could see all the sharp teeth inside his mouth. She closed her eyes as tight as possible, knowing what was coming next.

Alex felt the wolf's wide wet tongue lick her face over and over again—he was so excited to see her.

"Hello, Clawdius," Alex grunted under him. "It's nice to see you again."

"No, Clawdius! What did I say about tackling guests?" Red yelled.

A handful of Red's guards who had been standing along the edge of the room tried to remove the wolf from the young fairy but he growled viciously at them and they quickly backed away.

"Clawdius! Get off the heir of magic right now!" Red demanded.

Clawdius immediately jumped off Alex. Clearly Red was the only one who could control him. Alex got to her feet and Clawdius put his overgrown head in her hand so she would pet him.

"Look how big you've gotten, Clawdius!" Alex said as she scratched under his chin. "You get bigger every time I see you."

Clawdius retrieved Alex's wand, but when she went to take it from his mouth he pulled away—he wanted to play.

"Oh no, Clawdius," Alex said in a panic. "That's not something we can play with!"

"Clawdius, drop the nice fairy's wand right now!" Red ordered, but the wolf ignored her. *"I said, drop it! Don't make me shake the can full of coins!"*

Clawdius sat down and set the wand gently on the floor in front of Alex. Even when seated he was almost as tall as she was. Alex collected her wand and headed to the back of the room where Red sat.

Red was perched on a raised throne and dressed to the nines in a red ball gown and a tiara; she was drenched in diamonds. To her right were two rows of raised seats where nine people and animals alike sat, although the seats weren't raised as high as hers, of course. Alex assumed these must be the representatives Red had been talking about yesterday.

Alex immediately recognized the three sitting closest to Red as Red's granny; the Little Old Woman who ran the Shoe Inn; and the third Little Pig. There were also three blindfolded white mice who shared one seat, a bushy-haired black sheep; a nervous and jumpy young woman; and an obese man who wore a guilty expression as he ate a pie.

"Everyone, this is my good friend Alex," Red said. "Alex, let me introduce you to my House of Progress representatives: the Honorable Three Blind Mice, Sir BaaBaa Blacksheep, Lady Muffet, and Sir Jack Horner. And of course you know Granny, the Old Woman from the Shoe Inn, and the third Little Pig."

They all greeted her with warm welcomes, except the Old Woman, who was infamously hard of hearing.

"Who's complex?" the Old Woman asked.

"Not complex—*Alex*," Granny said directly into her friend's ear. "She's one of Red's friends."

"Wonderful to meet you all," Alex said. "I hope I'm not interrupting anything."

"Not at all," Red said. "We're just waiting for Charlie to arrive before we begin our weekly open-house meeting. I'm sure you saw all the townspeople lined up—they love coming to the House of Progress and voicing their concerns. I've become very good at figuring out ways to help the people; it's like a little game."

Just then they heard footsteps and saw Froggy entering the room carrying a large stack of papers. "Good afternoon, everyone," he kindly greeted the representatives. "And hello, Alex! I wasn't expecting to see you—*huuuh!*"

Clawdius tackled Froggy as soon as he came into the room. This was just how the wolf seemed to greet people. All of Froggy's papers flew into the air.

"Clawdius, I just saw you not twenty minutes ago—you have to stop this madness," Froggy grunted, pushing the wolf off him. "We need to start chaining him down!"

"I tried that but he ate through the chain." Red shrugged. *"Clawdius, come here, boy! Come to Mommy!"*

Clawdius ran to Red's side and happily plopped his big head in her lap. Froggy collected his papers but they were all disorganized now.

"Come sit by me, Alex," Red said, and patted the armrest of her throne. "We have so much to talk about!"

"Are you sure it's all right to visit during the open-house meeting?" Alex asked, taking a seat.

"Oh, it's more than fine," Red assured her. "Charlie leads the meetings while I supervise. They'll get my attention if they need me."

Froggy took his place at the front of the room and the meeting began. "Forgive me but the open-house forms you filled out prior to arriving are a little jumbled," he apologized to the townspeople. "So when it's your turn I'll need you to step forward and state your name and the nature of the pressing matter that you'd like us to deal with."

One by one, the townspeople stepped forward and told Froggy and the representatives about their dilemmas. Froggy and the representatives talked about the matter among themselves and then presented the villager with the best solution possible. It was a very nice process for Alex to witness; Froggy and the representatives genuinely seemed passionate about helping the townspeople.

"Wonderful, everything is going just splendidly," Red said, and then allowed Alex to become her sole focus. "Let's talk about your date this evening—have you picked out an outfit to wear? If not, I have a little pink dress somewhere in one of my closets that would look divine on you."

"I was thinking I would just wear this," Alex said, and gestured to the sparkling dress she wore every day. "I think he'd appreciate it if I just dressed as myself."

"Be careful of *that*," Red warned her. "Some of the best advice Granny ever gave me was never to be myself when meeting someone for the first time—you don't want to scare them away."

Alex thought about this for a moment. She was pretty sure Granny had meant that as advice for Red personally, not in general.

"He's a farmer's son," Alex said. "I'm afraid doing or saying anything over-the-top may scare him away just as easily. I'd rather he feels comfortable with me than intimidated by me."

"That may be, but you shouldn't make him feel too good about himself on the first date," Red instructed. "Men must always think they're inferior to you, otherwise they don't leave you any room to train them."

Froggy interrupted their conversation momentarily. "Darling, this man is from the south part of town," he said about the townsman standing in the middle of the room. "Apparently the south path has become so bumpy it's ruining all the carts that travel on it. They need a new path to be paved."

"Great, then pave a new one," Red said with a big smile.

"Unfortunately, they don't have the funds for it and the kingdom's pockets will be shallow until the new wall is built," Froggy explained. "What should the representatives and I suggest?"

Red knew just the thing. She took the diamond bracelet off her left wrist and tossed it to the man from the South Village. "Here, sell this and use the money to pave a new path; it should be more than enough."

The man was stunned the queen would give him something so valuable. Tears came to his eyes. "Thank you, Your Majesty! Thank you so kindly!" he said on his way out the door.

"You're very welcome!" Red said, then turned quickly back to Alex. "So where are you and Rook going on a walk to?"

"I'm not sure," Alex said. "I was just planning on following him."

Red shook her head. "Whatever you do, do not let him lead the walk," she said. "Men are natural-born leaders and it's our job as women to rid them of that animalistic trait. If you let him lead the first walk, soon he'll be leading the whole relationship."

"So is it a good sign if he wants *me* to lead the walk?" Alex asked.

"No, that's even worse!" Red said. "That means he's got no confidence and expects you to do all the work and hold his hand the rest of his life. You're way too young for that, Alex."

Alex scrunched her forehead. Red was only making matters

more confusing for her. "Do you really believe this advice, Red?" she asked.

"Oh, none of this stuff pertains to *me*," Red said. "I'm just looking out for *you*."

"Darling," Froggy interrupted again. "This woman is from the east part of town. She's a baker whose husband died a few years ago. She makes a decent living, but not enough to take care of her four children on her own."

Tears were streaming down the poor baker's face. She was clearly ashamed to be standing before them asking for help.

"There, there," Red said sympathetically. "There is no reason to cry! We all need a helping hand every now and then— especially me. I'm useless without my staff."

The queen scanned the dozen or so remaining townspeople in the line. She saw a frail and sad-looking man holding a pitchfork in the very back. "Excuse me, sir, are you a farmer?" she asked him.

The man was shocked his queen was speaking to him directly. "Yes, Your Majesty," he said with a quick bow.

"Let me guess, you're here because you can no longer afford to feed your family, am I correct?" Red asked.

"Why, *yes*, Your Majesty," he said, amazed she could tell so easily.

"Oh wonderful," Red said happily. Everyone in the room gave her a strange look. "Oh, I didn't mean *that* was wonderful, I meant it's wonderful that you're a farmer because I believe you and this baker can help each other out. Do you have cows on your farm?"

The farmer nodded. "Yes, I have six cows," he said.

"Terrific." Red then looked back to the baker. "I assume a financial burden for you is the cost of milk? Am I right?"

"Yes, Your Majesty," the tearful baker admitted.

"Then that's solved," Red said with a gleeful clap. "The farmer will supply the baker with as much milk as she needs and in return she will provide food for his family. Does that work for everyone?"

The farmer and the baker looked at each other and smiled; Queen Red had given them both a solution. Froggy and Alex exchanged a smile of their own—Red may have been clueless most of the time but when she was good she was *good*.

Froggy continued the open-house meeting and Red continued chatting with Alex.

"Now, if he wants to go on a second walk with you, you must act like you're too busy," Red said.

"Why?" Alex asked.

"To keep him grateful for your company," Red said as if it was obvious.

A hurried set of footsteps echoed through the room. A woman was causing quite a commotion as she entered, pushing past all the townspeople waiting in line. It had been such a pleasant day until this; the disturbance caught everyone's attention, especially Red's.

"Excuse me, you have to wait your turn," Froggy politely told the woman.

"I didn't come here to ask for any favors," the woman said as she stepped before them. "I've come here to make an announcement."

She was a very beautiful and determined young woman, who

seemed to be about the same age as Red. She had pale skin, blue eyes, and dark hair that was tucked underneath a yellow bonnet. She wore a matching yellow ruffled dress with a blue sash and carried a white shepherd's staff. She was the most stylish shepherdess Alex had ever laid eyes on.

"Who are you?" Froggy asked her. He was fairly new to the Red Riding Hood Kingdom and didn't recognize her.

"I'm Little Bo Peep, owner of the Bo Peep Family Farms," she declared.

A hush fell over the room. Little Bo Peep was a very powerful and respected member of the community. It was only on rare occasions that she was seen outside her farms. The townspeople and representatives knew there must be a very important reason she had come to the House of Progress today.

Queen Red eyed her up and down, and left to right. She refused to be intimidated by anyone in her own house. "Thank you for joining us, Little Bo," she said. "What brings you to the House of Progress today?"

Little Bo smiled. "To put it simply, I've come here before you today to challenge Queen Red for the throne of the Red Riding Hood Kingdom."

Everyone gasped. Never in the history of the Red Riding Hood Kingdom had someone so openly disrespected the queen. Little Bo smiled snidely at their reaction.

At this bold declaration, Red stood up from her throne. *"How dare you,"* she said coldly. "You think you can just walk into *my* House of Progress and threaten the throne of *my* kingdom? You're lucky I don't have you immediately locked up!"

"You think this is *your* kingdom?" Little Bo said without a trace of fear. "Then you're mistaken, Your Majesty. It may have your name on it but this kingdom belongs to the people. The sole purpose of the C.R.A.W.L. Revolution was to free ourselves from the Evil Queen, who was in power in the Northern Kingdom at the time. Now look at us, a decade and a half later we're standing in one of the many shrines to *another* self-obsessed queen. Well, I'm sick of it and I'm not alone."

She reached into the pocket of her dress and removed a scroll that she handed to Froggy.

"This is a petition signed by a hundred other citizens of the kingdom who agree it's time for a regime change," Little Bo said. "They also have stated that I am their chosen candidate for a new sovereign. We elected a queen before, we can elect a queen again."

"This is preposterous," Froggy said.

"It's the will of the people, sir," Little Bo corrected. "Are you going to ignore it—in the House of Progress of all places?"

Froggy looked over the list of names and shared it with the representatives.

"You're not actually humoring her, are you?" Red yelled, outraged that they would even read such a thing.

"The Little Peep girl has a point, dear," Granny said.

"Granny, whose side are you on?" Red asked in shock.

"I'll always be on your side, dear," Granny said. "But it's the people who gave you your throne, so if the people want to give it to someone else now, they have the right to do so."

All the other representatives seemed to agree with her; even the Three Blind Mice nodded along and they couldn't read the names on the scroll.

"What makes you think you're qualified to lead this country?" Red asked Little Bo.

"My farms make up over seventy percent of the kingdom and produce over eighty percent of the goods we trade with other kingdoms," Little Bo proclaimed. "Only for you to take ninety percent of those profits and use it to build castles and statues of yourself."

Red's nostrils flared. "Which keeps many builders and artists employed throughout the kingdom," she said in defense.

"Yes, but as you can see, there are no builders or artists seeking aid in this room," Little Bo pointed out. "I believe there is a more responsible way this kingdom can be managed that will benefit everyone equally—and I believe I am the woman to do it."

The townspeople and representatives began whispering among themselves. Red could sense some of them were starting to agree with Bo Peep.

"So what do you want, Little Bo?" Red said, crossing her arms. "You can't just waltz in here and demand to be queen."

Sir BaaBaa raised a hoof to join the conversation. "We could have another election."

Red was staring daggers at him. "Oh how typical, the *sheep* wants Little Bo Peep to run for queen. That's partisanship if I ever saw it."

"I think that's a good idea," Granny said. "An election would give the people of this kingdom a way to express their will."

"And what if I don't allow an election?" Red said. "I'm still the queen, after all. The last time I checked, my word was still the law."

Little Bo stepped even closer to her throne. "Then you would be proving to your kingdom that you are no different from the Evil Queen, and the next revolution that breaks out will be against *you*."

The statement was meant to scare Red and it worked. "So be it," Red said. "We'll humor this shepherdess with a little election. But if I recall, Little Bo, you have a reputation of not being able to find your own sheep, so I doubt you'll be able to find support that rivals mine. I was elected queen after the C.R.A.W.L. Revolution and I will be elected queen again."

"Then I'll see you at the polls, Your Majesty," Little Bo said with a coy smile. She turned on her heel and promptly left the House of Progress.

Red re-seated herself on the throne. Her cheeks were bright pink and a concerned scowl was frozen on her face. Alex had never seen her look so distraught. The thought of losing her throne had always been Red's greatest fear—but the idea that she might lose it to the people's will was obviously almost unbearable to her.

Alex couldn't imagine Red as anything but a queen. She put a hand on her friend's shoulder, wishing she had words to comfort her with.

Froggy ran up to the throne and kneeled at her side. "Are you all right, my dear?"

"Splendid, just splendid," Red said. She stared at the floor, quietly plotting her next move. "If it's an election that sheepherder wants, it's an election she'll get."

CHAPTER SEVEN

LITTLE BO PEEPING

Alex left Red's House of Progress, grateful to return to her own problems. The anxiety she felt about the Fairy Inaugural Ball and the walk with Rook was heavy to carry around, but not *life altering* like Red's afternoon had become, although Alex had a sneaking suspicion Red would find a way to drag her into the drama.

That evening Alex went to the field beyond the gardens to meet Rook. She was positive she arrived at the exact time they had agreed to meet but when she got there Rook was nowhere in sight. Alex sat on a boulder by the stream and waited patiently for him—or at least she thought she was being patient.

Every second waiting for Rook felt like a minute and every minute felt like an hour. The more she waited the more her head filled with doubts. Where was he? What was taking him so long? Had he forgotten about their walk? Had he changed his mind and decided not to come? Had she been stood up?

In between the negative thoughts she self-consciously straightened her headband or fixed a crease in her dress. After only five minutes of waiting Alex had convinced herself Rook wasn't coming. What was she going to tell Red the next time she saw her? How was she supposed to trust another boy again? How could she live with the embarrassment?

Just when she was about to call it a day and return to the Fairy Palace, she heard rustling in the woods beyond the field. Rook stepped into view, looking as happy, excited, and dreamy as ever.

"Hello, Alex!" Rook said with a big smile.

"Hi, Rook!" Alex said, and let out a relaxed sigh. Just seeing him had instantly switched off all the negative thoughts multiplying in her head. She had stressed herself out for no reason.

Neither knew if they should hug or shake hands or something else, so they stood a few feet apart and silently looked at each other for a moment. It was an awkward hello.

"How was your day?" Alex said, breaking the silence.

"It was pretty normal," Rook said. "I was planting carrots."

"How nice!" Alex said, as if it was the most fascinating thing she had heard in weeks.

Rook nodded. "I'm a good gardener," he said. "My secret is singing. I've discovered if I sing to the crops, they grow much healthier." Rook's eyes suddenly widened. "Oh no, I hope you find that charming and not crazy.... It's not like I have conversations with them or anything...."

Alex giggled. "Oh please, where I live, the plants often sing *back*."

Rook was relieved to hear this. "So...where would you like to take a walk to?" he asked.

"I was planning to follow you," Alex said. She wasn't obeying any of Red's advice and she knew Red would have killed her for saying that she'd follow Rook.

"Well, there's a trail through the woods that I know pretty well," Rook said.

"Terrific," Alex said.

They journeyed into the trees and found a small dirt path that snaked deeper into the woods. It wasn't a very scenic route but it didn't matter; their walk was more about getting to know each other. However, they were both afraid to be the first to say something to the other.

"What if we take turns asking each other questions?" Rook suggested. "This is going to be a very quiet walk unless we start talking about something. Or we could play charades."

"Sounds like a plan," Alex said. "But you go first."

"Oh, you're making *me* go first?" Rook said playfully. "All right, here's one—how long have you been practicing magic?"

"Less than a year, actually," Alex said. "Everyone says I've been learning very quickly, though. I didn't even know I was a fairy until I was twelve."

"Really?" Rook said. "How did you find out?"

"It's a long story," Alex said bashfully.

"Good thing we picked a long path," Rook said with a wink that made her melt inside.

Alex decided to tell him the shortest version of the story she could. "My twin brother and I grew up in a place very far away and different from all of this," she explained. "Our dad grew up here and felt that magic ruined people. He thought it made them lazy and entitled. He wanted us to learn how to take care of our problems without relying on magic. Then when we were twelve—well, to make a long story short, we followed our grandmother home one day and discovered who we really were."

Rook's eyebrows were raised so high they disappeared into his floppy hair. "That's incredible," he said. "No wonder you're so different from all the other fairies. What does your father think of you now?"

"I wouldn't know," Alex said sadly. "He died shortly before our eleventh birthday. He never got the chance to tell us the truth himself."

Rook nodded. "I'm very sorry to hear that. He must have been a very smart man to raise a daughter like you."

"Thank you," Alex said. She quickly straightened her headband to distract him from her blushing face.

"Is your brother a fairy, too?" Rook asked.

Alex couldn't help but laugh. "Conner? A fairy? Oh, heavens no. Being a fairy was the last thing he ever wanted to be. He still lives back home with our mom and stepdad. I think he'd be really good at magic if he ever tried, though."

"What about your grandmother? Does she live in the Fairy Kingdom with you?" Rook asked.

It took Alex a moment to respond. She hadn't realized how little he knew about her; it was really refreshing. He must have genuinely liked Alex for *her* and not who she was *going to be.*

"She does," Alex said. She wasn't sure how he would react to hearing who her grandmother was and she wasn't sure she was ready for him to know. "Now it's my turn to ask you a question. How old are you?"

Rook had to think about his answer. "I'm fifteen, but technically I'm one hundred and fifteen."

At first Alex thought he was joking and gave a small laugh, but when he didn't laugh with her she realized he was being serious. "Oh my goodness, because of the one-hundred-year sleeping curse!" She figured it out. "You must have been a toddler when it was cast."

"I was very young," he said. "I don't remember much about it. I was playing outside when suddenly for no reason I went to sleep. Then my dad and I woke up one hundred years later."

"What about your mother?" Alex asked. "What happened to her?"

Rook paused for a second before explaining. "It was my birthday and my mother and brother were in a field collecting berries for a special dessert they were making that night. The field was just outside the border of the Eastern Kingdom, so when the sleeping spell was cast it didn't reach them. By the time my father and I woke up . . . they were gone."

Alex placed a hand over her mouth. "I'm so sorry, Rook," she said. "It never occurred to me that families were separated because of the curse."

"Many people don't realize that," Rook said. "They just assume everyone went to sleep and awoke to their normal lives a hundred years later, but our whole lives changed when we awoke. I'd be lying if I didn't tell you I was happy to hear Ezmia had been killed. It brought a lot of closure for me. I don't think my father will ever be the same, though. That's why he hates fairies so much; he blames them for not being able to stop the curse."

Alex nodded. "I understand him a little better now." She wondered how Rook and Farmer Robins would take knowing she was the one who had defeated the Enchantress. Would it make them like her any more? Or would she just become a living reminder of what they had lost?

"My mother and brother took care of us for as long as they could while we slept," Rook went on. "They wrote us letters every day and left them for us to read when the curse was eventually broken. I'll read one or two when I find myself missing them the most. It makes it feel like they're still around."

Alex understood this more than he knew. One of the reasons she felt so comfortable in the Land of Stories was because everything there reminded Alex of her dad and made missing him less painful.

"My turn to ask you another question," Rook said, changing the subject. "How was your day? Tell me everything you did."

Alex didn't know where to begin. "Well, it started out very nice," she said. "I went to the Red Riding Hood Kingdom to visit Queen Red—we're old friends, believe it or not—but then the day took a very bizarre turn."

"What happened?"

"Her throne was challenged by Little Bo Peep," Alex told him. "She managed to convince everyone they should have an election for a new leader."

Rook was so intrigued his whole face lit up. "That's unbelievable," he said. "What would make her do that? I always thought Queen Red was loved by her people."

"Not by everyone, it seems," Alex said. "Apparently Little Bo has been unhappy for a long time with the way the kingdom has been managed and thinks she would be a much better queen. I would never want Red to lose her throne but I honestly think Little Bo had some valid things to say."

Rook scrunched his forehead and thought more about it. "What would you say possessed Little Bo to challenge the throne today of all days? If she's been unhappy for so long you'd think she would have done something about it sooner."

Alex thought back to the scene Little Bo had caused earlier that day in the House of Progress but couldn't come up with an answer. "That's a really good point," she said. "She didn't mention anything in particular. But something must have provoked her into demanding an election."

"Seems fishy, if you ask me," Rook said. He abruptly stopped walking and a sly smile crept over his face.

"What is it?" Alex asked, looking back at him.

"I just thought of something really adventurous we could do," he said, but then quickly said, "Never mind, it might not be your cup of tea."

Alex laughed—if he only knew the mischief she and her

brother had gotten into over the years. "I'll have you know I happen to be *very* adventurous," she teased. "Don't let the wand and sparkly dress fool you."

Rook shook his head. "I don't want to be a bad influence, especially to an up-and-coming fairy. It could get us both into a lot of trouble."

Alex was appreciative of this but was even more curious about what he was getting at. "Then tonight I'll just be *Alex*," she said. "What's on your mind?"

Rook laughed at her and caved in. "All right, but don't say I didn't warn you." He chuckled. "I was just going to suggest that if you're curious about Little Bo Peep's intentions, we could sneak onto her farm and have a look around. I know right where it is—it's on the southeast side of the Red Riding Hood Kingdom, not too far from our farm. Her farmhands sold my father some sheep once."

Alex's conscience instantly shot down the idea. As a respected fairy, it would be extremely irresponsible and childish of her to spy on Little Bo Peep. She would never want to do anything that could potentially jeopardize her reputation. But the answer she gave Rook took them both by surprise.

"Let's do it!"

Rook was shocked. He had been half kidding but the excitement in Alex's eyes was contagious. "Are you sure you're up for it? I'm not pressuring you, am I?"

In truth, the only thing pressuring Alex was Alex herself. It felt like ages since she'd experienced a true adventure. She craved the fear of getting caught and missed the thrill of being chased.

"Let's ride Cornelius," Alex said. "It'll take us a quarter of the time to get there."

She confidently turned around and headed back to the field. Rook froze for a moment before catching up with her—he liked her more and more with every moment they spent together. When they returned to the field Alex whistled for Cornelius and he appeared shortly after.

"Good evening, Cornelius," Alex said. "Rook and I are going to the Red Riding Hood Kingdom to spy on someone. Care to join us in a little mischief tonight?"

Cornelius was just as surprised as Rook had been. He had never seen this side of Alex before, but he liked it. He nodded his huge head as if to say, *I thought you'd never ask.*

Alex and Rook climbed astride the unicorn and the three took off toward the Red Riding Hood Kingdom. By the time they reached the kingdom's partially built wall, the sun had set and the moon was aglow in a twinkly night sky. All the stonemasons had gone home for the night, so Alex and Rook didn't have to worry about being seen entering the kingdom.

Rook jumped off Cornelius's back and began climbing the unfinished wall. "It's a little tricky but I think you'll manage in that dress of yours," Rook called down to Alex.

Alex didn't even bother trying to climb it. She removed her wand from the pocket of her dress and pointed it directly at the wall. A doorway appeared immediately and Alex effortlessly walked through it and into the kingdom.

"Oh, now you're just showing off," Rook said to her, and climbed down to meet her.

Cornelius tried to walk through the doorway but couldn't fit.

"Stay on the other side of the wall, Cornelius," Alex said. "We'll be back soon."

The unicorn slumped. He was disappointed he wasn't going with them but patiently waited as Alex requested. Rook took Alex by the hand and led her through the grassy hills of the Bo Peep Farms. It was the first time a boy had ever held her hand. She felt like her heart was doing cartwheels into her stomach.

About a mile past the wall, the rooftops of Little Bo Peep's quaint farm came into view in the distance. It was an adorable place and reminded Alex of a play set she and her brother had when they were toddlers. The barn was big and painted bright red with white trim. The farmhouse was wooden and small, the perfect size for one person, and had a wraparound porch. A metal windmill stood between the buildings, slowly turning in the night breeze.

Huge stacks of hay were scattered across the land and there were fluffy black and white sheep as far as the eye could see. It was like the farm was covered in little walking clouds.

When they got closer to the farm Rook pulled Alex behind a haystack to hide from a group of farmhands they saw ahead. The farmhands were collecting their tools and putting them away in the barn. They had finished their work for the day and were preparing to go home.

The front door of the farmhouse suddenly burst open and Little Bo Peep stepped onto the porch. She had taken her bonnet off for the evening and her dark hair was up in a tight bun. She wore a long blue cloak over her yellow ruffled dress and held her staff in one hand and a lantern in the other. Her pale skin glowed in the moonlight.

At first Little Bo appeared to be in a hurry, but she stayed on the porch once she realized the farmhands were still there.

"Good night, Miss Peep!" the farmhands called to her.

"Good night, gentlemen, thank you for all your hard work today!" Little Bo said back. "See you in the morning."

The farmhands tipped their hats to her and all climbed into the same wagon and drove off into the night. Little Bo smiled and waved to them, but once they were out of sight her smile faded into a somber expression. She did a full circle around the porch, scanning the farm to make absolutely certain that she was alone.

Once she was sure that every farmhand had left, Little Bo hurried down the steps of the porch and headed straight to the barn. She pulled open the heavy red doors and shut them behind her. Alex and Rook heard a scrape as Little Bo locked them from the inside.

"What do you think she's up to?" Alex whispered.

"Let's find out." Rook gestured for her to follow him.

They sprinted to the barn as quickly, as quietly, and as low to the ground as possible. Alex kept tripping over her dress and Rook had to help her up each time. They were both laughing and kept reminding each other to stay quiet. Alex couldn't remember the last time she had had this much fun.

They circled the barn until they found an open window. They slowly peeked over the windowsill to see inside.

The barn was lined with mountainous stacks of square hay

bales. Little Bo was standing before the largest stack, in the middle of the barn, tirelessly pulling the bales down one square at a time. She grunted and dabbed her forehead with the corner of her cloak. Eventually, a large rectangular object covered with a sheet was revealed. Little Bo had been hiding something in the hay.

She yanked off the sheet covering the object and Alex had to put a hand over her mouth to keep from gasping out loud.

"That's a magic mirror!" Alex whispered. "Little Bo Peep is hiding a magic mirror in her barn!"

"Are you sure it's magic?" Rook asked.

"I'm positive." The mirror had a thick silver frame with floral engravings and its reflection was too crisp to be a normal mirror's.

Little Bo examined herself in the mirror, fixing a few strands of hair that had fallen into her face. Once she was satisfied with her appearance, she gently placed an open hand on the glass. The mirror instantly rippled to life like a stone had been dropped in a still lake.

Little Bo leaned as close to the mirror as she could without touching it. "Are you there, my love?" she whispered softly. Her eyes were wide and anxious as she waited. She looked like a puppy waiting for its master to arrive.

A dark silhouette of a man appeared through the rippling glass. "I am," his deep and gruff voice declared.

Little Bo smiled and pressed both of her hands against the glass. "I missed you so much today," she said. "I would have come sooner but the farmhands were working late."

"How did it go at the House of Progress?" the man asked.

"Everything went exactly as we planned," Little Bo was happy to share. "I wish you could have been there to hear me; I was very convincing. No one would have thought I was anything but genuinely passionate about the kingdom."

"Good," the man said. "Make sure to keep it that way."

The man's harsh tone made Little Bo blue. "What's wrong? You don't seem yourself," she said, and peered closer into the glass to see his silhouette better.

"Every day I'm trapped in here is harder than the one before," he said. "I'm starting to have doubts that I'll ever be free."

"You don't trust me?" Little Bo said sadly.

"I trust your intentions, my sweet, but until you're crowned queen I can't get my hopes up," he said. "Misery fills the emptiness that hope leaves behind when the world disappoints you."

Little Bo passionately pressed her body against the glass. "I will find a way to get you out of there, if it's the last thing I do," she said. "Soon I'll be queen and I'll have a world of opportunity at my disposal. I'll exhaust every resource in my power until I have you in my arms again."

The silhouette went silent. "We'll see," it said coldly.

"You must believe in me," Little Bo said. "I can't do this without your trust."

The silhouette slowly faded away and the mirror's glass became solid.

"No, come back! Please come back!" Little Bo pleaded but the man did not return.

Little Bo slid down the glass and onto the ground. She sat

on her knees and buried her face in her hands, quietly sobbing. Once she stopped crying she stood up and re-covered the mirror and re-stacked the bales of hay to hide it.

"We should head back before she finishes," Rook suggested.

Alex agreed and they quickly crept away in the direction they'd come from. They stayed quiet until they reached the wall and then returned to the Fairy Kingdom on Cornelius's back.

As they traveled home on the swift unicorn, Rook asked, "What was Little Bo Peep doing with a magic mirror? And who was that man trapped inside it?"

Alex had been asking herself the same questions. "I have no idea," she said. "I feel so awful for her. Once someone is trapped in a magic mirror it's nearly impossible to get them out, and whoever that man was, it looked like Little Bo loved him very much."

"That's the real reason she wants to be queen, then," Rook said. "She thinks if she becomes queen it'll be easier to find a way to free him."

"And from the looks of it, that man hasn't been trapped in the mirror very long," Alex said. "After a while people imprisoned inside magic mirrors begin to lose themselves—their thoughts and memories fade and eventually all they can do is reflect the world around them. That man's mind was still pretty intact. He must have been cursed recently and that's probably what triggered Little Bo's decision to challenge the throne today."

"You sure know a lot about magic mirrors," Rook said.

"I've had some experience with them," Alex said. "And Little Bo's not the first person to think of a throne as the solution to getting someone out. Not many people know this but the man trapped inside the Evil Queen's mirror was her beloved, too. Her vanity and all the horrible things she did to Snow White were in one way or another just attempts to save the little of him that was left."

"Oh, good," Rook said with a smile in his eyes. "I was afraid you might have a collection of magic mirrors with all the other boys you've gone on walks with trapped inside."

They shared a laugh over the thought. "Stop giving me ideas," Alex teased. "Besides, you're the first boy I've ever taken a walk with, so my collection would be awfully small."

Alex's saying this made Rook feel like the most special boy in the world and the way he looked at Alex made her feel like the most special girl. The closer they got to the Fairy Kingdom, the closer they sat to each other on the unicorn. Soon they reached the field just outside the fairy gardens and Rook helped Alex off Cornelius. They looked into each other's eyes, knowing their night was coming to an end.

"It's getting late," Rook said, looking up at the night sky. "I should go home before my father worries."

"I had so much fun tonight," Alex said. "Thank you for taking me on an adventure. I really needed one."

"When may I see you again?" Rook had been waiting to ask since they left the Red Riding Hood Kingdom. "*If* I may see you again, that is."

"I'd like that very much," Alex said. "There's this fairy ball thing I have to go to tomorrow night but maybe we could see each other again at the end of the week?"

"I can't wait." He was looking so deeply into her eyes she felt like he was staring at her soul. He leaned closer to her and her heart began to flutter—was he about to do what she thought? Was she ready for it? But just before their mouths touched, Rook turned from her and began walking in the direction of his home.

"To more adventures," Rook said.

"To more adventures," Alex repeated.

"Good night, Alex," he said as he disappeared into the trees.

Alex sighed and leaned on Cornelius for support. Her heart was beating in time to a glorious symphony that played in her mind. She felt like she was floating above herself. She had never wanted to be with someone as much as she wanted to be with Rook. His presence gave her a purpose she couldn't explain.

Alex patted Cornelius's head good night and made her way back to the Fairy Palace. She couldn't help skipping as she walked; she was full of excitement, giggles, and butterflies. . . .

CHAPTER EIGHT

THE FAIRY INAUGURAL BALL

The day of the Fairy Inaugural Ball finally arrived and the entire Fairy Kingdom was united in celebration. Two years ago, when Alex first laid eyes on the fairy gardens and the Fairy Palace, she never would have thought the kingdom could look *more* magical than it already did. But when she awoke that morning and looked out her window and saw the results of all the hard work the fairies had put into making this day as special as possible, she realized she had been mistaken.

A double rainbow arched high above the kingdom without fading. The fluffiest white clouds imaginable slowly morphed into the shapes of flowers, animals, and insects as they floated through the sky. The air was filled with bubbles of all sizes and some transported the tiniest fairies from one corner of the kingdom to another. Every plant was bigger and brighter than normal and swayed in a light breeze. High geysers shot sporadically out of every pond and lake and never from the same place twice.

The kingdom only became more majestic as the sun set and all the stars appeared. They twinkled vividly in the night sky and with each shooting star a sparkly trail glistened down as if it were raining stardust. The Fairy Palace shimmered brighter than ever, as if it were covered in millions of miniature lights. Fireworks went off in slow motion above the palace, illuminating the gardens and bodies of water in bright colors.

The ball began downstairs in the main hall of the Fairy Palace and the sounds of celebration increased as more and more fairies from around the kingdom arrived. Alex was still in her chambers, too nervous to join the festivities. They were all waiting for *her*, they had all come to see *her*—it was more attention than she was comfortable with.

Alex had been standing in front of her mirror for hours. She magically transformed her dress into several different gowns, each more eccentric than the next, until she finally settled on a simple white gown with matching gloves. She even styled her hair up into a look Queen Red would have been proud of.

She looked beautiful and, more important, she *felt* beautiful. She wished her six-year-old self could see her now. Alex would have grown up with such confidence had she known this was where she would end up. She just wished her brother and her mom could see her.

The small piece of glass Alex had chipped off her mirror so she could communicate with her brother during his trip had been shimmering non-stop all day. She figured her brother was having the time of his life in Germany and wanted to tell her all about it. Alex couldn't wait to hear about it, but she ignored him, wanting to spare herself from any jokes or sarcastic comments he would make about her dress and the ball tonight—she was dreading it enough as it was.

There was a knock on her door and Tangerina and Skylene walked into her chamber.

"Hello, hello," Tangerina said. "We came to see how you were doing."

"Everyone is waiting for you downstairs," Skylene said.

Alex lost all confidence in her appearance as soon as she saw the enchanted outfits they were wearing. Tangerina was dressed in a square gown made entirely out of honeycomb. Live bees circled her neck and wrists like floating jewelry and honey dripped from her earlobes like teardrop earrings. Skylene wore her long hair up in the shape of a large water lily. Her dress was made of continuously flowing water; it started at her neck and flowed down her body, stopping just before it touched the ground—it was like she was wearing a waterfall.

"You two look amazing," Alex peeped.

"Is *that* what you're wearing?" Skylene asked. She and Tangerina exchanged a look that made Alex feel horribly underdressed.

"It is," Alex said confidently, trying to rebuild her self-esteem.

"You both said I should dress as I want to be remembered, right? This gown is elegant but simple and it does its job without being overly flashy and without stealing focus. That's exactly what I'd like my reputation to be."

The fairies just nodded. "It's *cuuute*," Tangerina finally said.

They weren't convincing and made Alex feel more discouraged than ever. "I can't do this," she said, and sat on her bed. "I'm not cut out for this kind of attention or pressure. I'm the kind of girl who just wants to be at the ball, not be the *belle of the ball*."

Tangerina and Skylene sat down on either side of her.

"You'll have to excuse the kingdom," Tangerina said. "The last Fairy Inaugural Ball was canceled when we discovered how destructive Ezmia was. It's been a very long time since we had something or someone worth celebrating. We're all just very excited, perhaps too excited."

"I can't imagine how over-stimulating all this must be for you," Skylene said. "And I don't think we've been much help. We may have given you the wrong idea about what tonight is truly about."

"Then I shouldn't dress how I want to be remembered?" Alex asked.

"Forget what we said about that, Alex," Tangerina said. "Being a fairy means you must be true to the goodness in your heart, and nothing is truer than wearing your heart on your sleeve."

"And the more honesty you show in your appearance, the more you will be remembered and admired for it," Skylene added.

Alex thought about that for a few moments but wasn't sure

she entirely understood. "So I'm supposed to wear my feelings?" she asked.

"So to speak," Skylene said.

"But if you truly believe this gown represents you, then you should have no regrets wearing this downstairs," Tangerina said.

"We'll give you a few moments alone to think it over," Skylene said. "There's no rush; come down whenever you're ready."

They each patted her on the shoulder and walked to the door.

"Oh, and Alex," Tangerina said before leaving, "don't think you're not worth celebrating."

The fairies smiled affectionately at Alex as they left her chambers. Alex stood before the mirror again, this time looking into her heart more than at her reflection.

In the past year Alex had experienced so many new phases in her life: living in a different dimension, learning magic, going on walks with boys, and being away from her family for the first time. Everything was as terrifying as it was exciting and Alex wanted her gown to reflect it all.

Alex closed her eyes and thought of the perfect thing to wear. She raised her wand and with a bright flash transformed her dress one last time....

The main hall of the Fairy Palace was decorated to perfection. The usually golden arches and pillars had been bewitched to change colors as the night went on. A small band of enchanted flutes and strings played music by themselves in the corner. The hall had been cleared out entirely and was lined with tables of food and drinks.

There were hundreds upon hundreds of fairies and not one of them was alike: water fairies sprinkled in dew, garden fairies wrapped in leaves, fairies with large colorful wings, fairies that glowed like they were made entirely of light, and small fairies the size of insects. The majority of them stood around mingling, while others hovered in the air.

The Fairy Godmother was in the center of the party, playing hostess and greeting everyone who came up to her. She was wearing her finest robes, which sparkled like the night sky, and tonight the air around her also sparkled, as if her aura had dressed for the occasion.

Mother Goose and Lester were camped out by one of the drink tables, trying to avoid the other fairies at all costs. Mother Goose poured herself and the large goose goblets of punch and topped them off with a splash from her flask.

Tangerina and Skylene waited by the foot of the stairs for Alex to arrive. "I hope we cheered her up," Tangerina said. "The poor thing looked terrified."

"She'll be down when she's ready," Skylene said.

"Oh look! Here she comes now," Tangerina said, and pointed to the top of the stairs.

Skylene eagerly tapped the side of her glass until the room went silent. "Ladies and gentlemen, boys and girls, we'd like to present the fairy of the hour," she announced. "She is the youngest fairy to ever join the Fairy Council and the Happily Ever After Assembly, the only fairy clever enough to outsmart the Enchantress, and she's the future Fairy Godmother! Please give a warm welcome to the one and only Alex Bailey!"

Skylene made a grand gesture toward the top of the stairs and the hall burst into applause. Alex walked down the stairs and the entire room gasped when they saw her gown. She was still wearing the white gown but it was now covered in thousands of vibrant live butterflies. The butterflies twitched and fluttered in time with Alex's nervous heart but they never flew away.

Tangerina and Skylene were the first to greet Alex and rave about her new dress. Mother Goose and Lester raised their goblets in her direction from the drinks table. The Fairy Godmother smiled proudly up at her from the middle of the room. She met her granddaughter at the foot of the stairs, took her hand, and led her into the center of the hall.

The palace was filled with fairies Alex had never seen before, but besides Tangerina and Skylene, the rest of the Fairy Council members were nowhere to be found.

"Grandma, where is everyone?" Alex asked. "Aren't Rosette, Xanthous, Emerelda, Violetta, and Coral coming to the ball?"

"They'll be here shortly," the Fairy Godmother said. "They're just waiting for us to start."

"Start *what*?" Alex asked, and gave her grandmother a suspicious look.

"You'll see," the Fairy Godmother said, hiding a smile.

Skylene tapped the side of her glass again to regain the crowd's attention. "Tonight we're here to celebrate a girl who over the past few months has shown wisdom and skill beyond her years. However, before she can officially join the Fairy Council and the Happily Ever After Assembly, there are four sacred tests she must pass: the test of *courage*, the test of *grace*, the test of *kindness*, and the test of *heart*."

The butterflies on the inside and outside of Alex fluttered intensely. "Grandma," she said with enormous eyes. "You never said I would be *tested* at the ball."

An amused grin appeared on the Fairy Godmother's face. "I didn't want to worry you," she said. "Just relax, sweetheart, you've already passed the first three without realizing it."

"Please clear the floor!" Skylene said, and the crowd of guests parted to the sides of the room, leaving Alex alone in the center. A bright flash of light filled the back of the hall and seven podiums and a seat on either side of them suddenly appeared. They were the official stations of the Fairy Council members— and if Alex passed the tests, she would be given a seat among them.

Mother Goose was to present the first test. She went to Alex and put an arm around her. "When Alex was thirteen years old she proved her bravery to the world by defeating the evil Enchantress," Mother Goose said to the guests. "Alex was able to do something five queens, four kings, and ten fairies combined could not; she figured out a way to outwit Ezmia. She didn't care if she lived or died in the process, all she cared about was saving the people she loved. So, Alex, it's my privilege to inform you that, without question, you have passed the test of *courage*."

The fairies applauded and Mother Goose took her seat by the

podiums. Once she was seated, four familiar people pushed their way through the crowd of fairies lining the room and stepped into the center of the hall next to Alex—it was the old lady and her three bratty granddaughters whom Alex had helped in the Charming Kingdom.

"Wait, what are they doing here?" Alex asked.

Suddenly, bright lights appeared and began swirling around the woman and her granddaughters. Alex watched in amazement as the woman transformed into Emerelda and the three granddaughters became Rosette, Violetta, and Coral.

"That was you four?" Alex asked in shock, and a smile came to her face.

All four looked as gorgeous as ever. Emerelda wore a long dress made entirely out of small emeralds. Rosette's gown was red and multi-layered, so the bottom of it looked like a giant rose wrapped around her legs. Violetta wore a purple dress with a high collar shaped like a violet. Coral's dress was made of pink flower petals and Fisher, her walking-fish pet, held tightly in her hands, wore a matching bow tie.

"Being a fairy doesn't mean you're always appreciated," Emerelda said. "But even when she was subjected to a rude and unwelcoming home, Alex was able to keep a calm and elegant demeanor. She understands that being a fairy isn't about *whom* you help, but *how* you help. She has passed the test of *grace*."

The fairies around the hall clapped again. Rosette, Tangerina, Emerelda, Skylene, Violetta, and Coral went to their respective podiums—there was only one fairy missing.

Before Alex knew it, Cornelius abruptly galloped into the

hall at full speed with Xanthous on his back. They stopped in the center of the room beside her, and Xanthous hopped down from the unicorn.

"Don't tell me *you* were a test, too!" Alex said to her unicorn, and playfully put her hands on her hips. The unicorn happily nodded his giant head.

Xanthous was wearing a crisp yellow suit with a long flickering cape of flames. He addressed the crowd, soaking up the attention for all it was worth. "Of all the unicorns in the forest she could have chosen as her method of transportation, Alex chose *this* one," he told the crowd.

Cornelius snorted loudly as if to say, *"I have a name."*

"Alex gave this unicorn a chance to prove himself even when the unicorns of his own herd had disregarded him," Xanthous continued. "She has proven that she believes passion is far more important than appearance and in doing so has passed the test of *kindness.*"

The fairies cheered again. Cornelius became emotional and had to wipe his eyes on a tablecloth. Xanthous joined the other fairies at the podiums, completing their rainbow of color. The Fairy Godmother was next to approach Alex. The entire hall fell silent, knowing the final test was about to be presented.

"Alex, there is one final test you must complete, and you must complete it in here in front of all of us," the Fairy Godmother said sternly, although it was mostly for show. "It's the test of *heart*, and it cannot be proven with a wand, but only with words. Are you ready?"

Alex's hands were trembling. She had been afraid a moment

like this would happen—a moment when she could possibly let down the entire Fairy Kingdom if she failed. Alex licked her lips and nodded. "Yes, I'm ready."

"In your own words, tell us why you should join the Fairy Council and the Happily Ever After Assembly," the Fairy Godmother said.

It was difficult for Alex to think with so many pairs of eyes staring at her. She looked inside her heart for the best answer. She thought about all the people she had helped as a fairy and all the people who had ever helped her before she was a fairy. She thought about the fairies around her, and about Farmer Robins and Rook, and tried to form an answer she thought would please them all.

"Because...because...," Alex said with a nervous quiver. "Because I know what it's like to live without magic. I know what it's like to struggle and work hard for things. Right now I think people outside this kingdom have a hard time believing in us because they don't see how any of us truly understand what it's like for them. And in time, I think I can be the fairy they will all trust and depend on because I'll always be one of them."

The hall kept very silent while they waited to hear the results. The Fairy Godmother turned away from her granddaughter and faced the room of spectators. "She has passed the test of *heart*," she declared.

The fairies erupted into thunderous applause. The Fairy Godmother took her seat by the podiums and the Fairy Council was complete. A brand-new golden chair appeared out of thin air beside the Fairy Godmother. Alex went to the chair and stroked the armrest. She was finally an official member of the

Fairy Council and the Happily Ever After Assembly and had her own seat to prove it.

The Fairy Godmother leaned in to her. "I told you there was nothing to worry about," she said.

Alex smiled at her. "I can't believe you've been testing me all week," she said to her fellow council members.

"We knew you wouldn't disappoint us," Xanthous said.

"Congratulations, Alex," Emerelda told her.

"Well done," Rosette added.

"Aren't you going to try your seat?" Coral asked.

Alex sat in her chair for the first time. She couldn't deny that sitting alongside the rest of the council members with purpose was a very good feeling.

The celebration went on and Alex was continuously congratulated by fairies she had never met. At one point she noticed someone lingering behind a pillar nearby. She could have sworn she knew him. He was taller than her and wore an old suit a tad too big for him. A feathered mask covered his face.

He had been watching her the entire night but never came over to congratulate her or say hello. The more Alex looked at him, the more anxious he seemed to become. Finally the attention she was giving him obviously worried him too much and he headed out of the Fairy Palace. Alex's curiosity got the best of her and she decided to follow him.

"Grandma, may I be excused from the party for a few minutes?" Alex asked.

"Of course, dear!"

Alex hurried out of the main hall and down the front steps

of the Fairy Palace. She felt something crunch under her foot and realized the fellow in question had taken off his mask and dropped it on the stairs. She looked ahead and saw him running into the gardens.

"Hey!" Alex called out, but he didn't turn around.

She chased after him as fast as she could in her gown. Every time she got close enough to see who he was, he would turn and run down another path in the gardens. Alex felt like she was chasing him in a maze of colorful plants and flowers. Eventually she caught up to him on a small bridge that crossed over a pond.

"Freeze!" Alex demanded. "Show yourself or I'll use my wand!"

He slowly turned around and his face was perfectly lit in the moonlight.

"Rook?!" Alex gasped.

"Hello, Alex," Rook said timidly.

"What are you doing here?" Alex asked.

"I'm sorry, I didn't mean to run from you," he said. "I just really wanted to see you again. I thought I would sneak into the ball and surprise you, but once I saw you and discovered it was *your* ball, I couldn't help but stay."

Alex didn't know what to say. She had never meant to keep the reality of who she was a secret from him but she hadn't wanted him to find out like this.

"Rook, I'm sorry I didn't tell you the whole story about who I am," Alex said. "I was afraid I would scare you away if I did."

Rook stared at her for a moment and then nodded. "So you're the next Fairy Godmother, huh?"

"Yes," Alex said sheepishly.

"And *you're* the one who defeated the Enchantress?" he asked.

"Guilty of that as well," she said.

Rook took a minute to wrap his head around it. He stared off at the gardens around them in absolute bewilderment. "This is bad," he said, shaking his head. "I don't know what I'm going to do about this."

Alex felt her heart drop into the pit of her stomach. "Rook, I'm still me," she pleaded. "I'm still the same fairy you met at your farm and who you went on a walk with yesterday."

To Alex's relief, Rook looked up at her and smiled. "That's not what I meant," he said, and stepped closer to her. "I thought you were amazing the first time I met you, and the more I think about you, the more amazing you seem. Now that I know just how incredible you really are, I'm not sure how I'm ever going to let you go."

"Oh," Alex said. Her heart began racing and her butterflies fluttered to life. "Well, that's very . . . very . . . *nice*."

"You make me really happy, Alex, in ways I can't explain," he said.

"You make me really happy, too, Rook," she said. "One of the reasons I'm wearing butterflies tonight is to match the butterflies you give me when I think of you."

Rook stepped even closer to her and placed a hand on the side of her face. He looked into her eyes for a moment and then slowly leaned his head closer to hers. Alex's heart was about to beat out of her chest. The butterflies fluttered more rapidly the closer he got to her. They flew off her dress just as Rook kissed her for the first time.

The celebration continued in the main hall despite Alex's absence. The Fairy Godmother sat in her chair and happily watched over the party around her. It had been a terrific night and she couldn't have been prouder of her granddaughter. However, the celebration had taken a toll on the Fairy Godmother and she was feeling very tired and a tad weak.

"It's a wonderful party," Mother Goose said, pulling up her own seat next to the Fairy Godmother. "Nothing will ever beat that mixer I threw during the Crusades but this might be a close second."

"Yes, I think everyone is enjoying themselves," the Fairy Godmother said softly.

"Are you feeling all right, FG?" Mother Goose asked. "You don't seem very festive."

"I'm just glad this day is finally here," she said. "The Fairy Kingdom can now rest assured that their future is in good hands."

Mother Goose took a good look at her. She knew something was wrong even if it wasn't plainly written on her face. "I've known you for centuries; I can tell when something is bothering you," she said.

The Fairy Godmother sighed. "Can I confide in you?" she asked her oldest friend.

"Of course," Mother Goose said. "If I gave you a gold coin for every secret of mine you've kept, I'd be broke."

The Fairy Godmother looked directly into her eyes. "Years

ago when I declared Ezmia as my heir, there was always something in the back of my mind that told me it wasn't meant to be," she said. "I ignored it, but then later that feeling proved to be intuition. Now that I've declared Alex as my heir, there is another feeling that's come over me that I can't ignore."

"What is it?" Mother Goose asked. "Do you have doubts about Alex, too?"

"On the contrary," the Fairy Godmother replied. "After months of training her and finally seeing her among the council tonight, I feel nothing but hopeful . . . and *tired*."

"How tired?" Mother Goose asked.

"More tired than I've felt before in my life," the Fairy Godmother told her.

Mother Goose's face fell. "Are you telling me what I think you might be?"

The Fairy Godmother nodded. "Yes," she said with a bittersweet smile. "You and I are the only ones old enough to know how magic works in these situations. We know what's to be expected. But please remember this is good news. It means we've finally found the true heir of magic and she's ready."

Mother Goose didn't say a word. She took the Fairy Godmother's hand into her own and smiled as widely as she could, given the news.

"I think I'm going to retire for the night," the Fairy Godmother said. "If you see Alex, please tell her I'll see her in the morning."

The Fairy Godmother slowly disappeared into soft glittery clouds, too tired to climb the stairs.

Suddenly the hall of fairies parted. Something was causing a ruckus, and they hurried away from it as fast as possible. Three boisterous witches had just arrived in the Fairy Palace, and they noisily made their way into the center of the hall.

Each wore a long, ragged black cloak, and they all smelled foul. One witch had cat eyes and twigs for hair, another was missing an eye but had two large noses, and the third had skin so loose, it appeared to be melting off her face like wax. They cackled loudly at the fairies cowering away from them.

The eight members of the Fairy Council formed a circle around the witches. It was obvious they had come to start trouble.

"What business do you have here?" Emerelda asked them.

"We came here for the Fairy Inaugural Ball, of course," the one-eyed witch said in a shrill voice.

"You weren't invited," Violetta said. "This celebration is for fairies only."

"You're breaking the laws of the Happily Ever After Assembly by being in our palace," Xanthous threatened. "Witches are not allowed to set foot in this kingdom, and you know it."

"Enforce those laws while you still have them, because soon there will be no assembly to threaten us with," the one-eyed witch warned.

The fairies whispered to one another. What did the witch mean by this? Xanthous grew impatient and didn't care to find out. "Leave at once, or we'll have you thrown in Pinocchio Prison," he threatened.

The witches cackled even harder at his attempt to frighten them. "But if we leave, you'll never receive our gift," the witch with cat eyes hissed. "We didn't come all this way empty-handed."

"We don't want your gift," Tangerina said. The bees flying around her neck and wrists flew at a quicker pace. "Go back to wherever it is you came from."

"Trust us—you want what we have to offer," the witch with waxy skin wheezed. "It's less a gift and more a *prophecy*. It's something the witches have kept to themselves for a great while, but since it's such a ceremonious night, we thought we'd share it with you."

"We don't want to hear your ridiculous prophecy, either," Rosette said.

"I do!" Coral peeped, speaking on behalf of all the curious fairies in the room. "It couldn't hurt just to listen to whatever information they want to give us."

The members of the Fairy Council looked at one another, but no one objected. "Very well," Emerelda said. "If the witches promise to leave us in peace when they've finished, they may share their message with us."

The witches scowled at the audience of fairies. They held hands and formed a circle. The witches cocked their heads up to the sky, and their mouths and eyes began to glow. A strong breeze swiftly blew through the palace as the witches chanted a rhyme in unison.

"Fairies, listen well,
For there is truth in the sights we foretell.
'Happily ever after' will not last,

When it's greeted by a threat from the past.
One by one, the kingdoms will fall apart,
From battles they'll lose and wars they'll start.
Fairy blood will be spilt by the gallons,
When you face the army of thousands."

The witches howled with laughter at the conclusion of their prophecy. All the fairies had to cover their ears from the screeching sounds.

"Get out of this palace before I turn you into ashes," Xanthous said, and his whole body burst into flames.

"Yeah, and then I'll kick your ashes into next week!" Mother Goose added.

The witches left the palace, cackling as loudly as they could the entire way. The fairies looked at one another anxiously. Did they have any reason to believe a word of what the witches had just said? Was an army of thousands really on its way? And from where?

"Do not worry," Emerelda told them. "This was nothing more than a foolish attempt to ruin our evening, and I refuse to let them succeed. I say we continue our festivities in the gardens where we can celebrate under the stars."

The fairies cheered, and Emerelda led all the guests through the hall and outside the palace.

"Aren't you coming, Mother Goose?" Coral asked as she left with the others.

Mother Goose was the only one who had stayed behind. "Sure," she said. "I'll be out in a minute."

"All right," Coral said, and flew off with the others.

Mother Goose's eyes darted left and right, and small beads of sweat appeared on her forehead. She was the only person to whom the witches' prophecy meant something. Everything the witches had foretold was connected to a dark secret Mother Goose had kept for a very long time, a secret she had never told anyone, not even the Fairy Godmother.

But years ago Mother Goose had done everything in her power to make sure the army wouldn't cross over. Was the threat still alive?

There was only one way to find out, and there was only one person who could help her—and he was worlds away.

Mother Goose took a giant swig from her flask and hopped onto Lester's back. She steered him to the window of Alex's room. Mother Goose climbed in through the window and had a look around. She found the magic mirror placed in the corner and touched its glass. There was no response and Mother Goose looked desperately around the room. On Alex's nightstand she found the piece of mirror that had been chipped off, and to her relief it was shimmering—*he* was trying to contact Alex at that exact moment.

Mother Goose picked up the piece of mirror and the round, freckled face of the person she was trying to contact appeared.

"Oh, C-Dog, thank God it's you," Mother Goose said to Conner. "Listen, we need to talk. I need your help. . . ."

CHAPTER NINE

ABANDON TRIP

Conner spent his last two days in Germany locked in his hotel room pretending to be sick. While his principal and schoolmates went to museums and historical landmarks, he worked around the clock trying to contact his sister. He lived off sandwiches and sodas from a vending machine down the hall and twenty-minute naps when he needed them.

He had never been so angry with his sister before in his life. He knew Alex was busy preparing for the Fairy Inaugural Ball but it couldn't have been going on for all of the past three days. When he finally got ahold of her—if he ever got ahold of her—she'd better have a good reason for why she had been ignoring him.

Unfortunately, the day of their departure finally came and Conner had no choice but to travel home with the others. He regretted leaving—somehow being close to the grave sites of the Brothers Grimm made him feel closer to the issue.

Their group loaded into the van and said good-bye to Berlin as they drove to the airport. Once they arrived at the airport Conner wouldn't let the woman behind the counter check Betsy. His piece of magic mirror was inside and he didn't want to be away from it in case Alex tried contacting him. His unexpected clinginess to the suitcase didn't go unnoticed. Everyone in his group raised an eyebrow, but no one's eyebrow rose higher than Bree's. She was carefully watching every move he made.

They landed in London's Heathrow Airport and found seats by the gate for their connecting flight home.

"Oy, governor! Oy, governor!" Cindy said in a horrible cockney accent to all the British people that passed them by. "That's how you say hello here," she whispered to the others like she was filling them in on a secret.

"No, it's not," Bree said, embarrassed for her.

The Book Huggers had been giving Conner dirty looks ever since they left Berlin but Conner was unaware of it. He had been staring off into space the entire time, clutching Betsy to his chest as if he were expecting someone to rip the suitcase out of his hands.

"How are you feeling, Mr. Bailey?" Mrs. Peters asked him as she read a newspaper.

"Better," Conner said, without looking up.

"I'm so sorry you missed out on all the other activities; you would have enjoyed them," his principal said.

"Next time" was all Conner could reply.

The gate's intercom buzzed as an announcement was made. "Attention, all travelers leaving on international flight 527, we will be boarding the plane in ten minutes, starting with our first-class passengers."

"Oh wonderful," Mrs. Peters said, and folded up her newspaper. "We'll be in the air on our way home in no time."

Conner knew it would be difficult to use the piece of magic mirror once he was on the plane. He decided to try reaching Alex one more time before boarding.

"I'm going to use the restroom before we get on the plane," Conner announced to the girls. He hurried across the waiting area to the nearest bathroom with Betsy in his arms.

The Book Huggers rolled their eyes at Conner just like every time he had said or done anything on the trip. Bree watched Conner as he went, curious about why he needed his suitcase to use the restroom.

Conner entered the men's room and looked under all the stalls to make sure he was alone. He locked himself inside one, put the toilet lid down, and had a seat. He opened Betsy on the floor in front of him and retrieved the piece of mirror. He pressed the glass with his finger and watched it shimmer for a few moments but had no luck reaching Alex. He was so frustrated and disappointed.

However doubtful he was about getting a different result,

Conner decided to tap the glass one more time before calling it quits. The glass shimmered for as long as it always did and right when Conner was about to put the piece of mirror away, his heart dropped. A face appeared in the mirror—but it wasn't the person he was expecting.

"Oh, C-Dog, thank God it's you," Mother Goose said. "Listen, we need to talk. I need your help. . . ."

Conner was so excited to finally be in contact with someone he almost fell off the toilet. *"Mother Goose! It's so good to see your face!"* He was in hysterics.

"If I had a gold coin for every time someone said that, I would be in debt," she cracked. "Listen, I have to talk to you about something very important."

She seemed just as flustered and worried as he was, but Conner figured her concern could wait, compared to the news he had to share.

"No! I have something I need to tell you that's *more* important," he said. *"Something major has happened and I need to tell someone in the fairy-tale world about it!"*

Mother Goose eyed him strangely. "Kid, are you in a bathroom?" she asked. "Because if so, I think you should maybe talk to a doctor about this and not me—"

"I'm in a bathroom because I'm trying to hide!" Conner said. "I'm in Europe on a class trip! This was the only place I could get privacy!"

"Europe?" Mother Goose asked. "Okay, kid, calm down and slowly tell me what's going on before you have an accident."

Conner took a deep breath and started from the beginning.

"I was in Germany for this thing with my principal and a couple other kids. The University of Berlin found three brand-new fairy tales in a time capsule left by the Brothers Grimm. They included careful instructions not to publicize or publish the stories until two hundred years later. We and a bunch of other people went to the cemetery where the Brothers Grimm are buried, and there was a special reading of the stories. The first two weren't important but I think the third one was a warning in disguise."

"A warning?" Mother Goose asked. "A warning about what?"

"That's what I've been trying to figure out," he said. "The story was too similar to real life not to have a bigger purpose."

"Tell me what the story was about," she prompted.

"It was about a pair of brothers who told stories just like the Brothers Grimm. They got their stories from a fairy who lived in a secret castle, *just like the Brothers Grimm got their stories from you, and from Grandma and the other fairies.* One day a greedy king forced the brothers to provide him with a map to the secret castle so he could conquer it. A magical bird that also lived in the secret castle, *who I'm assuming is supposed to be you,* gave the brothers an enchanted map to give to the king, so that it would take him two hundred years to get to the castle, leaving the people and magical creatures lots of time to prepare a defense. The brothers in the story were afraid the magical bird would forget to warn the others in the secret castle about the approaching king so they wrote a story about it, hoping the story would reach the secret castle before the king's army of thousands did."

"Wait, can you say that last part again?" Mother Goose interrupted.

168

"I said, they hoped their story would reach the secret castle before the king's army of thousands did, in case the magical bird had forgotten to warn the others," Conner repeated.

All the blood drained from Mother Goose's face and her eyes drifted off into a fearful trance. "But it's impossible," she said softly to herself.

"What's impossible?" Conner asked. "Does this story mean something to you? Because it sounds like something bad started two hundred years ago and the Brothers Grimm are warning everyone about it now."

Mother Goose didn't respond. All she could do was shake her head from side to side as she thought about what he told her.

"Mother Goose, if this story is real, then I'm afraid something horrible is about to happen in the Land of Stories and we need to stop it," he said.

She finally looked up and made eye contact with him again. "I'm afraid their story is based on something that is very real," she told him in a stricken tone.

Conner felt his heart descend deeper into his stomach. "What happened?" he asked.

Mother Goose sighed and then told Conner a secret she had managed to keep to herself for years—until this moment.

"Two hundred years ago in Otherworld time, there was a man named Jacques Marquis, a general in the French Empire's Grande Armée," she said. "General Marquis was a smart man; he knew the Brothers Grimm stories about mythical creatures and kingdoms were more than just fiction. He had them followed and discovered the truth about where their stories came from. He wanted to conquer the magnificent lands he read about, in the name of the French empire. So, he kidnapped the Brothers Grimm and demanded they provide his army with a portal into the fairy-tale world or he would kill their family."

"And did they give him one?" Conner asked.

"That's where I come into the story," Mother Goose said. "I never gave them a map like the bird in the story, but I told the Brothers Grimm of a portal they could lead General Marquis and his army of five thousand men to. But I bewitched the portal before the army arrived so that it would take them two hundred Otherworld years to cross through it and into the fairy-tale world."

"And that was two hundred years ago!" Conner exclaimed. "So why haven't they crossed into the fairy-tale world yet?"

"Because, after the Enchantress was defeated, your grandmother closed the portal between worlds, and just in the nick of time," Mother Goose said. "Thank God she did, because it meant I never had to tell her about the approaching army. I loved the Otherworld so much but I couldn't object to closing the portal since I knew that it would prevent that awful man and his soldiers from entering our world."

"Didn't anyone wonder where a group of five thousand soldiers disappeared to?" Conner asked.

"No, because shortly after, in the winter of 1812, Napoleon and the Grande Armée also invaded Russia," Mother Goose explained. "The French soldiers couldn't stand the cold and the retreating Russian soldiers hadn't left them any crops or livestock to survive on. The death toll was catastrophic and everyone assumed General Marquis and his men were among those that perished."

Conner sighed a deep breath of relief. "That's wonderful news," he said. "That means the army is still stuck in the portal and will never reach the Land of Stories, right?"

He expected Mother Goose to confirm his relief but instead her eyes drifted off again into another concerned gaze.

"The portal is closed permanently, isn't it?" Conner asked.

"It *was*," Mother Goose said. "But there is a chance the portal between the worlds may be . . . *re-opened*."

"How?" Conner asked.

Mother Goose knew the answer but decided it wasn't her place to tell him yet. "I can't tell you why or even that it will for certain, all I can tell you is that there is a chance," she repeated. "And the only way we'll know for sure is if we check whether or not the portal is working. If it can be opened from the Other-world side, that means it can be opened on the Land of Stories side as well, and the Grande Armée may cross into the fairy-tale world after all this time."

"Then tell me where it is! I'll check it myself," he pleaded.

"Absolutely not," Mother Goose said firmly. "I still haven't forgiven myself for telling Alex about the Enchantress—I couldn't live with myself if I sent you off on a dangerous chase as well."

Conner was so frustrated he wanted to throw the piece of mirror across the bathroom. He was still being treated like a child after all this time. But Mother Goose raised a hand to silence him before he could argue.

"But I may know someone *else* who can tell you," she said with a mischievously raised eyebrow.

"Who?" Conner said. "Someone in this world?"

"Yes," she said. "Where exactly in Europe are you?"

"I'm at an airport in London," he said.

This made Mother Goose extremely happy and she made an excited fist with her free hand. "Terrific, I have a friend in London—"

"It's not the queen, I hope," Conner said. "She'd be difficult to get to."

"No, the queen and I haven't spoken in years." Mother Goose waved off the idea. "This friend is very old but has been a confidant of mine for a very long time."

"Who is he?"

"He's more of a *what* than a *who*," Mother Goose explained. "Find the lion from the Red Lion Brewery. Tell him I sent you, and he'll tell you everything you need to know."

"The lion from the Red Lion Brewery?" Conner repeated to make sure he had heard her correctly. "Is he a real lion?"

"He's a statue," Mother Goose said. "He was the mascot of the brewery I spent most of the 1800s at—I met a lot of my closest drinking buddies there. Now I really need to go before your sister catches me in her room. We shouldn't tell anyone else about this unless we know for certain the portal has been re-opened. I don't want to dampen anyone's spirits around here if there's nothing to worry about."

"And what if it's open?" Conner said.

Mother Goose gulped. "Then we're in big trouble," she said. "Good luck, kid—oh and one more thing, do you still have that poker chip I gave you?"

"Yes, I take it everywhere with me," Conner said.

"Good—you'll need it," Mother Goose said, and then she faded from the piece of mirror in his hand.

Conner's head was spinning but he knew there was no time to waste. He quickly created a plan based on the tasks Mother Goose had given him. First, he had to sneak out of the airport and find a way into the city. Then he had to find the Red Lion Brewery and the lion and ask it where the portal was and how to check whether it was still closed. If the portal could be opened from the Otherworld side, then that meant it was open to the fairy-tale world, and the Grande Armée could be moments away from crossing over. His plan seemed straightforward. He packed the piece of mirror into Betsy and left the stall not wanting to waste another moment. However, his momentum came to a screeching halt as soon as he realized he wasn't alone in the bathroom.

"Bree?" Conner said in horror. Bree was standing just outside the stall and, judging from the bewildered expression on her face, she had heard every word of his and Mother Goose's conversation. "What are you doing in the men's bathroom?"

"They started boarding early," Bree said. "Mrs. Peters wanted me to check on you. When I got close to the bathroom I heard voices. I know you don't have a cell phone so I came in to see who you were talking to—and now after saying that out loud I realize how many privacy laws I just broke."

"How much of my conversation did you hear?" Conner asked.

"Enough," Bree said blankly.

Conner had no idea what to say to her. "Well, thank you for coming to check on me but I'm not going home," he said.

"I gathered," Bree said.

"Please don't tell Mrs. Peters where I'm going," Conner pleaded with her. "There is someone in London I really need to meet. It's really important."

Bree's face finally returned to normal. She quietly bobbed her head as she contemplated the situation. "I won't tell anyone," she said. "Because I'm going with you."

Conner shook his head in disbelief. "What? You can't go with me—you don't even know what's going on."

Bree crossed her arms. "I've known something was going on since the plane ride to Germany. Your sister disappeared last year with almost no explanation, you knew the plots of fairy tales that hadn't seen the light of day in two hundred years, and I just caught you somehow communicating with a woman called Mother Goose about an army invading another dimension."

Conner closed his eyes—there was no coming back from it now.

"With all that in mind, my best guess is that you are somehow connected to the *fairy-tale world*, and now you have to make sure an army from the 1800s isn't going to cross into that world and put your sister and grandmother in jeopardy. *Did I miss anything?*"

Bree said the whole thing in one breath without blinking. Conner was stunned. Reading all those mystery novels had paid off.

"Okay, I guess the dots aren't that hard to connect," Conner said. "But there's no way you're going with me. Do you know how much trouble you'd get into?"

Bree tipped her head back and grunted toward the ceiling. "I can live with trouble. I'll tell you what I can't live with—hearing one more conversation between the Book Huggers about a boy band or a fictitious relationship from a novel. I have three younger sisters—I went to Germany to escape all *that* and to have a European adventure. So far it seems you're the only person who can supply that and you could probably use help so I'm going with you, like it or not."

Conner's mouth and eyes were wide open. It was the most excited he had ever seen Bree get.

"How are you taking all of this so well?" he asked. "Don't you think the idea of another dimension seems insane?"

"Not at all," Bree said. "I'm a writer, too, Conner, and the reason I write is because I've always believed there is more to life than most people are willing to believe. You're just the first person to prove it to me."

Conner recognized the excitement in her eyes; he had seen it every day in his sister's eyes after their first trip into the Land of Stories. Now that Bree knew the truth, how could Conner tell her she couldn't go with him?

"All right, you can come," Conner told her. "As long as you promise never to share with another soul anything you've found out or anything you might see."

Bree slowly nodded, smiling the biggest smile ever. "I promise," she said, and Conner knew he could trust her.

"Good, now let's sneak out of the airport," he said.

They peered out of the men's restroom and glanced at the gate where their principal and schoolmates stood. The five of them were impatiently waiting for Conner and Bree to return before joining the line to board the plane. Mrs. Peters scanned the lounge, trying to see where they had gone. Then she looked down at her watch and Conner and Bree took it as a cue. They held on to their luggage as tightly as they could and bolted out of the bathroom, running down the terminal before she looked up. They followed the exit signs and went into customs.

"We got this—just follow my lead," Bree said. They got in line, keeping their heads down in case Mrs. Peters came looking for them. When it was Bree's turn, she walked up to the customs officer in the booth and presented her passport.

"Are you here for business or pleasure?" the officer asked her.

"Pleasure," Bree said casually. "I've come to visit my aunt and see a few shows in the West End."

She was good at this deception thing. The customs officer stamped her passport and sent Bree on her way. Conner went next, confident he had nothing to worry about.

"Are you here for business or pleasure?" the officer asked him.

"Pleasure," Conner replied. "I've come for the food."

The customs officer flinched and looked up at him awkwardly. "The *food*?" he asked.

Bree slapped her hand against her forehead. Conner wanted to put his whole leg in his mouth. Of all the things to say, he'd picked possibly the only thing Great Britain *wasn't* known for. Conner panicked, thinking fast.

"You've never heard of the Food?" he went on. "They're only the greatest singing quartet of chefs-turned-tenors on the planet! They have a concert at the Buckinghamshirevilleton Coliseum. Here, let me give you one of their albums."

Conner reached for his suitcase but the customs officer held up a hand to stop him. "Please don't," he said. He stamped Conner's passport and then sent him on his way, too. Conner had never been so thankful to be perceived as just a stupid kid.

Bree was appalled by Conner's stunt. *"Buckinghamshirevilleton?"* she whispered. *"Are you out of your mind? How are you supposed to save another dimension when you can't even get out of an airport?"*

"Give me a break—obviously I'm under a lot of pressure!" Conner whispered back.

They made it outside the airport and looked around at the sea of cars, taxis, and buses around the pickup zone.

"How are we going to get to central London?" Bree asked. "Are we old enough to take a taxi by ourselves?"

Conner looked down the curb and saw something that gave him an idea. A large group of obnoxious American teenagers was boarding a bus. They were looked after by only one chaperone that Conner could see and she was practically pulling her hair out trying to manage. "Everyone settle down and get on the bus!" the chaperone screamed. "I have your parents' phone numbers and I will use them!"

Conner gestured for Bree to follow him. "Keep your head down, I've got an idea," he said. They both looked at the ground and joined the line of students boarding the bus. The line was moving so quickly the chaperone couldn't keep up with checking the names on her clipboard and finally just gave up. Conner and Bree boarded the bus effortlessly and took a seat in the very back.

"All right, that was a good one," Bree said. "It almost makes up for Buckinghamshirevilleton."

"Thanks," Conner said. "This should get us into the city without a hitch."

The other teenagers aboard the bus were so busy taunting each other and taking pictures of themselves they didn't even notice the strangers in the back. The bus pulled away from the airport and headed into town.

"All right, I want to hear the whole story, and don't skip any details," Bree said to Conner.

"About what?" he asked.

"Everything I need to know before venturing out on this adventure with you," she said. "About you, your sister, that goose lady, and this dimension we're about to save."

Conner didn't know where to begin. "Okay, but it's a long story," he warned.

"Great," Bree said. "Long stories are my favorite."

Conner figured there was no use in keeping anything from her now. He told Bree his and Alex's whole story, starting with when they were magically transported into the Land of Stories for the first time and ending with their last good-bye when the portal between the two worlds was closed.

Bree hung on every word he said. It felt so therapeutic for Conner to talk to someone about it besides his family. He was very glad Bree had insisted on coming on this new escapade of his, and as Conner knew all too well, adventures were always best when there was someone to share them with.

CHAPTER TEN

THE SOUTH BANK LION

The bus finally arrived in central London and they all went quiet as they took in the first sights of the regal city. London was a multi-cultural maze of pristine buildings and proud tradition. It was difficult to differentiate the landmarks from the non-landmarks as everything was so well kept. Every building looked a hundred years old and brand-new at the same time.

The teenagers aboard the bus pointed to the landmarks they recognized as they drove past them—Buckingham Palace, Westminster Abbey, Big Ben, the Tower of London, and Tower Bridge.

"This is the most proper place I've ever been in my life." Conner nudged Bree. "Just being here makes me feel like I should be dressed up."

The bus stopped in a place called Trafalgar Square, near the passengers' hotel. The square was filled with tourists taking photos of the impressive statues and fountains in front of the National Gallery, which stretched across the back of the square like a grand backdrop. The teenagers raced off the bus to be amid the tourists outside and Conner and Bree exited with them.

Once they were on the street, the first thing Conner did was find an ATM.

"Forgive me, Bob," Conner said as he looked down at the credit card Bob had so kindly given him. He stuck it into the machine and took out the maximum amount of pounds in the maximum amount of transactions it would allow at a time.

"That's a lot of money—in any country," Bree said. She covered him from any onlookers as he stuck the money in the pockets of his jacket and pants and then put the rest of it in his suitcase. "But it's smart of you to take out a bunch of cash so no one can use your transactions to trace you. They do that to find suspects in the crime books I read."

"Oh, I never thought about that," he said with a shrug. "I just took out as much as I could because it was my first time using an ATM."

The first thing Conner bought was a map from a street merchant. He opened it up and scanned the tiny print depicting the streets and attractions around them.

"There's one!" he said happily, pointing at something on the map.

"What were you looking for?" Bree asked him.

"A library," Conner said. "We'll go to the library and look up where to find the Red Lion Brewery."

"Are you sure you don't want me to look it up on the Internet with my phone?" Bree asked.

Since Conner had never had a smart phone before, he hadn't considered this possibility. "No, I don't trust those things," he said. "I'd rather do it the traditional way—we're in London after all."

"Suit yourself," Bree said.

They followed the map a few blocks west, to the closest library, which was tucked away in the corner of St. James's Square. Conner and Bree walked up the front steps and pulled open its wooden doors. Conner had always found libraries intimidating and that feeling was heightened by being inside one in another country.

"Are you members?" a librarian at the front desk asked them. She glared at them over her thick-framed glasses. Conner always thought librarians could read minds and was afraid this one was going to prove his theory correct.

"No, but we're interested in joining," Bree said calmly. "May we have a look around?"

The librarian granted her request with a gesture for them to continue inside.

"Baggage is not allowed inside the library," the librarian said when she saw their suitcases.

"Oh, of course," Bree said. "May we leave them to the side here?"

She put her bag down near the front door and Conner placed Betsy beside it. The librarian permitted it with a nod and they continued inside. Conner and Bree found a table in the back of the first floor.

"I'll be right back; I'm going to find some books," Conner said, and disappeared into the rows of shelves. Bree sat down and made herself comfortable, looking at her phone while she waited. Conner returned twenty minutes later with a stack of heavy books.

"Look what I found," Conner said. He showed Bree the first book in his stack.

"Breweries of Britain," Bree read. "That's great, Conner, but I looked up the Red Lion Brewery on my phone and apparently it was demolished in 1949."

"You can't trust anything the Internet says," Conner said. He frantically flipped through the book until he found a page written about the Red Lion Brewery. "Oh no, according to this, the Red Lion Brewery was demolished in 1949."

"Shocking," Bree said sarcastically. "I don't mean to be a downer but I don't think the lion we're looking for is around anymore."

Conner let out a defeated sigh but he wasn't ready to give up just yet. He pulled out another book from his stack, titled *The Statues of London*, and began flipping through it. After a couple minutes Conner started fidgeting with excitement as he read.

"Check this out," Conner said, showing Bree the section he had just read.

The South Bank Lion
13 tons, 13 feet wide
As silly as it would be to say a statue has lived, of all the statues in London the one known as the South Bank Lion has lived many different lives. The statue was created in 1837 by W. F. Woodington, and was constructed of artificial Coade stone. The lion lived his first life as a symbol, guarding the Red Lion Brewery facing the River Thames in Lambeth, London. An intriguing aura of mystery surrounds the lion as it was one of the only sculptures in the area not severely damaged in the bombings of World War II, and when the Red Lion Brewery was eventually demolished in 1949, the lion was recovered from the demolition completely unscathed. King George VI took a liking to the lion and had him moved to Waterloo station. He spent his second life on display at the station for several years before being moved to his current resting place on Westminster Bridge in the South Bank area of central London. The remains of a secondary lion statue were also found in the demolition of the Red Lion Brewery. It was pieced back together and painted gold, and can now be seen at Twickenham Stadium.

Conner and Bree were both bubbling with excitement.
"That must be it! That's the lion we need to find!" Bree said.

Conner looked over the map at all the bridges crossing over the River Thames. "I found Westminster Bridge!" he said. "It's right by Big Ben and it's walking distance from here."

"Great," Bree said. "Let's go see the lion!"

The duo finished in the library just before wearing out their welcome. They collected their luggage and walked briskly through St. James's Square and followed the map to Westminster Bridge. They passed countless statues and sculptures of lions as they went, each looking more regal and ferocious than the last one. Conner grew anxious thinking about meeting the thirteen-ton, thirteen-foot-long South Bank Lion. He hoped the lion wouldn't be too frightening to approach—enchanted objects were always unpredictable.

Westminster Bridge began at the Houses of Parliament, at the base of Big Ben, and stretched across the River Thames to just below the giant Ferris wheel known as the London Eye. The bridge was busy with hundreds of tourists and citizens alike. Multitudes of cars and red double-decker buses continuously drove across the bridge as well.

Conner and Bree reached the end of the bridge and looked across the street. In the midst of the pedestrian chaos just below the towering London Eye, they found the South Bank Lion. He was massive and pale gray and stood on top of a tall pedestal. Something about him was different from all the other lions they'd seen in the city, and Conner and Bree picked up on it as soon as they laid eyes on him. Rather than a vicious and threatening scowl on his face, the South Bank Lion had a genuinely *concerned* expression. His eyes were wide and his mouth was open.

"That's got to be him," Conner said.

"What makes you so sure?" Bree said.

"Because I make that face whenever Mother Goose tells me a secret, too," Conner said.

Bree looked around at the crowds. "Are we supposed to walk over there and talk to him in front of all these people?" she asked.

"No, we'll have to come back later when they're all gone," he said. "We might have to wait until after midnight."

They left the bridge and got a bite to eat at a local pub. Bree insisted they have an authentic English experience and forced Conner to order fish and chips with her. After they were done eating they camped out in St. James's Park and waited until after nightfall before returning to the bridge.

They lingered across the street from the South Bank Lion until the traffic of cars and people was almost nonexistent. Then they crossed the street and stood directly below the lion.

"Say something to him," Bree said. She nudged Conner.

"What am I supposed to say?" he asked.

"I don't know, aren't you used to these kinds of things?"

"Enchanted statues in the middle of crowded cities? No, I can't say I'm an expert," he said.

"I have faith in you." Bree smiled at him.

Her smile made his rosy cheeks a bit rosier. He figured he had nothing to lose, so Conner took a deep breath and addressed the lion like he would anyone else.

"Hello up there!" he called. "I don't mean to disturb you, but my friend and I were wondering if we could speak to you."

The lion didn't say a word or move an inch. There was nothing to indicate Conner was anything but a crazy person talking to a statue.

"You must be exhausted," Conner called. "You've been on your feet for, like, what, a century and a half?"

Buttering up the statue didn't help. Knowing what an idiot he must look like talking to this statue didn't help matters, either.

"So, you like London?" Conner asked. "We just got here today and *whoa*—what a neat place!"

Bree grew impatient with both of them and stepped closer to address the lion herself. "Listen, pussy cat," she hissed. "We've got questions for you! We know you can talk, we know you're friends with Mother Goose, and we're not leaving here until you give us the answers we need!"

"What are you doing?" Conner whispered. *"You think he's going to talk to us if you treat him like that?"*

"We're playing good cop, bad cop," she whispered back. *"Trust me; it works every time in my crime novels."*

Conner rubbed his fingers through his hair, convinced this strategy was a dead-end. But when he looked back at the lion, he could have sworn the lion's face had changed; he looked *more* concerned.

"Bree, do you notice anything different about the lion?" he whispered.

She looked closer and her eyes lit up. "Yes."

"Say something else about Mother Goose," Conner instructed. *"I think he's afraid of her."*

Bree nodded and spoke to the lion again. "Hey! Mother

Goose told us that you would talk to us, but if you'd rather talk to her yourself, she can be here in five minutes."

There was no doubt about it: The lion was moving! They watched the South Bank Lion's face grow more fretful the more they mentioned Mother Goose. Eventually the statue couldn't take it anymore and shifted from its solid position.

"No, please don't call Mother Goose!" the lion begged, coming to life before their eyes. It startled Bree and she jumped behind Conner. It was her first magical sighting. Conner was used to seeing magic at its finest, but it never got old. He stared up at the lion with an amazed smile.

"So you *can* talk," he said.

"Yes, I can talk," the lion admitted. "I'll answer whatever questions you have, just please don't call that woman here."

Conner found his dislike of Mother Goose wildly amusing. "Why are you so afraid of Mother Goose?"

"I'm not afraid of *her*; it's her stories I can't stand." The lion shook his head. "Over the years she's told me some outlandish secrets that I never wanted to know—and she never spares any of the details! If you knew half the things I know, you would look differently at her, too. It's too much for one lion to bear!"

"Is that why you look so concerned all the time?" Conner asked.

"That's part of it," the lion said, and his face suddenly grew very sad. He whimpered, like he was about to cry. "I'm also afraid of heights and these people keep putting me on top of very tall things! And they separated me from my brother when the Red Lion Brewery was demolished and I don't know where he is!"

The stone lion sniffled into his large paws.

"Oh, you're talking about the second lion statue," Bree said. She had regained her confidence and stepped out from behind Conner. "He's still around! They painted him gold and put him on display at some sports arena."

The South Bank Lion was happy to hear this and looked a little less concerned than before. "That's such a relief," he said. "He always loved sports."

"Can he talk and move like you?" Conner asked.

"No, he's just a normal statue, but we're made of the same artificial stone," the lion said. "I was the only lion Mother Goose enchanted."

"Why did she enchant you?" Conner asked. They had several important questions to ask but he couldn't resist hearing the story.

"In the mid-1800s Mother Goose used to visit her friends at the Red Lion Brewery every Sunday night," the lion told him. "Around the same time she had just started training that horrible gander of hers to fly her around. He was a horrible flyer and every so often they would crash right into me on the roof. One night they were a little too careless and hit me so hard I was knocked off the roof and shattered into pieces on the ground. She magically put me back together and cast an invincibility spell on me so I wouldn't leave such a mess the next time they knocked me off the roof."

"Ah, so that's why you stayed in such good condition during the war and the demolition," Bree said.

"But that doesn't explain why you can talk," Conner pointed out.

"Well, after a few years Mother Goose's brewery friends started dying off," the lion explained. "She wanted a friend who would stick around and give her an excuse to come back to the brewery. And unfortunately she chose me. Although I still don't understand why she gave me the ability to speak when all I ever did was listen."

"Speaking of listening," Conner said, "do you remember her mentioning anything about the Brothers Grimm and sabotaging a portal?"

The lion scrunched his forehead and tried to remember. "It rings a bell," he said. "Was this the same time she led the French soldiers into a trap?"

"Yes! That's it!" Conner said with a happy jump.

The lion's eyes grew wider and he nodded his giant stone head. "Oh boy, do I remember *that* story," he said. "I wish I could forget it! It gave me nightmares for fifty years!"

Conner knew he needed to be very clear and careful as he got the information out of him to avoid making any mistakes later.

"Do you remember where the portal was that she trapped the soldiers inside?" he asked.

"I do," the lion said confidently. "It was deep in the Bavarian woods, between twin trees that grew between twin medieval castles. The only reason I remember is because I'm a twin myself."

"Where is Bavaria?" Conner asked.

"It's an old country that's now a state of Germany," Bree said. "Two trees between two medieval castles seems pretty easy to find."

"Oh, you wouldn't find the trees and the castles anymore," the lion told them regretfully. "They're gone."

"*What?*" Conner and Bree said together. "What do you mean they're gone?"

"After the Brothers Grimm tricked the soldiers into entering the tampered-with portal, Mother Goose grew paranoid that the soldiers would find a way out, back into this world, so she asked her friend Ludwig for a very large favor," he said.

"What was the favor?" Conner asked.

"She asked Ludwig to build one of his elaborate castles on top of the portal, so if the soldiers were ever to re-emerge from it they might be tricked into thinking they had arrived in the fairy-tale world."

"*He built a castle for her?*" Conner asked in disbelief. "That *is* a big favor."

Bree gasped and clutched her hands together. "Wait a second, are you talking about *King Ludwig II* of Bavaria?" she asked.

"That was his official name, I believe," the lion said. "Mother Goose always just called him *Ludwig* or *Wiggy*."

Conner was the only one who had never heard of Ludwig. "Who was he?" he asked.

"Haven't you ever heard of *the mad fairy-tale king*?" Bree asked. Conner shook his head. "He was addicted to building lavish palaces for himself, all inspired by other palaces he had visited around the world."

"He sounds like someone Red Riding Hood would be friends with," Conner said, but he dropped the subject when he remembered he was the only person there who knew her.

"The last home Ludwig built for himself was Neuschwanstein Castle," Bree continued. "It was inspired by all his favorite childhood stories and looks like something you'd find in a storybook. It's considered one of the wonders of the modern world."

"Wait, *is* considered, meaning the castle is still around?" Conner asked.

"Oh yes," Bree said. "It's easily one of the biggest tourist attractions in southern Germany. It's always been a mystery why Ludwig built the castle, but it makes sense now."

"But what happened to the portal? Is it somewhere inside the castle?" Conner asked.

"I'm assuming so, but I wouldn't know," the lion said. "I've lived within a five-kilometer radius my whole life."

"Do you know how we can check the portal to see if it's open or not?" Conner asked.

"Let me think, let me think," the lion said, and he closed his eyes while he remembered. "Yes! The Bavarian portal is accessed when a person of magic blood plays eight notes on a special ancient panpipe."

Conner made a mental note of this crucial information. "If it has to be played by someone of magic blood, then how did the Brothers Grimm open it for the French soldiers?" he asked.

The lion scrunched his nose; it was the part of the story he didn't like telling. "Mother Goose took a dagger and made a cut in her hand and one in Wilhelm Grimm's hand," he said. "They held their hands tightly together and let some of the magic from Mother Goose's blood flow into his. I really wish she had kept that part to herself—the thought of blood makes me incredibly squeamish since I don't have any myself."

"And where can we find this panpipe?" Conner asked.

"I believe it's with the rest of Mother Goose's Otherworld belongings in a vault in a Monégasque bank," the lion said. "And I only know that because she measured me one day to see if I would fit in the vault, too. Thank goodness I was too big."

"So, *where is the bank*?" Conner asked.

"Monégasque means it's in Monte Carlo," Bree said.

"Right," Conner said. "So where in Monte Carlo is this bank?"

The lion thought about it and seemed very disappointed when he couldn't come up with its location. "I don't remember," he said with a frown. "If only my mind were as concrete as the rest of me."

Thankfully, this was the only question the lion didn't have an answer to. Conner paced the sidewalk, concentrating carefully—the lion's words reminded him of something Mother Goose had said in the past. He felt he should know where the bank was....

He opened his suitcase and dug around until he found his lucky poker chip from Mother Goose. He looked closely at its design. The chip was dark blue and the symbols of the houses of cards circled around the edge: a heart, a spade, a diamond, a club. But in the very center of the chip, instead of a number to mark its value, there was an image of a small golden key.

"I think I know where to find the vault," Conner said eagerly to Bree. "What time is it?"

Bree looked at the screen of her phone. "It's almost four in the morning," she said. "Wow, time flies when you're talking to an enchanted statue."

Conner looked up at the lion gratefully. "Thank you so much for all your help, but you'll have to excuse us now," he said. "We have to get to the train station as soon as possible."

The lion seemed sad to see them go and his face returned to its trademark concerned expression. "Good luck," the lion said. "And next time you see Mother Goose, please tell her I understand she's a busy woman and there's no need for her to visit me... *ever again.*"

Conner took off along Westminster Bridge, speed walking as fast as he could. Bree said good-bye to the South Bank Lion and caught up with him.

"So where are we off to next?" she asked him with bright eyes.

"We're going to the *Lumière des Etoiles* casino," Conner replied.

"Where is that?"

"Somewhere in Monte Carlo, I guess," he said.

CHAPTER ELEVEN

THE LUMIERE DES ETOILES CASINO

Conner and Bree made it to the train station at St. Pancras a little before six o'clock that morning. They hadn't slept all night but neither showed any indication of being tired. They were living on adrenaline and determination. Conner had never run away before but now he understood why Jack and Goldilocks preferred a life on the run. Despite the circumstances, it had been a very exciting day.

Bree hadn't stopped smiling since they left the South Bank. *"I'm friends with a lion statue, I'm friends with a lion statue,"* she sang to herself over and over again.

They gawked at a large map over the ticketing counters and tried to make sense of all the colorful lines showing which trains traveled where.

"Doesn't look like there's anything direct to Monte Carlo," Conner said. "We'll have to stop in Paris where that thick blue line ends and then get on the thin dotted orange line."

"Your knowledge of travel terminology is so impressive," Bree joked.

They stood in line and zigzagged to the ticket counter with the other early-morning travelers. The ticketing agent had frizzy red hair and huge bags under her eyes. She drank coffee from an enormous mug like it was water.

"Next?" she said.

Conner and Bree approached her. "Two tickets to Paris, please," Bree said.

The agent looked at them like they had asked to borrow her car. "Do you have a guardian accompanying you? Or an unaccompanied-minor form signed by your parents?" she asked.

Bree and Conner froze. Both of them had somehow forgotten that being fourteen-year-olds might set them back on this trip.

"We . . . we . . . ," Bree began but nothing else came out.

Conner panicked and looked around the train station for a solution. In a far corner he saw a very elderly woman sitting in a wheelchair all by herself. Her hair was teased up into a large pouf and she had a full face of makeup on. She somberly stared at the floor as she held a purse and small suitcase on her lap.

"We're traveling with our *grandmother*," Conner said.

"We are?" Bree asked. Conner gestured to the old woman in

the corner. "I mean, *we are*," Bree continued. "Stupid me, make it three tickets to Paris," she said back at the ticketing agent.

"That's your grandmother?" the agent asked.

"Yes, that's *Granny Pearl*," Conner said. "She doesn't speak a lick of English so she's asked us to buy the tickets." Conner energetically waved at the old woman. "Just one more minute, Gran!"

Pearl, as they christened her, was rather confused as to why two young strangers were waving to her in the middle of a train station but decided to wave back with a friendly smile. She also appeared to be a little senile, which was working in their favor.

The ticketing agent shrugged and checked the ticket options. "The only availability we have for three on the next train is in a first-class compartment," she said.

"Great, how much?" Conner asked.

"Two hundred pounds each," the ticketing agent said.

Conner gulped. "Boy, that's a lot of weight, ha-ha," he said. "We'll take it. Good thing Granny Pearl gave us lots of money."

He exchanged cash for the tickets and walked quickly away from the ticketing counter and toward Pearl. Bree glanced over her shoulder and saw the ticketing agent suspiciously glaring at them over her coffee mug.

"She's still watching us; what do we do?" Bree whispered to Conner.

"Grab the old lady and get on the train, I guess," he whispered back.

"We can't kidnap an old woman!"

"What other option do we have?"

Their hearts were racing—they were about to commit the biggest crime of their lives. They leaned down to the old woman and quietly spoke to her.

"Hello there, would you mind doing us a favor?" Conner asked her.

Pearl just smiled blankly at them—he had guessed correctly; she didn't know a lick of English.

"Wer sind Sie?" she asked.

"What did she just say?" Conner asked.

"I think she said, 'Who are you?'" Bree said. "She's German."

"You speak German?"

"Only a little bit—my real grandma was born in Germany."

"Ask her if she wants to go on a trip with us," Conner said.

Bree licked her lips and tried translating. "Would you like ... um ... *eine Reise* with *uns*?"

Pearl blinked a couple times, causing her head to move slightly.

"I think that counts as a nod—grab her and let's go!" Conner whispered.

Bree grabbed the handles of Pearl's wheelchair and they pushed her toward the security line. Pearl smiled as cheerfully as ever, clearly without the slightest clue what was going on. They handed their tickets to the man at the security check and he carefully looked them over.

"Ich werde entführt," Pearl told the man casually.

Bree panicked and nervously burst into fake laughter. "Oh, Granny, you're so funny!" she said loudly. "You've been making jokes all day."

The man handed back their tickets and allowed them to move forward.

"What did she just tell him?" Conner whispered to Bree.

"She said, 'I'm being kidnapped,'" Bree whispered back.

"Oh," he said, and guiltily looked down at their captive. Pearl's big smile never left her face. "She's taking it very well, then."

They pushed her wheelchair all the way down the platform and boarded the car at the front of the train. The train attendant folded her wheelchair and stowed it with their luggage. Conner and Bree helped Pearl up the steps into the train and into their private first-class compartment. It was very luxurious for a pair of teenage runaways and a kidnapped old woman. It had red cushioned seats and white drapes over a large square window.

They gently sat Pearl down and took the seats across from her. Conner and Bree sat very still and watched Pearl like she was a poisonous animal until the train pulled away from the station. They were convinced at any minute she might start screaming for help, but she never did. Pearl just kept on smiling and contentedly watched the land move outside the window.

The train's speed gradually increased and soon they were zooming through the English countryside on their way to Paris. Conner found a pamphlet in their compartment and looked at the map on the back of it—it was exactly like the map in the station.

"So once we reach Paris we'll switch trains and head to Monte Carlo," Conner said.

Pearl looked away from the window for a second to tell them, *"Ich liebe Monte Carlo!"*

"I guess she likes Monte Carlo," Bree translated.

"Okay," Conner said cautiously, and then continued with his plan. "Then, once we reach Monte Carlo we'll try to find the Lumière des Etoiles casino and see if my chip means something to anyone there," he said.

Pearl turned to them again only to say, *"Ich liebe das Lumière des Etoiles!"* Apparently she was a big fan of the casino as well.

"Why are we going to a casino when we should be trying to find a bank?" Bree asked.

"Mother Goose said the poker chip would come in handy," he explained. "When she gave it to me she said that if I was ever in Monte Carlo I should take it to the roulette table in the northwest corner and bet it on the black. It made no sense to me at the time, but now I think we'll find something there that will help us. I've got a good feeling about this."

The train went dark as it swooped under the English Channel and the next time they saw light they were in the French countryside. France was only a couple hours from England, but once the train began decelerating into Paris they felt they had entered a completely different world. Paris made Conner and Bree feel like they were living in a painting. Every building was beautifully detailed, like it had been hand sculpted. Many were tall and narrow with iron railings at each of their multiple windows. Soon the train arrived at the Paris station, Gare du Nord.

Conner and Bree helped Pearl off the train and pushed her through the crowded station.

"We need to exchange our pounds for euros," Bree told

Conner. "We won't be able to buy tickets to Monte Carlo until we do."

They found a currency-exchange station and traded in all the pounds they had left. They proceeded to the ticketing counter to purchase tickets for the next train to Monte Carlo and once again pretended Pearl was their grandmother to avoid any suspicion.

"Would you like a first-class or an economy compartment, *monsieur*?" the Frenchwoman at the counter asked.

"Economy is fine if it's available," Conner said.

"Don't go cheap on me now, Bailey," Bree said.

"Fine, *first class*, please." Conner griped, "I'm gonna be so grounded when I get home."

Within the hour, Conner, Bree, and Granny Pearl were aboard another train enjoying another first-class cabin. It was a very long and bumpy ride and all three of them slept as much as they could. The train stopped in five or six cities along the way, and about six hours had passed by the time they reached the Monte Carlo station.

They gathered their luggage and Granny Pearl, and headed for the exit. They stepped outside the station and Conner and Bree caught their first sight of Monte Carlo.

The city was gorgeous. A cluster of colorful hotels, resorts, and residences grew down the Monégasque hills and stretched along the ocean side. The salty smell of the ocean was all around them. A bay a little ways along the shoreline was home to hundreds of boats and yachts that bobbed in the bluest water Conner had ever seen.

"So this is where postcards come from," he said in awe.

It was almost impossible not to enjoy the refreshing breeze and the warm rays of the golden setting sun. Pearl hummed a cheerful tune as they pushed her along the paradisiacal city.

They wandered aimlessly through the streets looking for a directory or a sign that pointed toward the Lumière des Etoiles casino. However, they soon realized the whole city was made up of casinos.

"It's like looking for a needle in a haystack," Bree said.

"Why don't you look it up on your phone?" Conner asked.

"I would but my battery died in Paris," she said.

Just when they thought their luck had run out, Pearl tugged at Conner's sleeve and pointed to a building at the end of the street.

"Das Lumière des Etoiles casino!" she said excitedly.

Bree and Conner were so happy they wanted to hug her, but since they still didn't even know her name they thought that might be too forward and just hugged each other instead.

"Granny Pearl, you're amazing!" Conner said as they pushed her toward the casino.

The Lumière des Etoiles casino was an enormous building with tall columns and was topped by a vast glass dome. If it wasn't for the electric sign blinking its name, Conner would have thought it was an old town hall that had been painted a sandy yellow to match the rest of the city.

Conner and Bree had difficulty pushing Pearl's wheelchair up the steps but they managed and then hustled inside. The casino had green marble floors and golden pillars lining the walls. A massive chandelier hung from the dome above and illuminated the sea of slot machines and card tables.

There wasn't a single guest at the casino who was under the age of eighty. Everywhere they looked they saw wheelchairs, walkers, and white hair. Grandmas showed other grandmas pictures of their grandchildren before taking each other's money. Old men showed off faded tattoos they had mistakenly gotten when they were younger. It was like they had stepped into a room full of Pearls.

"No wonder Mother Goose and Pearl like this casino so much," Conner said. "I feel like we've found their natural habitat."

They propped Pearl up in front of a slot machine and gave her a handful of coins to keep her busy. Just as Mother Goose had described, there was a roulette table in the northwest corner. It was the only table in the casino that was completely empty. Conner and Bree walked through the crowd of senior citizens, receiving the strangest looks from them as they did—they stood out like sore thumbs.

They got to the roulette table and Conner reached into his pocket for the poker chip. The roulette dealer wore a white button-down shirt with a black vest and bow tie. He put his hand up to stop them before they said a word.

"Sincerest apologies, *mademoiselle* and *monsieur*, but this table is reserved for special chips only," the dealer said. "And I do not believe either of you are old enough to be in this casino, anyway."

Conner showed him the blue poker chip. The dealer's eyes lit up.

"We didn't come here to gamble," Conner said. "But I would like to bet this on the black."

It must have been code for something because the dealer

dropped his hand and raised an eyebrow at the teenagers. He looked at them shrewdly.

"I see," he said. "One moment, please." He picked up the receiver of a telephone under the roulette table. *"Monsieur, nous avons quelqu'un avec un jeton noir,"* he said in French to whoever was on the other end of the phone, and then promptly hung up. "The manager will be with you shortly."

Conner and Bree didn't know whether this was good news or bad. Had the chip actually led them to something useful or were they just going to be escorted out of the casino by the manager?

A moment later the manager of the Lumière des Etoiles casino met them at the roulette table. He was a tall, burly man with a thick black mustache. He wore a sharp suit and straightened his tie as he greeted them.

"Bonjour," the manager said. "I believe I can be of some assistance?"

Conner showed him the poker chip. "Yes, this belongs to our grandmother," he said, and gestured to Pearl over at the slot machine. Pearl had proven to be a great cover thus far so Conner figured she couldn't hurt them here.

"May I?" the manager asked, and opened a hand. Conner handed the chip to him and the manager pulled a magnifying glass out of his lapel and examined the ridges of the side of the chip. "Very well, please follow me," he said, walking away from the roulette table.

Conner and Bree exchanged looks, each wanting the other to go first. Finally Conner followed the manager, with Bree right at his heels.

The manager led them through the casino and into an elevator, politely holding the door open. The elevator had a button for each of the building's five floors above them, but once the doors shut the manager pressed several at once, as if he were entering a secret code. When he was finished, the elevator took Conner and Bree by surprise—it started traveling *down* to an unmarked level.

"Are you enjoying Monte Carlo?" the manager asked casually as the elevator descended.

"Yup," Conner peeped nervously, terrified of where they might be going.

Finally the elevator came to a stop and the doors opened. "Right this way," the manager said, and escorted them out of the elevator.

To their amazement, Conner and Bree found themselves at the top level of a gigantic underground courtyard. It was like they were looking at a four-story cell block beneath them, but instead of prison cells the walls were lined with rows of *vaults*.

"So *this* is where her vault is!" Conner said.

"This isn't really a casino, it's a secret bank," Bree said.

"Oh no, it's still one of Monte Carlo's finest casinos," the manager reassured them. "But before it was a casino it was one of the world's greatest private storage facilities for hundreds of years. The building was bought in the early 1900s on the condition that it remain a working storage facility. The vaults are not rented or leased but purchased in perpetuity, like cemetery plots."

"So there are things inside these vaults that will never be seen again?" Conner asked.

"Usually the vaults and their possessions are inherited, but occasionally we have clients who pass on before naming a bene-factor," the manager explained.

"And those people's valuables will just be locked away for the rest of time?"

"Yes," the manager said. "But typically when people lock away something in an underground vault, it's because they don't wish to share it with the world."

Conner and Bree gulped in unison. The thought of what might be behind some of those metal doors gave them the chills.

"Now, please follow me and I'll show you to your grand-mother's vault," the manager said.

They followed him down two flights of stairs to the third-highest level.

"Here we are, vault 317," the manager said and stood to the side of the vault door.

"Wait, how do you know for sure this is our vault?" Conner asked.

"Each chip contains a small number on its side, and I examined yours before bringing you down here," the manager explained. "Each chip also acts as a key. The sides are not ridged like nor-mal chips but have several unique grooves and dents. When you place the correct chip into the center of a vault's lock and spin the handles, the vault will open. Place the incorrect chip into a lock and the chip will be destroyed when you spin the handles."

"But how do you know that we're the proper beneficiaries?" Bree asked. "How do you know we didn't steal the chip?"

"That is not a problem," the manager told her. "According to the three-hundred-year-old policy, whoever is in possession of the chip is the rightful beneficiary. We give one chip to each client. If it breaks or gets lost or is stolen, that is not our issue. We avoid many lawsuits and robberies that way."

Conner and Bree nodded their understanding. This was a very strange and serious storage facility; it wasn't a shock that Mother Goose had business here.

"Now please enjoy your time with whatever your vault possesses," the manager said. "It is also policy that I leave the room before you open it, to uphold our guarantee of the absolute privacy of your possessions. Please wait until I have entered the elevator before opening the vault. When you have finished with your possessions, please take the elevator to the main floor."

He spoke so casually even though there was nothing casual about this place. The manager walked off in the direction they had come from. He climbed up the stairs and disappeared into the elevator.

"This place is intense," Conner said.

"This place is awesome," Bree said. "Think about what might be in these vaults—think about *who* might be in these vaults!"

It dawned on Conner that what most people found frightening, Bree found intriguing. And knowing this about her both frightened and intrigued him.

"Fingers crossed this works," Conner said. He put the chip into the vault's lock. He spun the handles around the lock and the door opened with a *pop*. A gust of air carrying mixed scents came with it. Both of his hands were on the handles but he didn't pull the door fully open.

"What are you waiting for?" Bree asked.

"I just thought about all the potentially amazing and horrible things that might be waiting for us inside," he said.

"I know," Bree said. "Too bad my phone is dead; otherwise I'd take pictures."

Conner grunted as he pulled the heavy door open. He and Bree stepped inside the vault and looked around in astonishment at the treasures Mother Goose had acquired over the centuries.

It looked like they were in the storage room of a museum. There were large Egyptian busts, small Fabergé eggs, hundreds of rolled-up scrolls, portraits, canvases, dinosaur bones, clay pots and pans, and even a giant machine gun from World War II.

Conner and Bree began searching through the items. Some of them were so outrageous they completely forgot what they were looking for. Mother Goose had labeled many of the objects and they had a difficult time believing in their accuracy. A pair of wooden dentures had a note pinned to it that said "George Washington's teeth." A large rolled-up scroll was tagged "Map to Atlantis." A small envelope containing a telegram said "Amelia Earhart's Forwarding Address."

Bree's eyes were practically bulging out of her head when she read the tag on a small goblet. "You don't think this is actually *the Holy Grail*, do you?" she said, and raised the cup to show Conner.

"Probably not," Conner said.

Bree sighed with relief and tossed the cup aside. She unrolled a portrait and laughed. "Then this painting labeled 'The original *Mona Lisa*' with a note from Leonardo da Vinci probably isn't real, either," she said, showing it to him.

"Um...*that* one might be legit," Conner said, remembering Mother Goose's da Vinci stories.

Bree suddenly looked like she was holding an explosive in her hands and gently put it back where she found it. Conner was getting distracted by all the things he was finding. He had to keep reminding himself what they were there for.

"I wish Mother Goose wasn't such a hoarder. It'd be so much easier finding the panpipe if she had learned to recycle," Conner said. He pushed a stack of ancient maps out of the way and then leaped with excitement when he found a small wooden panpipe hiding underneath them.

"Bree! Get over here and look at this!" Conner yelled. *"I found it! I found it!"*

"You're amazing!" Bree said, and hugged him tightly. "Does it say what notes need to be played to access the portal?"

Conner inspected the panpipe and found a series of letters carved into the largest cylinder. "It says 'G-E-F-C, C-E-G-F,'" he said. "I'm assuming those are musical notes or maybe it's how you spell a sneeze."

"This is terrific! Now all we have to do is get to Neuschwanstein Castle and find the portal!" Bree said.

She was so excited she kissed his cheek and then hurried out of the vault. Conner turned bright red and almost passed out. She made him feel like the most special thing in the room of treasures.

Bree poked her head back into the vault. "Aren't you coming?"

"Yeah, sorry, be right there!" Conner collected the panpipe and his senses and followed her out.

They shut and carefully locked the vault behind them. Conner tucked the chip safely into his pocket. They rode the elevator up to the casino and thanked the manager for his assistance. As they raced down the front steps they plotted what their next move would be, although it was jarring to see the sun had already set while they were inside.

"Before we left the train station I took a look at the upcoming departures," Bree said. "If we can make it back in time, there's a nine o'clock overnight train to Prague that stops in Munich on the way."

"Perfect," Conner said. "There's only one thing we're missing."

"What's that?" she asked.

"Pearl!" he said.

They turned around and dashed back into the casino. Pearl was still by the slot machine where they had left her. However, she was clutching three buckets full of coins she had won while they were downstairs.

"Nicely done, Pearl," Bree said.

"Pearl, would you like to go on one last train ride with us?" Conner asked.

The old woman didn't seem to understand him but she nodded sweetly. Pearl was in it for the ride as much as they were.

They brought her down the front steps of the casino and journeyed to the train station as fast as possible. They made it just in time and were the last ones to buy tickets and board the train. Their compartment wasn't as nice as the other two had been but they didn't mind—as long as they were on their way to Germany everything was right in the world.

The compartment door abruptly slid open to reveal an aggressive-looking train attendant. His eyes narrowed when he discovered Conner and Bree behind the door.

"Passports, please," the attendant demanded.

"Why do you need to see our passports?" Conner asked.

The attendant squinted his eyes at Conner's reluctance. "We've just gotten word of two runaway American teenage tourists," he said. "It's protocol to check the identification of every passenger on board the train who matches that description."

Conner and Bree tensed up. They had come so close to getting to the portal but there was no way out of this now. Conner wondered if the train was moving too fast to jump out of it.

"But these are my grandchildren," Pearl said in perfect English.

Conner and Bree turned their heads so quickly they almost gave themselves whiplash. Had she been coherent the entire time?

"I understand that, *madame*, but we still need to check their passports," the attendant insisted.

"Fine, fine, fine," Pearl said. "Let me get my purse and I'll find them for you."

She slowly went through her bag: one pen, one piece of hard candy, and one coin at a time. She pulled out wads of tissue and folded-up notes and stamped letters she had forgotten to mail. The attendant grew impatient waiting for her to retrieve the passports.

"Where did I put those passports?" Pearl said. "We were just in Monte Carlo and I put them in my pocket, then when we got back on the train I put them in my suitcase—yes, they're in my suitcase! If you wouldn't mind kindly waiting another moment, I'll have a look for them in my suitcase."

"That's quite all right, *madame*," the attendant said. He had run out of patience for the day. "I trust you. Please forgive this disturbance." He slid the door shut and they heard his footsteps travel down the train.

Pearl put her belongings back into her purse and then looked up at Conner and Bree. Both were staring at her with wide eyes and open mouths as if she were on fire.

"So where are we off to next?" Pearl asked them sweetly.

"Have you been aware of what we've been doing this entire time?" Conner asked, completely mortified.

"I'm old but I'm not ancient. I can speak English, too, you know," she said.

"And you let us take you around the continent willingly?" Bree asked, just as horrified.

"Yes," Pearl said. "You seemed like nice kids at the train station in London. I wasn't sure what was going on at first but I knew it would be good fun once we got on the train."

Conner and Bree looked at each other. Both wore the same bewildered expression.

"I ran away on my own adventure when I was your age," Pearl said. "I fell in love with a circus clown named Fabrizio and followed him around the globe."

"Did you get caught?" Bree asked.

"No, and after six months of following him I finally had the courage to tell Fabrizio how I felt," Pearl said.

"What happened?" Conner asked. "Was he creeped out because you were stalking him? Did he break your heart?"

"No, we were married for sixty-four years—until he died," Pearl said. "Back then actions spoke louder than words. We just did what our hearts told us to. These days people act like love is an island—they all want to swim to it but no one wants to get wet."

"What were you doing at the train station in London?" Bree asked.

"I had been visiting my son," she said. "He dropped me off but I wasn't ready to go home yet. I think I'm ready now, though. Disappearing for two days is the perfect amount of time to get your children to value you a bit more. I've enjoyed our little adventure together but I'm very tired and I should probably get off at the next stop and take a train home."

Conner and Bree shook their heads and laughed. "What's your real name, anyway?" Conner asked.

"It's Elsa," she said with a big smile. "But I insist you call me *Granny Pearl*."

Conner and Bree liked the idea of having a new grandma. "Well, our names are—"

"Uh," Pearl interrupted. "If you don't tell me your names, I'll never have to tell anyone where I saw you."

Conner and Bree thought the woman sitting across from them was almost too good to be true.

"You're so much cooler than my real German grandma," Bree said.

"Now, it's none of my business why you're away from your parents, but promise me you'll stay safe while you're having this adventure of yours," Pearl told them. "It's all fun and games until someone gets hurt."

They nodded, knowing it was a promise neither of them could keep.

CHAPTER TWELVE

THE SECRETS OF NEUSCHWANSTEIN CASTLE

The train from Monte Carlo arrived in Munich at six o'clock the next morning, after making a few stops along the way. They tried sleeping as much as they could but didn't manage much rest. Conner and Bree made sure Pearl was safely aboard the train that would take her home before they left the train station.

When Conner and Bree left Germany two days prior, neither would have thought they would be returning so soon. And just like every other city they'd seen so far, Munich proved to be a world of its own. It was a city of spirals and clock towers and pointed roofs. There were beautiful buildings with stained-glass windows and handcrafted wooden doors. Statues of religious and mythical figures were mounted on the roofs and balconies to keep watch over the busy streets.

"I can't believe how close these countries are and yet they're all so different," Conner said.

"And you really don't know a place until you've been there," Bree said. "You can look at a hundred pictures and a dozen maps, but unless you've been to the city and felt its pulse, you really know nothing about it."

Conner couldn't have put it in better words himself. With no time to lose, they brainstormed how they were going to get from Munich to Neuschwanstein Castle.

"I've got some bad news," Conner said. "We're almost out of cash. I've got enough for food for a couple days, but that's about it. I don't know how we're supposed to get to the castle now."

"Don't worry, I've got an idea," Bree said. "Let's find a hotel and pretend we're staying there. Then we'll trick the concierge into giving us what we need."

"Let me guess, this happens in your crime books, too?" Conner asked.

"No, I figured this one out myself," Bree said proudly. "My grandma lives in a condo in Atlantic City next to a bunch of hotels—there were summers I never paid for lunch once."

They walked up and down the stone streets until Bree found a large and fancy hotel ideal for her plan. The hotel was painted yellow and had the flags of several different countries displayed around its front revolving doors. They pushed through the doors and Bree got in line to speak with someone at the front desk.

Conner waited a few feet behind her; she said she was confident enough to do this alone—or perhaps she just didn't want him hovering over her.

"*Guten Morgen, gnädige Frau,*" the man at the concierge desk said.

"*Guten Morgen,* it's good to see you again," she said, even though she had never seen the man before. "I was wondering if I received any messages while I was out."

"Oh?" the concierge said. He looked awfully confused, like he could have sworn they had never met. "What room number?"

"*It's 723,*" Bree said as if she had told him a hundred times already.

"And what's your name?" he asked.

"Bree Campbell," she said honestly, and acted a little hurt that he hadn't remembered. "But as you *should* know, the room is under my stepfather's name."

"Herr Hueber is your stepfather?" he asked.

"Oh, is *that* the name he checked in under?" Bree said with a massive eye roll. "Please ignore him, he's from Milwaukee. Every time we go someplace new, he likes to trick the locals into thinking he's one of them. He probably checked in with some ridiculous accent, too. *Now about those messages—*"

"Oh yes, of course," the concierge said, and went through the papers on his desk. "No messages for room 723."

Bree pouted and stuck out her bottom lip. "Not even from *Jacob?*" she asked sadly.

Conner did a double take—*who the heck was Jacob?*

"No, I'm sorry," he said.

"That's a shame," she said, then got down to business. "Well, since I'm here, I was wondering if you could tell me the easiest way to Neuschwanstein Castle. My dad has to work all day and I have nothing to do."

"There is a two-hour bus that can take you there," he said. "Unfortunately, it has already sold out for today and tomorrow."

Conner slumped after hearing this but Bree quickly thought of plan B.

"Does this hotel rent bikes?" she asked.

"Yes, madame," the concierge said. He was very happy to finally give her some good news.

"Terrific. I suppose a bike ride around the countryside will have to do," she said.

"One bike?"

"Make it two, please," Bree said.

"And charge it to the room?" he asked.

"Yes, please," Bree said. "And if you could please leave a note for my dad telling him I went on a short bike ride I would really appreciate it."

"Yes, I'd be happy to," the concierge said. "I'll have those bikes brought to the front of the hotel right away."

"Thank you so much," Bree said.

Conner had almost forgotten Bree wasn't actually staying there. He tapped his foot to get her attention. *"We need to know how to get there,"* he whispered.

"Oh, and one last thing," Bree said to the concierge. "Would you mind highlighting how to get to Neuschwanstein Castle on a map for me? Just in case I can convince my dad to take me there himself when he's finished with work?"

The concierge nodded, and highlighted the route for her on a small map. She thanked him again and then waited with Conner in the front of the hotel for their bikes to be brought out.

"You're really good at that," Conner said. "Like, *scary* good."

Bree's head was lost in the map. "Okay, judging from this map, the castle is roughly eighty miles away...meaning we're gonna be on these bikes *all day*," she said.

"Oh no," Conner said, looking down at the suitcase he had been lugging around the entire trip. "What am I supposed to do with Betsy?"

"Just check her at the front desk and tell them you're with me," Bree said and handed him her bag to store as well.

"I guess this is where we part, old girl," he said sadly. He removed the piece of mirror from the suitcase and put it in his jacket pocket. He had just realized that now, with being in Munich, he had taken Betsy on as many adventures as Bob had before him. He took her back inside and checked her under room 723, not knowing if he would ever see her again.

A man from the hotel brought Conner and Bree each a bike and they began their long ride to Neuschwanstein Castle. Bree took the task of leading. She steered her bike with one hand while constantly looking down at the map in the other.

It took them an hour or so to pedal away from the Munich traffic and enter the German countryside. As soon as they did, the magnificent Alps came into view. They were unbelievably tall, as if they had been painted against the sky. Their sharp and jagged peaks were sprinkled with snow like the white in an old man's beard. They stood imperially like giant soldiers guarding their homeland.

As they rode deeper into the scenery, the ground rose with the Alps' altitude. Conner and Bree looked in wonder at the grassy hills around them. They were convinced Germany was the greenest place on earth.

Occasionally a village appeared beside the road. Each was more picturesque than the last, with their orange roofs set against the high backdrop of the azure sky behind the Alps. The scenery was so beautiful it didn't seem real. Conner never knew the world could be so gorgeous and with every mile of their journey he saw something that reminded him of the Land of Stories and just how much he missed it.

Clouds began to roll in from beyond the mountain peaks and covered the countryside like a thick fluffy gray ceiling. It was hard to tell where the mountains ended and the clouds started.

After a few hours of biking, Conner and Bree pulled into a tiny town called Oberammergau to get a bite to eat. Every one of the cottage-like homes and shops were painted with murals of fairy-tale and religious art as if they were one and the same. Conner and Bree stopped to admire an adorable house painted with iconic scenes from the story of Little Red Riding Hood.

"I could never tell Red about this," Conner said. "She's already got a huge head; I can't imagine how she'd act if she knew she was painted on the buildings of the Otherworld, too."

They were delighted to see how well represented fairy tales were in the center of town. There were statues of trolls and Humpty Dumpty, shops were filled with toys and trinkets and puppets of all the classic storybook characters, and there was even a small inn called Hotel Wolf, where Conner and Bree chose to eat.

"I feel like we're eating in the Red Riding Hood Kingdom," Conner said over lunch.

"If these people only knew what we knew," Bree said.

Conner looked down at his food. "Yeah . . . ," he mumbled sadly.

"What's the matter with you?" Bree asked.

He was hesitant to tell her what was on his mind. "I would never want anything to happen to my sister or my grandmother or anyone in the Land of Stories," he said. "But there's a part of me that hopes the portal *does* open, so I can see them all again."

Bree smiled gently. "I don't think there's anything wrong with that," she said. "We'll just try to think of the situation as a win-win. If the portal is closed, your friends are safe, and if it's open, at least you'll get to see them again."

"Yeah, while they're being attacked by thousands of French soldiers," Conner said.

"Maybe the soldiers changed their minds while they were in the portal," Bree said. "Two hundred years is a long time for self-reflection; they could have re-thought their whole universe-domination thing."

"Maybe." He shrugged. They both knew it was a slim chance but Conner appreciated the optimism nonetheless. He wished he could live a life where there wasn't always a *cost* or a *choice*—he wished for once that when someone said, "And they lived happily ever after," they meant it.

They finished eating and continued their journey to the castle. It was impossible to keep track of time since the sun was hidden by the clouds. A few hours later, just as their bums and feet started aching from biking all day, they arrived in the village of Hohenschwangau.

Conner and Bree could see the tips of the towers belonging to Neuschwanstein Castle hidden by the trees in the hills above the village. It felt like a giant was peeking at them.

"We made it!" Bree said cheerfully. "And it only took us nine and a half hours!"

"Only?" Conner asked, groaning as he dismounted his bike. "I think I'm going to have a bicycle-seat-shaped dent in my butt for the rest of my life."

Hohenschwangau was an incredibly tiny place and mainly consisted of restaurants, inns, and souvenir shops for tourists visiting Neuschwanstein. The village was also home to another, smaller and older castle that sat on a hill across from Neuschwanstein. It was square and golden and almost completely forgotten by the travelers roaming the village.

Glass kiosks lined in the center of the village sold tours of Neuschwanstein. A long line of tourists waited outside for buses that took them up the path into the hills and to the castle.

"Okay, I think I've got a plan," Conner said. "We'll go on a tour of the castle and stay in the very back of our group so we're easily forgettable. When no one is looking, we find the perfect place to hide. Then at night, when all the guides and guests have gone, we give ourselves a tour of the castle and try to find the portal."

"That sounds like an excellent plan!" Bree said.

They chained their bikes to a bike rack and went to purchase their tickets. But just as they walked up to the kiosks, a sign written in many languages was placed in the window:

ALLE TOUREN VON SCHLOSS NEUSCHWANSTEIN
SIND FÜR DEN REST DES TAGES AUSVERKAUFT

ALL TOURS OF NEUSCHWANSTEIN CASTLE
ARE SOLD OUT FOR THE REST OF THE DAY

TOUS LES BILLETS POUR LES VISITES DU CHÂTEAU
DE NEUSCHWANSTEIN ONT ETE VENDUS
POUR LE RESTE DE LA JOURNEE

TUTTI I TOUR DI NEUSCHWANSTEIN CASTELLO SONO
ESAURITI PER IL RESTO DELLA GIORNATA

"Oh no!" Conner exclaimed. "What are we supposed to do now?"

"Let's see if we can get a better look at the castle," Bree said. "Maybe there's a window or something we could sneak into."

They walked down the road a little ways away from the village, and more of the castle's towers came into view.

"It's no use looking at it from down here, we'll have to go up the hill and get a closer look," Conner said.

He tried his best to fight the disheartening thoughts creeping over him, but the situation wasn't looking great. If the street below the castle was *that* crowded, the castle must be packed with people. It would be impossible to snoop around without looking suspicious.

Conner closed his eyes and prayed for a miracle. They just needed a way inside the castle, that was all! The fate of the fairy-tale world depended on what they might find inside. Luckily for Conner, there was still a bit of magic in his blood and it must have been listening to his request. . . .

"Hey, Conner," Bree whispered. *"That kid over there keeps staring at us."*

Conner turned in the direction she was referring to. A few yards ahead of them beside the road was a tiny cottage-like house. A boy sat on its front steps unapologetically watching them. He was very young, no older than ten, and had dark hair and very pale skin. He was skinny although his cheeks were plump and rosy, making him look like a puppet that lived in a cuckoo clock.

"Hi," Conner said, and waved awkwardly at their observer.

"Hello," the boy said in a cute German accent. "Are you guys American?"

"We are," Bree said.

A big grin stretched between his rosy cheeks and he giddily sat up.

"Do you like the United States?" Conner asked him.

"Yes!" the boy said with an animated nod. "That's where all the superheroes are from!"

"Have you ever been there?" Bree asked.

The boy's shoulders sank. "No," he said. "I go to school in Füssen down the road but other than that I've never been very far from here. But I'm saving all my money so I can visit Gotham City one day!"

Conner and Bree looked at each other like he was a precious puppy they wanted to keep.

"What's your name?" Conner asked. They walked up closer to his house to visit with him some more.

"My name is Emmerich," he was happy to tell them. "Emmerich Himmelsbach. What are your names?"

"I'm Conner and this is my friend Bree."

"What brings you to Hohenschwangau?" he asked, and then quickly corrected himself. "Oh, that was a silly question; you're here to see the castle, right? Everybody always comes to see the castle."

"Yes," Bree said. "Have you been inside it before?"

"Oh, *many, many, many* times!" he told them. "My grandfather used to give tours of the castle and my mother works at a gift shop in the village. So there isn't anything I don't know about the place."

"Well, we *were* here to see the castle," Conner said dejectedly. "We rode bikes all the way from Munich but the tickets are sold out."

This completely blew Emmerich's mind and he almost fell over just hearing it. "You rode bikes all the way from *Munich*?" he said with enormous gestures. "Why would you do that?"

An idea suddenly came to Conner's mind. He looked at Bree

and she could see the light in his eyes. She was prepared to go along with whatever it was he was thinking.

"Well, we would tell you but we wouldn't want to endanger you," Conner said.

"Yes, you're far too young," Bree added.

Emmerich's eyes grew and his mouth fell open. "Tell me *what*?" he asked.

"I'm afraid we can't tell you," Conner said. "It would blow our cover if anyone were to ever find out."

"What are you covering up?" Emmerich asked, desperate to know. "You can tell me—I don't have any friends to tell!"

Conner and Bree looked at each other; they had him right where they wanted him.

"Well, we came to Germany to *hide something*," Conner said. "We were hired by the United States government because no one would ever suspect kids of traveling with *it*."

Emmerich put his hands on his cheeks; the curiosity was eating him alive. "What are you trying to hide?" he asked.

Conner pulled the panpipe from his jacket pocket and showed it to him. *"This."*

Emmerich gasped before knowing what it was. "Wait, what is that?"

"It looks like a panpipe, but it's actually a weapon," Bree said. "And a very bad man wants to get his hands on it."

"And you want to hide it in *Hohenschwangau*?!" Emmerich asked.

They nodded. "We were going to hide it in the castle," Conner said. "That way no one would ever suspect it was anything but a historical item—but since there aren't any more tours, we'll just have to hide it somewhere else."

"Sorry to bother you, Emmerich," Bree said. "But we need to get going now. We need to be out of the country by nightfall so they don't find us."

They turned to leave but Emmerich ran to stand in front of them.

"No, wait, please!" he said. "I can take you into Neuschwanstein if you want!"

"But how can you do that?" Conner asked.

Emmerich looked around to make sure no one could hear him. "I know a secret passage into the castle," he explained. "My grandfather took me there once."

Conner's and Bree's spirits soared hearing this, but they had to remain calm to keep their cover.

"I don't know, I would hate to put your life in danger, Emmerich," Bree said.

"But I'm putting my own life in danger by offering!" he pleaded. "Please! I can even keep an eye on it for you after you leave!"

They took a few steps away and huddled with their backs to him, pretending to think it over.

"You're a genius!" Bree whispered to Conner. *"What are the chances we would find someone who could lead us to a secret passage into the castle?"*

"Yeah, what are the chances?" Conner whispered back with a smile. He knew deep down there was a bit of fairy magic inside of him, although he would never have admitted it openly.

They forced their excitement to fade from their faces and went back to Emmerich.

"All right, Emmerich, if you promise never to tell anyone about this, we'll let you take us to the castle," Conner said.

Emmerich jumped up and down. This was the most exciting thing that had ever happened to him in his young life. "I knew there was something special about you," he said. "I've seen enough movies to know a secret agent when I see one! When do you want to go?"

"Sometime after dark," Bree said. "So no one will see us there."

"Great! I can meet you at Mary's Bridge after dinner, in an hour or two," Emmerich said. "My mom would kill me if I missed dinner, even if it was to help save the world."

"Sounds good," Conner said. "Where is Mary's Bridge?"

"It's up the path to the castle," Emmerich said. "There are signs to guide you, you can't miss it. It has the best views of the castle."

"Terrific, we'll meet you there," Bree said.

Emmerich was bouncing and his cheeks were extra rosy. "I can't wait!" he said, but then became very still when another thought occurred to him. "If I'm leaving after dinner, I better clean my room before my mother gets home!"

He hurried past them and ran up the steps into his house. Conner and Bree sighed with relief at the same time.

"So far we've run away from our principal, kidnapped an old lady, lied to a concierge, and tricked an innocent German boy into believing we're secret agents," Bree listed. "Does that make us bad people?"

"Nah," Conner said, shaking his head. "Sometimes you have

to do the wrong thing for the right reason. Now let's go check out this bridge. I'm anxious to see this castle."

They returned to the village and followed the road up to the castle. There were many signs pointing to the various things that could be seen in the hills, but they followed the arrows that said "Marienbrücke" ("Mary's Bridge").

The bridge was very long and narrow. It was wood with an iron railing and stretched from one cliff to another. Several tourists braved the bridge and took pictures of the mountains and forest around it. Conner and Bree faced mild cases of vertigo during their first steps onto the bridge—they weren't expecting to see a waterfall and stream several hundred feet below.

When they got to the middle of the bridge they looked out and saw Neuschwanstein Castle in its entirety for the first time.

"Oh my gosh," Bree gasped, and put her hands over her mouth.

"I can't...I can't...I c-c-can't believe I'm seeing this right now," Conner stuttered.

It was easy to believe Neuschwanstein Castle was referred to as one of the wonders of Europe. It was a massive white structure with thousands of windows, dozens of tall towers, pointed roofs, and sharp spirals the color of the night sky. The castle sat on a stone base surrounded by trees at the peak of the hill, which made it look like it was growing out of the mountainside.

Conner had seen many impressive structures in the Land of Stories but never in his *own world*. Neuschwanstein Castle had been built brick by brick with the hands of man, using no magic whatsoever.

"I would say this is amazing but that would be an understatement," he said.

"You're right, there really are no words," Bree said. "It's funny that we're the only ones who know there's a portal into the fairy-tale world inside—you would think it's obvious."

Conner couldn't agree more. The luscious green mountains surrounding it, the clear lakes reflecting the thick gray clouds in the sky, and the small villages miles into the horizon made him feel like he was looking at something otherworldly. It was as if a piece of the fairy-tale world had penetrated through the seam of the Otherworld and had been named Bavaria.

The few short hours they waited for Emmerich to arrive went by quickly as they took in the sights around them. Night had fallen over the German countryside and the tourists slowly disappeared until Conner and Bree were the last ones on the bridge. They saw a small light in the trees and soon Emmerich emerged, walking toward them with a flashlight in his hand.

"Guten Abend," Emmerich said. "Are you ready to explore the castle?"

Emmerich led them to a path that crisscrossed down the hillside to an observation deck near the waterfall. They crawled over the railing of the deck and then followed the stream all the way down to the bottom of the hill the castle was perched on.

"Careful, don't get your shoes wet," Emmerich warned them. The closer they got to the hill, the farther the stream flowed into the land beside it, like an overflowing bathtub.

The bridge, the castle, and the mountains disappeared from view behind the thick trees that surrounded the base of the hill.

Built into the side of the hill, disguised by a layer of dirt and rocks, was a round door. Emmerich felt around for its steel handle and then heaved the door open.

"This way," Emmerich said happily.

Conner and Bree crawled through the door after him and into a long stone tunnel. The tunnel twisted and turned for what felt like miles under the castle. Without Emmerich's flashlight, it would have been pitch-black. Eventually the three arrived at the end of the tunnel and Emmerich pushed through another circular door and into the small storage room of a gift shop.

"This used to be the servants' quarters," Emmerich said. "Now stay close behind me, I just have to go punch in the code before the alarm goes off."

They went past the gift shop and into a hall dedicated to the history of the castle's construction and design. A large replica of the castle sat in the middle of the hall and the walls were covered with photos of the castle being built and illustrations of its early concept art.

Emmerich found a keypad behind one of the photos and typed in a long code. A green light blinked when he was finished.

"Neuschwanstein is ours!" Emmerich said.

"All right, Emmerich, take us on a tour," Conner said. "We want to see everything."

Emmerich marched them down the hall and up a spiral staircase, and the lavishness of the castle began. The circular walls around the staircase were covered in wallpaper patterned with dragons and symbols they didn't recognize.

"This place gives me the creeps," Conner said.

"Me too," Bree said. "I love it!"

"A lot of people think it's haunted," Emmerich said. "Many visitors have claimed to see ghosts moving past the windows at night or hear sounds coming from inside when it's completely empty."

Conner gulped and Bree grinned. At the top of the stairs they passed a statue of a dragon standing like an overgrown watchdog guarding the hallway.

"I'll show you the throne room first," Emmerich said, and guided them down the hallway.

Every inch of the hallway was decorated in wallpaper of diamond, checkered, or floral design. Pillars with animal carvings sat in the arches of the windows and each window was lined with gold. The colors may have faded over the years, but the castle remained a spectacle even more than a century later.

Emmerich escorted them through an open doorway and into the throne room. It had a towering domed ceiling. A gigantic chandelier hung from the ceiling and was rimmed with hundreds of wax candles. The walls were covered in beautiful paintings of mythological and religious figures. Every species of the animal kingdom appeared in the mosaic floor as if the circle of life was right under their feet.

Colorful arches and pillars surrounded the throne room. Balconies wrapped around the top of the room, facing a high platform under a large mural of Jesus Christ. The platform was the perfect place for a throne, but it was empty.

"So if this is the throne room, where's the throne?" Bree asked.

"He never had one," Emmerich said. "King Ludwig II had

an extravagant throne made to match this room but he was declared insane before it was finished."

"So the king never got to sit on his throne?" Conner asked. "That's tough."

"Most of the castle remains unfinished," Emmerich said. "Ludwig was spending all of Bavaria's money to build his luxurious homes and when that began running out he started borrowing money from other countries to complete them."

"I can see how that might lead to a bad reputation," Bree said.

Conner had been studying every square inch of the castle as they went, searching for anything that could possibly be the portal, but he wasn't finding anything that rang a bell in the throne room.

"Do you think this room would be a good place for the weapon?" Emmerich whispered even though they were the only three in the castle.

"No, not here," Conner said. "Let's keep looking."

"I'll show you King Ludwig's bedroom next," Emmerich said.

They followed him back into the hall and entered a pair of heavy wooden doors. The king's bedroom was covered from floor to ceiling in remarkable wooden craftsmanship. Everything from the washstand to the desk to the bed frame displayed intricate carvings of disciples, nobility, and harvest. Murals of *Tristan and Isolde*, one of the king's favorite stories, covered the areas of the walls not decorated in wood.

Then they took a quick look at a small artificial grotto tucked between two rooms; it was as if the king had kept a tiny cave in his closet. But even that wasn't appealing enough for Conner.

"See any place that works?" Emmerich asked.

Bree was just as interested; she wasn't entirely sure what they were supposed to be looking for, either. However, it wasn't something Conner could explain—part of recognizing a portal was being able to feel it.

"Not yet," Conner said. "I'll know it when I see it."

"Then I'll take you to the Singer's Hall next! There are many things to see there!" Emmerich said.

They returned to the spiral staircase and walked up to the fifth floor of the castle. When they walked into the Singer's Hall the first thing they heard was the sound of their footsteps echoing back at them. The hall was by far the largest room in the castle and stretched long and wide.

The Singer's Hall was such an over-stimulating sight it took Conner and Bree a few moments to differentiate all the artwork. The whole hall seemed to blend into one giant piece of art composed of paintings, statues, busts, carvings, engravings, and symbols of King Ludwig's favorite myths and legends. There were depictions of knights in shining armor, damsels in distress, royal weddings, and the punishment of evildoers. Candelabras lined the perimeter of the room while enormous chandeliers hung from the high ceiling.

Bree was looking up at a woman in one of the portraits. "Has anyone ever noticed that every woman in an old portrait looks like she's being tricked into something?" she asked.

"They still use this room," Emmerich said. "They fill it with chairs and instruments and put on concerts and performances to this day. This would be a convenient place to store your panpipe."

Hearing this struck a chord with Conner. Emmerich was right; it would make sense for the panpipe to be affiliated with this room. If Conner had built the castle, he would certainly have put a panpipe that gave access to a portal in a room that had something to do with music. The portal *had* to be in the Singer's Hall—he could feel it.

At the far side of the room was a platform four steps high. Four pillars of dark red marble stood on the front of the platform and held three colorful arches above them. Behind the pillars and arches, covering the wall, was the largest painting in the room. It was of a majestic forest with trees, flowers, squirrels, deer, and boulders.

Conner couldn't take his eyes off this area of the room. The painting looked familiar to him, like a place he had seen with his sister. There was something intriguing and inviting about it that he couldn't explain in words.

"What is this painting of?" Conner said.

"That's a painting of a magic garden," Emmerich said. "I don't know what it's from, though."

Conner smiled on the inside and out. "I do," he said, and then looked at Bree. "I think I've found it."

Bree and Emmerich joined him at the back of the room. They stood by his side and all three of them gazed at the painting behind the pillars.

"You want to put the weapon in there?" Emmerich asked excitedly.

Conner decided to tell his young tour guide the truth. "Emmerich, it's not really a weapon," he said. "And we're not really secret agents."

Emmerich looked sadly at the floor. "I know," he said. "But I thought it would be fun to pretend with you guys. I don't get many chances to have fun with other kids; everyone who comes to Hohenschwangau is only here for a day and then they always leave."

It broke Conner's and Bree's hearts a little to hear this. He was the second person on their trip to *let* them manipulate him or her due to loneliness. Bree leaned down so she could look him right in the eyes.

"Don't worry, Emmerich," she said. "We have to check something out now, and if it works, it's going to be much cooler than anything secret agents could show you."

Emmerich looked curious. Bree nodded to Conner and he took the panpipe from his jacket pocket. He looked over the notes carved into the back of it and double-checked that he knew which cylinder played which note.

"The middle cylinder should be middle C," Bree said. "At least that's how it works on a piano—my mom made me take lessons when I was younger."

"Here goes," Conner said. He blew the first four notes into the pipe and then paused for a second before blowing the remaining four. They were pure and chilling in the empty castle.

The notes echoed through the hall like all the noises they had made—only the notes never stopped. The sound only increased more and more, causing the whole hall to vibrate. The chandeliers above them began to sway and the floor started rumbling.

"What's happening?" Emmerich shouted. He covered his ears and looked around the hall in absolute horror.

Suddenly a bright flash of light appeared between the two pillars in the center of the platform. The light grew and started to swirl; the larger it became, the faster it spun. Soon the entire back of the hall was covered in the light.

"*Oh no*," Conner said, and locked eyes with Bree. "*It works! We can access it from our side. That means the portal has re-opened and the French soldiers are—*"

The three of them jolted forward against their will. The light had abruptly turned into a swirling vortex and was *pulling them inside it.*

"*Run!*" Conner yelled.

The three of them ran for the other side of the hall, but the vortex's pull was too strong. Emmerich grabbed Bree, Bree grabbed Conner, and Conner grabbed one of the candelabras bolted to the wall. They dangled in the air as the vortex only grew stronger. Emmerich lost his hold on Bree, Bree lost her grasp of Conner, and Conner's grip slipped from the candelabra.

All three of them flew through the air and were sucked into the circling light. Conner, Bree, and Emmerich disappeared into the vortex and vanished from Neuschwanstein Castle.

CHAPTER THIRTEEN

THE EVICTED QUEEN

The weeks following the Fairy Inaugural Ball turned out to be quite enjoyable for Alex. She attended the Fairy Council meetings every day, she rode Cornelius on her daily trips around the kingdoms to see who needed the helping hand of a fairy, and then she spent the evenings going on long walks with Rook through the woods. She couldn't decide which part of her day she liked best—except on the days when their walks ended with a good-night kiss: Then the walk was definitely her favorite part.

After weeks of agonizing over the ball and days spent worrying about Rook, Alex was so happy she could finally enjoy herself again. It had been so long since she was content about anything she had almost forgotten what relief felt like. She had been so occupied she hadn't even thought to ask Conner how his trip to Germany was.

However, as enjoyable as her carefree days were, she knew they were most likely limited. And one afternoon Alex received a letter from Red that proved just that.

Dearest Alex,

Congratulations on graduating Fairy School or whatever it was you've recently accomplished—I'm very proud of you! I'm positive you'll be a wonderful addition to the League of Fairies or whatever it is you're a part of now.
I'm writing to you because I need a favor. That dreadful Peep woman has struck again! She convinced the House of Progress to organize a debate between us before the polls open tomorrow afternoon. Isn't that the most barbaric thing you've ever heard of? What kind of kingdom wants to watch their ruler defend herself against a series of vicious personal attacks on her character? Do the words nobility and grace not go hand in hand anymore?
Anyway, I was wondering, if you weren't too busy with Fairy Court, if you wouldn't mind attending the debates in my support. Having a fairy publicly

on my side would do a lot for my image, and when the election results come in tomorrow evening and Little Bo Peep loses, you can turn her into a pumpkin and we can take turns smashing her with a sledgehammer.
Warmest wishes,
Her Majesty, Queen Red Riding Hood of the Red Riding Hood Kingdom
P.S. Charlie says hello. He's been guiding me through all of this campaign ridiculousness. I convinced the House of Progress to let him moderate the debate. He hopes to see you, too!

The letter had been delivered personally by one of Red's messengers and he looked very tired after traveling all night to deliver it.

"Please tell Queen Red I'll be there." Alex sighed.

Later that evening, Alex told Rook about the letter while they were on their walk.

"Are you going to tell Red what we saw in Little Bo's barn?" Rook asked her.

"No, I don't think I will," Alex said. "I can't fault Little Bo for not having noble intentions when Red doesn't exactly have the noblest intentions, either."

"So does that mean I won't be seeing you for our walk tomorrow?" Rook asked, making sad-puppy eyes at her.

"Probably not," Alex said. "But I'll see you the day after."

"That's all right, my father and I are pulling weeds tomorrow and that usually takes up the majority of the day." Rook let out a pitiful laugh.

"What's so funny?" Alex asked.

"I just compared our days in my head," Rook said. "You're going to be part of an election that will change a kingdom's future and I'm pulling weeds."

"We all do our part," Alex teased. "But if it's any consolation, Red's problems are a lot like weeds. No matter how many times you pull them, they just keep coming back."

The following afternoon Alex rode Cornelius into the Red Riding Hood Kingdom and arrived in town just as the debate was about to begin. From a distance it looked like the entire kingdom had been painted red, but when Alex got closer she realized it wasn't *paint* the town was covered in. Every shop, home, and tree was covered in Red's campaign posters.

The majority of them said VOTE FOR QUEEN RED and had a sketch of Red on them. Others were a bit catchier and said KEEP THE KINGDOM FED, VOTE FOR QUEEN RED or, A KINGDOM THIS GREAT MUST BE DOING SOMETHING RIGHT, VOTE FOR QUEEN RED. Others completely slandered Little Bo and said DON'T BE A CREEP, DON'T VOTE FOR PEEP or, more subtly, PEEP LOSES SHEEP.

Alex tried to find posters in Little Bo's favor but couldn't see any. She clearly wasn't campaigning as hard as Red, or perhaps all her posters had been covered by Red's.

The park in the center of the kingdom was lined with voting booths. Two podiums were set up on the House of Progress's front steps where most of the kingdom had gathered on the ground below. The representatives were seated at the bottom of the steps, privileged to have front-row seats to the debate.

Alex let Cornelius graze in the park and met Froggy at the steps. He paced around nervously, holding a stack of cards in his hands.

"Is she ready for this?" Alex asked him.

"As ready as she can be. I've been coaching her all week."

"I'm sure you were an amazing teacher," Alex said, and put a hand on his shoulder.

"I really love Red and I think she's an amazing queen in her own way," he said. "Her confidence is contagious and it's good for the kingdom. Getting others to see it that way is the challenge."

Queen Red and Little Bo emerged from inside the House of Progress and were greeted by warm applause as they walked down the steps to their respective podiums. Red moved a little faster than Little Bo and walked in front of her, taking in all the applause for herself.

Alex had a seat with the representatives and Froggy addressed the crowd.

"Hello, Hoodians, and welcome to the first electoral debate in the history of the Red Riding Hood Kingdom," Froggy said. "Our candidates will each be given a chance to express why they feel deserving of your votes and then we will conclude the debate with questions submitted by citizens from around the kingdom. Let's begin!"

Froggy took his position on the lower steps below the podiums and the debate began. Queen Red was the first to try to persuade the kingdom to vote for her.

"Fellow Hoodians," she declared. "That has such a nice ring to it, don't you think? What will you be called if Little Bo sits on the throne—*the Peepers*? I bet you would dislike that as much as I would dislike it. Now I know my opponent is going to spend the next few minutes telling you all *she understands you*

and she's *one of you* and *blah, blah, blah* . . . and you know what, she's right!"

The citizens were shocked to hear Red take this approach. Alex was afraid of where she was taking this.

"Little Bo Peep is just like you. And I couldn't be more *different* from you," Red continued. "But that's how you like your queen! You want your queen to *represent you*, not be one of you. That's why I was elected queen when I was a little girl, because as a young innocent victim I *symbolized* you. And now that our kingdom has become the prosperous nation it is today, I symbolize *that*. When other kingdoms think about the Red Riding Hood Kingdom, do you want them thinking about a leader who carries around a staff and probably does her own cooking and cleaning? *No!* You want them thinking of a rich and beautiful and fearless queen because *that* is what the Red Riding Hood Kingdom is! Thank you."

Red finished her speech and struck a pose with her hands in the air. Her citizens had been trained well enough by now to know they were supposed to applaud whenever she did this.

Little Bo cleared her throat; it was her turn to convince the citizens to vote for her.

"The reason I didn't put campaign posters up is the same reason I won't bore you with a long speech now: It's a waste of time," Little Bo said. "Queen Red may waste your time and your resources, but I will not."

A quiet whispering broke out through the crowd. Red was appalled by Little Bo's response. She kept looking into the crowd expecting someone to say Little Bo was breaking the rules. Little

Bo stayed as calm and collected as ever. She definitely wasn't the emotional mess Alex had seen in the barn a few weeks earlier. Red was desperate to get the crowd back on her side.

"May I just remind everyone that when I was younger and surviving horrendous attacks by wild creatures, *Miss High-and-Mighty* over there couldn't even keep track of her own sheep!" Red said. "And then her own sheep felt so sorry for her they came *back*, wagging their tails behind them, so she wouldn't feel so pathetic. And now *this woman* wants to be queen."

The spectators hooted and hollered at Red's feisty response—the debate was getting interesting. Froggy slapped his hand against his forehead. Alex could tell he had tried coaching her against having outbursts like this.

"For the queen's information, I lost my flock of sheep *one time* and it was a traumatic experience that inspired me to single-handedly turn my family's farms into the most productive in the kingdom," Little Bo stated. "We are now the number one wool-producing business in the world and, thanks to the flawless counting system I invented, my farm has *never* lost a sheep since."

Red greeted this response with an impressive eye roll. "Well, if traumatic experiences make someone a bigger person, I'm surprised I even fit through the doors of my own castle," she said. "I was inside the stomach of the Big Bad Wolf—inside him! Surely that deserves a little more credit than just being absentminded—"

"You walked into that forest wearing a bright red cape and carrying a basket of freshly baked goods," Little Bo interrupted.

"You were *asking* to be attacked by a wolf, and then we elected you queen. If a fish jumped into a boat with a hook in its mouth, would we have elected him king?"

A sprinkling of people in the crowd grunted their protest, feeling Little Bo was insulting their judgment now. Red quickly milked this for all it was worth.

"Are you telling the Hoodian people here today that they were wrong to elect me queen?" Red asked.

Little Bo's eyes darted around the crowd, who grew more insulted by the second. It was her turn to get them back on her side.

"What I'm trying to say is, Queen Red may have been a symbol at one point, but the Big Bad Wolves are gone now," Little Bo said. "The times have changed and so should the leader of this kingdom. The kingdom may have needed a symbol then, but we need a ruler now."

A hush fell over the crowd. The citizens started to look at Little Bo differently now, not just as someone brave enough to challenge the queen, but as a true leader.

"Let's read some of the questions," Froggy said. "We'll start with Queen Red and then Little Bo will follow. The first question is, *How will you help the farmers whose crops freeze in the winter?*"

Red perked up like she knew the perfect answer. "Not only would I supply the farmers with coats, I would supply their crops with coats as well," she said happily.

The entire crowd squinted at her—was she serious?

"I would supply the farmers with mulch to give their crops

a better chance of withstanding the cold as well as barrels of heated water to keep the crops from freezing over," Little Bo said. The citizens nodded to one another—they liked her answer better. Froggy moved on to the next question.

"Now Little Bo will answer first, followed by Queen Red," he prefaced. *"How will you make school a more meaningful experience for the children of our kingdom?"*

Little Bo was prepared with an answer. "You can only learn so much in a classroom," she said. "I would invite the children to my farm or have them visit the shops in town so they can experience different workplaces before choosing a field to go into—and it would give our poor overworked teachers a rest once in a while."

This answer was welcomed with a soft round of applause from the teachers in the crowd. Red thought about her answer before giving it.

"Actually, I like her answer," she said with a confident nod. "Yes, I would do the same."

Alex sighed—she didn't think this was going to end well for her friend.

"Next question," Froggy said, and flipped to the next card. "Queen Red will answer first. *What is your take on national security?"*

Red placed her index finger over her mouth while she formed an answer. Alex crossed her fingers, hoping she would deliver an answer the citizens could get behind.

"I like it!" was all Red said, and a large smile grew on her face.

Alex covered her eyes; it was like watching a carriage wreck.

A few citizens even laughed at Red. Little Bo waited a moment before answering the question herself, letting Red's embarrassment marinate.

"I believe the key to national security is having a strong army," Little Bo said. "No kingdom has ever experienced a downfall because it was too strong."

The Hoodian citizens started a round of healthy applause for Little Bo. *"Bo Peep! Bo Peep! Bo Peep!"* the crowd chanted. *"Bo Peep! Bo Peep!"*

Red looked sadly over her citizens; she didn't understand where she had gone wrong. Froggy immediately concluded the debate before it got worse for her.

"We'd like to thank you all for joining us in this debate," Froggy said. "Please cast your vote in one of the many voting booths in the park."

While the citizens voted for a queen, Alex and Froggy kept Red company in the library of her castle. They were all on pins and needles waiting to hear the results of the election. Alex and Froggy sat in the large comfy chairs by the fireplace but Red had been pacing for hours since they'd returned from the debate. Clawdius watched her sadly from a corner of the room, looking as if he wished there was something he could do.

"Little Bo is a pain in the shepherdess!" Red shouted, loud enough for her whole castle to hear. "She'd never be half the queen I am. Would *she* have been chased by a pack of wolves and lived to tell the tale? *No!* Would she have gotten into a flying ship and sailed around the world trying to save it? *No!* Could she have chopped down a beanstalk to save her citizens from being

devoured by a giant man-eating cat? *No!* Would *she* have refused to surrender her kingdom to the Enchantress? *No!* Does anyone except me remember the things I've done for this country?"

"Maybe they do, darling," Froggy said. "You have to be patient and hear what the results are. Don't declare your defeat yet."

"Your people might have more faith in you than you have in them," Alex said. "Just believe in them as much as they've always believed in you."

This comforted Red a little bit and the distance of her pacing shortened. There was a knock on the door and the third Little Pig entered the room. Froggy and Alex stood from their seats and Red stopped pacing altogether.

"Good evening, Your Majesty," he said.

"Have the votes been counted?" Froggy asked.

"Yes, they have," the third Little Pig said.

The room grew uncomfortably tense and Red didn't know what else to do but laugh. "Good," she said, pretending it wasn't a big deal. "Has all this election business finally been settled, then? Can we let Little Bo Peep know that I'm here to stay?"

The third Little Pig hesitated to respond and Alex and Froggy knew it hadn't gone in her favor. Red was about to hear the worst news of her life.

"Actually, Little Bo Peep has been elected the new queen," the pig said.

Red fell into the closest seat and clutched her chest; her heart had just broken into a million pieces. "I'm sorry," she said, trying to fight the tears forming in her eyes. "Can you repeat that?"

"Little Bo Peep has been elected the new queen, ma'am," the pig said again.

Froggy had a seat next to Red and held her hand tightly. Alex placed a hand on her friend's shoulder. Clawdius came and sat by her feet. Even though Red had heard the news twice she still had a hard time comprehending it.

"This isn't possible," Red said, shaking her head. "This is *my* kingdom. It has *my* name, after all."

"Actually, ma'am, the kingdom is going to be re-named," the pig told her regretfully, as if she hadn't heard enough bad news already.

"To what?" Alex asked.

"The Bo Peep Republic."

Red forced a laugh again. "Well, that's a ridiculous name," she said, desperately needing to make light of the situation for her own good.

"When does Little Bo officially take over?" Froggy asked.

"In one week," the pig said. "She's kindly asked that Red Riding Hood have all of her belongings out of the castle by then."

Even Red couldn't hold a stoic face after hearing this. She burst into tears and buried her face in Froggy's shoulder.

"I'll give you a moment to yourselves," the pig said, and left the room.

Sometimes it was difficult to be around Red when she was happy, but Alex had never expected it would be so painful to watch her be so miserable. Red sobbed for the rest of the evening. Her spirit had been broken and Alex was afraid it might never be salvaged.

"But I'm the queen...," she cried into Froggy's arms. *"I'm the queen... I'm the queen...."*

Seven days, one thousand dresses, eight hundred pairs of shoes, five hundred paintings, twenty-eight statues, and one wolf later, the entire castle had been cleared of any trace of Red Riding Hood. She spent her last moments in the castle alone in her empty bedroom looking at the bare walls she had once called home. She was so depressed all she wore was a simple red dress and a matching overcoat.

There was a soft knock on her door and Froggy peeked inside. "All the carriages are loaded, darling," he said. "It's time to go."

"All right, then," Red said, dabbing her eyes with a handkerchief. She stood up and somberly left the room. She shut the door behind her, not only to her old bedroom, but to her life as queen.

Froggy gave her his arm and escorted her down the grand staircase and through the castle. All of the servants lined the walls as she passed. They respectfully bowed to her one final time. Red and Froggy walked outside, where a parade of twelve carriages jam-packed with Red's belongings was waiting for them.

The carriages were very plain wooden—much different from the luxurious ones Red was used to traveling in.

Froggy and Clawdius climbed into the first carriage and

waited for Red. She looked up at the castle and admired the towers and windows she had personally designed. She thought about the happy and not-so-happy memories she had lived through inside and said good-bye to it all.

The parade of carriages left the Red Riding Hood Kingdom and traveled into the Fairy Kingdom to the Fairy Palace. Alex had invited Red to stay with her for a few days while she figured out what the next step in her life would be. Alex had to magically shrink Red's belongings so she could place them inside a tiny cupboard; otherwise they never would have fit in the palace.

Alex took Red, Froggy, and Clawdius up to the grand balcony of the Fairy Palace, hoping the remarkable view might cheer Red up.

"I suppose I took things for granted," Red said. She hadn't looked at the view once, her eyes cast down at the floor. "Just like I expected the sky to always be blue, I expected to always be queen."

"We have to take some things for granted every now and then," Alex told her friend. "Otherwise we would live life afraid of losing everything."

Clawdius whimpered on the floor at their feet—even he missed the castle. Froggy had been quiet since they arrived and hadn't been acting himself. He looked like he was getting sick but didn't have any symptoms yet.

"Are you feeling all right, Froggy?" Alex asked him.

"I'll be just fine," he said. "I'm a tad dizzy, that's all. I think the week is catching up to me."

He walked a little ways away from them, clutching the

balcony tightly as he went, but Alex didn't press the matter. She tried to think of something to talk about that would take Red's mind off her troubles.

"At least while you're here I can introduce you to Rook," Alex told her.

Red nodded but then quickly looked confused. "Sorry— who?" she asked.

Alex sighed. Red had been through such a wringer she couldn't fault her for not remembering his name.

Emerelda suddenly rushed onto the balcony and went straight to Alex.

"Alex, you need to come with me," she said in a serious tone.

"Why, what's wrong?" she asked.

"It's your grandmother," Emerelda said. "She's sick."

Alex didn't know what to say to this. As far as she knew, her grandmother had never been sick in her entire life. Could Fairy Godmothers even get sick?

A croaking sound unexpectedly came from the end of the balcony and interrupted her train of thought.

"Would this by chance have anything to do with my current situation?" Froggy asked.

They all turned to look at him by the railing and Red screamed. Without warning or reason, Froggy had transformed back into a frog.

CHAPTER FOURTEEN

THE ARMEE ARRIVES

Conner was spinning through a world of light. It was so bright he could barely see anything. He couldn't hear the sound of his own voice, either—all he heard was the air rushing around him. Occasionally he saw Bree or Emmerich fly past him. He reached for them but couldn't reach far enough to catch them. He knew they were in the space between dimensions; he had been here before when he and his sister traveled through the *Land of Stories* book two years ago. Only it seemed to be taking much longer to arrive than it had the last time.

Conner saw a flash and felt something brush by him as if he were falling through a curtain. The next thing he knew, he was lying on his back looking up at a hazy night sky. He stayed there for a moment and didn't move, waiting for his senses to catch up with him.

There were two more flashes nearby and he felt *thud*s on the ground—Bree and Emmerich had landed beside him. Conner sat up to check on his friends and saw that they were as discombobulated as he was.

"Well, now we know the portal is definitely open," Conner said.

Bree pulled herself up to a seated position. "Is it always this rough getting here?" she said.

"No," he said. "I don't know why that was so tough."

Emmerich was so dizzy he could barely speak. "I don't think we're in Hohenschwangau anymore," he said, and his head bobbed up and down.

Conner got to his feet and looked at the forest around them. The trees were tall and their branches stretched wide into the sky. But they were bare of leaves and almost looked dead. It was foggy so he couldn't see very far into the distance.

Bree got to her feet, too. "So this is it, huh?" she asked.

"A part of it," Conner said. "Although I'm not sure where."

Emmerich tried getting to his feet but kept falling. Conner and Bree dragged him to the closest tree and propped him up against the trunk.

"Will one of you please tell me where I am?" Emmerich asked. "And what happened in Neuschwanstein?"

"I told you it would be cooler than being secret agents," Bree said playfully.

"We're in the fairy-tale world, bud," Conner explained. "We accessed a portal that was hidden inside Neuschwanstein."

Emmerich looked around the forest with large amazed eyes. *"The fairy-tale world?"* he said. "As in Snow White, Sleeping Beauty, Rapunzel—"

"They're all here," Conner said. "My grandma and sister live here, too. The portal between this world and ours had been blocked for a while but a friend of mine asked me to check if it had been re-opened—and here we are."

Emmerich had so many questions he didn't know what to ask first. "Why did your friend ask you to check it?" was the question he chose.

"To make sure some bad people couldn't get in," Conner said.

Bree turned her head and looked at the forest around them. "Speaking of, if *we* got through the portal into the fairy-tale world, doesn't that mean the French—"

Bright lights abruptly flashed all around them. With each flash, something extremely heavy appeared in midair and crashed to the ground. Bree screamed when she realized most of the objects were *human.* Conner was afraid something or someone would fall on them and looked for someplace to take cover.

"Hurry! Climb the tree!" he yelled. They helped Emmerich to his feet and the three of them dashed up the tree, climbing as high as they could. From the treetop they got a better view of what was happening. It was as if a lightning storm had swept

over the forest and was raining cannons, carriages, horses, swords, long pointed guns, *and soldiers.*

"It's the army!" Conner whispered to his friends. *"They're here!"*

The storm of soldiers didn't show any sign of letting up. From the top of the tree the three kids saw flashes in the fog for miles around. The hundreds of men and pieces of equipment that rained from the sky turned into thousands as the storm increased. Many soldiers barely missed being crushed by the carriages or cannons or horses that fell beside them.

Eventually the storm dissipated and the thunderous crashes around the forest came to a stop. The sounds of thousands of men moaning and grunting took its place. The soldiers twitched and turned on the ground—they were a hundred times as discombobulated as Conner, Bree, and Emmerich had been. Most of them held their heads in agony or vomited.

They all wore black boots, white pants, and blue jackets. Most of them wore plain hats while others' were decorated with colorful accessories and feathers representing their rank. They stayed on the ground for a long while without attempting to stand.

One man appeared through the fog in the distance. He was smaller than the average man and wore a large curved hat. He gazed around at the suffering soldiers with disgust. A musky cologne smell filled the air as he got closer to the tree where Conner, Bree, and Emmerich were hidden. Although Conner and Bree had never seen him before, they were certain he had to be General Jacques Marquis, who Mother Goose had warned them about.

The general apparently had a much stronger stomach than

the soldiers and wasn't affected by the arrival. *"Debout!"* he shouted at the anguished men on the ground. *"Vous êtes une honte pour la France!"*

"What did he say?" Conner whispered to the others.

"He said, 'Stand up, you're an embarrassment to France,'" Emmerich translated.

"You speak French?" Conner asked.

"I can speak German, English, French, and Danish."

Conner was floored. *"Wow, I'm still struggling with English."*

Bree covered their mouths with her hands. *"This is not the time to be comparing party tricks!"* she snapped, and they both stayed quiet.

Many of the soldiers stumbled to their feet as their general commanded. Emmerich quietly translated what they were saying for Conner and Bree.

"Walk it off like men," the general told his nauseated soldiers. "This is nothing compared to the battle ahead."

Another man appeared through the fog. He was a very tall and broad man and wore a rounded hat just like the general's but it was turned to the side.

"General Marquis—congratulations, sir, we've arrived," Colonel Baton said.

"Yes, Colonel, I can see that," the general barked. "But there is no use congratulating me until we know *exactly* where we are."

Two other soldiers hurried through the forest to the general and colonel. They were dragging another man who didn't look like a soldier at all.

"General Marquis! Colonel Baton!" Captain De Lange said. "We've found someone!"

"This man was walking through the forest when we arrived!" Lieutenant Rembert said.

They pushed the weak old man onto the ground in front of General Marquis. He was terrified and looked around at the soldiers in complete shock. "I saw you all fall from the sky!" he said, trembling. "What kind of magic is this?"

The general had no time for his befuddlement. "Tell us where we are and you may keep your life," he said.

"Why . . . why . . . you're in the Eastern Kingdom, sir," the old man said.

Conner locked eyes with Bree; this was good information for them to know, too.

"And what is near here other than trees?" the general asked.

"The border of the Fairy Kingdom is west of here, but Pinocchio Prison is closer, just to the east," the old man said.

The general stepped closer to him, looking intrigued. "A prison, you say?" he said. "Home to what kind of criminals?"

"The worst criminals in all the kingdoms," the old man said, surprised the general did not know.

General Marquis's forehead went very smooth and the corners of his mouth curled to form a sinister smile. "Gentlemen," he said to his soldiers. "The gods have smiled down on us! Soon we shall have the fairy-tale world in the palm of our hands! Napoleon will be so proud!"

The soldiers mustered up enough energy to cheer.

"You're here to take over the world?" the old man asked. "Who are you people?"

The general bent low to look the man in the eyes. "Unfortunately, you already know too much," he said. "Get rid of him."

The old man screamed. *"No! Please! I have a family!"* he pleaded, but it was no use. The general didn't have an ounce of mercy to spare. Captain De Lange and Lieutenant Rembert dragged the old man into the foggy woods and his screams echoed through the trees around them. A moment later a gunshot was heard and the woods were silent again.

Bree had to cover her mouth to keep from screaming. Emmerich gazed around the woods like he had found himself in a nightmare. Conner looked at them with a grave expression in his eyes—they had to stay as quiet as possible or they could be next.

"Colonel Baton, we need to regroup with our men immediately," the general instructed. "Half will stay in the woods and set up camp, the other half will accompany us to the prison. We strike at dawn."

"What are we doing at the prison, sir?" Baton asked.

"Recruiting," the general said.

They walked back through the trees in the direction they had come from and disappeared into the fog. The other soldiers gathered their weapons that were scattered around the trees, hitched the horses to the wagons, and followed them into the woods. Conner, Bree, and Emmerich were the only ones left in the area.

Conner gestured to the others to stay quiet as he climbed down the tree. Once he made sure the coast was clear, he signaled for them to join him.

"That poor old man," Emmerich said with his eyes full of tears. "I can't believe the general would do that to him! I always thought if someone needed help I could save them like a super-hero in the movies, but I guess I was wrong."

Bree placed a comforting hand on his shoulder.

Conner's mind was racing as he thought about something the general had said. "Did you hear what he told the soldiers?" Conner asked the others. "He said, 'Napoleon will be so proud.'"

The same thought had occurred to Bree. "Yeah," she said. "Napoleon's been dead for, like, two hundred years. I don't think they realize how long they were in the portal."

"Then how do we know how long *we* were in the portal?" Emmerich asked.

Conner and Bree looked at each other and chills went down their spines. Could they have been stuck in the portal for longer than they realized, too? It was all the more reason to find someone they knew as quickly as possible.

Conner felt so guilty for exposing Bree and Emmerich to this; it almost brought him to tears. He knew he should get them out of the Land of Stories as soon as he could.

"I'm not going to lie; these guys are really scary," he said. "And right now we need to get to the Fairy Palace pronto so I can warn my friends that the army is here. Once we're at the palace, I promise I'll find a way to send you back to the Otherworld."

Bree and Emmerich both nodded.

"Now follow me," Conner said. "We have to travel west into the Fairy Kingdom—and we have to move fast."

Chapter Fifteen

A BITTERSWEET REUNION

Alex sat by her grandma's bedside holding her hand. The Fairy Godmother had been sleeping peacefully since she got there. She didn't look like she had a care in the world, but Alex knew this was her favorite façade to keep; even as she slept she couldn't be trusted to show her true feelings. Something was very wrong and Alex could sense it.

"Are you going to tell me what's the matter with her?" Alex asked. "Or are you just going to sit there and make me figure it out on my own like everything else?"

Emerelda and Mother Goose sat on the other side of the bed

keeping to themselves. Red and Froggy were there, too; they stood at the foot of the bed wishing there was something they could do to comfort their friend. The week had proven to be a difficult one for all of them.

"Your grandmother has been feeling very *tired* for a long time," Mother Goose said. "She asked me not to tell anyone—and then today she didn't wake up."

"Today is the first time I'm hearing about this, too, Alex," Emerelda said. "She was keeping it from everyone."

"But what does *tired* mean?" Alex said, becoming frustrated. "Does she just need to rest? Is there anything I can get or give her to wake her up? Or is she . . . is she . . ."

Alex couldn't bring herself to say it.

"I'm afraid there's nothing any of us can do," Mother Goose said.

"So she's *dying*," Alex finally said. "If that's what's happening why can't either of you just tell me?"

Emerelda sighed, not for Alex, but for herself. "Yes," she confirmed. "We believe the Fairy Godmother is dying."

Tears immediately ran down Alex's face. She had always known her grandmother wouldn't be around forever, but she'd never expected to lose her so soon.

"I am so sorry, Alex," Red said.

"Please let us know if there is anything we can do," Froggy said.

Alex didn't say anything. Of course there wasn't. The only thing that would comfort her now would be if her grandmother woke up.

"I haven't even lived here a full year yet," Alex said through her tears. "My grandma is the only family I have. I just don't understand why this is happening. . . ."

Mother Goose hoped it would supply the young fairy with a little comfort if she explained.

"Your grandmother has been around for a very long time, Alex," Mother Goose told her. "She's worked very hard to make the fairy-tale world what it is. She knew she wouldn't be around forever and over the past couple of centuries she's looked for someone to continue her work when she's gone. She's had many apprentices and all of them have failed but you. In you, she finally found someone she knows will continue her legacy and continue it well. And knowing this, she's given her soul permission to *move on*."

This only made it much worse for Alex. "So what you're saying is, it's *my fault*," she said. "Had I never come to live in the Land of Stories or joined the Fairy Council, she would still be looking for a successor and wouldn't be in this bed. *I'm killing her*."

"Good heavens, no," Mother Goose said. "I'm trying to tell you you're *saving her*. You're giving your grandmother the freedom to pass on, and that's a right every living creature deserves when it's their time to go."

It was a very hard thing for Alex to hear. Had she known that with every lesson or test she passed she was getting closer to losing her grandmother, Alex would have given it all up in a heartbeat. But she also knew that was the last thing her grandmother would have wanted.

"How much time do we have left with her?" Alex asked. "Will she wake up before she goes?"

"It's hard to say," Emerelda said. "There's always a chance. She could very well pull through this and live for another hundred years—it all depends on how much magic she has left in her. But given the information she shared with Mother Goose, we think it's very unlikely."

"And that's why Froggy turned into a frog again," Alex said, starting to make sense of it all. "As she dies some of her magic starts to die with her, so her most recent spells and enchantments will slowly start to fade and wear off."

"Correct," Emerelda said. "And it's our job to make sure the work she put into this world never fades away completely."

Alex gently touched the side of her grandmother's face. She was such an extraordinary woman; she wouldn't be surprised if there was still a bit of magic in her somewhere.

"Froggy, I'd be more than happy to change you back into a man," Alex said. "It may take me a couple tries but I think I can do it."

Froggy was touched by the gesture, especially given the situation, but he surprised the whole room with his answer. "No, that's all right," he said. "Red, my darling, I hope you can understand this but I've thought it over and decided to stay a frog."

They all were shocked to hear this, especially Red.

"What are you saying?" Red asked. "What would make you come to that conclusion?"

"Because no matter how many times I become a man I always change back into a frog," he explained. "I think the universe is trying to tell me something. And although I put on a good show, each transformation is more exhausting than the last. Constantly having to re-train yourself to walk and to eat and to function takes a heavy toll. I'd much rather just choose one form and stick with it, and it appears being a frog is what's meant to be."

Red tried her absolute best to take this news well, but after so recently losing her throne she couldn't put on a brave face.

"Forgive me," Red said, blinking back tears. "I don't mean to look as disappointed as I do. Charlie, you stood by me even as I lost my kingdom—I know I can support you through something as trivial as this—it's just going to take some getting used to, I suppose. Please excuse me; I'm going to get some fresh air."

Red left the Fairy Godmother's chambers intact but once she was out the door they heard her burst into tears. Alex gently placed her grandmother's hand on the bed and rose to leave.

"I need some air, too," Alex said.

"I'll walk out with you," Mother Goose said.

"I'll stay with the Fairy Godmother," Emerelda said.

"Me too," Froggy said, and took Alex's seat.

As Alex walked with Mother Goose through the halls of the Fairy Palace she could tell the news about her grandmother had spread. Every fairy who passed looked at her somberly, expressing sympathy and respect as she walked by.

"This is going to be so hard to get through without my brother," Alex said. "I would give anything to have him here with me."

Mother Goose's eyes darted up and down the hall. When they reached a vacant part of the hall, she quickly pulled Alex behind a pillar and out of sight.

"Alex, I need to tell you something," Mother Goose said. "It's about your brother."

"What is it?" Alex asked.

"When your grandmother first told me how she was feeling, I immediately contacted Conner," she explained. "I didn't tell him she was sick, but I sent him on a little errand for me—to check on something."

"To check on what?" Alex asked.

"Froggy's spell isn't the only bit of your grandmother's magic that might wear off," she said. "The spell she cast to shut the portal between the worlds may fade away as well. And I asked Conner to check it out."

A roller coaster of emotions ran through Alex's body. Was it possible a bit of good news could come with this tragedy? After all, if the portal could be opened, she might see her brother again.

"How long until we know?" she asked.

"I'm still waiting to hear from him," Mother Goose said. "Your grandmother's magic may be fading, but as long as there's the smallest bit left in her, there's no way of telling which of her spells will stick. It could take weeks, months, or even years before we know about the portal."

Red suddenly stormed down the hallway but stopped when she saw Alex and Mother Goose talking behind the pillar.

"Red, what's wrong?" Mother Goose asked her. "Are you just sad about Charlie being pro-frog or has Clawdius swallowed one of the pixies again?"

"I was on the balcony feeling sorry for myself when I spotted something," Red said with bright eyes. "I may be hallucinating from all the misfortune, but I could swear I just saw *Conner* running toward the palace!"

Mother Goose jerked her head back to Alex. "Or perhaps the portal's open and we'll know in a matter of minutes," she said, finishing her previous thought. *"Let's get to the balcony!"*

The three of them ran down the hall and emerged onto the grand balcony of the Fairy Palace. They scanned the gardens below until they saw a familiar young man running toward them.

"Conner!" Alex screamed down at him. Seeing her brother running through the gardens put her in a state of complete shock, as if she were seeing a ghost. Was she really seeing him or had the misfortune of the day caused her to hallucinate, too?

"Alex!" Conner yelled up at her. He was wheezing and sweaty, like he had been running for hours. *"I have to tell you something—"* His voice faded away, his eyes rolled into the back of his head, and Conner fainted on the spot.

Without missing a beat, Alex ran off the balcony, through the palace, and into the gardens to her brother's side. She kneeled on the ground next to him and placed his head in her lap. Mother Goose and Red arrived right after her.

"Is he dead?" Red asked, hiding behind Mother Goose.

"Conner, can you hear me?" Alex said to her unconscious brother. *"Can you hear me?"*

Mother Goose removed her flask from her hat and splashed his face with the liquid inside. Conner stirred to life and quickly sat up.

"Ahh! That burns!" he said, wiping the liquid out of his eyes. *"What's wrong with you?"*

"Sorry, but that usually does the trick," Mother Goose said.

Alex instantly broke into tears upon seeing that he was all right. She had spent months convinced she would never see him in person again—and now here he was, sitting on the ground in front of her. She wrapped her arms around his ribs and cried into his chest.

"Conner! You're here! You're actually here!" she sobbed. *"I've never been so happy to see someone in my entire life!"*

He was panting but still found the strength to hug her back. "It's good to see you, too, Alex," he huffed.

Mother Goose interrupted their reunion. "Kid, if you're here I'm assuming that means—"

"The portal's open!" Conner said breathlessly. *"And the army—they're here, too!"*

Mother Goose suddenly went pale as a ghost. She tipped her head back and drank whatever was left in her flask. Alex didn't understand what they were talking about.

"Conner, what army?" she asked. "And what have you been running from?"

"It's a long story," Conner said. "But first, I have two friends with me from the Otherworld who helped me find the portal. They're in the woods somewhere behind me; they couldn't run anymore so I left them behind—we have to find them and send them home as soon as possible."

"I'm on it," Mother Goose said, and whistled for Lester. A couple moments later the giant goose swooped down from the towers of the palace and landed on the ground next to them. Lester was just as surprised to see Conner as the rest of them.

"Squaaaw?" Lester squawked.

"Hi, buddy, long time no see," Conner said, and rubbed Lester's long neck.

Mother Goose hopped aboard the gander and they took off into the night sky to find Conner's friends. Conner got to his feet; he was still having a hard time catching his breath.

Froggy appeared at the top of the palace's front steps and looked across the gardens. He was amazed by what he saw. "Conner?" he gasped. "Is that really you?"

"Yes, Conner's back!" Red called to him. "The *porthole* has been re-opened or something."

Froggy leaped across the gardens and gave his friend a giant hug. He didn't care how Conner had managed to return; he was just happy something good could come out of this day.

"Hi, Froggy," Conner said. "It's so good to see you all again!"

"You look flustered, old chap," Froggy said. "What's the matter?"

"Please tell us what's wrong," Alex pleaded. "You're starting to scare me."

Conner took a few extra-deep breaths to calm his racing heart and then told them what was happening. He started with his trip to Germany and the warning the Brothers Grimm had left in their last story. He explained how he had tried to get ahold of Alex but eventually contacted Mother Goose. He filled them in on how the Brothers Grimm had tricked the Grande Armée into an enchanted portal. Conner told them about his trip across Europe to find the portal and to see if it was open—with Bree and Emmerich's help. And then, to their absolute horror, he told them that the army of thousands of men had finally arrived in the Land of Stories after two hundred years.

They were all at a loss for words. None of them wanted to believe their horrible week was gravely worse than they'd thought.

"Oh my gosh," Alex said. "This is unbelievable."

"Tell me about it," Conner said. "It's been a rough couple days."

Hearing this confused Alex. "A couple days?" she clarified. "Wait, you say you tried contacting me during the ball?"

"Yeah," Conner said, and rolled his eyes remembering his attempts. "It must have been a pretty busy ball since you couldn't speak to me for three days."

"I'm sorry about that, I was occupied with a lot of things," Alex said, not wanting to get into them. "But the ball was almost a month ago. Conner, you've been in that portal for *weeks*!"

Just when Conner's heart had calmed down it started racing again. Emmerich's suspicion was right—the soldiers weren't the only ones who had lost all track of time while they were in the portal. No wonder they had been so discombobulated when they arrived.

"Oh no," Conner said. "That means Bree and Emmerich have been away from their families for a month."

"Once Mother Goose brings them back, we'll take them to my chambers and send them home using our old *Land of Stories* book," Alex decided. "It should be working again since the portal has been re-opened."

A question suddenly came to Conner's mind. "But Mother Goose never explained to me *why* the portal has been re-opened," he said. "Do any of you know why this is happening now?"

Alex looked gloomily to Froggy and Red and they went silent. Conner could tell they knew something he didn't—something important.

"What is it?" Conner said. "Has something else happened that I don't know about?"

Alex took a deep breath before breaking the news to him. "Conner, the portal is open for the same reason Froggy is a frog again," she said. "Grandma's magic is fading because ... Grandma's dying."

Conner felt like he had been punched in the stomach. He fell to his knees and his eyes darted around the gardens surrounding him. This couldn't be happening. He had risked so much in the Otherworld trying to save his loved ones only to find out he *couldn't* save his grandmother after all. It was like he was trapped in a nightmare that he couldn't wake up from.

"Grandma can't die," Conner said, and tears formed in his eyes. "She's a Fairy Godmother ... fairies don't die...."

Telling him was almost harder than hearing it herself. "Apparently they do," Alex said through her own tears.

"How long does she have?" he whimpered.

"There's no way of knowing," Alex said. "Emerelda said as long as there's still magic left inside her there's always a chance she could pull through, but it looks unlikely since all her spells are fading."

A sudden gust of air blew by them as Mother Goose and Lester returned. They had found Bree and Emmerich and safely brought them to the Fairy Kingdom. The two were beside themselves as they looked around at the majestic gardens and stunning palace—they had never seen such a beautiful place.

"Wow, you don't see this every day," Emmerich said.

"Now *this* is what I was expecting!" Bree said happily.

Mother Goose hopped down from Lester and helped them off the large bird. They joined the others around Conner.

"That's a big frog," Emmerich said when he saw Froggy standing there. He stepped behind Bree and hid from him.

"Hi, Alex!" Bree said sheepishly; she almost hadn't recognized her. "I don't know if you remember me but we were in Social Studies together in the seventh grade. You look great, nice palace!"

"Hi, Bree," Alex said, vaguely remembering her. "Thanks for helping my brother find the portal."

"No worries," Bree said. "My schedule was pretty open."

Conner tearfully looked up at Mother Goose. "You didn't tell me the portal was opening because Grandma was sick," he said.

Mother Goose let out a long sigh. "I'm sorry, C-Dog, I didn't think I should be the one to tell you," she said.

Conner looked away from her. "No, you never want to take responsibility for anything," he said coldly.

Mother Goose went quiet and shamefully looked to the ground; he was right. Bree and Emmerich fell silent, too; they weren't sure what kind of drama they had walked into.

"Would it make you feel better if you saw her?" Alex asked her brother. "She's resting in her room."

Conner shook his head; he wanted to take care of his guilt before he moved on to his grief. "No, I want to get Bree and Emmerich home first," he said. "I don't want to expose them to more than I already have."

Alex led them into the palace and up the stairs to her chambers. She retrieved their old *Land of Stories* book with its emerald cover and gold writing from its special spot on her bookshelf. She placed the large book in the center of her bed. She tapped it three times with the tip of her crystal wand but nothing happened. She tried it twice more but got the same result.

"I don't understand," she said. "If the portal is open, why isn't the book working?"

Mother Goose picked up the book and inspected every inch of it. Her eyes lit up as she came to a sudden realization. "Because the portal is still *halfway closed*," she explained. "Your grandmother's magic has faded enough for the portal to open on the Otherworld side, but not enough for it to open on this side. It's like a doorway that's only been unlocked on one side."

"So you're saying Bree and Emmerich are stuck here?" Conner asked. The situation just grew more terrible by the hour.

"For the time being," Mother Goose said.

"Wait a second," Alex said, and looked up to all the guests in her room. Her eyes widened and a smile slowly appeared. "This is good news."

"How could this be good news?" Conner asked.

"Because if the portal is closed on our side, it means there's still a little bit of magic left in Grandma," she said happily.

CHAPTER SIXTEEN

THE MASKED MAN OF PINOCCHIO PRISON

Pinocchio Prison had just been restored following the Enchantress's vicious attack when it was faced with yet another threat. Like a swift bolt of lightning, the Grande Armée charged toward the fortress in the early hours of the morning and unleashed the full power of its nineteenth-century artilleries.

The heavy, spiked front doors of the prison were blasted into smithereens by the army's cannons. Only two hundred enchanted wooden soldiers guarded the prisoners inside and they were no match for the thousands of Frenchmen invading the prison. The Grande Armée forced its way inside and the wooden soldiers were blown into pieces by volleys of rifle fire.

After the wooden soldiers were completely obliterated and the smoke began to clear, General Marquis stepped inside the prison and had a look at his newest conquest. Pinocchio Prison was thirty stories high and open on the inside like a cylinder; from the center of the ground floor the general could see floor after floor of various creatures locked in their cells above him.

The prisoners were a rowdy bunch, consisting of ogres, witches, trolls, goblins, elves, animals, men, and women alike. Some welcomed the French soldiers who had destroyed the wooden guards by banging their chains against the bars of their cells. Others cowered in fear, afraid they would be targeted next.

Nothing was known about these intruders. They spoke and dressed differently from anyone the prisoners had ever seen. Judging by their weapons, the prisoners could only assume these men were soldiers of very dark magic.

The remains of the wooden soldiers were piled in the center of the prison. Many pieces, such as the legs and hands, still twitched. The general poured lamp oil over the pile of the fallen and lit it on fire so the prisoners above could watch the guards who had held them captive burn.

General Marquis circled the flames and a hush fell over the prison.

"Good morning," the general said to the prisoners above. "I am General Marquis of the Grande Armée of the French

Empire. I am certain many of you have never heard of the empire and its army before, so I would like to change that now. Where we come from, we are known as one of the greatest military forces in history. We have dominated every territory in our path and have defeated every nation that stood in our way. And now we have come to your world to claim it as our own."

The prisoners grew uncomfortable in his presence. The general didn't need to say anything further to convince them that he was a cunning and powerful man; they could sense it.

"Where we come from, we have a phrase," the general continued. *"The enemy of my enemy is my friend,* we say. Today I would like to give each of you a chance to *make friends* with the Grande Armée. We offer you a chance to join our conquest and be cleared of your crimes. Help us fight against the people who imprisoned you—help us seize this world in the name of France and become part of *the French Empire!*"

The majority of the prisoners cheered at what he was offering.

"Or you can stay here and rot as intended," the general said. "The choice is yours."

The prison vibrated as the prisoners roared with delight. Anything was better than spending another day in the prison—even joining an army. Finally they could experience the freedom and revenge they had only dreamed about.

Colonel Baton, along with Capitaine De Lange and Lieutenant Rembert, recruited the criminals one cell at a time. The inmates were given the options of pledging their allegiance to the French Empire or remaining locked in their cell. And to the general's pleasure, almost all the prisoners waited with bated breath to pledge their allegiance and be freed from their cells.

Only one prisoner gave the commanders an answer they weren't expecting. His cell was at the very top of the prison and he supplied them with a message for the general that was too enticing to ignore.

"General Marquis," Colonel Baton said. "There is a prisoner who wishes to speak with you, sir."

The general was irritated Baton would even bring him such a request. "And what makes this man worthy of my time?"

"He wishes to help you," Baton said. "And he says without his help, you cannot conquer the fairy-tale world."

Hearing the prisoner's message infuriated the general. Who would dare be so bold as to give General Jacques Marquis an ultimatum? But the general was so determined in his quest for domination, he allowed his curiosity to outweigh his ego. He decided to speak with the prisoner and see if he had anything worthwhile to contribute.

Baton led the general to the very top of the prison and showed him to the cell of the daring man. A large plaque displayed on the wall beside his cell read:

THE MASKED MAN
SENTENCED TO LIFE IN
PINOCCHIO PRISON
FOR ATTEMPTED ROBBERY OF THE
FAIRY GODMOTHER

The general peered into the cell to see the prisoner for himself. The Masked Man was tall but very frail. He wore a tattered suit and his tie was torn in half. A gray sack over his head concealed his face; holes were cut around the eyes and mouth.

"You are the Masked Man, I take it," the general said.

"Hello, General," he said. "I thoroughly enjoyed your speech down there. Boy, you sure know how to make an entrance. Did they teach you that in your military training?"

The general glared at this ridiculous man. "I do not have time for games," he said. "Make sure this man stays in his cell."

The general stormed off but the Masked Man desperately reached for him through his bars and begged him to stay.

"No, wait, General!" he pleaded. "I apologize! I didn't mean to offend you—I'm only trying to help you! I have information that will lead you to a certain victory!"

On this the general turned on his heel and faced the prisoner. "And how can a man like *you* possibly help a man like *me*?"

"Because you're not from this world, and I am!" the Masked Man said. "I know my way around it and how it operates. You have a very impressive army, but that won't be enough to take over. You're going to need something bigger, something much more powerful if you're going to stand up to the fairies. And I know where you can get it!"

The general took a step closer to the man, his interest sparked although his face didn't show it. "You have two minutes of my time," he said. "Explain yourself."

The Masked Man rubbed his hands together and began. He was a very odd and animated man and used lots of hand gestures as he spoke, most of which didn't go along with what he said. It was like his hands and mouth were describing two different things.

"The first thing you should know about this world is its history," he said. "The past is divided into three ages: the Dragon Age, the Age of Magic, and the Golden Age, which we're living in now. Hundreds of years ago, during the Dragon Age, this world was a mess! It was filled with tyrant kings and evil sorcerers and obviously *dragons*, lots and lots of dragons—they were nearly unstoppable and reproduced like rabbits!"

"What value does this history lesson have to me?" the general asked. He was starting to feel like his time was being wasted and it angered him.

"I'm getting there, General," the Masked Man assured him. "Like I was saying, there were dragons everywhere destroying everything—then the fairies got together and put a stop to them. That's how they came to power and the world entered the Age of Magic. They formed the Happily Ever After Assembly and there was peace on earth and *yadda, yadda, yadda....* Now the Fairy Godmother, the head of the assembly, and her fairies have been in charge since the dragons went extinct and no one has been able to overthrow them *because...*"

He was hoping the general would play along and finish his sentence but Marquis didn't break his stoic expression.

"*Dragons!*" the Masked Man said with mystical hand gestures. "No one has been able to overthrow the fairies because you need a dragon—and I know where to get one!"

General Marquis had expected his left eye to start twitching from the moment the Masked Man started speaking—but it didn't. There must have been some truth to what he was saying.

"So where do we get this dragon?" the general asked.

The Masked Man dropped his hands and an equally serious expression grew on his own face. "Let me out of this cell first, and then I'll *show* you."

General Marquis was impressed by the Masked Man's quick and calculated scheme. But he figured there was much more to this man than met the eye. He wanted to know more about him before he unlocked the door of his cell.

"How long have you been in this prison?" he asked.

"A decade," the Masked Man said.

"And why were you sentenced to life for *attempted burglary*?" the general pressed. "Surely even in this world that's an awfully harsh punishment for such a little crime."

The Masked Man lowered his head shamefully, not for committing the crime, but for failing to accomplish it. "It was *what* I was trying to steal that cemented the sentence," he said, and then looked into the general's eyes. "You and I are very similar men, General. We know an opportunity when we see one; otherwise neither of us would be standing here now."

There was eagerness in the Masked Man's pale blue eyes that the general found alluring. Perhaps this man could be of service after all.

"One last question," the general said. "Why do you wear that bag over your head?"

The Masked Man smiled coyly. "The same reason you wear that uniform," he said. "To cover something I don't want the rest of the world to see."

Normally a statement like this would outrage the general, but this time it made him smile. The Masked Man was a strange man, but he was one of the few the general could identify with.

"Colonel Baton," General Marquis ordered. "Remove this man from his cell. As soon as we leave the prison we will organize a traveling party and he will guide us to a dragon."

CHAPTER SEVENTEEN

THE ONLY WITNESS

Alex and Conner sat by their grandma's bedside all night. Neither of them could think about sleep at a time like this. They were afraid if they left their grandmother it would discourage her from waking up. They hoped that if she felt their presence for long enough, it might activate that last bit of magic inside of her.

An emergency Fairy Council meeting was called early the next morning to discuss the matters at stake. Since the Fairy Godmother was absent, Alex asked Conner to accompany her. The twins always thought best when they were together and they hoped they could help the Fairy Council assess the current situation. Alex took a seat in her chair and Conner leaned against its arm. Although their grandmother's seat was empty Conner wouldn't sit in it; he didn't want to feel like it was *available*.

The meeting had already started and they could tell the conversation was heated when they walked in. All the fairies were standing at their respective podiums staring daggers at Mother Goose.

"Let me get this straight," Emerelda said. "An army from the Otherworld has been trapped in a portal for two hundred years and now they've arrived and plan on taking over our world?"

"That's it in a golden eggshell," Mother Goose said. She shifted in her seat as the others glared at her.

"And why didn't you bring this to anyone's attention?" Tangerina said, absolutely infuriated. Her bees flew aggressively around her beehive. They would have attacked Mother Goose had she given them the word.

"I didn't want to worry the Fairy Godmother," Mother Goose said. "I thought I could take care of the situation myself and was too embarrassed to involve anyone else. The Brothers Grimm and I trapped them inside the portal and then, luckily, by the time their two hundred years were up, the portal had been permanently closed by the Fairy Godmother. I thought I was in the clear for good until she became ill."

"So you didn't tell anyone about this because you didn't want anyone to *worry* or *think less of you*?" Skylene asked. "That seems like jumping into a lake to avoid the rain if you ask me."

Mother Goose looked at the twins, especially at Conner,

and then told the council something she had never told anyone before. "A very long time ago, before any of you were on this council, before the Fairy Godmother and I lost the color in our hair, gained the wrinkles on our faces, and when we were both much thinner—before Ezmia and Alex—*I* was the Fairy Godmother's first apprentice," she confessed.

All the fairies looked at one another, floored. Of all the things they involuntarily knew about her, Alex and Conner were impressed she had managed to keep *this* a secret.

"It only took me a few months to realize I wasn't cut out for the job," Mother Goose explained. "Sure, I was *capable,* but I just wasn't *willing.* I was too much of a free spirit to take on that kind of responsibility. So I passed on the highest honor a fairy could have and became the laughingstock of the kingdom. The Fairy Godmother said she understood but I knew she was disappointed and it killed me. I promised myself I would never let her down again, so in the 1800s when I was careless enough to get caught by those greedy French fries, I tried to handle the situation the best way I could so I would never have to see disappointment in those eyes again."

None of the fairies knew what to say so they just shook their heads. Conner felt sorry for Mother Goose. After growing up with a sister as precocious as Alex, he knew very well what it was like to constantly disappoint people. Now he understood why Mother Goose hadn't been honest with him about the portal.

"Oh come on," Conner said to the fairies. "Give Mother Goose a break! You're all standing there shaking your heads as if you could have handled the situation better. Well, no offense, but at least she came up with a solution. I can't remember the last time I saw any of *you* solve anything. Every time there's a crisis it's usually Alex and me who figure out what to do."

"How are we *not* supposed to take offense at that?" Xanthous asked the others.

"My point is, glass people shouldn't throw stones," Conner said.

"The phrase is 'People in glass houses shouldn't throw stones,'" Alex corrected him.

"Oh yeah," he said. "Well, you get my point."

Mother Goose smiled at Conner and mouthed, *"Thank you, C-Dog."* Emerelda massaged her forehead as she thought about what to do next.

"There's no use in blaming anyone for what has happened—we need to move forward to find a way to fix it," Emerelda said. "Alex, what do you think we should do?"

She couldn't believe Emerelda was asking her. "Me?" she asked.

"Yes, of course you," Emerelda said. "Unless your grandmother miraculously recovers, you'll be acting as Fairy Godmother."

This was a heavy thing for both the twins to digest. When people referred to Alex as the next Fairy Godmother, she always assumed they meant someday in the distant future, not now.

Alex bit her thumb and looked at the floor while she thought it over. "We need to see this army first, so we know for sure what we're up against," she said. "The more we know about them, the easier it will be to find a solution."

"The last thing I heard them talk about was an attack on Pinocchio Prison," Conner said.

"Why would they be attacking a prison?" Rosette asked.

"The general said they were *recruiting*," Conner said.

Suddenly the room grew very tense. All the fairies eyed one another and frantically whispered among themselves.

"I told you, that General Marquis is a smart man," Mother Goose said.

"Wait, am I missing something?" Conner asked. "What use can he get from recruiting a bunch of criminals?"

"There are some pretty powerful characters in that prison," Mother Goose said. "Trust me, I know most of them. And the prisoners in Pinocchio Prison are only the ones who have been *caught*. The Dwarf Forests and the backwoods of every kingdom are crawling with criminals, and when they see their friends have joined an army fighting against us, they'll all want to join, too. If the general succeeds in recruiting them, we won't just be fighting an old army, we could be fighting a *war*."

Conner gulped. He was sorry he had even asked. Coral was having difficulty processing the information, too. She politely raised a hand and asked a question.

"So are you saying that it's possible the Happily Ever After Assembly may be up against—?"

"Everyone else?" Mother Goose said. "All the creatures in the other kingdoms have been waiting for an opportunity to over-throw the fairies and the humans. This could be their chance."

Coral looked like she was about to cry. She cradled Fisher even tighter in her arms at the thought of what tomorrow might bring.

"The witches, the ogres, the trolls, the goblins, the elves—

they've wanted us gone since the Dragon Age!" Violetta added. "They've just lacked the organizational skills to challenge us."

"And those are skills the general can provide," Mother Goose said.

While Conner and the fairies started to panic, Alex was adamant about her original plan. The more information they had, the more options they would have. She raised her wand and a bright bolt of light shot out of it, silencing the room of frightened fairies.

"We're worrying about a lot of *ifs*," Alex said. "We don't know *if* the prisoners have joined the general yet. Those criminals are in prison because they couldn't follow the rules of a society; what makes us think they'll follow the general's commands?"

She made a very good point—there was no use in worrying unless they had evidence to worry about.

"My brother and I will go to the prison and see if they were successful in recruiting the prisoners," Alex said. "We'll need a way to get there without being seen—and a flying ship or a unicorn isn't going to go unnoticed by men from our world."

"You can take Lester," Mother Goose said. "That's why I rode him around the Otherworld—if anyone sees him in the sky they just assume he's a normal bird."

"Great," Alex said. "We'll leave as soon as possible and get a better idea of what we're up against."

None of the fairies argued. For the first time Alex's word was final and it was respected. With no time to lose, Alex and Conner immediately followed Mother Goose up to the grand balcony. She whistled for Lester and he swooped toward them from the towers above. She pulled his reins down and whispered their plan into his ear.

Froggy and Red were also on the balcony, showing the view of the gardens to Bree and Emmerich. Bree walked over to Conner as soon as she saw him.

"Hi, Bree," Conner said. "How did you sleep?"

"Oh, you know," she said. "As well as anyone could their first night in a new dimension, I suppose."

Conner smiled; he remembered that restless feeling all too well. As tired as she was, Bree still had an excited light in her eyes as she looked around the palace.

"I'm so sorry you guys are stuck here. We're going to get you home as soon as possible," Conner said.

"It's my own fault for wanting an adventure," Bree said. "I made you take me, remember?"

This made Conner feel a little better. He looked over at Emmerich as Froggy pointed out the different parts of the gardens below—he looked like he was having the time of his life. He reminded Conner of himself during his and Alex's first trip into the Land of Stories. He would have given anything to face *those* problems again.

"I've just talked Lester through it," Mother Goose said. "He knows to fly high enough so no one will see you."

"*Squaaa.*" Lester nodded.

"Then let's get going," Alex said.

They climbed aboard the giant goose and took off into the sky, heading in the direction of the prison. They flew over the gardens of the Fairy Kingdom, over the sparkling waters of Mermaid Bay, and saw Pinocchio Prison at the center of the penin-sula in southern Eastern Kingdom ahead of them.

"There it is!" Alex pointed out. "Lester, circle the prison until we can see something!"

Lester nodded, and looped the sky above the prison. There was destruction everywhere—Alex and Conner could see the entrance had been blown to bits from all the way in the sky. However, there was no trace of prisoners or soldiers anywhere.

"I think it's safe to get a little closer," Conner said.

Lester gradually descended, circling the prison as cautiously as possible. The closer they got, the more certain they were that no one was around. They looked for somewhere to land but the prison was covered in enormous spikes to prevent anyone from doing just that. Alex waved her wand at the prison's roof and the spikes turned into tall blades of grass for Lester to land on.

"Okay, let's see if there's anyone left inside," Alex said. She pointed her wand at the roof again and a small hatch appeared. They opened the hatch and dropped inside, landing on the pris-on's highest floor.

The air inside was very smoky. All the cells on the top floor were wide open and empty. They looked down the center of the prison and saw that all twenty-nine floors below them were exactly the same.

"I don't think anyone's here," Conner said. "It's like they had a fire drill and never came back."

The twins jumped when they suddenly heard a voice that wasn't either of their own. Sitting in a cell on the top floor, by herself, was a woman.

"Pssst!" she said. *"Over here!"*

Alex and Conner approached the woman with caution. Whoever she was, she was still a prisoner and couldn't be trusted. The woman was only a few years older than Red but wasn't aging nearly as gracefully. Her hair was thin and messy and she had bags under her enormous eyes. She wore a plain black dress and no shoes.

"Down here!" the woman called up to them from where she was sitting on the floor. Her voice sounded alarmed but she seemed perfectly comfortable. "You've got to warn someone! An army raided the prison earlier today and took the prisoners with them! They're trying to take over the world!"

Alex and Conner leaned down to speak with her. She stuck her head through the bars as far as it would go.

"We know about the army and are trying to stop them," Alex said. "We've come here to find out more."

"Were the prisoners taken captive or did they join them?" Conner asked.

"They *joined* them," the woman said. "The soldiers opened every cell and gave each prisoner the option of staying or joining their army. And as you can see, it was an almost unanimous decision."

"Why didn't you leave with them?" Alex asked.

The woman looked at them like they were insane. "I'm not going out there," she said and shook her head. "There's nothing for me out there. I mean, perhaps at one point there was, but not anymore. I belong right here in my cell."

"You've been in here for a long time, haven't you?" Conner asked.

Alex thought there was something curious about her. She saw there was a plaque on the wall next to the woman's cell and Alex stood to read it.

THE LADY GRETEL SENTENCED TO LIFE IN PINOCCHIO PRISON FOR THE MURDER OF SIR HANSEL

Alex gestured for Conner to look at the plaque, too. *"Conner, it's Gretel from 'Hansel and Gretel'!"* she whispered to him. *"She killed her brother!"*

"What?" he whispered back.

"It's all right, you don't have to whisper," Gretel said. "I know what that plaque says. I know who I am. I know what I did."

Alex suddenly had so many questions. "Why did you kill your brother?"

Gretel dreamily stared off into the distance. "Because it was the only way I could be *free*."

"Free from what?" Alex asked.

"From 'Hansel and Gretel,'" Gretel said.

"The story?" Conner asked.

"No, *the label*," Gretel said. Their inquiring looks begged her to explain more. "After my brother and I survived the gingerbread house, all I wanted was to have a normal life—but that's not what Hansel wanted; he wanted us to be *heroes*. He told everyone we knew about what happened to us in the woods and then those people told everyone they knew and soon word spread and we became household names around the kingdoms. We were treated like royalty; parades were thrown for us, we were honored with medals everywhere we went, they even named a holiday after us."

"That sounds pretty nice," Conner said.

Gretel's eyes shot up at him. "No, it was *terrible*," she said. "Because no one cared about *me*, they just cared about 'Hansel and Gretel.' I just wanted to be Gretel, *just Gretel*, but no matter what I did no one would let me be just Gretel. It was like my brother had become an invisible ball and chain I was forced to carry around for the rest of my life."

"But he was your brother," Alex said. "Didn't you love him?"

Gretel grunted and stuck out her tongue like she had tasted something foul. "No, I couldn't stand him!" she said. "Hansel may have seemed like a nice young man but all he cared about was himself and the attention he got! He used to drag me around with him just so he could get more admiration! Hansel also took all the credit for what happened in the gingerbread house—even though *I* was the one who tricked the witch and pushed her into the fireplace! He wouldn't even be alive without me! Had I known then what I know now, I would have let the witch eat him!"

"So you killed him instead?"

Gretel nodded. "It was an accident. One day we were walking through the trees and he started mentioning all the places he had planned for us to go, all the people we would meet, and all the awards we were going to receive in the upcoming days. Well, I got so mad I pushed him—but I didn't see there was a cliff behind him!"

"Did you tell anyone that it was an accident?" Alex asked.

"I was planning to," Gretel said. "But then I realized this cell allowed me to be something that the rest of the world didn't— *just Gretel.* So I pleaded guilty and have been here ever since. And so, today when the soldiers asked me if I wanted to join their army or stay in this cell I didn't have to think twice."

Gretel sighed at the thought of all the peace her cell brought her. Conner looked at Alex and circled his temple with his finger. *"She's nuts!"* he mouthed.

But Gretel wasn't finished with her story. "The worst thing one person can do to another—besides eat them, of course—is to reduce their identity to being only *half* of something. When someone is treated as *half of* or *less than half of* one identity, they're not being treated like a human at all. Everyone should have the right to individuality."

Conner slowly stood up and walked away from the cell. "Well, thanks, Lady Gretel!" he said. "We should get going now. We need to figure out where this army went."

"Wait!" Gretel said. "I can tell you! The army and the soldiers went back to their camp, but the general and his men were headed somewhere else!"

"Where?" Alex asked.

"I don't know where, just somewhere else," Gretel said. "The prisoner across from me—they call him the Masked Man because of the sack he wears over his head—he was talking to the general before they let him out. He convinced the general that he needed a dragon to get rid of the fairies and take over the world! He said it was the only way the general would win!"

Alex and Conner exchanged the same confused look. "A dragon?" Alex asked. "But they've been extinct for hundreds of years. Our grandmother and her friends were the ones who fought them off during the Dragon Age."

"Apparently the Masked Man knows where to find one," Gretel said. "And I wouldn't be surprised if he did. He's a very unusual man. He's been in that cell for almost a decade now. He likes to talk to himself at night—sometimes I swear I heard someone else in there with him, but that would be impossible."

Conner walked to the cell of the Masked Man and peeked inside. "Hey, Alex, this guy has a lot of stuff in here."

Alex joined him at the cell. The door was still open and they walked inside together. Just being in it gave them the creeps. The walls were covered in bizarre carved illustrations of winged creatures, pirate ships, and animals with big ears and feet. There was a pile of coal and he had carved the pieces into the shapes of hooks, hearts, and swords.

An oval mirror in a silver frame hung on the wall.

"What does a Masked Man need with a mirror?" Conner asked.

"I have no idea," Alex said. "But we should get out of here. We need to fly by their camp and see what the army is up to."

They left the cell and went back to the hatch in the ceiling. Alex pointed her wand at the floor and the stones rose to form a small staircase for them to climb through the hatch.

"Good-bye!" Gretel called out. "I hope you can stop them!"

"Us too!" Conner said before climbing onto the roof.

"Good-bye, *just Gretel*," Alex said. "Thank you for your help."

By the time the twins climbed to the roof, Lester had eaten all the long blades of grass. They hopped aboard the giant goose and took off into the sky again.

"The general told half of his men to set up camp somewhere in the southeast where the portal spit us out," Conner told his sister. "I bet they've regrouped by now."

Alex took Lester's reins and steered him into the sky high above the south of the Eastern Kingdom. Alex and Conner searched the ground as they passed over it, not sure what they were looking for. However, as soon as the camp came into view they knew exactly what it was.

Hundreds of trees had been cut down to make way for the expansive camp the soldiers had built. There were dozens and dozens of large beige tents set up and the timbered trees had been used to build a wall around the camp.

There were thousands of soldiers setting up and marching around the camp and the soldiers weren't alone. A thousand or so recruits from Pinocchio Prison were scattered around the camp as well. Giant ogres did the heavy lifting as the soldiers built the camp, witches wove broomsticks out of tree branches, and soldiers trained goblins how to fire cannons and trolls how to shoot rifles.

To Alex and Conner's horror, their target practice was a line of wooden fairy dummies.

"Mother Goose was right," Conner said. "They're preparing for *war*."

CHAPTER EIGHTEEN

SENDING THE SWANS

Mother Goose stood by the railing of the grand balcony and watched the skies as she waited for Lester and the twins to return. Emmerich and Bree were standing a little ways from her, having the most fascinating conversation with Froggy and Red.

"So there are six kingdoms, two territories, and one empire?" Emmerich asked, wrapping his head around the lesson Froggy was teaching them on the fairy-tale world.

"Precisely!" Froggy said. "And the leaders of the six kingdoms, including the Fairy Council, make up the Happily Ever After Assembly."

Red cleared her throat. "There *used* to be six kingdoms, but now there are *five* kingdoms and one republic."

Bree almost went cross-eyed from all the information. "So Red used to be the queen of her own kingdom, which used to be part of the Northern Kingdom until the C.R.A.B. Revolution, was it?" she asked.

"The C.R.A.W.L. Revolution," Red corrected her. "It stood for Citizen Riots Against Wolf Liberty. The Evil Queen was in power in the Northern Kingdom at the time and she did nothing to stop the wolves terrorizing the farmers' villages. So we revolted and I got my own kingdom."

"Which you just lost in the election for queen," Bree pieced together. "But now the kingdom is a republic because the new queen changed the government. Can she do that?"

"Evidently," Red said, and pursed her lips at the thought of it.

"In our country we have a Congress and a House of Representatives to keep the president from doing things like that, I guess," Bree said.

"Yes, well, *I thought I did, too*," Red said with flared nostrils. "I hand selected representatives so I couldn't be blamed for my biased decision making and the whole kingdom *still* turned on me. I don't know where I went wrong."

"But who is the queen of your country now?" Emmerich asked.

"*Little Bo Bimbo*," Red replied without a hint of sarcasm. "She's the ugliest, most horrendous creature to ever live in the Red Riding Hood Kingdom and she scared all the villagers into voting for her."

"Now *that* sounds like politics in our world," Bree said.

"I've never heard of Little Bo Bimbo," Emmerich said, and shivered at the thought of her.

"Then you're a very lucky man," Red said. A small smile appeared on her face; it was very therapeutic for her to make things up about Little Bo Peep. She only wished she had done it *during* the election.

"They're back!" Mother Goose said, pointing to the sky.

A shadow passed over the balcony and they looked to the sky and saw Alex and Conner descending on Lester's back. They landed on the balcony and their friends eagerly approached them.

"Well, what did you find?" Mother Goose asked.

"The army recruited the prisoners!" Conner said as he hopped down from the giant goose. "The soldiers were training them for combat when we flew above their camp—there are thousands of them!"

Mother Goose placed a hand over her heart. "Oh dear," she said. "What should we do next?"

"I'm thinking," Alex said as she climbed down from Lester. "In the meantime, Mother Goose, please see that all the Fairy Council members gather in the hall as quickly as possible. Conner, go with her and tell the other fairies about what we've seen. The first thing I need to do is get the kings and queens to the Fairy Palace as quickly as possible so they can join in the conversation. This isn't a Fairy Council matter; it's an issue the entire Happily Ever After Assembly needs to discuss."

Mother Goose and Conner nodded and headed inside the palace. Alex raised her wand in the air and then cracked it like a whip six times. A series of shimmering lights flashed around the balcony and six enormous swans the size of Lester magically appeared in front of her. Alex spun the tip of her wand above the palm of her hand and a stack of papers appeared. She rolled the papers and put one in each swan's mouth.

"What are those?" Froggy asked.

"Invitations," Alex said, and handed Froggy an extra copy to read.

To the members of the Royal Families,

An emergency has occurred and all members of the Happily Ever After Assembly and their families must report to the Fairy Palace immediately. We will provide details of the matter upon your arrival.

Thank you,
Alex Bailey, Acting Fairy Godmother

"I need you to take these to the kings and queens of the Corner Kingdom, the Charming Kingdom, the Northern Kingdom, the Eastern Kingdom, and the Bo Peep Republic as quickly as possible and bring the rulers back," Alex instructed the first five swans, then turned to the sixth. "As for you, I have other acquaintances I'd like you to deliver this invitation to."

She whispered further instructions into the swan's ear so the others couldn't hear.

"If they don't cooperate, you have my permission to *persuade* them however you can," she said. "Bring them back by the ankles if you must—these invitations are not optional. Now go."

All six swans bowed and then launched into the air one at a

time. They flew off in opposite directions at speeds birds had never flown before.

"Now what?" Red asked. "Do you think the kings and queens will take your message seriously?"

"We'll have to wait and see," Alex said, hoping with all her heart they would.

After a few hours of waiting, Red and Froggy took Bree and Emmerich inside to give Alex some time to think alone. She paced back and forth so many times she almost left a mark on the floor. When she was studying wars in History in school, Alex had never imagined that one day she would be in one, let alone leading it. Was she equipped to lead the Happily Ever After Assembly into a war against a general of an empire?

She prayed her strengths of common sense and logic would be enough to make up for her lack of battle strategy. She kept thinking about the great war heroes from her world, like Franklin Roosevelt and Winston Churchill. What would they have done if they were in her shoes? What sort of plan would they have created? What would her grandmother have done if she wasn't ill?

Alex heard a commotion from above and looked up to the evening sky. One by one the swans came into view as they returned to the palace, bringing the kings and queens from opposite ends of the Land of Stories with them.

Alex sighed with relief as they all glided to her—she was so glad to see none of them had rejected her invitation.

Five swans landed on the balcony one after the other. The first swan carried King Chance, Queen Cinderella, and their two-year-old daughter, Princess Hope, from the Charming

Kingdom. The second swan carried Queen Sleeping Beauty and King Chase from the Eastern Kingdom. The third swan carried Queen Snow White and King Chandler from the Northern Kingdom. The fourth swan carried Queen Rapunzel and her husband, Sir William, from the Corner Kingdom. And the fifth swan carried Queen Little Bo Peep.

All the rulers appeared befuddled by their unexpected journey. Queen Little Bo Peep looked a tad intimidated at being among the legendary rulers on the balcony. It was the first time she had been called to participate in the Happily Ever After Assembly.

"Hello, Your Majesties," Alex said. "Thank you all so much for coming."

"Alex, I'm sure we'd all like to know: What is the meaning of this?" Cinderella asked. "And what happened to the Fairy Godmother? Why didn't she send for us herself?"

"Because she's fallen ill," Alex informed them. The royals took the news exactly as the twins had—they didn't even know it was possible for the Fairy Godmother to fall ill. "It's only one of many problems we face, I'm afraid, so if you please, quickly follow me into the hall so you can join our discussion."

She led the parade of monarchs into the Fairy Palace and down the stairs into the hall where Conner, Mother Goose, and the other fairies waited. They were all very surprised to see Conner there, especially Cinderella, who had witnessed the Fairy Godmother close the portal to the Otherworld right in her own kingdom. It didn't take them long to understand something was seriously wrong.

Froggy, Red, Bree, and Emmerich came down the stairs

to see what all the fuss was about. Although Bree and Emmerich had never met any of the kings and queens in person, it
didn't take them long to realize who they were looking at; Snow
White's pale skin and Rapunzel's long flowing hair were dead
giveaways. They stopped in their tracks and sat at the top of the
stairs, admiring all the beautiful royals.

Red's first instinct was to join them, but seeing Little Bo in
the group of her former peers was a painful reminder that she
didn't belong anymore. She sat next to Bree and Emmerich on
the stairs and glared at her nemesis from afar.

Froggy rushed down the stairs to say hello to his Charming
brothers.

"Charlie, what's happened to you?" Chandler asked.

"Why are you a frog again?" Chance asked, just as curious.

"It's a long story," Froggy told them. "We'll explain everything, I promise."

Alex decided to explain before any more confusion filled
the room. "The Fairy Godmother is very sick and her magic
is fading," she told everyone. "Her spell on Prince Charlie has
worn off and the portal into the Otherworld has been partially
re-opened. An army from our world has crossed over and plans
to dominate this world, but I'll let Conner tell you about the
army since he's seen them up close."

Alex gestured for her brother to take the floor but Mother
Goose suddenly rose from her seat.

"No, I'll do it," she said. "It's my fault they're even here,
after all."

Alex and Conner looked at each other—they were impressed

that she was willing to take responsibility in front of the entire Happily Ever After Assembly.

Mother Goose informed the kings and queens about the Grande Armée and how it was her fault that they had traveled through the portal into the fairy-tale world. She told them how they had raided Pinocchio Prison and recruited its criminals. And last, Mother Goose had the unfortunate task of telling the royals they could be at war very soon.

Alex sat in her chair as the monarchs were informed. She continued thinking of the horrors the future might bring and how they could best be prepared for them.

"So this army of five thousand men now has hundreds of additional soldiers—criminals that *we* put behind bars?" Snow White asked with a hand over her mouth.

"Correct," Mother Goose said. "And we have a suspicion that it will inspire all the criminals on the loose in the Dwarf Forests and throughout the other kingdoms to join the Armée."

"And how many criminals total would we say are currently unaccounted for within our kingdoms?" Sleeping Beauty asked.

"We've estimated around three thousand or so," Emerelda told the room.

Rapunzel quickly did the math in her head. "Then that gives the Grande Armée a total of close to nine thousand," she said. "That's more than *all our armies* combined."

"How many soldiers are in your armies?" Conner asked.

"The Northern Kingdom has an army of two thousand men," Chandler said.

"The Charming Kingdom has one thousand," Chance said.

"Many of the Eastern Kingdom's men perished trying to fight off the Enchantress's curses," Chase said. "We only have around one thousand five hundred soldiers left."

"The Corner Kingdom's army is very small as well, consisting of only five hundred men," Sir William said.

Little Bo Peep was the only one who hadn't responded. "I don't know the exact number, but I would say somewhere around—"

"Eight hundred and twenty-eight men!" Red called down from the top of the stairs.

Little Bo shot her a nasty look. "Yes, thank you, *former Queen* Red Riding Hood," she said.

The twins were shocked by the low numbers.

"Unlike your world, we've never had a real reason until now for large armies," Mother Goose said.

Conner added these numbers in his head. "So that means with all your armies together the Happily Ever After Assembly has roughly five and a half thousand men. That's *five and a half* versus a potential *nine thousand*—the Armée could grow up to twice the size of our forces!"

"And that's still not including the armies of the Elf Empire and the Troblin Territory," Mother Goose reminded them. "If General Marquis manages to convince them the way he convinced the prisoners, then it's over. We'll never win this war."

"Then we'll have to get to them first." Alex joined the discussion for the first time. "We need to do whatever it takes to make sure the elves and the troblins are on our side. They may not have a great relationship with the Happily Ever After Assembly but I doubt they want to see the world taken over by the Armée any more than we do. Does anyone know how large the elf and troblin armies are?"

"The trolls and goblins have an army of seven hundred, I believe," Tangerina said. "And the elves have a thousand soldiers."

"Then that's good news for us," Alex said. "After we convince the troblins and the elves to join us, that will raise our army to much better odds of survival. Plus, we have the fairies on our side; we can't forget to include them."

All the fairies behind the podiums objected at once but Xanthous was the loudest. "Fairies can't go into battle; it's against the Happily Ever After Assembly code of magic!" he protested.

"Screw the code!" Conner yelled, and the room went silent. "The code is there to ensure peace and prosperity for the fairytale world and soon there may not be a fairy-tale world left! If we want to win this war we will have to fight fire with fire, and Xanthous, no one has more fire than you—and no one can stir the waves better than Skylene—and no one can sting like Tangerina. We're going to have to use every resource possible."

The fairies were morally opposed to the idea with every fiber of their beings, but Conner was right. As long as they were using their magic for the greater good, they had no choice. Alex folded her hands together and looked at the floor as she thought more about what needed to be done.

"All right, I think I have a plan. Everyone listen closely," she said, and gained the room's undivided attention. "We don't know where or how the Grande Armée will strike first—we have to assume it could be anywhere. I want all the kings and queens to write to their commanding officers at once and tell them to split their armies in half. Half of each army will stay in its respective kingdom so nothing is left unguarded. The *other* halves will go into hiding—I don't care where they go as long as they stay out of sight—they are not to come out of hiding until they see my signal."

"But why split up the armies?" Xanthous asked.

"That way no kingdom is left unguarded, in case it's attacked," Alex explained. "And if a kingdom is attacked, its entire army won't be lost."

Alex turned to face the fairies. "I want you to be with the soldiers guarding the kingdoms," she said. "Rosette will go to the Corner Kingdom, Skylene to the Northern, Xanthous to the Charming, Tangerina to the Eastern, and Violetta and Coral to the Bo Peep Republic. Mother Goose and Emerelda will stay in the Fairy Kingdom and look after the Fairy Godmother."

Alex turned back to address the entire room for the conclusion of her plan. "My brother and I will personally go to the troblins and elves and plead with them to join our side. As soon as we recruit the elves and troblins, I'll signal all the remaining armies, the ones at home and the ones in hiding, and lead them in a strike against the Grande Armée."

Everyone carefully went over this plan in their heads. It may not have been a perfect strategy, but it was the only strategy they had.

"What's going to happen to us?" Cinderella asked. "Do we go home to our kingdoms or do we stay at the Fairy Palace?"

"Neither," Conner said, and stood by his sister. "If the Armée finds you, they'll kill you—they have a history of killing royal families and aristocrats—to them, death is the only surrender. We have to keep you moving at all times so they can never find you. I would suggest we put you all on a flying ship like the *Granny* but if the Armée saw that in the sky they would freak out and definitely shoot you down."

"Then what can we place them on that's both secretive and continuously moving?" Alex asked.

Her words rang a bell. Conner knew he had heard of something recently that met this description; he just had to think. He thought back to the very beginning of this whole ordeal, when he was standing in the cemetery listening to the Brothers Grimm stories, and the answer came to him. The Brothers Grimm hadn't just provided a warning, they had also provided a plan.

"I've got it!" Conner said. "We'll put them on *an enchanted path* just like in the story 'The Secret Castle'! The path could weave through the kingdoms like a snake, never traveling in the same direction twice and never leaving a trail behind it!"

"That's brilliant!" Alex said. "And the only people who will be able to find it are the people who know about it! As long as the Armée never knows about the path, they'll never find it."

Conner stepped closer to Alex and whispered something in her ear so only she could hear. *"Do you think you can create the path, Alex?"* He didn't want to fill the room with hope if Alex wasn't capable of the enchantment.

Alex took a deep breath. "Yes," she said. "I know I can." She looked up to the top of the stairs where the others sat. "Red, we can use the carriages you arrived in. They were very plain and didn't bear any symbols of royalty."

Red grunted. "Don't remind me."

Alex eyed the official robes, crowns, and jewels all the kings and queens wore. "We should also strip you down so you look less official," she said. "You can't wear any jewelry or be followed by guards or do anything that would make you appear royal."

"But surely we can't go on this path unprotected," Snow White said.

"We'll need *some* form of protection," Sleeping Beauty said. "Even if the path is as disguised as we are."

Alex looked to the sky to think about this. A big smile grew on her face for the first time all day. "I know the perfect people," Alex said. They were flying right above her. Everyone looked to the sky to see what Alex was smiling about.

The sixth swan was finally returning to the Fairy Palace; it landed in the hall. All the monarchs and fairies were stunned to see Jack and Goldilocks climb off the swan's back. Alex had secretly sent one of the swans to find her fugitive friends.

"You invited *them?*" Red yelled from the top of the stairs.

"Yes, I figured it wouldn't hurt having a few friends around," Alex said. "But now we have the perfect assignment for them."

They waved uncomfortably at the royals in the hall. Less than a year ago the kings and queens had agreed to clear them of all their crimes as a way of thanking them for helping to defeat the Enchantress—and since then, despite the gesture, Jack and Goldilocks had already committed multiple crimes in all their kingdoms.

"Hello, everyone," Jack said. "What's the occasion?"

"We got your letter, Alex," Goldilocks said. "We figured it had been sent to us by mistake, but the swan was *very* persuasive." She and Jack held up their arms and showed the bite marks they had endured trying to avoid the trip.

Alex and Conner quickly told them about the Grande Armée

and their plans to conquer the fairy-tale world. Jack and Goldilocks knew much more than they expected—word of the Grande Armée was spreading through the kingdoms.

"Many of the criminals we know have already joined them," Jack said. "The Armée is growing by the minute."

"Jack, Goldilocks, I need a big favor," Alex said. "We're sending the kings and queens away so the Armée can never find them. I'm going to ask that you go with them and protect them just as you protected my brother and me during our quest to stop the Enchantress."

Jack and Goldilocks looked at each other—it was a big favor. The kings and queens began mumbling their objections to one another. How were a couple of crooks supposed to protect them?

Red whistled from the top of the stairs to get the room's attention. "I know what you're thinking because there isn't a negative thought I haven't had myself about these two," Red declared. "But I can assure you there is no one in the world Goldilocks can't take on with her sword, or that Jack can't face with an axe at his side. We wouldn't have survived our trip around the kingdoms if they hadn't been there. You'll be well protected under their care."

Jack, Goldilocks, and the twins did a double take. They couldn't believe Red was defending them to all these people.

"Thank you, Red," Goldilocks said. "I would have never expected praise from you."

"Oh, I forgot to tell you, Goldie," Red said excitedly. "I have a new nemesis now! So you're off the hook!"

Red gave Goldilocks a thumbs-up. Little Bo rolled her eyes and crossed her arms.

"Very well," Cinderella said, and held Princess Hope a little tighter than before. "If you trust them, I suppose they're the best people for the job."

"Then it's decided," Emerelda declared. "Now we mustn't waste another minute. Let's get the kings and queens to safety."

The fairies magically transformed the royals' regal wardrobes into simple, common clothing. They were provided with parchment and scrolls and wrote to their commanding officers to inform them to split the armies as Alex had instructed. All the fairies, except Emerelda and Mother Goose, took the letters and disappeared into thin air, traveling to the kingdoms they had been assigned.

As they did this, Conner climbed to the top of the stairs to speak with Bree and Emmerich. "I want you guys to go with the kings and queens on the secret path," he said. "I would never forgive myself if anything happened to you. You'll be safe if you're with Jack and Goldilocks, I promise."

Bree and Emmerich both nodded, wide-eyed. The events of the past twenty-four hours had caused their heads to spin so fast they couldn't think straight. They would have agreed to anything.

"Certainly," Emmerich said.

"Sounds good," Bree said.

Conner smiled and then faced Red. "I want you and Froggy to go as well so Bree and Emmerich have someone they know with them," he said. "Besides, I know Alex and I will feel better knowing *all* our friends are safe."

"What?" Red asked sharply. "You want me stuck in a traveling party with *that Peep woman*?"

"I'm really sorry you lost your throne, Red," Conner said. "But if the Armée finds you, they won't care that you *used* to be queen. I know you love necklaces, but I don't think wearing a guillotine will be a good look for you."

"Fine," Red agreed. "But if we get captured I'm volunteering Little Bo for target practice."

Once all the monarchs had been disguised, everyone left the hall, following Alex outside to the front steps of the Fairy Palace. Three carriages were lined up in front of the Fairy Palace with two horses each.

King Chance, Queen Cinderella, and Princess Hope climbed into the first carriage with Queen Sleeping Beauty and King Chase. Queen Snow White and King Chandler joined Queen Rapunzel and Sir William in the second carriage. Froggy, Red, Emmerich, and Bree boarded the third carriage, and to Red's dismay, were joined by Queen Little Bo Peep.

"Will someone please put me *back* inside the wolf's stomach?" Red agonized.

"This is going to be a *long* trip." Little Bo sighed and shook her head.

Bree stepped outside the carriage before the door was shut and gave Conner a massive hug. "Please stay safe," she said.

The gesture made Conner turn bright pink. "Don't worry about me," he said. "I'm used to being in danger."

Conner shut the carriage door behind her with a tap for good luck. Cinderella poked her head out of the first carriage to get Conner's attention.

"I was just wondering if you've heard from my stepmother and stepsisters," she asked. "Are they all right in the Otherworld?"

"Oh yeah," Conner said. "The last time I talked to them Lady Iris and Rosemary had opened a diner and Petunia was working at an animal hospital. They seemed very happy."

Hearing this made Cinderella very happy, too. Conner was glad he could provide her with a bit of joy before she departed on the secret path.

Jack and Goldilocks mounted the horses attached to the first carriage so they could keep watch as they traveled. Emerelda bewitched the carriages to drive themselves while Alex stood in front of the first carriage, ready to create her biggest enchantment yet.

"Okay," Alex whispered to herself. *"Here I go."*

Alex visualized the path as clearly as she could. She imagined it snaking through the kingdoms, never giving any indication of where it was headed and leaving no trace of where it had been. She touched the ground with the tip of her wand and a shimmering golden path appeared on the ground ahead of her. It was less than a quarter mile long and disappeared at both ends.

Jack and Goldilocks held the reins of the horses and the parade of carriages took off down the secret path. Alex joined Emerelda, Mother Goose, and her brother on the front steps and they waved the travelers off until the golden path and the carriages snaked out of sight.

Emerelda placed a hand on Alex's shoulder. "Your grandmother would be very proud of you."

"I know," Alex said sadly. She just wished she could have been there to see it.

Emerelda, Mother Goose, and Conner went back into the

Fairy Palace. Alex was just about to turn and go with them when she saw someone she had completely forgotten about for the past few hours.

"*Rook!*" Alex said. He was peeking out from behind one of Rosette's magically enlarged roses.

"Alex, are you coming inside?" Conner asked.

"Yes, I'll be there in a minute," she said, and ran into the gardens to see Rook. She pulled him behind a giant patch of tulips and threw her arms around his neck.

"Sorry to intrude again, I just haven't seen you in a while and was worried. What were all those carriages for—" Rook said, but his cheerful expression quickly faded once he saw the seriousness in her eyes. "Alex, what's wrong?"

"Everything," she said, and fought back tears. She had held it together very well today, but Rook was the only person she didn't feel like she had to be brave in front of. "My grandmother is sick and there's an army that's invaded and trying to take over the world!"

"*What?*" Rook said. "What do you mean there's an army—"

Alex grabbed his shirt and pulled him closer to look directly in his eyes. "You and your dad have to get as far away from here as possible," she said. "You have to leave before you get hurt!"

"I hope this isn't your way of letting me down gently," Rook said, trying to make her laugh.

"I'm serious, Rook," Alex said. "Please, you have to go! I couldn't live with myself if anything happened to you! Promise me you'll get out of here!"

"All right, all right. I promise to get my dad and we'll leave."

Alex sighed and looked to the ground. "Good," she said. "I have to get back to the palace now; there are so many things we still need to plan."

Rook looked at her with the saddest eyes Alex had ever seen. "But when will I see you again?"

"I don't know. I'll find you once all of this is over and done with. Now please go so I don't worry about you on top of it all."

Rook nodded. He kissed her on the cheek and then headed home.

Sitting behind the tulips, it was the first time Alex had been out of sight all day. She kneeled on the ground, closed her eyes, and just breathed. She had put on a good show for the fairies and the royals and her brother, but after seeing Rook, all the emotion built up inside her young body suddenly surged through her.

"Just breathe, Alex, just breathe," she said to herself. "You can handle this, you can handle this."

She stayed behind the tulips until she felt the fear fade from her eyes and her brave face returned.

CHAPTER NINETEEN

AN ICY TRADE

The soldiers shivered in the freezing winds. The elements had grown too harsh for their horses so they were left behind and the soldiers were forced to trek through the thick snow on foot. For hours and hours they climbed higher and higher into the steep mountains of the north without a disclosed destination or an anticipated time of arrival.

"How much farther?" General Marquis demanded.

"Once we see the lights, we'll know we've arrived," the Masked Man called to the men behind him.

A unit that started out as twenty Grande Armée soldiers had

been reduced to less than a dozen. The soldiers were dropping like flies as the Masked Man led them through the cold. Every few hundred yards a soldier would faint from the elements and disappear into the snow. They were ordered to keep moving and the fallen were left behind.

General Marquis and Colonel Baton wore thick coats over their uniforms as they traveled, and although the withering soldiers behind them were given very little to shield themselves from the cold with, they were scolded for slowing the expedition down. The Masked Man had only been given a raggedy old blanket to stay warm but he still moved more agilely than the rest of them. He had braved these mountains many times before.

"You lot certainly don't handle the cold very well." The Masked Man chuckled.

"I am starting to lose my patience," the general threatened.

"Don't fret, General, we're almost there," the Masked Man assured him.

Soon the northern lights he had described came into view. They illuminated the dark sky in bright shades of green and circled above the glaciers ahead. By the time they reached the glaciers, the unit had been reduced to six men including the general and Colonel Baton. The Masked Man led the remaining men through an opening between two glaciers and into an enormous icy maze. They zigzagged between the glaciers and eventually stepped into a wide crater.

"Gentlemen, welcome to the Snow Queen's lair," the Masked Man announced.

The soldiers gazed around at the crater in bewilderment.

Several pillars of ice surrounded the crater, a frozen lake acted as its floor, and a frozen waterfall spilled inside from the mountains above and flowed around a giant icy throne. The Snow Queen sat on the throne with her faithful polar bears, one sitting on either side of her. She wore a large white fur coat and a snowflake crown. A cloth was wrapped over her empty eye sockets. The Snow Queen and the polar bears were eerily quiet, as if they had been waiting for the soldiers to arrive.

"The Masked Man has returned again," the Snow Queen said in her raspy crackling voice. "We've been expecting you."

"Hello, Your Majesty," the Masked Man said, and gave a shallow bow. "It's been a very long time but you look as frigid as ever."

"Compliments will get you nowhere," the Snow Queen said. "If it's a trade you've come to make, you know what I want in return."

"No, I understand," the Masked Man said. "The last time I was here, you made it perfectly clear what you wanted in exchange for the *item of interest*, and with great pleasure I have returned with the means of finally making that trade."

The general suddenly grew very tense. "You never said anything about a trade," he sneered.

The Masked Man gestured for him to remain calm. "Your Majesty, this is General Marquis of the Grande Armée," he introduced.

"I know who he is," the Snow Queen snapped. "I prophesied the general and his Armée entering this world long before you were born."

Something about this was very unsettling to the general and

he motioned for his soldiers to stand alert, but the Masked Man assured him this was good news. "Splendid," he said. "Then you know that in exchange for the dragon egg, he can provide you with what you've always wanted."

"Capable he may be, but faithful to keeping his end of a bargain I've yet to see," the Snow Queen said. "The future is filled with many certainties and many uncertainties for the general. Long ago I foresaw him and his Armée sweeping across the land and conquering everything in their path, but I do not see him rising against the fairies. If he wishes to claim this world, he'll need my trust in the deal we're about to make."

"And what exactly is the deal?" the general asked, stepping closer to her.

The Snow Queen smiled and her jagged teeth were exposed. "Many years ago I was the ruler of the Northern Kingdom until my throne was stolen from me. If the general wants my dragon egg so he can conquer this world as intended, he must promise to give me back the Northern Kingdom when he succeeds."

This was news to the general and it infuriated him. "Excuse me for a moment, Your Coldness," he said to the Snow Queen. He grabbed the Masked Man by the lapel and threw him against a pillar to the side of the crater.

"You never mentioned anything about a trade!" he whispered.

"General, you have to trust me," the Masked Man whispered back. *"This is the only way you can win this war. Make this trade with the Snow Queen and it won't matter what she is promised in return—once you have a dragon in your power, you'll be unstoppable! You can obliterate her and anything in your way."*

The general thought it over but the anger never left his eyes. "Very well," he said. He faced the Snow Queen. "If you supply me with a dragon egg now, when we take over you have my word that the north shall be yours again."

A deep and raspy celebratory laugh erupted out of the Snow Queen's mouth. "Music to my ears," she said. "Your offer is accepted, but it comes with a warning. I foresee nothing but greatness for you if you keep your end of our bargain, but if you betray me I foresee your quest ending with a scorching demise."

The general's left eye started to twitch. Clearly the Snow Queen was trying to trick him with visions she hadn't seen. He quickly glanced at the Masked Man, who silently urged him to proceed.

"Understood," the general said. "We have a deal."

The soldiers felt a rumble beneath them. They looked through the ice under their feet and saw bubbles appear as something large and round slowly floated toward them from the depths of the lake. A dragon egg surfaced and bobbed against the ice below the frozen lake.

General Marquis turned to his men. "Don't just stand there! Retrieve it!" he ordered.

The soldiers went to the dragon egg and beat the ice above it with the backs of their rifles. The ice began to break and General Marquis and Colonel Baton stood away from it. One of the soldiers fell through the cracking ice and into the freezing water underneath. The Snow Queen laughed, wildly amused by their attempts to get the egg. The man's fall created a huge hole in the ice and the dragon egg soon drifted into it and floated to reaching distance.

"No one move!" the Masked Man yelled, and the two remaining soldiers stood still. He carefully got to his hands and knees and slid across the icy floor and pulled the dragon egg out of the water. *"Cold—cold!"* he shrieked. He juggled the egg back and forth between his hands and wrapped it in his raggedy blanket. The egg was so cold his hands burned from its touch.

The dragon egg was twice the size of the Masked Man's head. It was the shape of a regular egg but was covered in a black shell with the same rough texture as coal. Cracks the egg had received over the years were covered in gold to preserve it, like a rotting tooth. The Masked Man stared down proudly at the egg as if he were holding his firstborn child—he had dreamed about this moment for a very long time.

General Marquis promptly approached him and took the egg out of his hands. "Wonderful," he said, and stared down at the egg with wide inquisitive eyes, as if he were looking into a crystal ball at his future. "Colonel Baton, please shoot the Masked Man; his services are no longer needed."

Colonel Baton retrieved a pistol from inside his coat and aimed it at the Masked Man.

"Whoa, whoa, whoa," the Masked Man said, and raised his hands. *"You can't kill me! You still need me!"*

"We have acquired the egg and will not waste another moment on your nonsense," the general said, and nodded for the colonel to fire at will.

"But someone's got to take care of the egg—and I doubt you or any of your men know how to properly hatch and raise a dragon," the Masked Man said.

"And what makes you an expert?" the general asked spitefully.

"I've spent years trying to get my hands on this egg," the Masked Man said. "I know everything there is to know about dragons! Now we have to get the egg into something very hot. The hotter the environment, the faster and stronger the dragon will grow—and I have a *very hot* place in mind if we keep working together."

A noise came out of General Marquis that was half a grunt and half a sigh. He had been looking forward to getting rid of the Masked Man since they left the prison, but now he would have to wait a little longer. He shook his head at Baton and the pistol was put away.

"It seems the Masked Man has proven himself useful again," the general said. "You may stay alive long enough to properly hatch and raise the dragon for me. Now escort us out of these icy mountains before you cause my irritation to trump my need for efficiency."

General Marquis glared at him and then headed toward the opening in the crater they had entered from. Colonel Baton and the remaining two soldiers followed him. The Masked Man rubbed his chest to calm his beating heart—he would have to keep himself as useful as possible in the days ahead if he wanted to keep his life.

"Thank you, Your Shiveringness," the Masked Man said to the Snow Queen. He bowed and quickly caught up with the rest of his party. As soon as he and the soldiers were gone, another raspy laugh erupted from the Snow Queen and echoed through the canyon.

"What do you find so amusing, My Grace?" the polar bear to her left asked.

A malicious smirk grew on the Snow Queen's face. "I suddenly foresee something very certain in the forthcoming days for our masked friend," she said.

"What does Your Highness see?" the polar bear to her right asked.

"His mask has successfully concealed who he is for an impressive length of time," she said. "But by the time the week is up, his worst fear will be realized when his identity is revealed to the person he most wishes to keep it secret from."

CHAPTER TWENTY

THE GREAT TROBLIN LAKE

The twins barely slept after sending the royals and their friends on the secret path, and were both up before sunrise. The few hours they'd managed to sleep were from worrying their bodies to the point of exhaustion, and had little to do with rest. They met Mother Goose on the grand balcony of the Fairy Palace just as the sun rose over the Fairy Kingdom. She was prepping Lester to take them on their journey to the Troblin Territory and the Elf Empire.

"I want you to listen to Conner and Alex and do exactly what they say, fly very carefully, always be aware of the sky around you, and make sure every landing is as safe and secure as possible," she instructed him. "In other words, do everything you don't usually do for me."

Lester nodded, and ruffled his feathers, making them nice and fluffy for their upcoming flight.

"Are you sure you're up for this, Lester?" Conner asked. "We could take one of those enchanted swans if you're having any hesitations."

Lester opened his beak and glared at him—insulted just by the thought of it. He grabbed his own reins with his mouth and shoved them into Conner's hand. He was definitely ready for this.

"I'll take that as a yes," Conner said with a laugh. He and his sister each swung a leg over the large goose. They sat on his back with Conner in the front.

"Our first stop is the Troblin Territory, Lester," Alex said. "And after what I hope will be a successful visit, we'll be on our way to the Elf Empire."

"Who's in charge of the Elf Empire?" Conner asked.

Mother Goose huffed uneasily just at the mention of it. "Elvina the Elf Empress," she said.

"She's *not* a friend of yours, I take it," Conner said.

"Just be cautious around her," she warned them. "Empress Elvina is just as cunning as she is beautiful. She's like a poisonous flower, pretty and peaceful on the outside but dangerous on the inside. Don't let her fool you; no matter what she promises, her loyalty will always be to her own people before it is to the greater good."

Conner gulped. "Poisonous flower, gotcha," he said.

"Elves are very sharp and known for their long memory—and

boy, can they hold a grudge," Mother Goose continued. "They'll be very hesitant at first to cooperate but don't let it dishearten you. They've never forgiven the Fairy Council for not including them in the Happily Ever After Assembly and have not talked to us since."

"If they haven't talked to you in so long, what makes you think they'll talk to us?" Alex asked.

Mother Goose shrugged. "Beats me," she said. "Good luck, kiddos. I'll be right here as soon as you get back."

Her words of advice did the opposite of comforting them. Lester took a few steps backward and stretched out his wings. He waddled forward and began flapping until he and the twins lifted off the balcony and flew into the sky. Soon Mother Goose and the Fairy Palace were out of sight.

"Who would have thought you and I would be saving the world again so soon after the last time," Conner said with a nervous laugh to break the tension.

"I always hoped the portal between our worlds would re-open somehow, but never at this price," Alex said. "It's like *an eye for an arm* is our trading standard."

"I know what you mean," Conner said, and thought of something to lighten their spirits. "Do you ever think about what our lives would be like if we had never discovered the Land of Stories? Do you ever wonder what you and I would be doing right now if Grandma and Dad weren't from the fairy-tale world?"

Alex smiled at the thought. "I'd probably be thinking about colleges and careers instead of wars and battles."

Conner laughed at his own prediction. "And I'd just be trying to survive Algebra, not an army of thousands."

His sister laughed along but her smile quickly faded. They had experienced many extraordinary things but had also given up a lot because of who they were.

"Think of all the normal teenage things we could be experiencing," she said with a sigh so heavy it was obviously carrying more than one thought. "After this chapter of our lives, I wonder if I'll ever enjoy anything without the constant fear of losing it."

"By the way," Conner said, reading between the lines of what his sister was saying. "Who was that guy you were talking to last night in the fairy gardens?"

Conner felt his sister's body tense up behind him. "What are you talking about?" Alex said, attempting to play dumb. "The boy in the gardens? Oh, you're talking about *Rook Robins*—the farmer boy from the Eastern Kingdom. He's just a friend I made recently."

"Rook Robins?" Conner said. "He sounds like a baseball player. Are you sure he's *just* a friend?"

For a reason he couldn't explain, Conner instantly disliked everything about the guy.

"Oh please, Conner," Alex said defensively. "As if I've had time for anything like romance while joining the Fairy Council and leading the Happily Ever After Assembly into a war."

Alex hated lying to her brother but she would never hear the end of it if he knew the truth, especially if he knew Rook was one of the reasons she had missed his attempts at contacting her while he was in Germany. Conner was glad Alex was sitting behind him so she couldn't see the look he was giving her. He knew exactly what was going on whether his sister wanted to admit it or not.

"You know, you could tell me if he was more than a friend—I promise I wouldn't tell Mom," Conner said, already anxious to tell their mom everything he knew.

Alex laughed it off. "You'll be the first person to know if my relationship with Rook unexpectedly progresses into anything more, but it doesn't look like that will be possible at the moment," she said sharply.

"That's good, but if he breaks your heart I'll beat him up for you," Conner said.

Alex burst into laughter. "Now that's something I'd pay to see," she said, and quickly changed the topic so she'd feel less exposed. "But while we're on the subject, I've been meaning to ask you, do you have a crush on your friend Bree?"

Had Lester been a car, Conner would have slammed on the brakes. Instead he abruptly grabbed ahold of the reins and caused Lester to squawk. He blushed so much Alex could see it on the back of his neck and ears.

"Do I have a crush on Bree?" Conner said like it was a preposterous thought. "Come on, Alex, just because I asked you a couple harmless questions about your love life doesn't mean you have to be rude."

Alex grunted at the double standard her brother set. "I'm not being rude, I just figured I would ask since you turn bright red whenever you're around her or her name gets brought up," she pointed out. "Last night when she hugged you good-bye I thought your head was about to explode—I wouldn't be surprised if she had a crush on you, too."

Conner started smiling and couldn't stop. *Did Bree have a*

crush on him, too? He'd never thought it was a possibility until now. Had she traveled around Europe with him not only because she wanted to have an adventure but also because she wanted to spend time with him? He quickly forced his smile to diminish when he remembered he was in the middle of defending himself.

"Rest assured, I don't have any feelings whatsoever for Bree," he said. "To be honest, she was starting to get on my nerves when we were in Europe. The way she always second-guessed me, the way she remained so calm in any situation, the way she wore her hair under a beanie with her streaks of blue and pink in the front, the fact that she surprised me every day with a new interesting fact about herself... it was all so annoying."

Alex didn't have to question further—it was obvious how Conner really felt. She was glad he couldn't see her raised eyebrow. "Uh-huh, sounds like you haven't given her much thought at all," she said. "I'm actually glad there's nothing going on."

"Why is that?" Conner asked, and became overly defensive in the opposite direction now. "You don't think I'm mature enough to have a crush on someone or for someone to have a crush on me? For your information, I'm a catch, too—"

"No," Alex interrupted. "Because we're about to visit our old friend Trollbella, and we're not leaving without the support of her army—even if it means you have to marry her."

Conner moaned a long weary sound under his breath. He had almost forgotten about the young troll queen who had been madly in love with him since they met.

"Gosh, I hope divorce exists in this world," he said.

The twins remained fairly quiet for the remainder of their trip into the Troblin Territory, fearing they would expose more about themselves than they were willing to. They knew each other so well it was a wonder why either ever tried fooling the other.

The mountainous boulders surrounding the Troblin Territory appeared on the horizon and Lester began his gradual descent. As they flew closer Conner was surprised to see that the land between the boulders was covered in water. The entire territory looked like a massive aboveground pool.

"Wait a second," Conner said. "They never drained their territory after the Enchantress flooded it?"

"Nope," Alex said. "The fairies offered to completely restore the land but Queen Trollbella had something else in mind."

"What was that?" he asked.

"You'll see," she said.

Lester swooped into the territory and landed smoothly on the water. He was like a miniature boat as they traveled across the giant lake the territory had become.

"No way," Conner said in shock when he saw what his sister was talking about. Queen Trollbella had turned her territory into a vast floating city.

Hundreds of forts crafted from the wreckage of their ruined underground home floated in the waters ahead of them. Troll and goblin families occupied the smaller forts while the larger forts served as common areas shared between them. Some of the goblins swam from fort to fort while trolls glided over the water in wooden floating devices. Many sat on the edges of the forts with their enormous feet in the water, and held fishing poles— although the twins were pretty sure there were no fish to catch. The trolls and goblins were darker than usual now that they lived above the ground. The sun had tanned their skin to dark shades of green and blue and brown.

Despite the environmental change, all the creatures looked incredibly bored as they drifted in the water. Alex and Conner floating past them on the giant goose was the most interesting thing they had seen in weeks and caused quite the scene.

"They sure are hard up for entertainment," Conner said, and his sister nodded.

The twins heard a familiar voice as a long and wide boat traveled toward them.

"*Row, troblins! Row!*" Queen Trollbella ordered. She lay leisurely across the front of the boat and took in the sun. A dozen trolls and a dozen goblins were seated in the center of the boat and rowed long oars as they were ordered. The boat drifted slightly to one side since the trolls' arms were shorter.

A young male troll stood at the back of the boat and monitored the rowers. He was short and stout just like Trollbella and wore a large horned helmet and a breastplate. All the rowers came to an abrupt stop as soon as they saw the twins floating on Lester in the water beside them. They pointed at the large goose and whispered among themselves as all the creatures on the surrounding forts had.

"Did I say you could stop rowing?" Trollbella said. When the rowing stayed at a halt, she agitatedly sat up to see what the concern was. She cupped her gaping mouth when she laid eyes on what the others had seen.

"Hi, Trollbella," Conner said sheepishly, with a wave. "Miss me?"

"Butterboy!" She gasped. "Am I really seeing you or are you a mirage in the water?"

"He's here," Alex said. "We're *both* here."

"But I thought I had lost my Butterboy forever," Trollbella said in complete shock. "You went home through that portal and I thought you'd never return! Was our love too strong for the portal to contain? Did our affection for each other break it open? Have you finally returned to be the king of the Great Troblin Lake?"

"Um...*no*," Conner clarified. "But the portal *has* been re-opened—that's why I'm here."

"The Great Troblin Lake, huh?" Alex asked. "Is that what you're calling this place now?"

"Yes, fairy girl," Trollbella said with a scowl. "And I expect all the maps to be changed at once! I've always wanted to live near the water and the Enchantress unintentionally made that dream come true. Now you must come aboard my boat so I can properly embrace my Butterboy."

Lester swam to the side of the boat and Alex and Conner were helped aboard by two of the troll rowers. Trollbella leaped onto Conner like a spider monkey hugging a tree and almost knocked both of them into the water. He figured it would take her a while to let him go but she detached much sooner than he was expecting. She looked up at him and her big eyes were full of concern rather than the usual lust. Something was very different about Trollbella but the twins were too pressed for time to find out what.

"Look, Trollbella," Conner said. "We've come to talk to you. Something very bad has happened and we need your help."

Trollbella put both of her hands on her hips. "It puts a strain on our relationship when you only come to me to share devastating news, Butterboy," she said. "Just once I wish you'd bring flowers or chocolates instead."

"For the millionth time, we don't have a *relationship*!" Conner said.

"Yes, I know our love is too strong for childish terms," she said. "Our love is bottomless...it's forever...it's indestructible...." The troll queen suddenly burst into tears.

"Trollbella, what's the matter with you?" Alex asked.

"There is something my Butterboy must know before we speak any further," Trollbella said. "While you were gone, *I found someone else.*"

"What?" the twins said together. This was the last thing they had expected to come out of the troll queen's mouth.

Trollbella's eyes darted around the boat guiltily and she turned away from them—what she had to confess was too painful to say while looking them in the eyes. "I knew after you disappeared into another dimension forever it would be challenging to keep our love alive. I tried to stay faithful to you for as long as I could and it was the hardest six days of my life. I was weak without you, Butterboy, and my heart strayed. I couldn't bear the thought of being alone forever so *I gave my heart to someone else.*"

Alex and Conner exchanged the same dumbfounded look. With everything else going on at the moment, Conner was surprised by how much relief he felt upon hearing this.

"I always thought that one day if the impossible should happen and you returned to me I could easily give my heart back to you, but now seeing you in front of me, I realize I was mistaken,"

Trollbella said. "Once I've invested my love in someone I cannot get my love back unless I know it's a dead end, and I'm afraid I've planned a long, joyous road with my new love."

"Okay, I've got to know, who is this poor guy?" Conner couldn't help but ask.

"His name is Gator, and he commands my army as well as my heart," Trollbella said. She dreamily looked to the back of her boat and waved at the small troll in the horned helmet. Gator waved back uncomfortably—apparently *reciprocation* wasn't something Trollbella looked for in a relationship.

"Congratulations," Conner said to them both.

"But I've failed you, Butterboy!" Trollbella said, and she fell to her knees. "I promised myself our love would be eternal and I've broken that vow! You'll never love anyone else as much as you've loved me! I feel so terrible to leave you alone in this cruel world! Please tell me if there is anything I can do to make it up to you!"

Alex nudged Conner and cleared her throat. *This was their chance.*

"I don't know," Conner said, and gave his best heartbroken performance. "I'm in shock, complete shock. My heart feels like it's been ripped out of my chest, trampled by a stampede of wolves, and chewed up by an ogre. I'm going to need some time to get over this—"

"But there is something you could do for him that would make him feel *much* better in the meantime," Alex said, trying to speed things up.

"Oh yes, Butterboy!" Trollbella groveled at his feet. "I'd do anything to ease your broken heart! Please, the guilt is too much to bear! Just say the word!"

"Well...," Conner said melodramatically. "If you're serious about healing my emotional wounds, mending the pieces of my heart, and sewing the seams of my soul...access to your army would help me greatly."

"You want my army?" Trollbella asked. She looked up at him questioningly. Even her Butterboy might have overstepped his boundaries with this request.

"Yes, but there's an even bigger reason why we need it," Conner said.

"Trollbella, an army of thousands of men has invaded this world and they plan on taking over—" Alex tried to explain, but Trollbella interrupted her.

"Hush, fairy girl!" the troll queen demanded. "This has nothing to do with you. Keep your wand out of our business!"

Alex rolled her eyes and gestured to her brother to explain the rest. Conner quickly told her about the Grande Armée and how they needed the troblins' help to stop them. His explanation may not have captivated the troll queen but it sparked the interest of all the other creatures around.

"I'll go!" said one of the rowing goblins.

"That sounds terrific!" an eavesdropping troll said from one of the forts nearby.

"I'm not even in the army but I'll help you fight!" said a desperate goblin.

"Me too!" said another troll.

The twins were so excited to see their enthusiasm. Life on a floating city must have been really dull if the idea of war sounded intriguing.

Trollbella squinted and crossed her arms as she thought about it. "But still, an army in exchange for a broken heart seems like a pretty steep deal," she said.

Without missing a beat, Conner clutched his chest and fell to the deck in pain. "Oh my broken heart! It hurts so much! Oh the pain, the miserable pain!" he screamed.

"Your heart is on the other side of your chest, Conner," Alex whispered down at him and he quickly made the correction.

Tears formed in Trollbella's eyes at the sight of her Butterboy in pain she had caused him. "Oh no, Butterboy!" she said, and rushed to his side. "If my army will help ease your pain, then my army you shall have!"

Conner quickly sat up, completely fine. "Thank goodness," he said. "I really appreciate it! Now we need to gather up your army and fill them in on our plan as soon as possible."

Queen Trollbella got to her feet to address the rowers aboard her boat. "Take us to the army fort at once, troblins!" she ordered. "My Butterboy needs to speak with our army and start his healing process."

The troll and goblin rowers turned the boat completely around and headed in the direction of the army float. Alex gestured for Lester to follow the boat, and helped Conner to his feet.

"Nice going," she whispered in his ear.

"Thanks," Conner said, but his face fell into a pout.

"What's wrong?" she said. "We recruited the troblin army and it was easier than either of us expected!"

"I know," Conner said sadly. "I just can't believe Trollbella picked that troll over *me*."

Chapter Twenty-One

FROM THE ASHES

The secret path weaved through the countryside, crossed rivers without bridges, and climbed over mountains that roads had never been built on as the carriages traveled through the kingdoms. Jack and Goldilocks were very attentive to the land surrounding them and so far they hadn't encountered any problems during their covert tour. However peaceful the land outside the carriages was, though, the inside of the third carriage was another story.

Red had managed to bite her tongue since they left the Fairy Kingdom. She and Little Bo hadn't said a word the entire trip and the others stayed just as silent, afraid any conversation might send the two into a vicious argument. Instead, as if they were watching a tennis match, Froggy, Bree, and Emmerich watched Red and Little Bo exchange spiteful looks back and forth.

The silence finally became too much for Red and she tried speaking to Little Bo as diplomatically as she could.

"So, Little Bo," Red said. "Have you enjoyed being queen of my kingdom—excuse me—*your* kingdom?"

"Yes" was all Little Bo replied. She stared at Red stoically and didn't look away, as if Red was playing a childish game she didn't want to participate in.

The others in the carriage traded uncomfortable looks. It was inevitable that this conversation would end in disaster.

"Good to hear," Red lied through a clenched jaw. "Have you fulfilled all the promises you made to the people during the election?"

"Almost," Little Bo said, and still her stoic expression didn't fade.

"Wonderful," Red peeped. "And how are the House of Progress representatives?"

"They were all replaced with actual representatives from the village," Little Bo informed her.

Red couldn't help but let a high-pitched snicker escape her mouth. The others relaxed a bit seeing her so amused—perhaps there was a chance they could be civil to each other.

"Well, they had it coming," she said. "And what about the castle? Have you grown accustomed to it yet? I'm sure it took some time getting used to it compared to that farmhouse you lived in before."

"I still live at my farm, actually," Little Bo said.

Red suddenly gagged as if she had swallowed a bug. "*Do you?*" she asked, trying her best to remain calm. "Then why did you ask me to move out of it?"

"Because I turned it into an orphanage," Little Bo said with a snide smile.

Red sat incredibly still while her brain processed this. Then, as if her animalistic instincts had taken over her body, she lunged toward Little Bo with her fists raised in the air.

"*I'm gonna kill her!*" Red yelled.

Froggy had been preparing for this moment and immediately grabbed ahold of her before any damage was done. It took Bree and Emmerich's help to keep her in her seat.

"You lousy piece of sheepherding trash! You did that on purpose! You knew giving my castle over to a bunch of brats would hurt me the most!"

"Red, how can you say that about orphans?" Bree scolded.

"Oh, don't let the word fool you! I've met all of those delinquents myself and each one is more awful than the last! Most of their parents are alive and well—those kids were just too horrible for them to raise on their own," Red said.

Little Bo didn't deny the reasoning behind her actions. She just sat across from Red and smiled mischievously. Red eventually cooled off enough for the others to let her go. Emmerich decided to change the subject before anyone got hurt.

"What is your necklace?" Emmerich asked Little Bo.

No one had ever pointed it out before and Little Bo was surprised he'd noticed it. A chain so thin it was almost invisible rested around her neck and was tucked neatly away into the top of her dress. She pulled the necklace out and showed him the small heart-shaped rock hanging from it.

"It's a stone heart," she said.

"Why do you wear it?" Emmerich asked.

Little Bo didn't know what to tell him since no one had ever asked before. "I lost someone I loved very much once," she said. "I wear this necklace to remember them. In a strange way, it helps me from missing them too much."

"Did they die or just *run away* from you?" Red remarked with a snort.

Little Bo didn't respond. She played with the necklace in her hand and just smiled at the former queen. Her presence alone aggravated Red much more than anything she could say.

Things weren't quite as lively in the first carriage but the passengers were starting to grow restless. Princess Hope was very agitated from being cooped up for so long and began to cry. Cinderella held her daughter tenderly in her arms and rocked her until she fell asleep. Sleeping Beauty admired her mothering skills as she sat across from her.

"You're so good with her," Sleeping Beauty said. "It makes me miss my own mother so much."

"Me too," Cinderella said. "There are so many times I wish my mother was still alive so I could ask her if I'm doing the right thing."

"If a better mother existed in the world I certainly haven't seen her," King Chance told his wife. "And that includes our own mother."

King Chase laughed at his brother. "Yes, our mother was a good person at heart but she was rather cold at times," he said.

Sleeping Beauty smiled and then gazed out the window sadly. The subject of mothers had recently become a very sore one for her.

"Do you think if all the chaos ends—" Cinderella said but quickly corrected her choice of words. "*When* all this chaos ends, will the two of you want to start a family?"

Chase placed a comforting hand over Sleeping Beauty's and she fought against the tears forming in her eyes. There was something they hadn't shared with them yet.

"I'm so sorry, I didn't mean to—" Cinderella said, but she didn't know what she was apologizing for.

"No, it's quite all right," Sleeping Beauty said. "Unfortunately, due to the effects of the sleeping curse, I and many women in our kingdom have been left unable to bear children."

Cinderella and Chance were devastated to hear this. "Oh, my dear friend, I am so sorry," Cinderella said, but there was nothing she could say to comfort her.

Sleeping Beauty looked back out her window before their sympathetic faces awoke any more of her pain and frustration. "Some things are just not meant to be, I suppose," she said.

The carriage became very quiet. The secret path curved across the border between the Northern and the Eastern Kingdoms and Sleeping Beauty recognized the landscape around them.

"We're home," she announced to her husband. "I would recognize these hills from miles away—"

Her voice faded and her mouth fell open. Something suddenly came into view in the distance that sent shivers down her spine. Before she could tell the others what she was seeing, she opened the window and stuck her head through it.

"Stop the carriages!" Sleeping Beauty yelled up at Jack and Goldilocks.

Jack and Goldilocks pulled on the reins and the carriages started to slow down but Sleeping Beauty had jumped out before they came to a complete stop. She ran straight toward what she had seen as fast as she could.

"Wait! Where's the fire?" Jack called after.

"Where are you going?" Goldilocks asked. But the queen didn't respond to either of them.

The others in the traveling party stepped out of their carriages to see what all the fuss was about. Once the royals saw Sleeping Beauty running in the distance, they sprinted after her but didn't go very far. Sleeping Beauty stopped at the edge of a village no one else had seen and stared at it in horror.

The village had been viciously attacked. Most of it had been burned down but smoke still filled the air from parts of the village still ablaze. Not a living soul could be seen or heard. The damage was so severe all the kings and queens knew it must have been caused by the Grande Armée. Only their weapons could have left such an ugly mark on an innocent town.

"I don't understand," Sleeping Beauty said. "Why does my kingdom seem to suffer the most during times of crisis?"

Snow White stepped forward and placed a hand on her shoulder. "The Eastern Kingdom may be the first to see the sun set, but it's also the first to see the dawn," she said.

Her comforting words were unheard as Sleeping Beauty was distracted by a noise among the flames. It was a sound so faint she couldn't tell if she was actually hearing it or if her mind was playing a trick on her.

"Did you hear that?" Sleeping Beauty asked.

"Hear what?" Snow White asked.

"It sounded like *crying*," she said.

The others didn't hear anything. The sound came again and this time Sleeping Beauty bolted toward the village.

"Beauty, come back!" Chase called after his wife.

"It's too dangerous!" Cinderella said.

"Don't worry, we'll get her," Goldilocks said, and she and Jack ran after the queen.

Sleeping Beauty let the sound guide her; the closer she got, the louder it became. She pushed through the door of a crumbling and burned-out home and stepped inside. She had to cover her mouth from all the smoke in the air. The crying was so loud she knew it must be real.

Jack and Goldilocks found the queen and heard the noise themselves, as clear as day.

"What is that?" Goldilocks asked.

"It sounds like a *baby*," Jack said.

"Over here!" Sleeping Beauty called out.

A small chest was buried under a pile of debris that had fallen from the ceiling. Jack and Goldilocks helped Sleeping Beauty lift the rubble off the chest and open the lid. An infant girl had been hidden inside the chest and was surely the sole survivor of the Grande Armée's raid.

"I don't believe it," Goldilocks said in amazement.

"How did you hear her crying?" Jack asked.

Sleeping Beauty couldn't explain it, either. "I suppose I was meant to hear her," she said. She scooped her up into her arms and the crying infant went silent.

Goldilocks was eyeing the roof above them. "We need to get out of here fast."

The three of them ran out of the home with their new discovery just as the roof collapsed. Sleeping Beauty had saved the baby's life seconds before it would have been lost. They returned to their traveling party, which was still waiting at the edge of the village. They were all just as astonished to see the surviving infant.

"Whose baby is that?" Bree asked.

"As far as we know, she's an orphan," Sleeping Beauty said.

"Well, I know of a great castle you can send her to if you need an orphanage," Red said, and gave Little Bo a dirty look.

Sleeping Beauty was smiling down at the baby she cradled with a warmth in her eyes the others had never seen. "I do, too," she said. "She's coming to live with us."

Chase stepped toward his wife to talk sense into her, but once he saw the infant's face he felt what his wife was feeling. The child had been *waiting* for them to save her.

"What about the royal bloodline?" Chandler asked what the rest of the group was thinking.

"If any of you are concerned with blood, I invite you to take a look around the village and see all the blood of my people that has been spilt," Sleeping Beauty said. "This child is a survivor and a child of this kingdom and therefore a worthy heir to our throne."

Although Cinderella and Chance were the only royals who knew Sleeping Beauty couldn't have a child of her own, none of them objected. The child was a beacon of light in a very dark time—if she could survive the wrath of the Grande Armée, they could, too.

"What will you name her?" Cinderella asked.

Sleeping Beauty exchanged a smile with all the kings and queens around her and tears of joy came to her eyes. They all accepted the child of this spontaneous adoption as one of their own.

"Since she was found in the ashes of her village, I think I'll name her Ash," she said.

"Princess Ash of the Eastern Kingdom; it has a nice ring to it," Froggy said.

"She's beautiful," Rapunzel said.

Red stared at the ransacked village and a heavy pile of guilt filled the pit of her stomach. All her anger and woes about losing her throne seemed so small in comparison to what the world was facing. This attack could have happened in *her kingdom,* and that thought angered her more than anything ever had.

Red marched up to Goldilocks. Everyone expected her to start an argument but she surprised all of them with a request.

"Teach us to fight," Red said.

"Excuse me?" Goldilocks asked.

"I want to learn how to fight this army myself," Red explained to the others. "This could have happened to any village in any of our kingdoms—this wasn't an attack on the Eastern Kingdom, it was an attack on us all. I refuse to sit back and watch this Grande Armée destroy everything we love so much. If I die, I don't want to die in a cozy carriage or throne room, I want to die fighting alongside our people."

The royals all looked to one another as her words touched each of them. They were surprised, impressed, and, most important, *inspired* by what Red said. They all took a step toward Goldilocks, united in the request.

"I do have pretty decent upper-body strength from cleaning my stepmother's house every day," Cinderella bragged.

"And we *could* use a break from being cooped up inside those carriages." Snow White shrugged.

Goldilocks was impressed by their interest and withdrew her sword from its scabbard. "All right, then," she said. "Your Majesties, each of you please find a large stick. The first thing I'm going to teach you is how to use a sword."

Mother Goose stood on the grand balcony of the Fairy Palace and gazed at the stars in the night sky. She quietly prayed that wherever the twins and Lester were, they were succeeding in their efforts to recruit the armies. But most of all, she prayed that they were safe.

Emerelda rushed onto the balcony. "Mother Goose," she said breathlessly. "It's the Fairy Godmother, she's awake."

Mother Goose's spirits soared so high she almost floated into the air. "For good?" she asked.

"From the looks of it, I would say only momentarily," Eme- relda said. "She seems extremely tired and she's asking for you."

Without wasting a second, Emerelda and Mother Goose ran to the Fairy Godmother's chambers. Mother Goose kneeled by her bedside and took her hand into her own. Her eyes were open but very heavy, as if she had just awoken from a deep sleep and was about to fall into another.

"Hello there, my dear friend," Mother Goose said softly to her.

"Emerelda, would you please give Mother Goose and me a moment alone?" the Fairy Godmother asked weakly.

Emerelda nodded and left the chambers.

"Mother Goose, I have something I need to ask of you before I go," the Fairy Godmother said.

"Go? But where are you going?" Mother Goose laughed. "The Poconos? Martha's Vineyard? Palm Springs?"

"You know where I'm going," she said.

"I do," Mother Goose said sadly. "But I was hoping there was still a chance you'd be sticking around. What is it that you need to ask me?"

The Fairy Godmother's eyes grew heavier the more she tried to speak. "Over the years I have kept many secrets for you," she said. "I've only asked you to keep one of mine, and I'm asking you to keep it even after I'm gone."

Mother Goose knew what her friend was referring to without having to ask. "I assume you're talking about the *other heir*," she said.

"Yes," the Fairy Godmother said with a deep breath. "If Alex hadn't proven herself to be the *true heir of magic*, I wouldn't be lying in this bed. Her compassion is both her greatest strength and her greatest weakness. If she ever knew there was another—if she ever found out who they are—she would be fooled the same way I was and it would destroy her."

"I understand," Mother Goose said. "You have my word: I will keep your secret and Alex will never know."

The Fairy Godmother smiled at her oldest friend. "Thank you," she said with relief. Her eyelids became too heavy to hold open and she drifted back into a very deep sleep. She slept even more peacefully than before, now that this had been addressed.

Mother Goose sighed and squeezed the Fairy Godmother's hand. Keeping the Fairy Godmother's secret would be the hardest challenge she would ever face.

CHAPTER TWENTY-TWO

TO THE CORE

In the middle of the night three villages in the south of the Eastern Kingdom found themselves under attack. Soldiers of the Grande Armée invaded the towns and robbed the villagers of all their supplies. The villagers themselves were imprisoned and taken back to the soldiers' camp.

Only one village had the courage to stand up against the Armée and it was destroyed in the process. As far as the soldiers knew, not a single soul had survived the ruthless attack. When the enslaved villagers arrived at the camp, they were lined up and each given a shovel. Their only instructions were to dig.

"How far do they dig?" General Marquis asked the Masked Man. They watched the villagers work from the general's comfortable tent.

"Until they hit magma," the Masked Man said. He cradled the dragon egg in his hands and never let it out of his sight. "It shouldn't take them very long to reach it. During the Dragon Age the Eastern Kingdom was consumed with volcanoes. Dragons laid their eggs in the magma because their offspring grew at rapid rates in the heat."

"And what happens after the egg is placed in the magma?" the general asked with a sideways glance at him.

"I'll let you know," the Masked Man said, and held the egg even tighter. He was very tight-lipped, knowing his knowledge of dragons was the only thing keeping him alive.

"You're smarter than you look," the general said.

"General Marquis," Colonel Baton called from the back of the tent. "We have finalized our plan of attack for tomorrow."

The colonel and Capitaine De Lange were standing over the general's desk. A large map of the fairy-tale world had been spread out across it with several flags and figurines placed in strategic clumps throughout the kingdoms.

"Does the plan follow what we discussed?" the general asked him.

"Yes, sir," the colonel said. "Tomorrow at dawn, we will strike the kingdoms and seize their capitals. Capitaine De Lange and his men have successfully spied on the kingdoms' armies and we're pleased to inform you our army of soldiers and recruits is more than twice the size of their armies put together."

"Go on," the general instructed.

"The ogres and one thousand soldiers will be sent to the Elf Empire to defeat their army—we didn't obtain the exact number of the elves in the Elf Empire's army, but we estimate it's only a thousand or so. The witches and three hundred soldiers will be sent to the Corner Kingdom to defeat their small army of two hundred or so men. The goblins and one thousand soldiers will be sent to the Northern Kingdom to defeat their army of one thousand men. The fugitive animals and four hundred soldiers will be sent to the Red Riding Hood Kingdom to defeat their army of four hundred men. The trolls and five hundred soldiers will be sent to the Charming Kingdom to defeat their army of five hundred men. The remaining criminal recruits and eight hundred soldiers will be sent to the Eastern Kingdom to defeat their army of seven hundred or so men. The Troll and Goblin Territory is worthless to us—they have no authority in this world so we won't waste our men on them."

"We outnumber each of the armies, sir," Capitaine De Lange said. "That will leave you two thousand soldiers to lead into the Fairy Kingdom and seize the Fairy Palace."

"And a dragon!" the Masked Man reminded them. "You'll have two thousand soldiers *and* a dragon."

"How soon will the dragon be ready?" Baton asked.

"Raising dragons is all about timing," the Masked Man told them. "Depending on the temperature of the magma and how much we feed it, it could grow to full size in a couple days—as long as you keep me around to properly raise it, that is."

The general carefully looked over the map on his desk.

The other commanders in his charge were practically claiming victory already based on the information they had, but the general wasn't pleased. There was something about their strategy that didn't sit well with him.

"Are you sure we haven't miscounted the armies?" the general asked. "When the Brothers Grimm described each of the kingdoms to us, their forces felt much bigger."

"My men returned only yesterday, shortly after you returned from the north, sir," Capitaine De Lange assured him. "The armies of the kingdoms have been seen preparing for war in the capitals and they were all accounted for."

The general still wasn't sold on the idea. He had a hunch they would need to charge the Fairy Palace with more than soldiers and a dragon if they wanted to succeed.

"Very well," the general said. "But I want more leverage than soldiers and a dragon before we strike the fairies. I want each of the rulers brought back alive once their kingdom is seized, is that understood?"

"Yes, sir," Colonel Baton said. "We will attack the Fairy Kingdom last—once all the rulers of the other kingdoms have been successfully retrieved."

"Capitaine De Lange, make sure the villagers are digging as quickly as possible," the general ordered. "I want to put the egg in the magma no later than sunrise tomorrow."

Capitaine De Lange saluted and headed to the digging site. General Marquis rubbed his bald head, worrying there was information his men had missed. Lieutenant Rembert hurried inside with wide eyes and exciting news to tell the general.

"General Marquis, a discovery was made in one of the nearby villages. I thought you would like to see it, sir."

"What is it, Lieutenant?" the general asked as if it was impossible for anything to excite him.

"We've discovered a magic mirror, sir," the lieutenant said.

This sparked the general's interest. He knew magic mirrors held intuitive knowledge about the world. Perhaps the mirror could ease his doubts about the battle ahead. "Bring it in," he ordered.

The lieutenant left the tent and returned a moment later instructing two soldiers as they dragged something square and heavy inside. They propped it up in a corner of the tent and pulled off the protective sheet wrapped around it. The mirror had a thick golden frame with floral carvings and the purest glass any of them had seen.

The general walked toward it like he was approaching a poisonous snake. The Masked Man knew very well what kind of mirror it was but he didn't warn the general—he was much more interested to find out what the general would see.

General Marquis stood in front of the mirror for a long moment and nothing happened. He waved his hand in front of it and nothing changed in the reflection.

"Idiot, you've been tricked," he shouted at Rembert. "There is nothing magical about this mirror at all."

Just as the general turned away, the other men in the tent gasped. The general's reflection in the mirror had changed. Instead of a grown man wearing a uniform decorated with badges of honor, a weak little boy appeared. The boy was dreadfully skinny, filthy, and he trembled; he was a starving and scared peasant. His clothes were covered in holes and tears and he didn't have any shoes. His left eye was swollen shut from a severe beating.

The general had spent his entire life trying to forget this boy but he knew who he was the instant he saw him.

"Lieutenant," General Marquis said in a soft but threatening tone. "I want this mirror to be taken out of my tent at once and destroyed, and if you disturb me with garbage like this again, you'll be next."

Rembert and the other soldiers quickly removed the mirror from the general's sight. Although he hadn't even raised his voice, none of the men had ever seen the general so affected by something before. The general continued staring into the corner even though the mirror had been taken away.

"Colonel Baton," the general said sharply. "I do not want to wait until dawn—send the armies out to the kingdoms as soon as they're organized."

"Yes, General," Colonel Baton said. He left the tent, and the Masked Man and the general were alone.

"What kind of magic mirror was *that*?" General Marquis asked.

"It was a Mirror of Truth," the Masked Man said. "It reflects who someone truly is rather than how they appear."

The general became very quiet and very still.

"I assume you must have grown up very poor," the Masked Man said. "I guess that explains where your drive comes from— a lifetime of having to prove yourself—"

The general jerked his head toward him. "Don't you dare

analyze me," he barked. "You think you know me, but you don't know the first thing about me. You have no idea where I came from, what I came from, or what I had to do to become who I am today. That boy in the mirror is a reflection from the past and nothing more. He will never have to prove anything to anyone again."

The Masked Man knew better than to play with fire. "You're right, I don't know you," he said. "So please allow me to ask you this—a question I've had since we first met. Why conquer this world? Claiming a different dimension must seem a tad extreme even where you come from."

The general walked to his desk and pulled out a thick book he kept in the top drawer. He flipped through the book and the Masked Man could see the pages were filled with maps and portraits—it was a history book.

"Where I come from, each era is defined by the greatness of one man," he said. "Alexander the Great, Julius Caesar, William the Conqueror, Genghis Khan... they were the greatest conquerors of their times. Soon a man named Napoleon Bonaparte will join that list of men... unless another man conquers something beyond Napoleon's wildest dreams."

"Ah, I see," the Masked Man said. "You're trying to outdo him. But surely you'll both be remembered as great contributors to the French Empire?"

General Marquis slammed the book shut and put it away in his desk. "Perhaps," the general said. "But there is only room for *one man* in the history books."

CHAPTER TWENTY-THREE

THE ELF EMPIRE

alf of the Happily Ever After Assembly armies are in hiding while the other half stand guard over their kingdoms," Alex explained to the Troblin Army. "Once we've recruited the Elf Army, all the armies in hiding, as well as the ones left guarding the kingdoms, will unite and charge the Grande Armée together. Wait for my signal, and then join us in the Fairy Kingdom. Any questions?"

The Troblin Army consisted of a little more than eight hundred out-of-shape trolls and goblins, many of whom had recently joined, just out of boredom. They were seated in front of Alex in a wooden amphitheater that looked like a doughnut floating in the Great Troblin Lake.

Only one troll raised his hand with a question regarding Alex's explanation.

"Yes, *you* with the bone through your nose," Conner called on him. "What's your question?"

"If we join the armies of the Happily Ever After Assembly, what's in it for us?" the troll asked.

The troblin soldiers started exchanging whispers with one another. Alex hadn't mentioned anything they would get in return for helping them.

"What do you want?" Conner asked. "We could hook you up with some sheep or maybe some solid ground?"

"We want our freedom back!" a goblin in the back row yelled.

"Yeah! We want the right to leave our kingdom!" a troll in the front growled.

The entire Troblin Army agreed. *"Freedom! Freedom! Freedom!"* they chanted.

"Silence, troblins!" Queen Trollbella demanded. The amphitheater went quiet. "I am insulted you want to leave the water world I have built for you! Especially since we just recently gained our sea legs!"

A goblin in the center of the amphitheater leaned forward and vomited all over the troll sitting in front of him.

"Well, *most* of us have gained our sea legs," Trollbella corrected herself.

Conner rolled his eyes at their request for freedom. "You were put here because you wouldn't stop enslaving people! My sister and I were enslaved not once but *twice* by you! Do you really expect us to grant you your freedom?"

Trollbella crossed her arms. "I'll never understand why humans take being enslaved so personally," she said. "What if my troblins promise to never enslave anyone again? Will you reconsider, Butterboy?"

Conner looked over at Alex. They didn't really have a choice—they needed the troblins.

"I guess," Conner said.

Queen Trollbella happily clapped her hands. "We'll give you a sacred troblin pinkie swear," she said. "Everyone raise your right hand, if you have one, and point your pinkie to the sky. Repeat after me: *I, Queen Trollbella—*"

"*I, Queen Trollbella,*" the Troblin Army repeated.

"No, troblins, you're supposed to say your own name," she said, and they quickly made the correction. *"I promise to never kidnap, imprison, enslave, or forcefully borrow any human without their permission for as long as I live."*

The troblins reluctantly repeated after her, word for word.

"Wonderful," Trollbella said. "Good job, troblins, you may rest your pinkies. Is that good enough for you, Butterboy and fairy girl?"

The twins sighed. "It'll have to do," Alex said.

A goblin in the front raised his hand.

"Yes, *you* with the missing ear," Conner called on him.

"What will the signal be?" the goblin asked.

Everyone turned to Alex and waited for the answer, including Conner.

"Um . . . um . . . I'm not sure yet," Alex said. "But don't worry; you'll know it when you see it."

Trollbella raised an eyebrow at her. "Has anyone ever told you you're a little *too* confident?" she said.

By the time the Troblin Army was up to date on Alex's strategy the sun had set. Trollbella insisted they stay the night, and Alex and Conner were given a private area on the troll queen's floating fort to sleep on—which consisted of the wooden floor and a blanket. Alex was worried if she made beds appear with her wand it would tip the whole fort over.

Besides the water rocking them and Trollbella spying on them every ten minutes, the twins had a difficult time sleeping because of all their worries.

"Conner, are you awake?" Alex whispered to her brother.

"Do you really have to ask?" he said. "What's on your mind?"

"I was just thinking about the Elf Empire," she said. "If the trolls wanted something in return for their help, I'm afraid the elves may ask for something in exchange, too."

"They'll probably just want a bunch of shoes," Conner said. "Aren't elves obsessed with shoes?"

"Gosh, I hope it's that easy," Alex said. "I'll have to think of something the empress wants so desperately she would be willing to give up her army for it."

"Good thing you're the next Fairy Godmother," Conner said. "It gives you a lot to work with."

The next morning the twins woke up with very sore backs from sleeping on the wooden floor. They said good-bye to Trollbella and climbed aboard Lester. He spread his wings and took off from the water and soared into the sky.

They flew northwest through the clouds toward the Elf Empire. The twins were reminded of their voyage on the *Granny* from up here. The world looked so peaceful and safe from above the clouds. They hoped that after meeting with the elves they would be one step closer to making the world below the clouds just as peaceful. After a few hours of flying, they arrived in the northwestern-most kingdom.

"Look, Conner!" Alex exclaimed. "There it is! That's the Elf Empire!"

"Whoa," Conner said. "Elves really do live in trees."

The entire empire was inside an enormous tree the size of a mountain. As the twins flew closer, they saw hundreds of homes built throughout the branches. Some were built on the tree like tree houses, some homes swung from the branches like birdhouses, and some were even built *into* the tree like squirrel nests.

The leaves were the size of the twins' bodies. It was as if they had shrunk and entered a miniature world. Lester carefully landed on a strong branch and the twins climbed off him. They walked along the branch, which was like a street, to all the different homes and toward the center of the tree where they figured the empress must live.

"I really hope this giant tree doesn't come with any giant bugs or birds," Conner said, and quivered at the idea.

"Squaaa!" Lester squawked, offended by the remark.

"Not *you*, Lester, I'm talking about giant crows or spiders," Conner said. "I don't want to become something's lunch."

Lester suddenly looked terrified of the tree. He waddled much closer to the twins for protection.

"I don't think we need to worry about that," Alex said. "Look around, there's *nothing* here."

The twins searched the branches below, above, and ahead, but didn't find anyone or anything. Every tree-home was vacant.

"They must have heard about the Grande Armée and left," Conner said.

Defeated, Alex took a seat on one of the smaller branches. "But where did they go?" she asked. "How are we supposed to find them?"

Conner looked around the tree while he thought on it. "Well, a whole empire couldn't have just uprooted and gone too far without someone noticing—" He froze. Before he could finish his thought, another one had interrupted.

"What is it?" Alex asked.

"Do you remember that time last year when you found me in the school library reading fairy tales?" Conner asked her.

"Maybe, why?"

"You said reading fairy tales was *returning to our roots*," Conner said. "Then you went on to tell me that certain species of birds and insects hide in their tree's roots when their home is being threatened. What if elves are one of those species?"

Alex got to her feet and started jumping up and down. "Conner, you're a genius!" Alex said. "I bet the elves never left! I bet if we fly to the bottom of the tree, we'll find the elves hiding!"

Conner started jumping up and down with his sister—he never missed an opportunity to celebrate his own cleverness. "I'm so glad I remembered that," he said happily. "Because I gotta tell you, most of the stuff you say to me goes in one ear and out the—*AAAAH!*"

CRACK! The twins had been jumping on a weak part of the

branch and fell straight through it. To their surprise, the tree branch was hollow and they landed on a long wooden slide. The slide traveled through the branch and coiled down the giant tree trunk. The twins screamed and tried to grab ahold of anything they could but the slide was too slick, so they slid deeper and deeper into the bottom of the tree.

The slide finally ended and Alex and Conner piled on top of each other on the ground. The giant tree trunk was hollow and they found themselves in a secret chamber at the tree's base. Alex and Conner looked up and could see the slide was one of many that spiraled upward into the different branches of the tree. They had fallen into an escape route.

The twins were also startled to see that they were no longer alone. Thousands and thousands of elves were hiding at the bottom of the tree just like they had predicted and they were just as surprised to see them.

They were all short but very thin. Everything about them was pointed: They had pointed ears, pointed jaws, pointed shoes, and some even wore pointed cone hats. Their clothing was black and white and asymmetrical. They wore vests that buttoned sideways; their pant legs and sleeves were different lengths.

"What's up with their clothes?" Conner whispered to his sister.

"Don't you remember the story 'The Shoemaker and the Elves'?" Alex whispered back. "Elves are horrible at making their own clothes."

Upon their arrival the twins were instantly circled by a dozen elf soldiers. They pointed their wooden crossbows at them and Alex and Conner threw their hands up.

"What are you doing in our empire?" one of the elf soldiers asked.

"We don't mean any trouble!" Conner said.

"We've come to speak with your empress," Alex said.

The elves shoved their crossbows closer to them. "Who are you?" the soldier demanded.

"I'm Conner Bailey and this is my sister, Alex," Conner whimpered. He panicked. "My sister's a big deal—she's sort of the Fairy Godmother at the moment."

"Conner!"

"What else am I supposed to say? They're about to shoot us!"

"Liars!" the elf shouted.

Alex reached for her wand and with one *swoosh* magically turned all their crossbows into bouquets of flowers. All the elves in the tree gasped and stepped back from her.

"She's a witch! She's come to grind our bones for her potions! Seize her!" the elf ordered. The soldiers lunged toward them and the twins braced themselves.

"STOP!" said a stern voice from the other side of the tree. All the elves quickly turned toward the direction it had come from. Across the secret chamber a female elf sat on a throne made of leaves.

"I'm guessing that's the empress," Conner said under his breath.

Empress Elvina was the largest elf in the room and when she stood from her throne she towered over everyone, including the twins—she was like a queen bee in a hive. She had a pointed jaw, pointed ears, large brown eyes, and very long earlobes. Her dark hair was wrapped in two buns on each side of her head and she wore a large headdress made of branches that stretched high and wide above her. The empress's gown was very tight and made entirely of sticks and twigs as if they had been individually glued to her lean body. She looked like a walking tree.

A fluffy but massive red squirrel was perched at the side of her throne like an overgrown dog. The empress slowly sauntered toward the twins and the elves parted as she moved through them.

"If she says she's the Fairy Godmother, then let her prove it," the empress challenged. She was exactly like Mother Goose had described, very beautiful on the outside but the twins could tell there was much more behind her intimidating eyes.

Alex didn't know what to do. She may have been a girl with a wand, but how was she going to convince the elves that she was legitimately acting as the Fairy Godmother?

A loud squawking echoed from above them. The entire empire looked up and saw Lester sliding down into the base of the tree. He was flapping his wings madly but was sliding too fast to stop. He plopped on the ground beside Alex and Conner, beak first. He greatly regretted his decision to follow the twins into the tree.

"We have a giant goose; does that help our case?" Conner asked with a nervous laugh. He meant it as a joke but the empress was taken by the large gander.

"I recognize this bird," she said. "He belongs to Mother Goose."

"Mother Goose is a friend of ours," Alex said. "She loaned us her goose so we could travel here safely to speak with you. I'm the Fairy Godmother's granddaughter, and since she's ill at the moment, I'm filling in for her."

Empress Elvina's eyes darted back and forth between the twins. Perhaps they were telling the truth after all.

"I hope you realize being the Fairy Godmother means nothing here. The Happily Ever After Assembly has no power or authority in my empire," she said.

"Yes, we understand," Alex said. "We've come here to warn you about an army that has invaded our world and plans to start a war—"

"We've heard about this Armée," the empress said. "That is why we have taken refuge inside our tree and we will stay here until the Armée is gone."

Conner took a step toward her. "But they won't go away unless we fight them together," he said. "The Happily Ever After Assembly needs the help of your army to defeat them. The fairies and humans can't do it alone."

An angry murmur broke out among the elves. The twins could see how outraged the empress was to hear this, but instead of getting angry, Elvina batted her eyelashes and a smile came to her face.

"Help?" She laughed. "You want our *help*? Did everyone hear that? The fairies have sent children to ask us for our help."

Only a few of the elves laughed with her. The rest of the chamber glared at Alex and Conner. They weren't making any friends.

"Look, Empress Tree Lady," Conner said. "We understand you're still upset that the elves weren't included in the Happily Ever After Assembly, but if we don't work together, the Grande Armée will destroy us all—"

"My dear boy," the empress said, and all the amusement faded from her face. "Is that what they told you—that we were upset because we weren't invited to join their little fairy club? Well, if so, it appears they've re-written history."

Alex and Conner exchanged a concerned look. "Then what else are you mad about?" Conner asked.

The empress knew their ignorance wasn't their fault and decided to educate them.

"The elves were tormented by dragons during the Dragon Age just as much as any other race," she explained. "Our ancestors helped the fairies defeat the dragons. Once the dragons were gone and the world entered the peaceful era of the Age of Magic, the fairies forgot everything we had done for them. They divided the world up among the surviving species. The humans were given several vast kingdoms but the elves were given only a tiny unlivable piece of land isolated from everyone else. We had been ostracized just as much as the trolls and goblins, but for no reason other than not being human."

The twins had never heard about this before. They'd always assumed the elves lived in the far northwest because they wanted to.

"When the elves objected to our assigned home, the fairies ignored us, and because the elves questioned them we weren't invited to join the Happily Ever After Assembly," Empress Elvina continued. "The northwest was full of predators that hunted elves, and witches that picked our bodies apart for potions, but the elves had no choice but to live here. Our ancestors grew this giant tree and built this empire high in its branches, far away from the dangers. And we've been here ever since."

Alex and Conner didn't know what to say. Could they apologize for something that happened so long ago?

"Well, you guys really screwed us over last year when you surrendered to the Enchantress!" Conner said, and folded his arms. "So I think we're even."

"Why were we expected to clean up a mess we didn't create?" the empress asked. "There is no difference between the Enchantress and this army—they're both your problems. The humans and fairies want to choose which issues the elves are involved in based on what's convenient for them—"

Alex interrupted her before the situation became worse. "Your Majesty, every nation will always remember history differently, and that's just how it is," she said. "We all live in the same world and it won't do anyone any good if we continue to play this game of *who was the bigger jerk* for eternity. Right now, more than ever, this world needs to stand united against a force that threatens us all. We weren't expecting you to cooperate just because we asked you to, so I'm willing to offer you something in return if you help us fight the Grande Armée."

"And what is that?" the empress asked mockingly.

"Yeah, what is that?" Conner asked, just as curious.

Alex knew she was going to regret making this offer for the rest of her life but they were running out of time. "Once this Armée is destroyed with the help of the elves, as the new Fairy Godmother I will abolish the Happily Ever After Assembly," she declared.

The entire chamber was astonished to hear this come from her mouth.

"What?" Conner shrieked.

"What did you just say?" the empress asked.

"You heard me," Alex said. "The Happily Ever After Assembly is unfair, it's exclusive, and it has proven to be inefficient in times of crisis. This world needs to march into the future *together.* So I'm inviting you to help me build a fresh and more inclusive assembly. Join me in creating the Happily Forever After Assembly."

This was shocking news to everyone in the room—especially to Alex. She had never dreamed of starting a new assembly to unite the fairy-tale world, but she knew the idea of one would be the only way to get the elf empress's attention.

The empress sauntered even closer to the twins. The whole empire was on pins and needles waiting to hear her answer.

"If the elves join this new assembly, I want to lead it," Empress Elvina said.

"You should have stuck with shoes, Alex!" Conner said. He slapped his palm against his forehead.

"The new assembly won't have a *leader,*" Alex said. "But you can manage it *with* me. The assembly will look to the Fairy Godmother and the empress of the elves for guidance and we will advise them *together.*"

Alex offered her hand to the empress. Elvina sneered down at it; she had never trusted a human before, but she knew Alex was a woman of her word. Empress Elvina shook Alex's hand and the deal was made. There was no going back now.

"My army is at your disposal, Fairy Godmother," the empress said with a small bow.

"Terrific," Alex said. She looked over at her brother, who sighed with as much relief as she did. Now that the elves were on their side, they could actually win this war.

"Now I want the Elf Army to follow me into the Fairy Kingdom immediately," Alex said. "I'll signal the other armies throughout the kingdoms to join us and we'll strike the Grande Armée before they—"

A deafening noise filled the giant tree as it was hit with a cannonball that blew part of the tree trunk to bits. The twins and the elves hit the ground, and sunlight filled the dark chamber, pouring in from the enormous hole that had just been created. They were too late—the Grande Armée had started their attack.

Another thunderous sound erupted as another cannonball hit the tree, followed by another and another.

"What's happening?" the elf empress screamed.

"It's the Grande Armée!" Conner yelled. "They're here! The Elf Empire is under attack!"

The elves started to panic and ran around the tree in hysterics.

"Everyone remain calm!" Elvina shouted. "I want everyone to climb to safety at once! Our army will stay behind and fight these invaders!"

Alex looked to her brother like a deer in headlights—in a matter of seconds their entire plan had gone astray.

"Conner, what do we do now?" Alex asked. "We need the elves to go with us so we can strike the Armée as a whole!"

"We have to get out of here and come up with a new plan, then!" Conner said. "If the Armée is attacking, I doubt the elves are the only ones they're targeting!"

"But the elves!" Alex pleaded. "We need them if we want to win!"

"We don't have a choice! We need to leave now!"

Conner grabbed Lester's reins and forced his sister onto the large bird. He climbed on the goose's back himself and they flew higher into the hollow tree. A cannon blasted a hole through the trunk near the top and Conner steered Lester through it and outside the giant tree.

The twins could see a thousand soldiers and hundreds of ogres surrounding the Elf Empire's tree. The soldiers re-directed their cannons toward Lester and the twins as soon as they were spotted emerging from the tree. The ogres grabbed boulders from the ground and threw them at the goose along with the cannonballs.

Lester squawked in terror as he narrowly dodged the cannonballs and boulders jetting toward him. He flew as fast as he could away from the Elf Empire's tree. They created a distraction as the Elf Army began firing their crossbows at the soldiers from inside the tree. The citizens of the Elf Empire also began dropping giant acorns and twigs on the Grande Armée from the branches above them.

Just when the twins thought they had flown out of the cannons' reach, a rogue cannonball bolted through the sky and blasted through Lester's right wing. The gander squawked in pain and he and the twins began rapidly descending toward the trees on the horizon. Lester flapped his left wing as hard as he could but it wasn't enough to keep them in the sky.

They crashed hard onto the forest ground. The twins were thrown off Lester's back and into separate directions through the trees. Conner hit a tree and then landed in a large shrub underneath it. Alex skidded across a grassy field and heard a crunch underneath her. When she came to a stop she reached for her wand but it had snapped into several pieces in her pocket.

Alex and Conner were too wounded to get to their feet. They both had broken several bones in their bodies from the crash. They heard Lester squawking in the distance—he was perhaps in even more pain than they were. They heard the attack on the Elf Empire continuing in the distance but there was nothing they could do. They looked at the trees around them and wondered where they had landed but their vision faded away as they both slowly lost consciousness.

The war had begun.

CHAPTER TWENTY-FOUR

THE FORGOTTEN ARMY

The Grande Armée's divided troops spread out across the fairy-tale world to attack the kingdoms they had been assigned. Hundreds of Armée soldiers and trolls crossed into the Charming Kingdom preparing to take the capital by storm.

Xanthous hovered in the air high above the spirals of the Charming Palace clock tower and saw the soldiers marching in the distance. The moment they had feared the most had come—the Charming Kingdom was facing its first attack and its defenses were outnumbered. Xanthous pointed his finger into the air and a fiery flare shot from it. It signaled Sir Lampton and his men below and they quickly assembled on the front lawns of the Charming Palace.

"How many are there?" Sir Lampton asked Xanthous as he descended to the lawns.

"They outnumber us by a few hundred trolls," the fairy said. "The stakes are high but it could be much worse."

"We must signal the other half of our army to come out of hiding," Sir Lampton said. "If they only outnumber us by trolls, we could win this battle! Not as many of my men will have to lose their lives today."

"Lampton, we can't," Xanthous said. "We have to fight the Armée off with the men we have while we wait for the signal. Trust me, this is only the first battle we'll face and if we use all our forces now, there may be no one left to fight the horrors of tomorrow."

Sir Lampton's face grew serious and he stepped closer to him. "How am I supposed to tell these men they're about to die in battle while their brothers stay in hiding?"

"We may not win this battle but if we want to win the war we have to follow the plan," Xanthous said.

Sir Lampton reluctantly nodded. "God, I hope that little girl's plan works," he said to himself.

"Me too, sir," Xanthous said. "I don't want to think about what the world will look like if we fail."

Sir Lampton mounted his horse and rode it through the lines of Charming soldiers. "My good men," he shouted. "The enemy has arrived in our beautiful home sooner than we expected. We may be outnumbered by soldiers and by trolls, but they can never outmatch us in heart, in courage, or in love for our country!" Lampton withdrew his sword and raised it high above his head. "Let's be the first ones to show these monsters that the Charming Kingdom is not for sale! Let's give them a taste of the Charming Army so they cower in fear when our brothers return from hiding to finish them off!"

The Charming soldiers all raised their swords with him. They cheered Lampton's words even though they knew the odds of surviving this battle were against them. Like true soldiers, they turned their fear into bravery and courageously faced the oncoming threat to protect the country they loved.

"But we're not outnumbered!" a voice called out from behind the soldiers.

Lampton and his soldiers turned toward the voice and they saw it wasn't alone. Slowly emerging from behind the Charming Palace and from the streets surrounding the capital were hundreds and hundreds of civilians. The men and women carried pots and pans, pitchforks and hoes, rolling pins and knives, scissors and shears, mops and buckets. They were bakers and farmers, locksmiths and seamstresses, teachers and butchers, maids and butlers—and they all had come to stand proudly with the soldiers of their kingdom.

"What's going on?" Xanthous asked the civilians.

"We've come to join the fight!" a farmer declared, and all the men and women of his party cheered.

"This is our home, too!" a seamstress yelled.

"We won't let our kingdom fall into the hands of anyone else but our king and queen," a butcher shouted.

Their enthusiasm befuddled the soldiers. In his entire military career, Sir Lampton had never seen anything like this before. The Charming citizens were perhaps more eager to fight the Armée than the soldiers were.

"Ladies and gentlemen," Lampton shouted, gesturing for them to quiet down. "We respect your intentions, but this is a matter for the Charming Army and we morally cannot ask this of you!"

A maid dramatically looked around at her crowd of servants. "*Asked?* Was anyone here *asked* to fight for this kingdom?" she said. "I don't have to be *asked*—I'm here of my own accord because I want to protect my home and I'm not leaving until the Armée is gone!"

The civilians burst into a thunderous roar. Their enthusiasm was unyielding. Nothing Lampton said or did was going to convince them to leave.

Xanthous looked at Lampton and shrugged. "It won't hurt to have more numbers," he said.

Sir Lampton gazed around at the willing crowd. His army had almost doubled right before his eyes. It was a sight that warmed him to the center of his heart. The people he had spent his entire life loyally protecting had come to *his* aid. They cared about their kingdom's prosperity as much as he did.

Lampton raised his sword to the bigger and stronger army now surrounding him. "Then let us fight these invaders together and show them what the Charming Army *and* the Charming Kingdom are made of!" he declared.

The soldiers of the Charming Army raised their swords,

their brooms, their rakes, their hammers, their rolling pins, their knitting needles, and whatever other objects they had brought with them for battle. They cheered so loudly together the sound was heard miles away and the soldiers and trolls of the approaching Armée quivered in their boots.

CHAPTER TWENTY-FIVE

THE HEALING FLAMES OF HAGETTA'S FIRE

Conner wasn't expecting to wake up. When Lester crashed into the forest, he figured it was *the end*. He hoped that the Happily Ever After Assembly could win the war without them, and if they did, he hoped he and his sister would be remembered as war heroes. The last image in his head as he slowly lost consciousness was the statue they would erect in his honor. The statue was much taller and more muscular than he was in real life and the sculptor had added a cleft in his chin—it was exactly how Conner wanted to be remembered.

But to Conner's surprise—*he woke up*. His eyelids slowly opened and his blurry vision took a moment to adjust. He was lying on a cot in a small and cluttered cottage. A large wooden table and an iron cauldron were in the center of the cottage and a thick stack of mirrors had been placed between them. The walls were filled from floor to ceiling with shelves of jars: jars of dirt, sand, plants, flowers, colorful liquids, insects, small reptiles, and pieces of bigger animals, like pig ears and cow hooves. A small fire of peach-colored flames burned in a tiny brick fireplace.

"Where am I?" he asked himself. He felt a tingling on the side of his torso and looked down to see his entire left side was engulfed in the same peach-colored flames. *"AHHH! I'm on fire! I'm on fire!"*

Conner screamed and looked around the cottage for something to extinguish them. He didn't see anything and beat the flames with his sleeves. He figured his whole body was in shock since he didn't feel any pain.

A woman appeared from another room in the cottage and rushed to Conner's side.

"Calm down," the woman said, and grabbed his hands. "You're doing more damage than the fire is," she said. The woman was middle-aged and wore dark red robes. Her hair was the same color as her robes and she had bright green eyes.

"What's happening to me?" Conner yelled.

"You broke your ribs in the fall," the woman said. "The fire is healing you."

"The fire is *healing me*?" he asked.

The woman walked to the fireplace. "It's a magic fire. Look," she said, and held her hand over the flames. They flickered around her hand but didn't burn her. "See? Are you satisfied?"

Conner stopped panicking but he was anything but relaxed. Seeing his body covered in flames was incredibly unsettling, however helpful they were.

"Did you see us crash?" Conner asked the woman.

"Yes," the woman said. "You were all hurt pretty bad. I brought you back here to heal your wounds before they got worse. You're in the Dwarf Forests, but don't worry, you're safe in my cottage."

"Where's my sister? Is she all right?" Conner asked.

"She's banged up worse than you but she's coming around," the woman said.

The woman moved her cauldron out of the way so Conner could see his sister resting peacefully on a cot behind it. Alex's leg and wrist were covered in flames healing her broken bones.

"Who are you?" Conner asked. "Are you a witch?"

"My name is Hagetta," the woman said. "I prefer the term *healer* these days, but yes, I'm a witch."

Her name instantly rang a bell. "Hagetta?" he repeated. "Any relation to the witch named Hagatha?"

Hagetta nodded. "She was my much older sister," she said. "Hagatha taught me everything I know about witchcraft. But I was never interested in dark magic like she was, so we parted ways shortly before she died."

Alex stirred to life and slowly sat up. She looked around the cottage as her eyes adjusted. "Where am I?"

"You're safe, dear," Hagetta said.

"Hey, Alex, heads-up—you're also on fire! But don't worry, it's helping your leg and wrist heal," Conner warned her.

Alex's eyes grew twice in size as she saw the flames engulfing her wrist and leg. *"Okay,"* she peeped. Nothing could make her entirely comfortable with this. "Sooo...what kind of fire am I on exactly?"

"They're healing flames from the breath of an albino dragon," Hagetta explained. "The albino dragons were very rare and just as awful as regular dragons, but their flames had unique healing qualities. My great-great-great-great-grandmother acquired some of those flames during the Dragon Age and my family has kept them burning from generation to generation."

"Wow," Conner said. "I can't even keep a Chia Pet alive."

Alex became less anxious knowing this information but she was still uneasy from waking up in the strange cottage. She couldn't stop staring at Hagetta—she could have sworn their paths had crossed in the past.

"Do I know you from somewhere?" she asked.

"Her name is Hagetta and she's Hagatha's younger sister." Conner filled her in.

Alex was shocked. "You're *Hagatha's* sister?"

"I am," Hagetta said. "But I believe we saw each other at Jack and Goldilocks's wedding."

"You're right!" Alex said, putting the pieces together. "How do you know Jack and Goldilocks?"

Hagetta laughed at the thought. "I've known Goldilocks since she was a very little girl and started her life on the run. We first met when I caught her trying to rob me. I scared her off and thought I'd never see her again, but then a few weeks later I found her in the woods—she had been attacked by some creature and barely survived. I brought her back here and healed her wounds but she refused to stay any longer. She insisted she didn't need my help and told me she could take care of herself. I knew she was too stubborn to convince, so I gave Goldilocks her first sword. I told her she would have to learn to defend herself if she was going to live on her own."

"You gave Goldilocks her first sword?" Conner asked, tickled pink by the story. "That's like giving Shakespeare his first pen!"

Hagetta smiled. "She returned the favor a few years later. A gang of trolls cornered me in the woods and tried to enslave me. Goldilocks heard my pleas for help and she came out of nowhere on that horse of hers."

"Wow, talk about karma," Conner said.

"Indeed," Hagetta said. "And since then, I've tried to assist anyone I met who needs a helping hand. I never thought a wanted fugitive would teach me the power of a clean conscience."

"We can't thank you enough for helping us," Conner said, then quickly looked around the room. "Wait, where's Lester?"

The twins heard a *squawk* as Lester drowsily popped his head up from under Hagetta's table. Flames covered his busted beak and his left wing was ablaze as the peach-colored fire slowly re-grew his wing one feather at a time.

"That is the most stubborn gander I have ever met," Hagetta said. "He wouldn't let me touch you when I first found you— it was like he was protecting his own chicks. I told him I only meant to help but still had to sedate him with a sleeping potion to calm him down. It should be out of his system by now."

Conner made an affectionate frown and rubbed the giant goose's neck. "Thanks for looking out for us, bud," he said. "Mother Goose will be very happy to hear that."

Alex searched her dress pockets and suddenly gasped. "Oh no," she said. "My wand broke and the pieces must have fallen out of my pocket!"

"No worries, child, your wand will be back to normal soon," Hagetta said. She pointed to the fireplace and Alex saw her crystal wand had been placed directly on the firewood and the flames were slowly mending it.

Alex was so relieved she laid back down and almost forgot she was on fire herself.

"You're the nicest witch we've ever met," Conner said. "I thought all witches were terrible, but you've proven me wrong."

"All it takes is one bad apple to disgrace a whole tree," Hagetta said. "I come from a very long line of witches and I've only ever heard of *one* witch who eats children—but thanks to the story 'Hansel and Gretel,' the whole world thinks *all of us* live in gingerbread houses and lure innocent youths to their deaths."

"That's an interesting point," Conner said. "I've met just as many ugly humans as I have ugly witches but *we're* not stereotyped."

"Most witches don't start out as ugly," Hagetta said. "Dark magic leaves its mark on its dealers. My sister Hagatha was the most beautiful woman I had ever seen. Men traveled across kingdoms to woo and court her. But after devoting her life to harmful witchcraft, its effects began to show on her face."

Alex sat straight up. "Wait a second, how long have we been here?" she asked.

"A few hours," Hagetta said.

"Oh no," Alex said. "Conner, we've got to get back to the Fairy Palace at once! Now that the Grande Armée has started attacking we have to form a new plan!" She made the mistake of stepping on her bad foot and yelped in pain before falling back onto the cot.

"You two are no good to anyone in the condition you're in," Hagetta said. "Wait for the flames to finish doing their job. Once they burn out, you'll be healed."

As much as it killed her to sit still at a time like this, Alex had no choice. Their plan had been compromised, and she slumped as if they had already lost the war.

"It was really smart of you to keep half of the armies hidden, Alex," Conner said. "At least no one was unprepared for this to happen. As soon as we get back to the Fairy Palace we'll find out who has and hasn't been attacked—maybe our first plan can still work."

"I'm not sad because of our plan," Alex said. "You saw how viciously they opened fire on the Elf Empire. There's no way the Corner Kingdom or the Bo Peep Republic stands a chance against forces like that—"

Hagetta couldn't help but interrupt. "Did you just say 'Bo Peep Republic'?" she asked. "What on earth is that?"

"It's the new name of the Red Riding Hood Kingdom," Conner said. "They changed the name because Little Bo Peep was elected queen."

Hagetta raised both of her eyebrows and looked off into space, completely flabbergasted. "Was she now?" she asked.

"Do you know Little Bo Peep?" Alex asked.

It was obvious from her expression that they were acquainted. "Very well, I'm afraid."

"How do you know her?" Conner asked.

"She sought me out when she was a little girl," Hagetta explained. "Apparently she dozed off one afternoon on her farm and lost track of her sheep. The whole thing was a great embarrassment for her so she found me in the woods and paid me five gold coins to make her a potion that would keep her awake."

"Did you make her the potion?" Conner asked.

"I did," Hagetta said. "And it was one of the biggest mistakes I ever made."

"Was something wrong with the potion you gave her?" Alex asked.

"No, there was just a lot wrong with the customer," Hagetta said. "The potion worked so well that Little Bo came back to me many times, expecting fixes for all of her problems throughout the years. She needed a potion for her sheep to grow the fluffiest wool, she needed a potion for her cows to give the sweetest milk, she wanted seeds to make her chickens lay the biggest eggs—it never stopped! Especially when *that man* came into the picture."

The twins looked at each other, equally intrigued.

"Which man?" Conner asked.

"The man Little Bo fell madly in love with," Hagetta said. "He was older than she was and a total crook."

"Are you talking about the man trapped inside her magic

mirror?" Alex asked. Her curiosity had completely taken over her body and she couldn't help asking.

Conner and Hagetta both stared at her. Conner had no idea what she was talking about but Hagetta was astonished she knew anything about it.

"How did you know about the magic mirror?" Hagetta asked.

"What magic mirror?" Conner asked, hoping one of them would fill him in.

Alex hesitated as she tried to make the explanation as harmless for herself as possible. "During the election a friend and I thought it would be fun to spy on Little Bo," Alex said. "We weren't looking to cause any trouble, just to have some fun, but we saw a magic mirror inside her barn and there was a man trapped inside it."

Conner raised a suspicious eyebrow. "Is this the same friend you're *not dating*?"

Alex didn't respond. All her attention was on Hagetta.

"The magic mirror in Little Bo's possession is a mirror of communication, not of imprisonment," Hagetta said. "I should know—I made it for her. The man you saw wasn't trapped in the mirror; he was locked away in prison many years ago. I gave them each a mirror so they could still communicate."

Alex covered her mouth. It had never occurred to her that the mirror in Little Bo's barn might be a communication mirror like the kind she and her brother had.

"Wait a second," Conner said, making connections of his own. "There was a mirror in one of the cells in Pinocchio Prison! Is Little Bo Peep in love with *the Masked Man*?"

"She never told me his real name but yes, that is the name

he chose for himself," Hagetta said. "He was the youngest son in a very powerful family—but he longed to be more powerful than all of them. He tried everything he possibly could to gain the control he desired; he lied and stole, he made promises he couldn't keep, and bargained deals he couldn't afford. He's the most conniving type of man there is."

Alex nodded as everything began making sense to her. "Little Bo wanted to be queen because she thought being the ruler of a kingdom would give her the authority to free him from prison."

Hagetta grunted. "I'm sure she also couldn't live with the guilt," she said. "Little Bo is the reason he was caught in the first place—*she turned him in.*"

Conner gasped. "She turned in the man she loved?"

"He may have cast a spell on Little Bo's innocent heart, but even she couldn't deny how dangerous he was. She warned me about him just as many times as she confessed her undying love. She betrayed him because Little Bo was protecting someone *else* she loved," Hagetta explained. "Little Bo and the Masked Man had a *child.*"

Both the twins shook their heads in disbelief. "Little Bo is a mother?" Conner asked.

"She was," Hagetta said. "Little Bo was terrified of what the Masked Man would do if he found out she was carrying his child. He was so obsessed with power she was afraid he would see an heir as a threat. So she wrote an anonymous letter to the Fairy Palace warning them of his plans to steal from the Fairy Godmother, and he was caught in the act. Little Bo gave birth to a son while he was locked up and he never knew about the baby or the betrayal."

"What happened to the baby?" Alex asked.

Hagetta sighed and shook her head. "Little Bo came here while she was in labor and delivered the child right in this room," she said. "She begged me to take the child somewhere the Masked Man could never find him. She was so young at the time I couldn't argue that the child should be raised by someone else. So I took him to a place I will never reveal for as long as I live, so his father will never find him. It broke Little Bo's heart to be separated from the child and the Masked Man. I tried soothing her with the healing flame, but even the flames of an albino dragon can't fix a broken heart."

"Did you do anything else to help her?" Conner asked.

"I did," Hagetta said. "And it was the only time I ever performed dark magic. I followed a spell I saw my sister perform on a lovesick maiden a long time ago. I cut out a small piece of Little Bo's heart, the part that was full of hurt and longing for the men in her life, and I turned it into stone. The maiden my sister used the enchantment on turned into a soulless monster, and I wanted better for Little Bo, so I gave Little Bo the piece of her heart on a chain and told her to wear it when she was ready to face the loss that comes with love. For her sake, I hope he stays in prison for the rest of his life."

It was a tragic story and it made Alex even more nervous about the chapter of the story they were still in.

"Hagetta, the Masked Man was recruited by the Grande Armée," Alex said. "He promised the general he could take them to a dragon egg. We were told it was impossible, but if he is as powerful as you say, do you think he actually knows where to obtain one?"

Hagetta went very quiet and her face became still. Horrific images flashed behind her eyes that she didn't share with the twins.

"I pray he doesn't," Hagetta said. "The fairies were successful in ridding the world of dragons, but there have always been rumors that there were one or two eggs left behind. No one would know how to kill a dragon anymore if one should arise—all those fairies are either dead or too old to slay a dragon now. If the Masked Man were to get his hands on a dragon egg, it wouldn't matter what kind of plan you formed, the world would be over."

CHAPTER TWENTY-SIX

<hr />

FEEDING THE CREATURE

The villagers dug so deep into the earth they created a canyon beside the Grande Armée's camp. A villager by the name of Farmer Robins had the misfortune of being the first to uncover the magma below the dirt. As soon as his shovel broke the ground, the lava gushed out and burned his hands. He screamed and fell to the ground in agony.

Although Rook had been warned to leave the south of the Eastern Kingdom, by the time he convinced his father that they should take Alex's advice, the Grande Armée had occupied their farm and the villages nearby. Rook and his father were taken captive and brought to the camp to dig along with the other imprisoned villagers.

"Father!" Rook cried, and rushed to his father's side.

Lava rapidly filled the canyon and the villagers frantically climbed out of it to safety. Rook and another man hoisted Farmer Robins onto their shoulders and helped him up out of the canyon just as its base filled with lava. The lava was so hot the abandoned shovels caught on fire before it even touched them.

General Marquis peered through his tent at the commotion and a small smile appeared on his face. He knew it was time to hatch the dragon egg.

The villagers were gathered in a group at the side of the canyon by the soldiers who observed them. They panted and sweated profusely from their quick climb. Rook held his father's head in his lap; he was moaning in pain from his burns. He needed help but as Rook looked around the camp he realized there was no one there who could help his father. He had to figure out a way to escape the camp as soon as possible.

A few moments later General Marquis and Colonel Baton stood over the edge of the canyon looking down at the orange lava at the very bottom. The Masked Man was sent into the canyon to place the dragon egg in the lava and the commanders waited impatiently for him to return. Finally, they saw his covered face appear as the Masked Man crawled up the canyon wall.

"Oh boy, we've got a lively one!" he happily shouted up at the commanders. Parts of his tattered clothing had been burned off and the edges of his mask were smoky. Apparently the hatching process hadn't been seamless.

"Did the egg hatch?" the general asked.

"Yes, it did!" the Masked Man said. "Congratulations, General, it's a boy! And he's a feisty lad! He nearly scorched me to death with his first breaths alone."

The Masked Man surfaced and reached out a hand for them to help him up but the general and the colonel didn't offer him any assistance. He pulled himself out of the ground and onto his feet and brushed all the dirt and ash from his clothes.

"And now what do we do?" the general asked.

"We feed him," the Masked Man said. "He's napping in the lava right now but he's going to be very hungry in a few minutes. The key is to keep as much food down there as possible. As soon as he runs out he'll climb up here to hunt, and we don't want him to do that until he's grown. Dragons are most aggressive when they first emerge from their nests, and we want him to save that energy for when he attacks the fairies."

The general grunted after learning he would have to wait even longer. The Masked Man continued to test his patience more than any battle ever had. "What does it eat?" the general asked.

"Meat," the Masked Man said as if it were obvious.

The general eyed the Masked Man peculiarly, hoping this might offer a chance to finally get rid of him.

"Don't look at me," the Masked Man said. "I'm nothing but skin and bone—he's going to need protein to build his strength. Besides, once he emerges, you'll still need me to show you how to declare dominance over him."

"Lieutenant Rembert?" General Marquis ordered.

Rembert was among the soldiers keeping watch over the villagers and stepped forward. "Yes, sir?" he asked.

"Round up all the livestock we took from the villagers and bring them to the edge of the canyon," the general said. "Gradually push the animals into the canyon as the Masked Man instructs."

"Yes, sir," Rembert said. "And what do you want us to do with the villagers now?"

General Marquis snuck a menacing glance at their captives. "Keep them alive for the time being," he said. "We may need more food for the dragon later."

Although the villagers couldn't hear the general, it was obvious what he was plotting with the lieutenant. They whispered frantically among themselves and the families held each other a little tighter than before. Rook looked around the camp, trying to think of something—*anything*—to save his father and the other villagers from this nightmare.

A repetitive and turbulent vibration moved through the ground as a galloping horse traveled toward the camp. The soldiers and the villagers looked into the forest and saw Capitaine De Lange charging toward them on his horse, returning from battle. He was in a frenzy and covered a wounded arm. He jumped off his horse and ran up to General Marquis.

"General Marquis! General Marquis!" the captain cried.

The general was anything but pleased to see him. "Why are you not leading the battalion in the Charming Kingdom, Capitaine De Lange? Have you led your men to a victory already?"

De Lange fell to his knees and stared up beseechingly at him. "Sir, my battalion did everything we could, but we were outnumbered!" he told him.

"*WHAT?*" the general shouted.

"Outnumbered?" Baton shouted as well. "But that is impossible! We sent more than enough trolls and soldiers into the Charming Kingdom!"

Capitaine De Lange began sobbing at the general's feet. He knew what the failure would cost him. "We counted the army correctly, sir! But we weren't expecting that hundreds and hundreds of citizens would be fighting with them! The trolls surrendered or fled into the Dwarf Forests upon seeing them. *We were defeated!*"

The general took a step closer and stared into De Lange's eyes. The lava at the bottom of the canyon behind him was nothing compared to the fire in Marquis's eyes.

"Are you telling me our Armée was defeated by the *peasant men and women* of the Charming Kingdom?" General Marquis asked. His nostrils had never been so wide and his head was so red he looked like he was about to catch on fire himself.

Capitaine De Lange shook his head; he had much worse news to tell him. "Not just in the Charming Kingdom, sir! Civilians stood with their kingdom's armies in *all of the kingdoms*. All of our calculations and predictions were correct—but we never could have seen *this* coming! Please believe me when I say we did everything in our power!"

The general turned his fiery gaze toward Colonel Baton, who was shocked by the news. "General, I oversaw the plans myself," Baton said. "We were positive they would lead to victory."

The general looked away from the colonel and promptly walked away from the men who had failed him. He had never been so disappointed in his entire military career.

"Lieutenant Rembert, your pistol," General Marquis demanded.

The lieutenant followed his instructions and retrieved his pistol for the general. In the blink of an eye, General Marquis turned to Colonel Baton and Capitaine De Lange and shot them both in the foot. They fell backward and slid down the canyon walls. They moaned as they tried to get to their feet. A low growling noise vibrated up the canyon walls and the commanders' moaning increased. A series of deafening screeches echoed next from the canyon, but they weren't human. The sound was like a thousand nails were being dragged across metal.

"The dragon's awake!" the Masked Man said, and the entire camp covered their ears.

In between the earsplitting screeches, the camp heard the colonel and the captain scream as they were eaten alive. The general's wrathful stare never left his face.

Marquis handed Rembert back his pistol. "Congratulations, Rembert, you're a colonel now," he said. "Now feed those animals to the dragon once it's finished with its appetizer."

"Yes, sir," Rembert said, and ran off to fetch the stolen livestock.

General Marquis paced up and down the edge of the canyon. He was experiencing the greatest failure of his life—and the general did not take failure well. More than half of his army was gone and it had been defeated by *peasants* of all things. He quietly plotted how his army was going to come back from this catastrophe.

The Masked Man approached him but kept his distance.

"You started this war and you can still win it," he said. "I'll tell you again, once you have the dragon—"

"If you tell me one more time all I need is a dragon to win this war, I will feed you piece by piece to the dragon myself!" the general warned. "Any hunter knows you cannot kill a boar with one arrow alone. You need one for the head and one for the heart. The dragon may be an arrow I'll fire into the head of this world, but if I had seized the capitals and the rulers of the kingdoms, I would have had this world's heart. This army would have been unstoppable."

Rook had been intently listening to their conversation the entire time. He realized he had information that the general wanted. "General!" he declared, standing with his hand raised. "If it's the kings and queens you're after, I know how you can get to them."

He couldn't believe what he was doing—it was as if his sense of survival had overridden all his other senses.

The general scowled at the boy and laughed at his pathetic attempt to get his attention. "Silence, before you are fed to the dragon next!"

"I'm serious," Rook said. The other villagers pleaded for him to sit and stay quiet but he resisted. "The kings and queens were sent away long before your men arrived at the capitals. I saw it happen and I know where they are."

General Marquis was already angry enough as it was and this village boy claiming to have answers *he* did not, was not helping. "Then tell me where they are," he said, and walked closer to him.

Rook shook his head. "I'm not telling you unless you set all the villagers free," he said.

The general was so upset by the mention of another bargain he looked as if lava were going to erupt from inside of him. "Perhaps I'll kill each of the villagers in front of you *until* you tell me where they are?"

"Excuse me, General?" the Masked Man said. "With all due respect, what the boy is asking for isn't very much. The villagers are useless so you wouldn't be losing anything by granting him what he wants in exchange for whatever he might know."

General Marquis gave the Masked Man the ugliest scowl yet. *"You don't have the right to give me advice!"* he said, and struck him across the face.

The Masked Man fell to the ground and spit out a mouthful of blood. "I'm only trying to help, General," he grunted. "If you lose this war, I lose this war, too! I'll be sent back to prison! I want to see you conquer this world as much as you do!"

The general slowly caught his breath and walked over to the boy. "All right, tell me and I'll let these people go free," he said calmly.

"No," Rook said. "Let them go first and then I'll tell you where the royals are."

The general stared directly at the boy, waiting for his left eye to twitch, but it didn't. "Fine," the general said. "But if you don't supply me with the rulers, I will kill you myself."

Marquis gestured for his soldiers to let the villagers go and Rook watched as one by one they were set free and ran into the forest. Many of them were hesitant to leave Rook with the soldiers but he assured them he would be fine. Farmer Robins was scooped up by two villagers and escorted out of the camp.

"Don't do this, Rook! Don't be a hero!" Farmer Robins cried out. He tried resisting the men helping him escape but his wounds were too painful for him to put up a fight. Rook waited until he was safely out of sight before giving the general the information he needed.

"I don't know where they are, but I know how to find them," Rook said.

"Then show us the way," the general demanded.

Rook closed his eyes and let out a sigh. It wasn't until after the deal had been made that he realized what he had done, or that by saving a few he had put many at risk. "Forgive me, Alex," he said to himself.

Had the world been in a better state, traveling down the secret path would have been quite an enjoyable trip. The kings and queens aboard the carriages were exposed to areas of their own kingdoms they had never seen before. They visited with one another and discussed how to make life easier for their kingdoms by reforming the treaties of their trading agreements and they considered how their armies could work together to manage the criminals who traveled between their borders.

The plans were bittersweet, though, knowing as they did that the Armée was still at large and that it would be a while before life would return to normal and they could return to their kingdoms.

Every few hours they stopped to stretch their legs and Goldilocks showed the travelers a new self-defense trick or two as they had requested, and she was impressed by the progress they made in such a short amount of time.

The voyage down the secret path had become a unique bonding experience for all the men and women involved. Goldilocks seemed to be enjoying it the most. She was practically glowing after every lesson and her smile never left her face.

"May I just say, you have never looked more gorgeous," Jack told his wife. "I've never seen you look so happy before."

"You know me, I love a good adventure," Goldilocks said. "Especially when I'm accompanied by my dashing husband."

Jack laughed and squinted at her. "I know you too well to believe that for one minute," he said. "There's something else you're not telling me, isn't there?"

"All right, I'll tell you," Goldilocks said. "Although I would never admit this in front of Red, being around the other queens—the strong, smart, and confident women that they are—has been highly enjoyable."

Jack's mouth fell open dramatically. "You mean to tell me my wife is enjoying *girl time*?" he asked with large mocking eyes.

"I think I am," Goldilocks said, just as amused to confess it as he was to hear it.

"I think there's even more behind that smile," Jack said. "You only make that face when you're about to surprise me with something. Come on, Goldie, you know I don't like surprises. Just tell me if you have a secret."

Goldilocks's smile grew even wider. "Perhaps I do," she said. "But like all good secrets, it deserves to be kept quiet until the right moment."

Jack laughed and shook his head. "You and your secrets," he said. "We could be married for one hundred years and I still would learn new things about you every day."

"I hope that doesn't bother you," Goldilocks said with a wink. "I am a woman of *many* secrets and you're just scratching the surface."

An endearing smile came to Jack's face. "Actually, everything I learn about you only makes me love you more."

Goldilocks leaned in to kiss him but the horses pulling their carriage suddenly dashed forward and began galloping much faster than they normally did. They looked forward and saw that the secret path, which usually curved and looped across the land ahead of them, had become perfectly straight and shot directly into the horizon.

"What's going on?" Goldilocks said.

"We're headed southeast," Jack said after glancing up at the sun. "Maybe Alex and the others want us back? Maybe the war is over?"

The carriages raced through the countryside and into the forests of the southeast. The horses began to slow down, however, when a young man came into view on the path ahead. He was in his mid-teens and was tall with floppy brown hair.

Red poked her head out of her carriage window to see what was going on. "I know I've never met that boy before, but I could almost swear I know who he is," she said, wondering how.

The carriages stopped directly in front of him. The young man looked up at them with tears in his eyes.

"Who are you?" Jack asked.

"I'm sorry," the young man said.

"Sorry about—" but Goldilocks didn't have a chance to finish her sentence.

A hundred soldiers suddenly emerged from the trees and surrounded the carriages. Jack and Goldilocks quickly retrieved their weapons but there were too many of them to fight. The kings and queens in the carriages screamed as rifles and swords were pointed at them. There wasn't anything anyone could do—they had been ambushed by the Grande Armée.

General Marquis was the last to appear out of the trees. He stood behind Rook and patted his shoulder. "Well done, my boy," he said. "Well done, indeed."

CHAPTER TWENTY-SEVEN

THE SIGNAL IN THE SKY

The flames on Alex's and Conner's wounds faded as the sun set and night fell upon the tiny cottage in the woods. Soon the flames dimmed more, burning so low only a thin glow covered the healing parts of their bodies.

"The flames are almost gone," Alex said. She stood from the cot and finally could put weight on her leg without any pain.

"My ribs feel good, too," Conner said. He twisted his torso and touched his toes without any difficulty. "I've never felt better! Looks like the fire did the trick!"

"We really need to get going," Alex said to Hagetta.

Hagetta didn't argue with her this time. She retrieved Alex's crystal wand from the fireplace and handed it to her. "Here you are, my dear."

Alex examined her wand and didn't find a scratch on it—it was as good as new. "We'll never forget this kindness," Alex said. "If there is anything we can ever do, please don't hesitate—"

Hagetta raised her hand. "The best thing you can do is to promise me you'll take care of yourselves," she said warmly. "I don't understand why such heavy burdens have been placed on your young shoulders, but the taller you stand, the less weight you'll feel. Don't ever let anything break your spirit, children. Courage is something no one can take away from you."

Alex and Conner exchanged a kindhearted smile with her. Goldilocks had told them the same thing once, and now they knew who she had learned it from.

"We always seem to land on our feet," Conner said. "Except that one time you saw us crash and we almost died—but thanks to you, we even bounced back from that!"

Alex leaned under the table. "Are you ready to go, Lester?"

"Squaaa!" Lester squawked and happily fluttered to his feet, almost knocking the table over in the process.

"Great, then let's go—"

Suddenly, a heavy knock came on Hagetta's door. All four of them immediately turned to it.

"Are you expecting company?" Conner asked.

"No," Hagetta said. She was just as alarmed as the twins were by the sound of a visitor. "Quick, hide behind the cauldron so no one will see you."

The twins crouched behind the cauldron. Lester dived under the table again and Hagetta placed a large tablecloth over it to shield him better. Alex pointed her wand at the door, preparing for the worst.

Hagetta opened the door only a sliver and peeked outside. "Can I help you?" she asked the caller.

"Hello, sorry to disturb you but I'm looking for a young girl and boy. The goose they were flying was shot from the sky and they were spotted landing in the woods around this area," said a familiar voice. "Have you seen them?"

Hagetta cautiously opened the door a bit wider so the twins could see who was on the other side.

"Xanthous!" Conner exclaimed, and popped up from behind the cauldron.

"It's all right, Hagetta, he's a friend," Alex said.

Hagetta let him inside and he greeted the twins with enormous hugs. He had never been so happy to see them.

"Alex! Conner! Thank the heavens you're all right! I've been looking for you everywhere," he said.

His cheerful demeanor confused the twins—weren't they in the middle of a war? Did he not know the Elf Empire and other territories had been attacked?

"Xanthous, why aren't you in the Charming Kingdom?" Alex asked. "The Grande Armée has started their attacks! We saw them strike the Elf Empire!"

"We were just about to warn you and the other fairies," Conner said.

"We already know! *All* the kingdoms have been attacked except for the Fairy Kingdom," he informed them.

Alex covered her mouth and tears instantly filled her eyes. "Oh no!" she said. "We never expected they would attack all the kingdoms at once! We didn't plan for that! I told everyone to split their armies in half! I left everyone outnumbered!"

Xanthous placed his hands on her shoulders and looked directly into her eyes. "Alex, you don't have to be upset. Even with half the armies in hiding, *we* still managed to outnumber *them*!"

Both the twins' hearts started racing, but for the first time in a while they beat in a good way. Was he telling them good news or were they just imagining it?

"Did you just say you outnumbered the Armée?" Conner asked. "But how is that possible? They were double the size of us."

A proud smile came to Xanthous's face. "It seems both sides made a mistake in counting," he said. "They counted the kingdoms' armies *after* they were divided and only sent enough soldiers to match those numbers. And it seems we didn't incorporate the *forgotten army* in our estimates."

"What forgotten army?" Alex asked. Her head was spinning trying to recall a kingdom or territory they hadn't counted.

"The citizens!" Xanthous exclaimed. "I've never seen anything like it! As soon as the Grande Armée and their recruited criminals crossed into the Charming Kingdom, all the average civilians left their homes to join the army in the fight! And it didn't just happen in the Charming Kingdom; I've heard word from Skylene, Rosette, Tangerina, and Coral—the same thing happened in the other kingdoms as well!"

"That's awesome!" Conner said with a celebratory fist pump.

It sounded too good to be true and Alex wanted to get all the facts straight before she got her hopes up. "Wait a second. You're telling me the majority of the Grande Armée has been wiped out and we still have *half* of the Happily Ever After Assembly armies in hiding waiting to reappear?"

"Yes!" Xanthous nodded.

"So that means *we* outnumber them now! And by a lot!" Conner happily concluded.

"We do!" Xanthous said, and picked up both the twins and whirled them around the cottage. "We just might win this war after all!"

The twins were so happy to hear this they hollered and jumped around the cottage. Their celebration was cut short when Alex remembered there may have been more than just soldiers at stake.

"Xanthous, the war isn't over yet," she said. "There is a chance the Grande Armée has obtained a dragon egg! We still need to rally every last soldier we can and get to the Fairy Kingdom before the Armée does! I bet they're planning to strike it last!"

"But that's impossible," Xanthous said. "Dragons have been extinct for hundreds and hundreds of years."

"I'm afraid it's very possible," Hagetta said. "I've never seen one myself but there have been rumors among the witch community for a very long time that one or two were preserved."

Xanthous sighed and the flames on his head and shoulders went low as he thought about it. "Then let's not waste another minute," he said. "Alex, it's time for the signal. Let's get back to the Fairy Kingdom—it should only take the kingdoms' armies a day or two to meet us there."

"No, that's not good enough," Conner said. "We need a way to get all these men to the Fairy Palace *now*. As soon as the general hears his units have been defeated he'll want to strike again soon."

"But you can't get thousands and thousands of men to the same place at one time," Xanthous said. "There isn't a flying ship or a secret path large enough."

Alex went very quiet and thought to herself. "It'll have to be a spell—possibly the biggest act of magic ever done in the history of the fairy-tale world," she said. "The signal has to alert all the soldiers and transport them to the Fairy Kingdom at the same time."

"But who or what is *that* powerful?" Conner said. "I don't think Grandma or the Enchantress could pull off something like that."

Xanthous and Alex looked at each other but neither of them had an answer or an idea. Alex thought back to her magic lessons with her grandmother—if Alex could just visualize something well enough, she knew she could make it happen. But what could she possibly visualize that would accomplish this?

Hagetta cleared her throat. "If I were you, I would use the night sky as an ally," she said. "During times of trouble, most people look to the stars for guidance."

It was exactly what Alex needed to hear. Her eyes grew and she looked up to the cottage ceiling as the idea came to her. She imagined it perfectly, as if she were seeing it projected on the ceiling above her. "I know what the spell has to be!" she said. "I'm going to need help, but I think it's crazy enough to work!"

"You've never let us down before," Xanthous said.

His words were encouraging and Alex needed encouragement now more than ever. "Xanthous, I want you to collect all the fairies stationed throughout the kingdoms and meet us back in the Fairy Kingdom," Alex said. "Conner and Lester, you'll come with me."

Xanthous bowed to Alex and Conner. "I'll see you there." He burst into bright shimmering sparks and disappeared into thin air.

"Where are we going?" Conner asked, but before she could answer, Alex raced out of the cottage and onto the grassy lawn outside. Conner and Lester quickly followed her out and Hagetta watched from the doorway.

Alex climbed onto Lester's back and took his reins. She gestured for Conner to do the same and this time he sat behind her on the goose.

"Lester, I want you to fly as high into the sky as you possibly can," she instructed him, and he nodded eagerly.

"So what are you going to do?" Conner asked Alex. "This might be the single most important spell you'll ever cast in your life—no pressure or anything!"

Alex looked over her shoulder with a twinkle in her eye. "It's not what *I'm* going to do, it's what *we're* going to do."

"Huh? What am I supposed to do?" Conner asked.

"You'll see," Alex said with a mischievous grin. "All right, Lester, let's go!"

Lester spread his enormous wings and lunged forward. The twins waved back to Hagetta as he soared into the sky.

"Thank you for everything, Hagetta!" Conner called behind them.

"Best of luck, children!" she said, and waved them off.

They flew so high into the night sky Hagetta's cottage disappeared from view. All they could see was a sea of trees that stretched into the distance for miles around. Lester tirelessly flapped his wings until the air became too thin and he couldn't fly any higher.

"This is good, boy," Alex said, and raised her wand over her head. "Conner, hold my wand with me—you're helping me do this."

"Me? I don't know how to do magic!"

"Yes you do," Alex assured him. "You're just as capable as me—you just have to believe it! No matter how much you deny it, there is just as much magic in your blood as there is in mine. Grandma taught me that the key to magic is having confidence—and with your help, I know we can make this spell work."

Conner was hesitant. "Okay, but if this doesn't work, it's not my fault."

"I know it will!" Alex said. "Just believe you can do this! And hold on, we're about to go *very fast!*"

Conner reluctantly grabbed the end of his sister's wand and they raised it together.

The world appeared to go in slow motion as they raised the wand above their heads. The twins could feel magic rush through their bodies and into the wand in their hands. Not only did they feel it surging from inside of them, but they also felt it traveling through the air around them. It was as if they were summoning all the magic in the world to help them cast this spell.

The twins pointed the wand into the sky directly ahead of

them and a gigantic blast of white light erupted from the tip and surrounded them. Like a cannonball, they shot through the air and headed toward the Fairy Kingdom. Alex and Conner had turned themselves and Lester into a shooting star that bolted across the sky faster than anything had ever traveled before.

It was so bright everyone and everything in all the kingdoms below stared up at it in bewilderment. Upon seeing it, every soldier of the Happily Ever After Assembly armies, on duty or in hiding, turned into his or her own sphere of light and instantly shot through the sky to join the twins. The more kingdoms they traveled across, the more soldiers were attached, and the larger the star became. It was as if thousands and thousands of shooting stars had been launched from the ground and then came together to form a massive comet.

With one flick of a wand, Alex and Conner had performed the greatest act of magic ever achieved. They united all the armies in the world so they could finish off the Armée who had threatened their home. Together they flew across the night sky, heading to the Fairy Palace with enough light to re-start the sun.

CHAPTER TWENTY-EIGHT

THE BATTLE FOR THE FAIRY KINGDOM

Emerelda and Mother Goose paced on the grand balcony of the Fairy Palace. One by one, the other fairies of the Fairy Council appeared beside them. Xanthous was the last fairy to arrive after retrieving the others and immediately ran to the railing and searched the gardens below.

"Have Alex and Conner arrived with the other armies yet?" he asked the others.

"What do you mean 'with the other armies'?" Emerelda asked.

"Xanny, calm down for a second and tell us what's going on," Mother Goose said.

Xanthous turned back to the other fairies and his flames flickered as he grew anxious. "Alex and Conner were going to collect the armies of the other kingdoms and bring them here before the Grande Armée arrived."

"But it would take days for all those soldiers to travel here," Violetta said.

"Alex was going to cast a spell so they would all arrive at the same time," Xanthous explained.

"What kind of spell could do that?" Skylene asked.

"That would take more magic than all our powers put together," Tangerina added.

Xanthous was frustrated by their lack of faith and his flames rose. "Ladies, we've trusted her since the beginning; we can't start doubting her now."

Mother Goose went to the railing and became fixated on something moving in the trees beyond the gardens. "Well, I sure hope whatever spell she tried works, because the Grande Armée is here!" she said.

The fairies joined her at the railing and looked into the distance. Two thousand of the remaining Grande Armée soldiers appeared through the trees. They came from all directions and completely surrounded the gardens and the Fairy Palace. Soldiers positioned themselves in rows and raised their rifles. They wheeled cannons and directed them toward the palace.

At the edge of the gardens, a dozen or so soldiers planted seven tall poles into the ground and stacked piles of hay and dried twigs around the base of the poles.

"What on earth are they doing?" Rosette asked.

Three carriages appeared and were steered to the poles. Only the first carriage had horses while the other two followed behind it magically. The fairies on the balcony screamed and covered their mouths as soon as they realized they were the same carriages that had been sent on the secret path. They could see the kings, queens, and others trapped inside them.

The kings and queens were yanked out of the carriages and taken to the poles. Princess Hope and Princess Ash were forced out of their mothers' arms and thrown into a carriage with Emmerich and Bree.

Queen Cinderella and King Chance were tied to the first pole, Queen Sleeping Beauty and King Chase were tied to the second, Queen Snow White and King Chandler were tied to the third, Queen Rapunzel and Sir William were tied to the fourth, and Queen Little Bo was tied to the fifth. Jack and Goldilocks were even included, and were tied to the sixth pole. Froggy and Red were tied to the seventh.

"If you would just listen to me for one second, I could explain I'm not the queen anymore," Red tried telling one of the Armée soldiers. "*She's* the queen now—she won the election and therefore being publicly executed is one of *her* responsibilities, not mine!"

She rapidly jerked her head in Little Bo's direction, but the soldier wasn't listening to a word she said.

A handful of the Armée soldiers began drumming while others lit torches and stood near the royals. The Fairy Council was about to witness a horrible execution. General Marquis stood on top of the center carriage and made an announcement to all the fairies in the gardens and at the palace before him.

"Fairies! This is your one and only opportunity to surrender to the Grande Armée!" he declared. "Take this opportunity and I will spare the leaders of your world. Fail to surrender and you will watch them die horrible deaths!"

"Choose the first option!" Red cried up at the Fairy Council.

The fairies living in the gardens peeked out from the plants and trees. They were horrified by what they saw, but there were too many soldiers for them to do anything.

"You have until the count of three," the general shouted. *"One . . ."*

The fairies in the gardens looked up to the Fairy Council members on the balcony. They silently pleaded with them to do something.

"Two . . ."

The Fairy Council whispered among themselves but no one had a solution.

"Three!" the general shouted with a dissatisfied frown. He had been expecting the fairies to surrender but to his surprise, they stayed on the balcony and did nothing. "Your time is up! *Les graver sur!*"

The soldiers threw torches onto the piles of dried hay and sticks around the poles and the executions began. Many of the queens screamed, and the kings yelled for help. The flames climbed higher and higher. They were seconds away from being burned at the stake unless the fairies helped them.

"Mother Goose, stay here and watch over the palace," Emerelda said. "The rest of you, follow me. We will not surrender but we must stop this before someone gets killed."

"Please hurry, Alex," Xanthous whispered to himself.

Several flashing lights appeared at the edge of the gardens and Emerelda, Xanthous, Tangerina, Skylene, Rosette, Violetta, and Coral appeared in front of the soldiers. All the cannons and rifles were raised at them, waiting for orders to fire. Emerelda lowered her hands and the fires at the base of the poles faded.

"Stop putting out those flames unless you want my men to open fire!" the general yelled.

There were too many guns and cannons pointed at them for the fairies to properly shield themselves in time. If the general ordered his men to fire, there was no way the fairies would survive.

"You are an evil man, General Marquis," Emerelda called back to him. "And unfortunately for you, you've attempted to dominate a world that does not tolerate the wicked. We may not be able to stop your Armée from taking our kingdom today, but *you will be stopped.* You will not win this war—this world will not let you! This world doesn't want you here! Untie these men and women at once and admit your failure with dignity, or suffer the consequences when the other armies arrive."

The Grande Armée soldiers looked around the fairy gardens nervously, but the general's attitude was not affected in the slightest. Emerelda's warning only made him angrier. He had been given so many ultimatums he couldn't tolerate one more.

"Fire at will!" he roared at his men.

The Armée loaded their cannons and cocked their rifles. The gardens buzzed with panic as the observing fairies feared the Fairy Council were about to be murdered in front of their eyes.

Suddenly, a bright light filled the sky as a shooting star

appeared. It caught everyone's attention, especially that of the general and the Grande Armée soldiers. They had never seen anything like it in their world—but neither had anyone in the fairy-tale world. It was too bright to be an average star and it grew bigger and bigger as it traveled closer and closer to the Fairy Kingdom.

"Take cover!" the general ordered his men, and dove off the carriage. All the Grande Armée soldiers fell to the ground and covered their heads. The Fairy Council and the fairies in the gardens stayed still as they stared up at the star in amazement— they knew this was an act of magic. Alex and Conner had arrived.

The star hit the center of the fairy gardens with such a strong impact it caused a massive breeze to sweep through the plants and extinguish the flames growing around the poles. Once the breeze faded and the dust lifted, the Fairy Council could see Alex and Conner aboard Lester in the center of the gardens and they were surrounded by the armies of the Charming Kingdom, the Bo Peep Republic, the Eastern Kingdom, the Northern Kingdom, the Corner Kingdom, and the Great Troblin Lake. The twins' spell had worked.

It was one of the most spectacular things anyone in the Fairy Kingdom had ever witnessed. Everyone looked around in astonishment—especially the incoming soldiers. Only seconds before this they had been in their own kingdoms.

"That was one heck of a spell, Alex!" Conner said. He was a little dizzy from the journey himself.

Alex looked around their new surroundings and a big smile came to her face. "We did it, Conner! We brought the armies here!" she said, and gave her brother a giant hug.

"It looks like the Grande Armée beat us, though." He pointed ahead of them.

All the pride in their accomplishment drained away when they saw the Fairy Council standing in front of the Grande Armée at the edge of the gardens. To their absolute horror, they saw the Armée had captured the kings and queens and their friends, too, and they felt sick to their stomachs.

"They have everyone from the secret path!" Conner shrieked.

"How is that possible?" Alex gasped. "Someone must have betrayed us! The only people who could have found them were the people who saw them embark on the secret path!"

The Armée soldiers quickly got to their feet and aimed their rifles and cannons, not just at the Fairy Council, but at everyone they surrounded in the gardens.

"I think that's a mystery we'll have to save for later," Conner said.

"You two come up with a plan and take cover! I'll hold them off for as long as I can!" Emerelda yelled at the twins over her shoulder.

"Fire!" General Marquis demanded as he got to his feet. *"Kill them! Kill them all!"*

Emerelda raised her hands and the gardens and palace were surrounded with a thick sheet of emerald light. The sheet acted as a temporary force field against the firing cannons and rifles. It took every last bit of Emerelda's strength to conjure it.

"Hurry!" Emerelda grunted. *"I can't hold it for very long!"*

Alex couldn't think—she was in a state of shock knowing one of their own had told the Grande Armée about the secret path.

Conner didn't wait to consult with his sister; he jumped off Lester's back and began instructing the soldiers and the fairies around them. They had to strategize as quickly as possible.

"All right, men, I know I'm half your age and size but listen to me!" he shouted. "I want all of you to line the edge of the gardens and don't let the Grande Armée through. The soldiers from the Northern Kingdom will guard the north side with Skylene. The Charming Kingdom army will protect the south side with Xanthous. The Eastern Kingdom army will protect the east side with Tangerina. The Corner Kingdom army will take the west side with the soldiers from the Bo Peep Republic. We cannot let them get to the Fairy Palace."

The armies were hesitant to take orders from a fourteen-year-old boy.

"What? Did I stutter?" Conner asked.

"You heard the boy!" Sir Lampton said, coming to Conner's rescue. "Let's surround the gardens!"

The armies followed Lampton's lead and separated into the directions Conner had instructed. Conner felt a tug on his shirt. He turned around and saw Queen Trollbella standing behind him.

"What about us, Butterboy?" she asked, and batted her eyelashes. "What do you want the Troblin Army to do?"

"Trollbella? Who invited you to this war?" Conner asked hysterically.

"I couldn't stay home while my troblins came and had all the fun, so I joined my own army," she said, and then pulled him down closer to whisper in his ear. *"I also couldn't let my Gator go to war by himself—he would miss me too much."*

Trollbella blew a kiss to Gator, who stood a few feet away, and he gulped—the relationship he had never agreed to had gotten way out of hand. Conner eyed the anxious Troblin Army around him and thought of the perfect assignment.

"Rosette! Violetta! Coral!" he called to the remaining fairies. "Before the Elf Empire was attacked, they agreed to help us—we have more than enough men here but since they didn't arrive with us I assume it means they're still fighting the Grande Armée in their own territory. I want the three of you to take as many troblins as possible to the Elf Empire and help them."

Rosette couldn't stop herself from shaking her head at his request. "You want us to help the *elves*? But they would be outraged if we showed up—"

"They can file a complaint later!" Conner said. "We've got to get rid of *all* these guys no matter how many bridges we burn!"

Rosette, Coral, and Violetta shrugged and agreed to the task.

"All right, troblins, everyone grab hands and hold on tightly," Coral instructed.

The Troblin Army joined hands and formed three groups, one around each fairy. They slowly disappeared into sparkling clouds of colorful dust as they traveled to the Elf Empire. Trollbella had joined hands with them, too, but Conner grabbed her and Gator out of the group before they disappeared with the others.

"Not you, Trollbella!" Conner said. "I want you, Gator, and the remaining troblins to wait by the Fairy Palace. It'll be safest there."

Trollbella looked at him like it was the sweetest thing anyone had ever told her. "Even during war, my safety is your biggest concern," she said. "I feel your love like a warm blanket over my body, Butter—"

"Yeah, yeah, yeah—just go!" Conner pushed her and Gator toward the palace.

"Everyone take cover!" Emerelda screamed. She couldn't hold off the bullets and the cannons anymore and collapsed to her knees. The sheet of emerald light faded as quickly as it had appeared. The armies of the Happily Ever After Assembly took cover behind trees and boulders as they moved to their positions between the Grande Armée and the gardens.

Conner jumped back onto Lester, and with one large flap of his wings, Lester flew the twins to Emerelda's side. Alex pointed her wand at the soldiers shooting at them and their rifles turned into large snakes that wrapped around their hands.

Emerelda was so exhausted she could barely stand. The twins helped her to her feet and placed her on Lester's back.

"Lester, take Emerelda to the Fairy Palace," Alex said.

The gander squawked and took off with the green fairy draped across his back. Conner looked around the gardens and saw that most of the armies had made it to their assigned posts.

"Now what do we do?" Alex asked her brother.

"We'll get the royals and our friends to safety," Conner said.

The twins ran toward the front of the gardens where the carriages and poles had been placed.

"Kill them!" the general demanded as the twins charged toward them.

"But sir, they're children," Colonel Rembert said.

"If they want to fight like men, then they can die like men," General Marquis said. *"Now fire!"*

The Grande Armée soldiers around him guarding the captive royals pointed their rifles directly at the twins. Alex raised her wand and waved it toward their feet. Vines like leafy nets shot out of the ground and pulled the general and his men to the earth. They struggled against the vines but Alex knew they wouldn't hold them down for long.

"Good job, Alex!" Froggy said.

"Nice one!" Jack said.

"Untie me first!" Red cried.

Alex pointed her wand at her brother's palm and a long, shiny, silver sword appeared in his hand. He used the sword to slice open the ropes binding Froggy's and Red's hands together first. As Conner cut the ropes, Alex stood guard.

Several Grande Armée soldiers ran to their general's aid and Alex swished her wand through the air at them. Their rifles were transformed into long-stemmed roses that pricked their fingers before they could shoot.

"Jack," Goldilocks whispered to her husband, who was tied next to her.

"Yes, my love?"

"I have something I need to tell you, and now might be the only chance I get."

"This may be the worst predicament we've been in yet, but there's no need for good-bye," he said.

"No, that's not it," Goldilocks said. "It's what I kept from you on the secret path. Jack, *I'm pregnant.*"

As if the world had suddenly been paused, Jack lost all sense of sound and thought. All he could see was his beautiful wife beside him and all he could think about was the beautiful news she had shared with him.

"*What?*" Jack said with an enormous smile. "You mean it?"

Goldilocks smiled and happily nodded. "Yes—does it make you happy?"

Jack laughed and tears filled his eyes. "Even though we just barely survived an execution and war is all around us, you've made me the happiest man in the world," he said.

Conner ran to Jack and Goldilocks next and sliced open the ropes around their hands and feet. "You two look *way* too happy to be in the middle of a war right now," he said, and stared at them oddly.

"Alex, do you mind supplying us with hardware?" Goldilocks asked, and she and Jack held out their empty hands. Alex flicked her wand at each of them and supplied them with a sword and an axe.

"We'll finish untying the royals; you two get the kids to safety," Jack told the twins. He gestured to the carriage behind them, where Bree and Emmerich were trapped inside. The carriage door had been locked but Conner sliced it open with his sword in one strike—he was impressing himself with this sword business.

"Conner! It's so good to see you!" Bree threw her arms around his neck.

"Are you guys all right?" Conner asked his friends.

"Besides jumping out of our skin with fear, we're fine," Emmerich said with large eyes.

He was holding Princess Ash in his arms and Bree helped Princess Hope out of the carriage after her. Conner whistled for Lester and the goose returned from the palace in a matter of seconds. "Lester, take these four to the palace, too! Make sure they get inside safely—they mean a lot to me."

Lester saluted him with the tip of his wing and crouched down so Bree and Emmerich could climb aboard his back.

"Are you coming?" Bree asked Conner.

"I'll be there soon." He winked at her. "But don't worry."

"Impossible," she said.

It made Conner feel like a million bucks but he knew this was no time to be sentimental. He nodded at Lester and the goose took off toward the palace with his friends before Bree could see him blush again. Bree and Emmerich held on to the little princesses tightly as they flew. Conner watched them go until he saw them land safely on the grand balcony in the distance.

Sounds of gunfire and cannons came less and less as the Grande Armée began running out of bullets and cannonballs. Most of the French soldiers tossed their firearms aside and charged toward the gardens with their swords. The Happily Ever After Assembly armies ran out from the trees and boulders shielding them and fought them. The echoes of gunfire were replaced with the clashing of swords—the real fight had begun.

Jack and Goldilocks sliced through all the ropes binding the kings and queens to the poles. Little Bo was the last one freed, but being saved seemed like the last thing on her mind. She searched the rows of Grande Armée soldiers surrounding the gardens as if she had lost someone in a crowd. Once Jack cut through the ropes around her wrists, she ran straight into the gardens with no explanation of where she was going.

"Come back! It's not safe!" Froggy yelled at her.

"We should have kept her tied up," Red said.

"I think she may be in shock," Froggy said. "Come on, dear—we have to catch her before she gets herself killed!"

"Do we *have to*—or is it just *the right thing to do*?" Red asked with a snide look. Before she could argue anymore, Froggy pulled Red into the gardens with him, determined to save the queen.

Cinderella and Sleeping Beauty ran to the carriage their daughters had been placed in and were alarmed to see they weren't there anymore.

"Where are the girls?" Cinderella asked desperately, looking at the trees around them.

"Don't worry, I sent them with my friends, back to the palace," Conner said. "They're safe."

"Oh, thank the stars," Sleeping Beauty said, and placed a hand on Cinderella's shoulder. Their postures sank almost a foot knowing their daughters were safe.

"We should escort the kings and queens to the palace, too," Goldilocks suggested.

"No! We said we wanted to help our armies fight and we meant it!" Snow White insisted.

All the kings and queens nodded eagerly along with her.

"Your Majesties, with all due respect, this is an actual war and a few roadside lessons with large sticks is no match for what we're fighting tonight," Jack said.

Rapunzel quickly turned to Conner. "Was it true about our people fighting off the Grande Armée at home?" she asked him, and the question gained all the royals' attention. "We heard soldiers talking about it when we were taken prisoner, but is it true?"

"Yes," Conner told them. "You should be very proud of your citizens—they kind of rock."

The kings and queens looked at one another and the same confident smirks appeared on their faces. "Then I have no plans of seeking refuge," Chance told the group. "If our people could be so brave, then we can as well!"

The general and the soldiers lying on the ground started breaking through the vines holding them. Alex waved her wand and more vines grew, but there wasn't time for Jack and Goldilocks or the twins to argue with the eager royals.

"All right, we'll lead our own little fleet into battle," Goldilocks said. "But everyone follow closely behind us and watch each other's backs!"

"Don't go unprotected!" Alex pointed her wand at each of them and swords and shields appeared in their hands.

"I never thought I would ever say this, but *let's fight*!" Cinderella raised her sword in the air. The other kings and queens did the same and Jack and Goldilocks led them into the gardens to fight alongside their armies.

Conner looked around the gardens. The Happily Ever After Assembly armies were now fighting the Grande Armée soldiers all over the gardens. It was hard to tell which soldier belonged to which kingdom. They were doing well holding the enemy back, but the troblins at the front steps of the palace looked very worried as the battle crept toward them.

"We should get to the palace and help the troblins," Conner said.

"I agree—" Alex nodded, but something suddenly distracted her. A persistent beating noise was coming from somewhere close behind her.

"Alex! Help me!" said a familiar voice.

Alex followed the sound and found Rook. He had been locked in one of the carriages. Her heart dropped and she immediately went to free him.

"Rook? What are you doing here?" Alex asked. "How did you get inside the . . . *carriage?"*

Before she could finish asking the question it suddenly dawned on her. Other than the fairies and her brother, Rook was the only person who had witnessed the kings and queens being sent down the secret path.

"Alex! Please let me out!" Rook pleaded.

All the color drained from her face and she didn't move. Her hand had been a second away from unlocking the latch. *"It was you,"* she gasped. *"You told the general about the secret path."*

Although she knew there was no other possible explanation, Alex prayed she was wrong. She wished for the first time in history there could be an alternative version to the truth.

Rook didn't even try to deny it. "Yes, it was me, but I didn't have a choice!"

She burst into tears as her heart burst into pieces. He was the person she had thought she could depend on for anything. She had never allowed someone so deep inside her heart before. The joy she had thought was evolving into love was just the foreshadowing of a stab in the back.

"I can't believe this," she sobbed. "I trusted you, Rook! I trusted you!"

Tears formed in Rook's eyes seeing her so hurt. "Alex, I never meant to betray you! You have to listen to me—my father was hurt so I told the general where the secret path was so he could get help! Now please, you have to let me out—there's something the general is planning that I have to tell you about—"

"How am I supposed to trust you now?" she asked.

"Alex! Behind you!" Conner shouted.

Alex turned around and saw a dozen Grande Armée soldiers sneaking up behind her. Half of them cut the general and his men free from the vines and the other half came at the twins with their weapons raised. Without thinking, Alex took her heartbreak out on the soldiers charging at her. She cracked her wand like a whip and a burst of white light sent the soldiers flying into the air.

Conner was just as terrified as he was impressed. "Alex?" he said meekly.

"I don't know what came over me...," Alex said breathlessly. "I...I...I just hurt all of those men!"

"Alex, it's all right!" Conner said, and cautiously approached his sister. "They were about to do the same to you!"

Alex's eyes darted around the gardens. In a matter of seconds she had completely lost sight of who she was. The anger and heartbreak consuming her had turned her into another person entirely.

The soldiers finished cutting the vines around the general and his men.

"Let's get to the palace now!" Conner said.

"Alex, please let me out!" Rook pleaded.

Freeing him was the last thing Alex wanted to do. She pointed her wand at the carriage door and five more latches appeared.

"No, Alex!" Rook said. "Don't do this! I have to tell you about the—"

"I never want to see you again," she told him.

Conner ran up to his sister and grabbed her arm. They dashed into the gardens ahead and disappeared from Rook's view.

General Marquis got to his feet and brushed off the vines. He looked at the battle around him and his nostrils flared. His men were horribly outnumbered. It was only a matter of minutes before the Grande Armée would be defeated entirely.

"Colonel Rembert!" he cried out.

"Yes, General?" Rembert said, running up to him.

"It's time we started phase two of our plan," the general ordered. "Get the Masked Man! Tell him to bring the dragon here at once! It's time we finished this war."

The thought of the dragon surfacing sent shivers down Rembert's spine. "Yes, sir," he said.

The twins zigzagged through the gardens, headed for the palace. Alex was crying so hard she couldn't run anymore and fell behind a giant patch of daisies. Conner kneeled down beside her and she buried her face into his shoulder.

"I'm assuming Rook was more than a friend," Conner said, and wiped his sister's tears with the corner of his shirt.

"Oh, Conner, I feel so stupid," she said. "This is all my fault! I let my heart get in the way of my head and it almost got our friends killed!"

"Hey, hey, hey," he said. "Everything's okay. We got to them and everyone is safe—as safe as possible, that is."

"I feel like a piece of glass that's been stepped on," Alex cried. "I feel so broken inside I don't know how to be myself anymore. Now I understand why Ezmia was the way she was—you saw what I did to those soldiers! I'm no better than she was."

Conner pulled his sister up so he could look her directly in the eye. "Alex, stop talking like that!" he said. "You are not going to let one stupid boy who needs a haircut change who you are, do you understand me? The Alex I know would kick herself for even saying something like that! Ezmia was a whiny and narcissistic wench and you will never be her no matter what happens to you. Now you're going to snap out of it and we're going to help our friends win this war!"

Alex sat up and slowly nodded. "All right," she said.

"Good. Now let's get to the palace and help the troblins."

He helped his sister to her feet and they continued through the gardens. Everywhere they looked they saw that the battle was persisting—but from the looks of it, *the Happily Ever After Assembly was winning*!

They saw seven Grande Armée soldiers surround Skylene with their swords exposed. Just as they went in for the kill, Skylene spun her hands above her head and the water from a nearby pond jetted at the soldiers like an enormous fire hose.

Soldiers chased Tangerina through the gardens and cornered

her against a tall hedge wall. They raised their rifles at her and she raised her hands toward them. A thousand angry bees flew out of her sleeves and beehive and attacked the men. They fell to the ground as the bees stung them over and over again. A smirk appeared on Tangerina's face—it was almost therapeutic for her.

Cannons were aimed at Xanthous and the Charming Army fighting alongside him. Small balls of fire grew in Xanthous's hands and he threw them at the cannons, causing them to explode before they could be set off. The men around him cheered and one burned himself when he tried to pat Xanthous on the back.

The fairies who lived in the gardens did their part, too. Fairies of all sizes pulled the soldiers' pants down or stole their hats as they wandered by. Some fairies even enchanted the giant plants in the gardens to grab the soldiers with their leaves and hold them tightly against their stems.

The twins saw Goldilocks and the queens go back to back as they fought off a group of Frenchmen circling them. The soldiers were cocky and laughed at the women challenging them.

"We'll do that trick I taught you in the Northern Kingdom meadow—on three," Goldilocks instructed the women. "One, two, *three*!"

The women dove to the ground and somersaulted into the soldiers, knocking them down. Two soldiers scuttled to their feet but Cinderella and Snow White tripped them using Rapunzel's hair.

"Well done, Your Majesty!" Sir Lampton called across the gardens.

"Thank you, Sir Lampton!" Cinderella called back.

Sir Lampton was battling his own group of Grande Armée soldiers with Jack and the kings. The Charming brothers were competitively seeing which of them could knock the most soldiers to the ground and they counted each man they disarmed.

"That's sixteen for Chandler, fourteen for Chance, and twenty for me," Chase declared.

Jack hit the ground and kicked a soldier's legs out from under him. "Nice try, boys," Jack teased. "But that was my *fiftieth*!"

Mother Goose flew through the air on Lester's back. She couldn't stay cooped up at the palace any longer and had decided to join the fight.

"All right, Lester! Just like that time we narrowly escaped those kamikaze pilots during World War II!" she instructed the gander.

The giant goose stretched out his wings and spun in the air like a fighter jet. Mother Goose held a basketful of empty bottles of bubbly she had been saving and threw them at the Grande Armée soldiers as they flew over them. Cannons were aimed at her but Mother Goose snapped her fingers and the cannonballs were transformed into big soapy bubbles.

One of the cannons fired at Mother Goose went astray and blasted a hole in the side of the carriage Rook was locked in. Had he been just a few inches to the left, he would have lost his life. Instead, Rook climbed through the hole in the carriage and rolled onto the ground. He ran into the woods away from the battle zone. He had tried to warn Alex but she wouldn't listen—the fairies were no match for what was coming their way.

Alex and Conner were a few yards from the front steps of the Fairy Palace when they saw Little Bo run past them. She was followed closely by Froggy and Red and didn't show any sign of stopping.

"Your Highness—" Froggy called after her.

"Your *Elected* Highness," Red corrected him.

"Little Bo, please stop running!" Froggy pleaded.

Alex and Conner chased after their friends. Little Bo sprinted just as determinedly as ever.

"What's going on?" Alex asked them.

"Isn't it obvious? Little Bo Peep has lost her sheep and doesn't know where to find them!" Red yelled back at them.

"That's not funny, Red!" Froggy reprimanded.

"And by sheep I mean *her mind*! She won't stop running!" Red said.

Little Bo frantically raced through the gardens on the search for someone or something. She scanned row after row of Grande Armée soldiers; once she realized whoever she was looking for wasn't among them she would dart across the gardens toward another row.

"Where are you?" Little Bo said to herself as she ran.

Froggy and Red were starting to lose energy and they slowed down. Little Bo's pace never slowed and she broke free of the group trailing her and ran farther into the gardens.

"It's no use," Froggy said, and stopped running. "She won't listen to reason."

Red and the twins caught up to him. Conner glanced back at the palace behind him and saw a cluster of Grande Armée soldiers had snuck through the gardens and were now battling the troblins on the front steps. Trollbella sat on the steps just behind Gator and cheered him on as he fought off a soldier.

"Go, Gator, go! Go, Gator, go!" she chanted and happily clapped like she was at a sporting event. "Get him with your sword! Get him with your sword!"

"Oh no," Conner said. "I've got a bad feeling about this!"

Conner bolted to the Troblin Army's aid but didn't get there fast enough. Gator was too small to fight the soldier off alone and lost his balance. The soldier stabbed him in the stomach and Gator fell to the ground.

"GATOR!" Trollbella screamed.

"Nooo!" Conner yelled. He lunged toward the soldier with his sword. The soldier was much stronger than Conner and he nearly suffered the same fate. Alex pointed her wand at the soldier dueling her brother and a bright red blast erupted from the tip and hit him in the chest. The soldier flew into the air and the other Grande Armée soldiers retreated in fear.

Trollbella placed Gator's head in her lap while he took his last breaths.

"Don't leave me, Gator," Trollbella said with tears spilling from her big eyes.

"Trollbella?" Gator said, looking up at her. *"Before I go, I just needed to tell you—"*

"You want to marry me, I know!" Trollbella cried hysterically. "Yes, Gator! I want to get married, too!"

Gator was shocked the troll queen had interrupted his dying words. It wasn't what he had intended to say, but the little troll died before he could say another word. Trollbella rocked him in her arms and tears rolled off her face and onto his.

"Come back, Gator!" she cried. "Please, come back!"

Alex, Froggy, and Red joined Conner and the troblins at the front steps of the palace and they all stared quietly at the sad troll queen.

"No war is without its casualties, I'm afraid," Froggy said.

As the twins looked around the gardens they saw more and more Grande Armée soldiers retreating into the woods. Xanthous appeared beside them, followed by Tangerina and Skylene.

"The Grande Armée has fled from the south gardens," he told the twins.

"They've left the east side as well," Tangerina said.

"And they've retreated from the north and west, also," Skylene said.

Xanthous looked sadly to the ground. "Many of our men were lost, but I think it's safe to say this battle is over."

Rosette reappeared from the Elf Empire with good news to share as well. "It was a bit of a mess when we arrived, but the soldiers and the ogres accompanying the Grande Armée fled into the Dwarf Forests," she told the others. "The empire's tree is severely damaged and a lot of the elves lost their homes, but Empress Elvina is safe. Violetta and Coral stayed behind to help them clean it up."

"That's good to hear," Alex said. "We're in about the same shape here."

Soon the armies gathered alongside their kings and queens as they made their way from the gardens and regrouped with others at the front of the palace. Mother Goose and Lester landed next to the twins and Jack and Goldilocks joined them, too. Every man, woman, troll, goblin, and fairy looked exhausted—but an underlying pride was felt among them: They had fought off the Grande Armée together.

Conner walked through the crowd and headed to the center of the gardens.

"Conner, where are you going?" Alex asked.

"To end this," he said.

He walked until he was halfway between the Happily Ever After Assembly armies at the front of the palace and the general and his men at the edge of the gardens. Only a couple dozen Grande Armée soldiers remained with the general and each looked more exhausted than the last. They leaned against the carriages and poles and one another. They were completely out of bullets and cannonballs and most of them had lost their swords.

General Marquis was the only one who seemed to have any life left in him. He stood as tall and as spiteful as ever—as if he still thought there was a chance the Grande Armée could win.

"The war is over!" Conner shouted at the general and his men. "It's time to surrender, General, before one more life is lost."

A menacing smile grew on General Marquis's face. "The Grande Armée never surrenders!" he said.

Conner threw his sword on the ground to further prove his point. "The Grande Armée is gone," he said. "You and your men were trapped in that portal for two hundred years! There is no French Empire for you to go home to! Napoleon is dead! You and your men aren't fighting for anything anymore."

The Grande Armée soldiers whispered to one another—was it true? Had they really lost all sense of time in the portal? The general held his stoic face and laughed at Conner.

"You stupid, pathetic, ignorant little boy," Marquis said. "Do you insult my intelligence trying to fool me with these lies? I did not travel all this way to be defeated! This war has only begun!"

A thunderous pulsing vibrated through the ground like a massive heartbeat. Conner looked at the ground and saw his sword quivering as if something gigantic was heading their way. The tremor grew with every beat and the Fairy Palace began shaking as if the kingdom was being rattled by earthquakes.

Smoke filled the sky above the treetops in the distance. A horrible screeching noise erupted through the air. Everyone standing at the palace covered their ears from the dreadful sound.

"Oh no," Alex said, and her face went pale.

"It can't be," Mother Goose faintly whispered to herself.

The Happily Ever After Assembly watched in horror as the silhouette of a gargantuan creature appeared above the trees. The rumors of the egg were true; a dragon had risen in the Land of Stories.

CHAPTER TWENTY-NINE

THE DRAGON AWAKES

The dragon emerged from the trees and landed at the edge of the fairy gardens. He was almost as tall as the Fairy Palace. Red scales covered his body and a forked tongue slipped in and out of his sharp teeth. He had two horns and sharp spikes covered his head and traveled down his spine. Two large wings grew out of the dragon's back and a long tail whipped around behind him. Smoke continuously floated out of his enormous nostrils as if they were the exhaust pipes of a steam engine.

Alex and Conner could never have imagined a creature so

big. There wasn't a dinosaur or monster they had ever read about that could compare to the beast coming toward them.

The dragon arched his back and roared at the Happily Ever After Assembly. It was so loud many of the windows shattered. All the fairies in the gardens ran or flew to the trees beyond the gardens to avoid being trampled by the creature. General Marquis laughed hysterically at the frightened fairies fleeing their homes.

Conner grabbed his sword from the ground and joined his sister and the men and women at the front of the palace.

"Mother Goose, what do we do?" he asked.

Everyone turned to her.

"Why is everyone looking at me? I've never killed a dragon before!" she said.

"Weren't you and Grandma some of the fairies who hunted them during the Dragon Age?" Alex asked, trying her best not to panic.

"I just wrestled the smaller ones," Mother Goose admitted. "Your grandmother was the one who knew how to slay them."

Conner rubbed his fingers through his hair. "Okay, everyone think! There's got to be a way we can kill this thing!"

General Marquis could feel their anxiety all the way across the gardens. He enjoyed seeing how helpless his new pet made them feel and forced them to wallow in it for a little longer before ordering it to attack them.

The Masked Man appeared through the trees just below the dragon and had never looked so happy. He gazed up at the dragon as if he were looking at an embodiment of his life's work. He had waited his whole life to possess an actual dragon, and it was bigger and better than he could ever have imagined.

Unfortunately for General Marquis, the Masked Man had more control over the dragon than he realized.

"That's enough waiting," the general shouted. "Send the dragon to attack the Fairy Palace! I want to watch it burn!"

The Masked Man turned his head sharply to the general. "No," he said.

The general rotated his whole body to face him. No one had ever defied him so bluntly before.

"What did you say?" General Marquis asked him.

"I said no, Jacques," the Masked Man said.

He walked toward the general but the dragon stayed right where he was. There was something very different about the Masked Man; he didn't seem as frail or as odd as he usually did. Having possession of the dragon made him stand taller and much more confidently—he didn't have to please anyone anymore.

"I've taken a lot of orders from you recently and I've had enough of it," he barked at the general.

"You work for me!" General Marquis shouted.

The Masked Man burst into laughter. "Now comes the part when I tell you the truth, General," he said. "From the minute I saw you and your men storm into the prison, you started working for *me*. I've waited a long time for someone like you to come my way—someone as power hungry as me but who was blinded by his determination and could be easily manipulated. This whole time you only *thought* I was working for you when actually you were giving me exactly what I wanted. Thank you for your services, General Marquis, but you are no longer valuable to my cause."

The Masked Man was the only person who had ever deceived

him. For the first time, the general of the Grande Armée looked *afraid*.

"Don't just stand there! Seize this man!" the general demanded—but the soldiers stayed still. In this moment the man with the dragon was the one they didn't want to cross.

"Wise choice," the Masked Man said to the soldiers. "Goodbye, General."

He opened his hands and the soldiers discovered he had kept the shells of the dragon egg. He clutched them very tightly. He raised his hands toward General Marquis and the dragon jerked his head in his direction. The dragon took two steps closer to him and the general tried running away.

"Nooooo!" General Marquis screamed.

The dragon took a deep breath and exhaled a long and powerful fiery geyser from his lungs. The geyser hit the general and he was consumed in its vicious flames. When the dragon stopped, the ground beneath the general had been scorched black and General Marquis was gone.

"What just happened?" Conner shrieked.

"The Masked Man—he has the dragon's eggshell!" Mother Goose exclaimed. "When a dragon is born and develops its sight, it assumes that whoever it first sees with its eggshell is its mother—meaning whoever holds the pieces of the eggshell becomes the dragon's master! The Masked Man is in control of the dragon!"

"Oh great," Conner said. "More good news!"

The Masked Man raised the eggshell pieces toward the Fairy Palace. "Kill them," he instructed the dragon, and the creature took a step forward. Suddenly, Little Bo Peep emerged from the gardens and put herself in between the dragon and the palace.

"Wait!" Little Bo screamed. *"You don't have to do this!"*

The Masked Man dropped his hands and the dragon stopped.

After searching the Grande Armée soldiers for hours, Little Bo had finally found the Masked Man. She slowly walked toward him with tears running down her face.

"I know your life has been difficult and unfair and you've been tossed aside by your own blood, but I also know there is a loving and caring man under that mask somewhere," she said. *"That's* the man I fell in love with! This is your chance to show the rest of the world that you're not the conniving and revenge-seeking lunatic they think you are—for my sake, show them the man I love so there is still hope we can be together! Don't ruin the world just because it has ruined you!"

The others watched her with bated breath. They felt their hearts pounding out of their chests. Had her words meant something to him? Did the Masked Man love her enough to call off the monster? If the Masked Man's face hadn't been covered, they would have seen a very conflicted expression surface as he thought about what Little Bo had said.

But he raised the eggshells toward the palace again. *"Kill them ALL!"* the Masked Man shouted.

Little Bo's pale skin went even whiter. Tears stopped rolling down her cheeks and she stopped breathing altogether. She stared at the Masked Man in a daze and clutched the left side of her chest. Despite her heartfelt appeal, the man she loved more than anything else in world didn't care if she lived or died. With no one else to live for, Little Bo collapsed on the ground and became very still.

Sir Lampton and Xanthous ran to her and carried her back to the others. They laid her down on the steps and Alex and Conner leaned beside her. Conner checked her pulse.

"She's dead," he gasped. The women covered their mouths and the men removed their hats at the news. Even Red was upset to hear it and buried her face in Froggy's shoulder.

Alex pulled Little Bo's necklace out from the top of her dress. She inspected the tiny heart-shaped stone at the end of the chain and saw that a crack had formed across it. Little Bo Peep had died of a broken heart.

The dragon slowly crept toward the Fairy Palace. He scorched the gardens beside him with his fiery breath as he went.

Alex couldn't stand waiting around like a sitting duck for another second. Her grandmother was the only living person who knew how to defeat a dragon—and as long as she was still alive there was a chance she could give them the answer. Alex ran up the front steps and into the Fairy Palace, praying her grandmother could give them a solution before all was lost.

"Alex, where are you—" Conner said, but was distracted before he could finish.

"Look!" Goldilocks yelled.

A herd of unicorns emerged from the forest behind the dragon and circled the enormous creature, preventing the beast from reaching the palace. The herd was led by Rook, who rode Cornelius at the front of the charge. He had returned just in time.

The dragon was agitated by the unexpected obstacle. "Destroy them and get to the palace!" the Masked Man ordered.

The unicorns stabbed their horns into the dragon's feet and he roared in pain. The dragon picked the unicorns up with his front claws and threw them into the forest in the distance. He kicked Cornelius and he was sent soaring into the gardens with Rook on his back. The dragon grew impatient and scorched the remaining unicorns with his breath. They had only slowed him down—but thankfully they had bought Alex some time.

Inside the palace, Alex raced into the chambers of the Fairy Godmother and fell to her knees at her grandmother's bedside. Even though the fairy-tale world was in the middle of the greatest crisis it had ever faced, the Fairy Godmother slept peacefully as if she hadn't a care in the world.

"Grandma, I need you to wake up!" Alex begged. "There's a dragon outside and I don't know how to stop it!"

The dragon's roars shook the chamber and Alex buried her face into her grandmother's mattress until the sound passed.

"Grandma, I know you think I'm ready to be the Fairy Godmother, but I'm not," she cried. "How to defeat a dragon is only one of the many things I still need you to teach me! If there is a little magic left in you, I need you to wake up! We need you more than ever!"

Alex listened for a sound different from that of the chaos outside but didn't hear one. She waited for a whole minute but nothing came. She wiped her tears on the mattress and looked up at her sleeping grandmother—*but her grandmother was gone!*

"Grandma?" Alex asked in astonishment, and looked around the chambers. *"Grandma?"*

She glanced at the nightstand and saw her grandmother's

wand was missing, too. The Fairy Godmother had left the room without making a sound.

Once the dragon had dealt with the unicorns, he sped toward the palace. His wings spread out on either side as he went in for the attack.

"What do we do now?" Jack asked the men and women around him.

Conner was the only one to respond. *"Pray,"* he said.

Mother Goose took a giant swig from her flask and walked toward the oncoming dragon. "I'm going to distract it—the rest of you run for the forests!"

"You can't! You'll get crushed!" Conner pleaded.

Mother Goose looked back at him. "It's all right, C-Dog," she said with sad eyes. "It's my fault this even happened in the first place—it's time I took a little responsibility."

Before she could take another step forward, the dragon roared violently and the sound knocked everyone to their knees. As they helped one another to their feet they heard a familiar voice behind them.

"Step aside, Goose. Slaying dragons was never your cup of tea," said a woman's soft and sweet voice. Everyone turned to look at the top of the Fairy Palace's front steps and couldn't believe their eyes.

"Grandma?" Conner panted.

The Fairy Godmother had appeared, wearing nothing but

her nightgown. "Forgive my appearance; I only just woke a few moments ago and didn't have time to dress for the occasion," she apologized.

The dragon stopped in his tracks when he saw the Fairy Godmother. She was the only thing that intimidated him in the slightest—as if it was in his DNA to fear her. He roared at her, knocking everyone back to the ground except for the Fairy Godmother.

She walked barefoot down the steps and into the gardens toward the gigantic beast with her wand ready. Alex ran out of the palace and joined Conner at the front steps. She gasped and dropped to a seated position when she saw what the others were witnessing.

The sight was unbelievable—their tiny grandmother gingerly walked toward a massive fire-breathing dragon as if she were taking a trip to the grocery store.

"Grandma! Wait! You can't do this!" Conner yelled.

"Grandma, you're sick! Please come back!" Alex cried after her.

Their grandmother looked at them with a twinkle in her eye. "Don't worry, children, I still have a little magic left inside me and I couldn't think of a better way to use it," she said. "This is going to be fun."

The men and women, soldiers and fairies, kings and queens, and trolls and goblins watched in disbelief as the old woman walked closer to the dragon. The giant creature screeched at the Fairy Godmother and blew a fiery geyser in her direction. She blocked it with her wand and the fire was sent in all directions except to the palace behind her.

"You've picked the wrong yard to make a mess in," the Fairy Godmother said to the dragon.

"Don't just sit there—*destroy her*!" the Masked Man demanded from the other side of the gardens.

The dragon blew his strongest gusts of fiery breath at the old woman, but she blocked every one of them with her wand. The twins clutched each other, terrified they were about to see their grandmother get hurt, but on the contrary, their grandmother laughed as the dragon attempted to harm her.

"The key to slaying a dragon is to always remember you're much smarter and more powerful than he is," the Fairy Godmother called to the men and women behind her. "He may seem scary, but he's really nothing but a large winged reptile with horrid breath."

A long silvery trail erupted from the tip of the Fairy Godmother's wand. She happily waved her wand in the air as if she were conducting an orchestra and the trail slashed through the air like a giant whip. The trail grew longer and longer by the second. The dragon jumped back and forth, trying to avoid it. Eventually the trail was so long the dragon tangled himself in it when he tried flying away.

The Fairy Godmother had the dragon exactly where she wanted him. She cracked her wand like a whip again, and the trail that was wrapped around the dragon grew brighter and brighter. The others covered their eyes at the blinding sight and the dragon burst into clumps of ash.

"*NOOOOO!*" the Masked Man screamed, and the sound echoed throughout the entire kingdom. He turned back to the

Grande Armée soldiers with infuriated eyes—it was a face much more frightening than any the general had ever made. "Don't just stand their gawking at me, you idiots! We need to get out of this kingdom immediately!"

None of the soldiers questioned the Masked Man's leadership, and they hurried behind him and escaped into the forest before the fairies came after them.

The Fairy Godmother took a deep, satisfied breath and closed her eyes. Her knees gave way and she slowly fell to the ground, landing softly on her back.

"GRANDMA!" the twins shouted in unison. They ran to her side and propped her head up in their laps.

"Grandma, are you all right?" Conner asked.

"Are you hurt?" Alex asked.

Their grandmother smiled warmly up at them. "I thought I would go out with a bang," she said weakly. "I knew there was a reason I hadn't passed on yet, and I'm so glad you got to see your old granny in action before I did."

"Grandma, that was the coolest thing I've ever seen in my life!" Conner said.

"You're amazing, Grandma," Alex said. "Please don't leave us."

"Leave?" their grandmother said, and she made a funny face at them. "Who said anything about leaving?"

"Aren't you dying?" Conner asked her softly. "Isn't that why you wouldn't get out of bed?"

The Fairy Godmother put her hands on her grandchildren's faces. "Yes, children, I am dying," she said. "But what the other fairies didn't explain is that a fairy never really *dies*. When a fairy's time is up, his or her soul simply *returns to magic*. They become the very substance that helps the fairies make the world a better place. Even when I'm gone I'll still be with you both. Every time you wave a wand, or cast a spell, or use an enchantment, I'll be watching from afar with enough pride to light the sky."

Tears spilled out of the twins' eyes and rolled down their faces. Their grandmother's voice gradually became softer and softer as she spoke. They weren't sure if this was true or if she was just trying to make them feel better, but they knew it would only be a few moments before she was gone.

"We love you so much, Grandma," Alex said. "I don't know what our lives would have been like without you."

"Boring, that's for sure," Conner joked. "You were the most magical grandmother a couple kids could ask for—*literally*! I think you pretty much have that title in the bag."

The twins saw their grandmother's trademark smile that wrinkled her eyes appear one last time on her face. It was the same smile as their dad's, and it was their favorite smile in the whole world.

"I love you, children," she said. "Take care of each other— and remember, I'll never be further than a thought away."

The Fairy Godmother's eyes closed for the final time. Her body became weightless in their hands and transformed into hundreds of bright sparkling lights. The lights floated through the air and joined the starry night sky above them.

Alex and Conner had never seen anything like it. Even as she passed away, their grandmother found a way to leave the twins fascinated—perhaps she had indeed returned to magic after all. The twins hugged each other and cried in each other's arms as the sun rose above them. The Fairy Godmother was gone, but the Fairy Kingdom had lived to see another day.

CHAPTER THIRTY

RETURNING TO MAGIC

A beautiful ceremony was held the following night in what was left of the fairy gardens. It celebrated the lives lost during the war and was attended by all the fairies in the Fairy Kingdom and all the citizens who wished to join from the neighboring kingdoms.

Special tributes were paid to Gator, Queen Little Bo Peep, and the Fairy Godmother. Plaques were placed in the gardens bearing Little Bo's and Gator's names and a giant statue of the Fairy Godmother was erected at the front steps of the Fairy Palace. Conner was pleased to see it was an exact likeness of his grandmother, and wasn't made taller or more muscular like the memorial he had envisioned for himself.

The ceremony reminded the twins of their father's funeral, but this time, thankfully, all the attention wasn't on them. They shared this loss with the fairy-tale world and were able to mourn with everyone they knew. The incredible impact their grandmother had left on the Land of Stories could be seen in the eyes of all the people who attended the ceremony. Gratitude radiated from their faces as much as grief.

Everywhere Alex went, people bowed to her and referred to her as the Fairy Godmother. It was going to take her time to get used to it.

Alex asked the kings and queens to stay an extra day so she could hold her first official Happily Ever After Assembly meeting as Fairy Godmother the day after the ceremony. The war was over but there were still so many battles ahead—private and public.

Bree and Emmerich asked Conner and Alex if they could stay for the ceremony but agreed with the twins that they should go home as soon as it was over. They didn't want their parents to worry any more than they already had.

"I am so going to be grounded when I get home." Bree laughed. "Too bad my parents would never believe the truth—they might go easy on me."

"What will you tell them?" Conner asked her.

Bree shrugged. "That I fell in love with a circus clown and followed him around Europe," she said. "We know it can happen."

"Would you mind letting my mom and stepdad know where I am?" Conner said. "They'll probably know already—Alex and I aren't strangers to going missing now and then."

"Sure," Bree said. "Maybe they can talk to my parents and soften the blow of my punishment. They can tell them what a horrible influence you are or something."

A playful smile appeared on Emmerich's face. "I bet all the kids in Füssen are so worried about me," he said. "I'm going to tell them I was kidnapped by secret agents—which isn't that far from the truth."

"What will you tell your mom and dad?" Bree asked.

"It's just my mom and me," Emmerich said. "I never knew my dad. But when my mother was a little girl my grandfather used to tell her about strange things he had seen in Neuschwanstein Castle. She probably wouldn't even be too surprised if I told her the truth. I'll still have to do dishes for months regardless of where I was, but it was worth it! Even though my life was put in danger several times, I've never had so much fun!"

"I agree," Bree said. "This has certainly been the adventure of my life."

That night Conner, Bree, and Emmerich followed Mother Goose to one of the tallest towers of the Fairy Palace. The circular room was very dusty and cobwebs stretched between walls. Clearly no one had been up there in a very long time. An empty archway was the only thing standing in the tower.

"This was one of the original portals we used to travel into the Otherworld during the heyday of fairy tales," Mother Goose told them. "Those were the good old days."

Conner put his arms around Bree and Emmerich. "You know, now that you two have seen the fairy-tale world, it's your responsibility to help us keep fairy tales alive in the Otherworld," he said.

Both were excited about the task. Having this responsibility made them feel like they were taking a piece of the Land of Stories back with them.

"I think I'm up for that challenge," Bree said.

"Me too!" Emmerich said.

Mother Goose pulled a lever on the wall and a transparent blue curtain appeared in the doorway. It was bright on the other side of the curtain and Conner recognized the zone of light between the two worlds.

"Looks like the old portal is back in action," Mother Goose declared.

"Where does it lead to?" Emmerich asked.

"Somewhere in the Netherlands," Mother Goose said but then second-guessed herself. "Or was it Nevada? Oh well, just ask someone once you get there. Let's make this quick. I'm not getting any younger despite the potions I drink."

Conner hugged his friends a bittersweet good-bye.

"Thank you both so much for helping me get here," he said. "I promise to visit you once we get everything straightened out here."

"I'll miss you, Herr Bailey," Emmerich said. He didn't want to leave.

"Take care, bud," Conner said.

Emmerich was first to step through the curtain and disappear into the Otherworld. Bree lingered by the archway before following him. Just saying *good-bye* didn't seem good enough.

"I'll see you around" was all she mustered.

"Yeah, definitely," Conner said, and looked around the tower as he blushed.

Bree kissed his cheek and stepped toward the portal. Conner was feeling a little daring since he knew he wouldn't be seeing her anytime soon, so he decided to send her off with a secret.

"Hey, Bree," he said. "Before you go, there's something I've wanted to tell you."

"What's that?" she asked.

Conner scrunched his whole face as he told her. "After a lot of thought and self-reflection, I've come to the conclusion that I might—possibly—maybe—*do* have a crush on you," he admitted.

Bree laughed. "I know you do," she said. "And by the way, *I have a crush on you, too.*" She winked at him and quickly stepped through the curtain before either of them could say another word.

Conner's mouth dropped open and his heart felt like it was going to flutter out of his chest. He was happy and confused at the same time. If they both liked each other, *what happened next?* It was an electrifying yet misery-inducing mystery and Conner didn't know what to do with himself.

Mother Goose turned the lever and faced Conner with a very serious expression in her eyes. "C-Dog, I've got to talk to you."

"I know," Conner said bashfully. "I don't know how to talk to girls—but in my defense, Bree is the first girl I ever met that I understood whatsoever!"

She stared at him peculiarly. "Puppy love has nothing to do with what I'm about to say," she said. "It's about the portal in Neuschwanstein Castle the three of you traveled through. There was a minor detail I forgot to mention when I was telling you about it."

"What's that?" he asked, trying to think of what she could be referring to. "We were stuck in it for a couple days but once the portal opened all the way we got here pretty smoothly."

"That's the thing—you weren't meant to," Mother Goose explained. "I told the Brothers Grimm to lead the Grande Armée into the Bavarian portal because I had bewitched it. I enchanted it so only someone of magic blood could travel through it easily. Any mortal traveling through it would be stuck inside for two hundred years; that's how we trapped the Grande Armée. You would have traveled here without a hitch, but if Bree and Emmerich were mortal they would still be in it."

Conner's eyes blinked rapidly as he wrapped his head around what she was saying. "Are you telling me that Bree and Emmerich have magic in their blood?"

"That's the only explanation," she said. "Although I don't know how it's possible."

Conner thought for a moment. An answer surfaced in his mind, based on all the information he had acquired during their journey.

"Wait, the lion statue told us you transferred some of your blood into Wilhelm Grimm's so he could play the panpipe and access the portal," he said.

"That's right," she said.

"Then is it possible Bree and Emmerich are descendants of Wilhelm Grimm?" he asked.

Mother Goose nodded as she pondered the conclusion. "Anything is possible," she said.

It was mind-boggling. Magic always worked in mysterious ways but it was astonishing that Conner had somehow crossed paths with the two people out of billions in the Otherworld who had magic in their blood. Bree and Emmerich must have been destined from birth to find the Land of Stories, just as Alex and Conner were.

"But if they're not related to Wilhelm Grimm, I wonder how else magic became a part of their DNA," Mother Goose said. "Someone else may have slipped between dimensions undetected in the past... but who?"

Alex walked through the halls of the Fairy Palace alone. It had been a very long and sad day and she desperately wanted to find a place she could be by herself. Regardless of her quest, Alex was faced with unwanted company when someone popped out from behind a pillar and startled her.

"Hello, Alex," Rook said.

He was the last person she wanted to see. "What are you doing here?"

"I snuck into the palace to see you," he told her. He adjusted his right arm, which was in a sling. He had received an injury fighting the dragon with the unicorns.

"I heard about you and the unicorns," Alex said. "How is Cornelius?"

"He's fine," Rook said. "He chipped his horn in the fall but you can't really tell."

"It was very brave of you and I'm thankful," she said. "There's a witch named Hagetta in the Dwarf Forests. Take your father to her. Tell her I sent you and she'll heal both of your wounds—but I can't help you anymore. I meant what I said in the gardens, I don't want to see you again."

She continued down the hall and Rook limped after her. Apparently he had sprained his ankle in the fall, too, but Alex didn't trust him enough to believe his injuries were genuine.

"I know I broke your trust, but I did it to save my father and the other villagers," Rook said. "You have to understand I had no choice."

Alex quickly turned back to him. "I know someday I'll understand that," she said. "But there is always a choice, and as the Fairy Godmother I'll *always* have to make the most difficult ones—who to help and who not to help, whose life to save and whose life not to save, which kingdom to protect and which kingdom not to protect. Those are the terrible decisions I have to make and it's a burden I shouldn't expect you to carry with me. I can't blame you for making choices I wouldn't. I can't share that responsibility with you, and that responsibility is my *life*."

"So that's it, then," Rook said sadly. "After all the wonderful talks and walks we've shared, one bump in the road comes along and we call it quits?"

"It's not a bump, it's a fork," Alex said. "We'll never be able to stay on the same path—it wouldn't be fair to either of us. I'm sorry."

She walked briskly down the hall from him so he couldn't keep up. Rook called after her but she didn't look back.

"I'll change your mind one day, Alex!" he cried. "That's a promise!"

Alex pushed through two heavy doors and walked into the Hall of Dreams. She knew she would find privacy there. She sat down on the invisible floor and looked out at all the bright orbs representing people's hopes and dreams. Unfortunately, the endless room wasn't as full as it had been when her grandmother showed it to her. Many people had been disheartened during the last few days, and their hopes and dreams were casualties of war.

A knock came from the other side of the doors.

"I said I didn't want to see you anymore!" Alex shouted.

Conner poked his head inside. "Jeez, sorry!"

"No, wait, Conner! I'm so sorry!" she apologized. "I thought you were someone else."

Conner had come to find his sister to tell her what he had learned about Bree and Emmerich, but he was so captivated by the Hall of Dreams he completely forgot what he was going to say. He shut the doors behind him and sat next to her.

"What is this place?" Conner asked.

"It's called the Hall of Dreams," Alex said. "It keeps a record of every hope and dream of every person and creature in the world."

"Neat," he said. "It's like a big fairy database."

"It used to be much fuller but I'm afraid the war discouraged a lot of people and they stopped believing," she said. "It's my job to restore that belief now that Grandma's gone."

"You mean it's *our* job," Conner said. "I'm not going anywhere."

Alex looked at him in confusion. "What do you mean you're not going anywhere? What about the Otherworld?"

"It'll still be there waiting for me," Conner said. "But right now my job is being here with you. I know you're worried about being the Fairy Godmother so I'm going to stay with you until you're comfortable enough to be on your own. Besides, I don't want to go home until Mom and Bob have forgotten about how much money I withdrew with my credit card."

Alex smiled. It was the sweetest thing her brother could do for her.

"You mean it?" She wasn't even going to pretend for a second she wasn't pleased and relieved to hear this.

"Absolutely," Conner said. "We're sort of unstoppable when we're together—and there's still a lot of work to be done here."

"All right," she said. "But on one condition."

He was afraid to ask. "What's that?"

"*You* have to be *my* apprentice," she said. "Every Fairy Godmother needs one."

Conner grunted. "Oh come on, Alex! Let's not get carried away," he moaned.

"Just think about it, Conner," she said excitedly. "I can teach you spells, how to make enchantments, and how to grant wishes! And if anything should ever happen to me, the Land of Stories would fall into your hands, just as it should."

He rolled his eyes and made a face like it was the worst idea in the world. "Fine," he said. "But I will not be called *the next Fairy Godmother.*"

"You can choose whatever title you want." She was so excited by the idea she didn't care what he wanted to be called.

Conner thought about it for a moment. "I want to be called *the Head Fairy Dude.*"

Alex smiled and nodded. "I can live with that," she said. "*Conner Bailey, Head Fairy Dude*—it has a nice ring to it."

CHAPTER THIRTY-ONE

THE DAWNING

The following day the entire Happily Ever After Assembly gathered in the main hall of the Fairy Palace. All seven fairies stood nobly behind their podiums, Mother Goose sat in her chair across from Alex, and the kings and queens stood on the floor before them. Jack, Goldilocks, and Trollbella had also been asked to attend the meeting, although none of them knew what for. They figured Alex had something up her sleeve.

The Fairy Godmother's seat remained in the hall by Alex's request—she wasn't ready for it to be moved. Every time she looked at the chair she imagined her grandmother sitting there smiling back at her. It inspired Alex and kept her motivated to continue her grandmother's work.

"Looks like we're all here," Mother Goose told the room after conducting a head count. "Shall the meeting proceed?"

"Not yet," Alex said. "We're still waiting for one person to arrive."

No one but Alex knew who they were waiting for. The rest of the hall joined her as she looked upward. Their curiosity increased with every moment that passed. Two giant swans appeared in the sky and descended into the hall. Empress Elvina rode one of the swans while two elf soldiers escorted her on the other.

The assembly exchanged wide-eyed glances as if they were looking at a ghost—the majority of them had never seen her in person before. The elf soldiers dismounted their swan and helped the empress down from the other. It was the first time in hundreds of years that elves had touched fairy soil.

"Thank you so much for coming to our meeting, Empress," Alex said with a cordial bow.

"I was very surprised to receive an invitation since I didn't fulfill my end of our agreement," the empress said.

"I'm just glad you and your elves are safe," Alex said.

The empress and her soldiers stood apart from everyone else in the hall. She was the tallest person in the room and glared at the other monarchs. The elves hadn't come with the intention of making friends.

"I just love your branches," Snow White said, trying to break the ice.

Empress Elvina stared at her as if the compliment was a horrible insult. "This is the sacred crown worn by every ruler of the Elf Empire since the Dragon Age," she stated as if it were obvious.

"Well, it's just lovely," Cinderella added.

Now that everyone had finally arrived, Alex began the assembly meeting.

"I've called you all here today to make an announcement," Alex said. "I've decided my first act as the new Fairy Godmother will be to abolish the Happily Ever After Assembly."

The hall immediately erupted in protest. Empress Elvina was the only one not surprised by the news and she found the others' reactions very amusing. It was the first time in a great while that the elves were in the know before the humans.

"Have you lost your mind?" Tangerina asked.

"I think you need a vacation, kiddo," Mother Goose said.

Xanthous tried reasoning with her. "Alex, we've stood behind you on every decision but this is one we can't support."

"Everyone calm down and hear me out," she said. "My grandmother formed the Happily Ever After Assembly as a way of uniting the world, but as the Grande Armée proved, the world is far from being united. The war wasn't the last threat we'll face. We have to be prepared for whatever the future may bring and we can't do that if some of us are left out of the conversation. So today, I am founding the Happily Forever After Assembly, and I'm asking the troblins and the elves to join us."

The hall went very quiet but no one objected. The men and women looked back and forth between the troll queen and the elf empress, waiting to see how they would react to the offer.

"You want the *troblins* to join?" Trollbella asked in shock.

"Yes," Alex said. "Your people come from a long line of horrible behavior and you've done a wonderful job of restoring their dignity, Trollbella. However, the trolls and goblins will never respect us if we don't respect them, too. I learned very valuable lessons from two unlikely teachers over the course of the war—one was a prisoner and the other was a witch. They taught me that every creature is an individual and we can't punish an entire race for mistakes made by individuals. As easy as it is to label large groups with the reputations of their ancestors, it isn't right. As we forgive the trolls and goblins, I hope the elves can forgive the humans and fairies for the treatment they have received from the fairies in the past."

"Our agreement wasn't based on *forgiveness*," Empress Elvina said. "But it was a very gracious gesture on the fairies' part to assist us during the Grande Armée's attack, and we are grateful. If this new assembly will benefit future generations of elves, then we will gladly join it."

A smile came to Alex's face. The fairies around her were stunned that she had convinced the elf empress to join forces with them.

"Are we all in agreement, then?" Alex asked the room. She made eye contact with every ruler and fairy in the hall and each nodded.

"I believe we are," Emerelda announced. "Let today mark the dawning of the Happily Forever After Assembly."

The hall burst into a round of applause. Even the empress couldn't resist clapping. Trollbella was so excited by the union she did a cartwheel. Alex had secured a very promising future for the fairy-tale world.

Jack cleared his throat. "Excuse me, but we're still wondering why we were called here."

"That leads me to my second order of business," Alex said. "The majority of the criminals the Grande Armée recruited fled from battle, which means more criminals are at large throughout the kingdoms than ever before, not to mention the remaining Armée soldiers that escaped. We need to work together to round them up and put them behind bars. With the assembly's permission, I would like to ask Jack and Goldilocks to form a team to track these criminals down."

Jack and Goldilocks looked at each other.

"Us?" Jack asked.

"But we *are* criminals," Goldilocks said.

"Which makes you the perfect candidates," Alex said. "You think like criminals—you know where they'll hide and who they'll make alliances with."

"We'll have to think about it," Jack said, speaking on their behalf. "Recently we've been toying with the idea of settling down."

This was news to Goldilocks. "When did we have that conversation?" she asked her husband.

"Well, I just assumed, because—" He raised his eyebrows suggestively so she knew he was thinking of their unborn child without saying it aloud.

Goldilocks smiled at him and held his hand. "Just because a bird builds a nest doesn't mean its wings are clipped," she said, and then quickly turned to Alex. "*We're in.* Jack and I want this world to be a better place as much as the rest of you do. Besides, it will allow us to live our lives much like we always have, except we'll be acting for the greater good instead of for ourselves."

"I agree," Jack said. They had both gained a sudden interest in the future, knowing they were bringing a child into the world. "We accept your offer."

"Then I would recommend the first person you track down is the Masked Man," Mother Goose said. "There is no limit to his ruthlessness or his greed—he tried stealing from the Fairy Godmother herself. I bet he's out plotting his next strike against the fairies even as we speak."

"Mother Goose, what did the Masked Man try to steal from her?" Alex asked. "Surely Grandma didn't have a dragon egg in her possession."

Mother Goose shook her head. "I'm afraid I don't know, but it was enough to have him put behind bars for life."

"We'll get together a team at once and track him down," Goldilocks said.

Unfortunately, the Masked Man was much closer than they all realized.

With nothing further to discuss, Alex concluded the first Happily Forever After Assembly meeting. She waved her wand and several more large swans appeared and took the kings and queens home to their own kingdoms.

Alex was completely drained after the meeting and desperately needed some time to rest and decompress. Rather than going back to her own chambers, she decided to go to her grandmother's instead. Soon her grandmother's old room would become hers and Alex wanted to spend a little time in it before it was changed.

The door was already ajar when Alex got there.

"That's odd," she said to herself. She hoped her things hadn't been moved to the chambers already.

Alex went inside and her grandmother's scent greeted her at the door. She was happy to see all of her grandmother's belongings were still there. Alex gazed around the chambers at her grandmother's things. She looked forward to going through them with her brother, and wondered what they would learn about her as they searched through her spell books and organized her cabinet of potions.

When Alex's eyes landed on the cabinet of potions she was confronted with an alarming sight. All the drawers were open and had been rummaged through. Broken glass bottles covered the floor around it—someone had searched it in a hurry. The cabinet door was still swinging—*whoever it was was still here.*

Alex raised her wand and cautiously moved about the chambers. "Who's in here?" she demanded.

She scanned the room though it appeared empty. But Alex's gut told her she wasn't alone.

Alex searched every corner of the room but didn't find a soul. The only place she hadn't looked was behind her grandmother's desk on top of the platform in the back. Her heart beat faster and faster as she approached it.

"Show yourself!" she ordered. "This is a private room and you don't belong in here!"

A tall and menacing figure suddenly jumped up from behind the desk. Before Alex could identify the Masked Man, he roared at her and shoved the desk in her direction. It toppled down the platform steps toward her and shattered on the floor—she barely avoided it crashing on her. He ran toward the door but Alex pointed her wand at it and it slammed shut.

"Freeze!" she yelled. "Don't move or I'll blast you into next week!"

The Masked Man raised his arms with his back to her. She noticed a small blue bottle dangling from one of his hands.

"So you're the new Fairy Godmother," he said. "It's nice to finally meet you."

"What did you steal?" Alex asked.

"I didn't *steal* anything."

"Then what's in your hand?"

"Something that was *owed* me a long time ago," the Masked Man snarled.

"Turn around!" Alex ordered.

The Masked Man slowly turned to face her. There was something very familiar about the pale blue eyes behind his mask—she could have sworn she had seen those eyes before.

"Take off that ridiculous disguise," Alex said, and gripped her wand even tighter.

"You don't want me to do that," the Masked Man said in a playful tone.

"Now!" she yelled.

The Masked Man reluctantly pulled off the sack over his head and exposed his face for the first time in over a decade. Alex gasped and dropped her wand. She was right—they had met before.

Conner, Froggy, and Red stood on the grand balcony watching the sun set over the gardens. The fairies across the lawns cleaned and restored the damage their homes had received during the battle.

"Even though more than half of the gardens were destroyed, the gardens are still beautiful," Red said dreamily. "I would love to plant my own garden just below the balcony of my bedroom at the castle—" She suddenly grew very sad and stopped herself from finishing the thought. "Oh silly me, I keep forgetting I'm homeless now."

"Have you thought about what you want to do now that you aren't queen anymore?" Conner asked.

"Besides becoming a recluse like the Snow Queen as I wait for someone to restore my throne?" Red said. "No, I'm afraid not. Although I hear Queen Sleeping Beauty is in the market for a nanny."

Froggy put his arm around her. "You'll come home with me to the Charming Kingdom," he said. "I can't offer you a kingdom, but I'm sure I can arrange for you to have a private garden all to yourself."

Red sighed at the idea. "I suppose that will have to do. It could be a lot worse—I'd rather be an evicted queen than a dead one. Poor Little Bo Peep, I almost feel guilty for saying all those horrible things about her."

A carriage traveled through the gardens toward the palace. They didn't pay any special attention to it until it got closer and they saw the passenger riding inside of it.

"That's the third Little Pig!" Conner said and pointed to the carriage.

"What's that brick-obsessed runt doing here?" Red asked.

"Let's find out," Froggy said. He led Red and Conner through the Fairy Palace and they met the third Little Pig on the front steps.

"Hello, Your Majesty," the third Little Pig said, and graciously bowed. "It's so good to see you again."

"Cut to the chase, piggy, what are you doing here?" Red asked, crossing her arms. He had been the bearer of bad news lately and she wasn't looking forward to hearing why he had come to them.

"The Bo Peep Republic is still mourning the tragic death of the queen, but a new election was held yesterday afternoon and I've come here to tell you the results," he said happily.

Red couldn't be less interested. "I wonder what baboon they replaced Little Bo with—they deserve whatever oaf they put on the throne—" She suddenly stopped talking and her eyes grew so large they took up half her face. "Wait one moment; did you just address me as *Your Majesty*?"

Froggy and Conner shared an excited smile. Red's hands started shaking and she jumped up and down. Had all her dreams come true? Had her people given her back the throne?

"Was Red re-elected queen?" Conner asked.

"Yes, am I the baboon? Am I the oaf they deserve?" she asked as she anxiously bounced.

"No, ma'am," the third Little Pig said. "I was speaking to Prince Charlie."

Froggy turned a pale shade of green. "Me?" he asked. "I was elected?"

"Him?" Red said, just as shocked as he was.

"Yes, sir," the pig said. "Congratulations, you've been elected king. Little Bo hadn't named a successor and there wasn't time for any candidates to properly run, so the citizens were given fill-in ballots. Your name was written down the most."

Conner gave a hearty chuckle and patted his friend on the back. "Way to go, King Froggy!"

Froggy was speechless. His pupils almost disappeared into his big glossy eyes. He turned around and looked guiltily at Red.

"My dear, I'm so sorry," he said. "I feel as if I've stolen something from you."

"Are you *kidding*?" Red said. "This is fantastic news! Do you know what this means?"

"You'll be secretly plotting my death now?" Froggy asked with a gulp.

Red laughed with delight. "No, Charlie!" she said with a gigantic smile. "This means I'll be queen again! *Once we're married, that is.*"

Froggy shook his head, positive he had misheard her. "Come again?" he peeped.

"Did you guys get engaged and not tell us?" Conner asked.

"Not to my knowledge," Froggy said, and stared at Red, horribly confused. "Was that a proposal, my love?"

"It was if it makes me queen again!" Red said, throwing her arms around him. "Oh, Charlie, our wedding will be beautiful! We'll have it right after your coronation in the new gardens you plant for me at the castle! It's so funny how life works out sometimes, isn't it?"

Froggy glanced at Conner with a fearful look on his face—his life had just taken a very unexpected and frightening turn.

The celebration was cut short when a cannon was fired in the distance. They all dove to the ground just in time to miss the cannonball that blew the front steps of the palace into smithereens. When the dust had cleared, Conner got to his feet and looked toward the edge of the gardens. A few dozen Grande Armée soldiers left over from the war, led by Colonel Rembert, were attacking the Fairy Palace.

"We're being attacked again!" Conner yelled.

"Again?" Red squealed.

Xanthous and Skylene emerged from the palace and climbed down the destroyed steps to where Conner and the others were.

"What's going on?" Xanthous asked.

"The Grande Armée soldiers have returned!" Conner said.

"How many of them are there?" Skylene asked.

"Not too many," he said. "Only a couple dozen or so."

The fairies looked across the gardens as another cannonball was fired in their direction. Xanthous shot a fiery burst out of his finger and the cannonball was destroyed in midair.

"Skylene and I will handle this," Xanthous told Conner. "Tell everyone inside the palace not to panic."

The fairies ran through the gardens toward the soldiers. Conner helped Froggy, Red, and the third Little Pig to their feet.

"A few dozen soldiers hardly seem large enough for a proper attack," Froggy said.

"I know," Conner agreed. "It's more like a *distraction.*" His heart suddenly fell into the pit of his stomach. "Oh no, that's exactly what this is! The Masked Man is back! I've got to find my sister!"

Conner climbed up the ruined front steps of the palace and darted inside. He was like a fish swimming upstream as all the fairies inside made their way out to see what was causing the commotion. He raced up the stairs but didn't find his sister in her chambers. He tried his grandmother's room next, and burst through the door.

The first thing Conner noticed was the desk lying in pieces on the floor and the broken glass surrounding the potions cabinet. Alex was sitting on the steps of the platform in the back of the room. Her face was ghostly white and she panted as she stared off into space. Her wand was on the floor a few feet away from her—something was very wrong.

"Alex, are you all right?" Conner asked, and ran to her side. "What the heck happened in here?"

She was trembling and didn't make eye contact with him. *"The M-m-masked M-m-man was here,"* she stuttered.

"Did he hurt you?" Conner asked.

Alex shook her head. *"He—he—he stole a potion. I—I—I caught him and made him take off his m-m-mask!"*

"And what happened?"

"I—I—I saw his face!" Alex shrieked. Tears spilled out of her eyes.

"What was wrong with it?" Conner asked. "Alex, you're scaring me! Tell me what you saw!"

She turned to her brother and looked him directly in the eyes. He had never seen her so petrified.

"Conner," she gasped. *"The Masked Man—it was Dad!"*

Acknowledgments

I'd like to thank Rob Weisbach, Alla Plotkin, Rachel Karten, Glenn Rigberg, Derek Kroeger, Lorrie Bartlett, Meredith Wechter, Joanne Wiles, Meredith Fine, and my second brain, Heather Manzutto. Thanks to Alvina Ling, Melanie Chang, Bethany Strout, Megan Tingley, Andrew Smith, and everyone at Little, Brown.

My parents, my sister, Grandma, Will, Ash, Pam, Jamie, Jen, Melissa, Babs, Dot and Bridgette, Romy, Roberto, Char, Whoopi, Brian, and the rest of my friends and family who have provided material for this book without realizing it.

Jerry Maybrook for spending countless hours with me recording audiobooks and for baking the best homemade bread I've ever tasted!

The people at St. Matthäus-Kirchhof cemetery and Neuschwanstein Castle. And to all the readers who send me artwork of their favorite characters and book reports—nothing makes me smile more!

Turn the page for a peek at the next adventure in the Land of Stories!

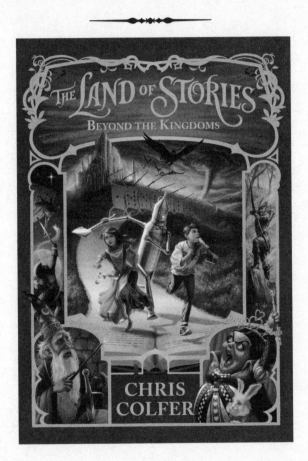

CHAPTER ONE

THE WITCHES' BREW

The creatures of the Dwarf Forests knew to avoid Dead Man's Creek tonight if they valued their lives. At midnight of every full moon, witches from the forests and neighboring kingdoms gathered at the creek. The meetings were strictly for witches only, and they enjoyed making gruesome examples out of those who disturbed them.

Dead Man's Creek was shrouded in mystery, making it an ideal place for the witches to assemble. Every so often, without any warning or explanation, the creek redirected itself to flow *uphill* into the forest. And every time the rerouting occurred, dead bodies floated in from an unknown location.

The bodies were never identified, nor was who or what had sent them—not that any time was given for an investigation. When corpses were found, the witches picked them apart like vultures, taking home what they needed in jars to stock their potion supplies.

The midnight gatherings were held at the Witches' Brew, an old tavern made entirely of twigs and mulch that sat in the middle of the creek like a giant beavers' dam. Smoke rose from the tavern's single chimney, filling the air with a foul odor and signaling to the witches traveling to the creek that the meeting was about to begin.

The gatherings were usually uneventful and low in attendance. However, due to a recent crisis that had taken the kingdoms by storm, tonight's attendance was expected to be much higher than usual.

Some witches traveled to the creek on foot or by mule. Flocks of witches flew toward the tavern's smoky signal on broomsticks. A few sailed down the creek by boat or on makeshift rafts. Some even slithered through the water like serpents.

At half past midnight, the tavern was fuller than it had ever been. A hundred or so witches were seated around an enormous cauldron in the center of the tavern, while the latecomers stood in the back.

Dark magic was known for leaving a mark on those

who partook of it, and each woman's appearance had been affected differently. Some witches had warts, enlarged noses, decaying flesh, or eyeballs that hung out of their sockets. Others had been transformed past the point of appearing human and resembled other species. They had hooves and horns, tails and feathers; some even had snouts and beaks.

A short and stout witch with skin made of stone approached the cauldron. She threw a handful of rocks inside and the liquid glowed, illuminating the room in a menacing green light: The meeting had begun.

"Welcome, sisters," the stone witch said in a gruff voice. "I am Gargoylia, the Stone Mistress of the Dwarf Forests. I assume we've all come tonight to discuss the same matter, so let's not waste any time."

The witches looked around the tavern and nodded to one another. They may have been a diverse group, but they were united in paranoia.

Serpentina, a witch with scaly green skin and a long, forked tongue, took the floor.

"We're here to *dissscusss* the *missssing* children," she hissed. "*Ssso* let me be the *firssst* to *sssay*, whichever witch *isss* taking them *needsss* to *ssstop* at once before *ssshe getsss usss* all killed!"

Most of the tavern was outraged by her remarks. Charcoaline, a witch made of ash and soot, hit the side of her seat so hard that part of her fist crumbled off.

"How dare you blame us!" she hollered at Serpentina.

Embers flew out of her mouth as she spoke. As her temper rose, a lava-like glow filled the cracks of her skin. "We're always the first ones accused whenever there's a crisis! I expect better from someone of our own kind!"

Arboris, a witch whose hair was made of sticks and whose body was covered in tree bark, stood by Serpentina's side. "Twelve children from the Corner Kingdom and twelve children from the Charming Kingdom have disappeared without a trace," Arboris said. "Only a witch would be stealthy and brave enough to commit such a crime, and she's probably among us in this tavern!"

Tarantulene, a large witch with fangs, four hairy arms, and four hairy legs, descended from the ceiling on a web produced from her abdomen. "If you two are so certain a witch kidnapped the children, perhaps it was one of you!" she growled, pointing with all four of her hands.

The tavern grew increasingly loud as each witch voiced her opinion on the matter. Gargoylia threw another handful of rocks into the cauldron and a blinding flash of green light hushed them.

"*Silence!*" Gargoylia yelled. "It doesn't matter which witch is responsible, the kingdoms will hold *all of us* responsible when they're caught! I've heard rumors that a witch hunt is being organized throughout the villages. We must prepare ourselves!"

A witch wearing scarlet robes stepped forward.

"May I offer a suggestion?" she asked calmly. She lowered her hood and a few witches gasped. She was a completely normal-looking middle-aged woman—and a pretty one at that.

"*Hagetta!*" Gargoylia said with a dirty gaze. "After all this time, you've finally graced us with your presence."

"*Ssshe* doesn't belong here!" Serpentina hissed.

"She's an embarrassment to all *real* witches," Charcoaline said.

Chastising Hagetta was the only thing all the witches could agree on, but Hagetta had come to the tavern expecting to cause a fuss.

"Practicing white magic doesn't make me any less of a witch than you," Hagetta said. "And I guarantee you, no one outside this tavern will care what kind of witchcraft I practice if more children disappear. Angry mobs will sweep through the woods until every last witch is found. We'll *all* be rounded up and burned at the stake. So, unlike the rest of you, I've come to present a *solution* that will hopefully prevent a witch hunt from happening."

The witches mumbled and grunted insults at her. Gargoylia tossed another handful of rocks into the cauldron to quiet them.

"None of us want a witch hunt, so if Hagetta thinks she can save us from one, let her speak," she said. "But make it quick—I'm out of rocks."

Hagetta looked around the tavern, making eye contact with as many witches as possible. She knew it would be a challenging audience, but she wasn't going to leave until she convinced them.

"I say we stop assigning blame and put our efforts into finding the perpetrator," she said. "The world has always blamed all of us for individual witches' mistakes. None of you would have come tonight if you were responsible, so let's work together and turn over the one who *is* responsible. We'll prove our innocence if we decide to *help* the kingdoms solve the mystery of the missing children."

"We can't turn in one of our own! This is a sisterhood!" Charcoaline yelled.

"It won't be much of a *sssisssterhood* if we're all dead," Serpentina said.

"The last thing the humans want is help from witches!" Arboris argued.

A witch standing in the back with a large stomach and a carrot-like nose burst into tears, and the entire tavern turned to her.

"I'm sorry," the emotional witch said. "I just relate to what Hagetta is saying. I'm not a saint, but I've been blamed my entire life for things that I'm innocent of."

She blew her nose into the cloak of the witch standing next to her.

"THERE'S NO SUCH THING AS AN INNOCENT

WITCH!" shouted a deep voice no one was expecting to hear.

Suddenly, the front doors of the tavern burst open, causing all the witches to jolt. A man wearing a sack over his face strolled into the tavern as if he owned it. A dozen soldiers in red-and-white uniforms followed behind him. All the witches jumped to their feet, outraged by the intrusion.

"Forgive us for interrupting, *ladies*—and I use that term loosely," the Masked Man said with a cocky laugh. "I've been listening to your discussion all night, and I'm afraid I can't keep quiet any longer."

"How dare you disturb us!" Gargoylia shouted. "No one disrupts us and lives to tell—"

He raised a hand to silence her.

"Before you turn us into mice for your familiars to feast on, please allow me to introduce myself," he said. "They call me the Masked Man—for obvious reasons. The men behind me are what's left of the Grande Armée that nearly conquered the world five months ago. Perhaps you've heard of us?"

Although none of them had been directly involved with the recent war, the witches knew very well about the pandemonium the Grande Armée had caused.

"This man is a joke," Hagetta said, knowing she had to intervene somehow before the witches' curiosities grew any more. "He'll fill your head with tales of grandeur about how he led an army and raised a dragon, but in the end, a dying old fairy made him run for his life."

The Masked Man scowled at her. "So *you've* heard of me, at least," he said. He looked Hagetta up and down—there was something very familiar about the witch. He was certain their paths had crossed a long time ago, but he didn't want to waste any time venturing down memory lane. He had come to the tavern with a purpose, and the witches weren't going to give him much time.

"I haven't come here to impress you; I've come here to establish a *partnership* by offering you a warning," he said.

"We don't need partnerships with the likes of you," Gargoylia said.

The Masked Man continued his pitch despite her unwillingness. "You have the right to be worried," he said. "It's widely believed that a witch is responsible for the missing children, and the villages that lost their young are not taking it lightly. I've lived in hiding for months and even I've heard about their upcoming retaliation. They aren't planning a witch hunt—they're planning an *extermination!*"

The news was heavy for the witches. Was the Masked Man trying to rile them up, or was the situation even worse than what they feared?

"Which is why we need to find the witch responsible while we still can," Hagetta said.

The Masked Man shook his head. "I'm afraid there's nothing you can do to prevent this," he said. "Even if you proved every witch was innocent, this massacre will happen. They don't want justice for the missing children; they want justice for every crime your kind has ever committed against theirs. They're using the missing children as an excuse to seek centuries' worth of revenge!"

The witches went quiet. None of them could deny the likelihood of what he was telling them. Relations between witches and mankind had never been easy, and the missing children may have angered the kingdoms of man past the point of no return.

"You try to start wars wherever you go," Hagetta said, desperately trying to belittle the info he was presenting. "We cannot listen to this man! He won't be satisfied until the whole world burns!"

The Masked Man smiled. "There'll be battles and fights, but you're giving yourself too much credit if you think there'll be a war," he teased. "Witches won't stand a chance once they're targeted—you're too outnumbered! Soon, your kind will be as extinct as the dragons."

The emotional witch in the back burst into tears again. She hunched over and vomited on the floor. "Sorry," she peeped. "I overwhelm easily."

Colonel Rembert, who stood among the soldiers of the Grand Armée, raised an eyebrow at her. Something about this witch didn't sit well with him.

"I think the Happily Forever After Assembly is behind the kidnappings!" the Masked Man said. "The fairies have always wanted to get rid of the witches, and inspiring a massive witch hunt would do the trick! I wouldn't be surprised if the new Fairy Godmother kidnapped the children herself!"

"The Fairy Godmother would never kidnap two dozen children," said one of the heads of a two-headed witch in the back.

Rat Mary, a mousy witch with thick bushy hair and enormous buckteeth, stood on her seat to get the tavern's attention. "Even if the fairies aren't behind it, I'm sure they'll encourage it!" she said.

"They want to live in a world without witchcraft!" Arboris said.

"They want magic *sssolely* for *themssselvesss*!" Serpentina hissed.

The witches were easily convinced the missing children had been a scheme concocted against them, and soon the entire tavern roared with hatred for the fairies. The Masked Man had the witches exactly where he wanted them.

"It's time the witches fought back!" the Masked Man said.

The witches cheered, but Gargoylia shook her head, acting as the voice of reason. "That would be suicide," she said. "You just said we're outnumbered, especially if the fairies are involved."

The Masked Man rubbed his hands together. "Not if you make the right friends," he said snidely. "With my help, we can raise *another* army!"

The witches cackled at him. The idea seemed ridiculous.

Hagetta quickly reclaimed the floor. "An *army*? An army of *what*?" She laughed. "Besides, you already had an army, and it failed miserably. Who would trust you to handle another?"

The Masked Man jerked his head toward her. Clearly she had touched on a sore subject.

"I'VE NEVER FAILED!" he yelled. "I have spent my entire life planning a way to abolish the fairies! So far I have succeeded in every step of my plan! The Grande Armée, the dragon, and the attack on the Fairy Palace were never meant to defeat them—just weaken them! Once they thought the fight was over, I snuck into the palace and retrieved a potion I've been after from the very beginning! Now that the potion is in my possession, the real war can begin!"

Beads of sweat soaked through the sack over the Masked Man's face. He took a few deep breaths to calm himself down.

"But before I can begin the next phase of my plan, I need your assistance," he continued. "There was something else in the Fairy Palace I meant to steal along with the potion—a collection of sorts, but the late Fairy Godmother must have gotten rid of it. I need your help finding where she put it. Once we find it and combine it with the potion, I'll be able to recruit the new army."

Gargoylia crossed her arms. "But what *kind* of army?" she asked. "If the Grande Armée and a dragon weren't enough to obliterate the fairies, what is?"

"An army beyond your wildest imaginations!" the Masked Man said with theatrical gestures. "An army that will make the Grande Armée look like a gang of children! I've been dreaming and scheming about it since I was a boy, and with your help we can bring it here. We can lead this army together and this world will be *ours*!"

The witches couldn't tell if the Masked Man was insane or if there was merit to what he was saying.

The emotional witch couldn't contain herself after hearing his speech. "I'm sorry. It's just so nice to see a man so passionate about something," she cried, and tears spilled down her face.

Colonel Rembert eyed the witch suspiciously. As the witch cried, her carrot-like nose was washed away by her tears—*it was a disguise!*

"Sir, I believe we are in the company of more than just witches!" Rembert shouted to the Masked Man. He quickly retrieved his pistol from inside his vest and aimed it at the witch.

Suddenly, the emotional witch leaped into the air and somersaulted toward Rembert, drawing a long sword from inside her cloak. She sliced the tip of the pistol off as she landed at Rembert's feet.

The witch moaned and held her stomach. "Somersaulting is more difficult when you're pregnant," she said.

The Masked Man stared down at the impostor—she wasn't a witch at all.

"GOLDILOCKS!" he screamed.

"Goldilocks, what are you doing in the tavern?" Hagetta said.

"Hello, Hagetta," Goldilocks said. "We followed you here. We knew the Masked Man couldn't resist an audience with the witches."

"*We?*" Hagetta asked.

The Masked Man backhanded Rembert across the face. "You idiot! You've led us right into a trap!" he shouted. *"Seize her!"*

The soldiers of the Grand Armée rushed toward Goldilocks with their weapons raised.

"NOW!" she yelled.

Four witches in the back threw off their disguises. Jack, Red Riding Hood, Froggy, and the third Little Pig had been among them the entire time.

The two-headed witch charged toward the Masked Man, separating into two different people as she closed in—*Alex and Conner Bailey.* The two circled the Masked Man. Alex pointed her crystal wand at him and Conner raised his sword.

"You aren't the only one with masks, dude," Conner said.

Alex didn't say anything. She was clutching her wand so hard she was afraid it might break in her hand. After months and months of agonized searching, they had finally found him. She would finally unmask the Masked Man and expose his true identity to the world.

"It's over," Alex told him. "And no one is going anywhere this time!"

PRAISE FOR

THE LAND OF STORIES

SERIES